WOLF OF CLONTARF IS
"BRAVEHEART" AS A LEGENDARY IRISH
WARRIOR AND YOUNG WOMAN SPY HELP
THEIR KING DEFEAT HORDES OF VIKING
INVADERS.

Praise for Thomas J. Howley's New Novel WOLF OF
CLONTARF

"A little known but momentous medieval battle and the few years preceding it, along with memorable characters drawn from the Irish annals and Norse sagas will thrill avid fans of historical fiction."—*Steven Pressfield, author of the national best seller Gates of Fire;" The Legend of Bagger Vance, "The Warrior Ethos;" and many other fiction and non-fiction books*

"Vikings versus a medieval Terminator. Wolf of Clontarf echoes with the explosive clash of axes and swords interwoven with tales of first loves. Howley has delivered an epic of heroic combat, subtle romance and high adventure."—*Mack Maloney, author of the Bestselling "Wingman" series and many others*

"In the grand mythmaking tradition of Bernard Cornwell, here is a medieval epic of Irish Warriors and Viking raiders, filled with high adventure, bursting with characters, and bathed in the atmosphere of ancient Ireland. Thomas Howley delivers it all in first novel."—*William Martin, New York Times Bestselling Author of Cape Cod and Bound for Gold*

"The life of Ireland's most mysterious and badass warriors comes to life in white-knuckle details, as the Norse invaders of Ireland discover that the only thing bigger and more badass than a heavily-armed band of Viking berserkers is a man known only as Wolf the Quarrelsome."—*Ben Thompson, Badass of the Week*

"This is a work of grand historical fiction that weaves a tale full of characters, causes and plots that more than rivals Game of Thrones. And its backdrop is real - the chaotic and complex early medieval world locked in a clash of cultures and values. Flush with action and drama, it is ultimately the characters, both historic and fictitious, who determine the destiny of cultures which are at war but also inexorably entwined."—*S. W. O'Connell, author of "The Patriot Spy" and "The Cavalier Spy"*

When Vikings invaders from across Europe storm into Ireland, her aging king, Brian Boru, must somehow protect his nation. Nordic sagas tell us an obscure and unlikely hero arises to save his people. Wolf the Quarrelsome leaps into history as a nightmare to the Norse and avenger for the Celts. This is Wolf's story spanning 15 years and leading up to an underrated and arguably most decisive battle of the Middle Ages. It is also the story of a young woman who develops a vast network of female spies and two young Irish men who lead medieval special operations forces.

The gargantuan figure stood erect to its full height and turned to face the two, its eyes burning, prognathous jaw grinning horribly. Despite the lack of armor, Thorbrand saw that the black lacquered and elegantly ornamented helmet of a Beserker chieftain adorned the head of the giant. The thing must have ripped off the visor because its terrible, scarred face was fully exposed.

"Ulf!...Fenrir!...Brian's Wolf from Hell!" cried Thorbrand to his dispirited comrade. "When we go now to Valhalla, our fathers' fathers will not disclaim us. Die now with pride and honor by my side!"

WOLF OF CLONTARF

Thomas J. Howley

Moonshine Cove Publishing, LLC
Abbeville, South Carolina U.S.A.
First Moonshine Cove edition May 2020

This book is a work of fiction. Names, characters, places and incidents are products of the author's imagination or are used fictitiously. Any resemblance to actual events, locales or persons, living or dead, is entirely coincidental.

ISBN: 978-1-945181-825
Library of Congress PCN: 2020906362
© Copyright 2020 by Thomas J. Howley

Cover image and design by Cathy Helms, Avalon Graphics LLC; cover and interior design by Moonshine Cove staff

Thomas Joseph Howley, born in Boston to an Irish immigrant family, is a retired U.S. Army officer. He began in tanks in  Armor branch and transferred later to Military Intelligence, spending the bulk of his career abroad, frequently supporting or leading counter-espionage and counter-terrorism operations.. Key tours of duty included U.S. Special Operations Command and as the only U.S. officer on the primary staff of the United Nations Protection Forces (UNPROFOR) in former Yugoslavia during the height of the civil wars there.

Earning a Master's Degree in Management, after military retirement he was employed as a civilian operational intelligence analyst supporting U.S. Defense, Federal Law Enforcement and the Intelligence Community. In the course of his career, he has deployed to or supported security and intelligence operations in every continent except Antarctica.

With an extended Irish family on both sides of the Atlantic, and his training and experience in intelligence and military matters writing about <u>Clontarf</u> was a natural extension of a life-long interest. He lives in New Hampshire with his wife where he is struggling through his sixth year of Irish Gaelic language studies. When not working on a project or in the gym, he can be found making his way through the trails in the deep New Hampshire woodlands with an Irish wolfhound at his side.

Tjhowleybooks.com

For my father, Thomas C. Howley, U.S. Army WWII; maternal grandfather, William A. Norton, U.S. Marine Corps WWI; and paternal grandfather, Patrick Howley, Irish Republican Army, Easter 1916 and beyond.

Acknowledgment

It seems inevitable to me that I would eventually write a book about a little-known Irish warrior and the Battle of Clontarf. My upbringing and later military experiences around the world, along with devouring Robert E. Howard's and Morgan Llywelyn's books and stories compelled it. There are others I'd like to recognize though. My fantastic agent Gina Panettieri of Talcott Notch Literary was and is invaluable. My writer friends; Brian, Bill and Scott; Ben Thompson, whose "Badass" historical book series challenged and motivated me to bring Wolf the Quarrelsome to life, and another legendary author, Steven Pressfield helped me immensely in this alien authoring environment. Steve was one of the very few who answered an email from a stranger and supplicant writer before I'd started and assured me how difficult it would be.

I can't leave out the Sisters of Saint Joseph and the Christian Brothers who made me *wicked* smart in the mean streets of Boston and imbued a love of history and literature. My boxing and wrestling coaches provided a then small-statured city kid confidence and early martial skill. And I must thank my Irish language teachers; Peadar, Bob, and Domi. Any Irish mistakes are mine not theirs. Finally, I have a formidably large extended Irish American family, and most importantly my wife, Marion, and sons, Kevin and Conor, all of whom inspire me.

Preface

Hostile Viking incursions into Ireland began around 795 A.D. and lasted several hundred years until generally coming to an end after the Battle of Clontarf. The invaders came from separate groups in Denmark and Norway. The Irish considered them both to be *Gaill* (foreigners) regardless of where they may have originated in Scandinavia. In this book, I use the terms Vikings, Norse and Northmen to apply to both types.

The Viking language of the time is supposedly most similar to modern Icelandic. My favorite Professor of Linguistics says all of the Scandinavian languages are actually variations of something called "Mainland Scandinavian." I use the term Danish to describe the Viking language of the time. The Irish I use in this book is almost always modern Irish Gaelic, regrettably not the Old Irish which was used around the first millennium.

Author's Note

The Vikings

"Now on one side of the battle were the shouting, hateful, powerful, wrestling, valiant, active, fierce-moving, dangerous, nimble, violent, furious, unscrupulous, untamable, inexorable, unsteady, cruel, barbarous, frightful, sharp, ready, huge, prepared, cunning, warlike, poisonous, murderous, hostile Danars; bold, hard-hearted Danmarkians, surly, piratical foreigners, blue-green, pagan; without reverence, without veneration, without honour, without mercy, for God or for man."

The Irish

"But on the other side of that battle were brave, valiant champions; soldierly, active, nimble, bold, full of courage, quick, doing great deeds, pompous, beautiful, aggressive, hot, strong, swelling, bright, fresh, never-weary, terrible, valiant, victorious heroes and chieftains, and brave soldiers, the men of high deeds, and honour, and renown of Erinn..."

James H. Todd, Cogadh Gaedhel re Gallaibh

Around the time of the millennium, 1000 A.D., European civilization and all the rudiments of Greco-Roman and Judeo-Christian knowledge and tradition were on the verge of being violently extinguished. The common people fully believed their world was coming to an end. Viking marauders were pouring down from the north, pillaging from Russia across Britannia and France to Iceland. Magyars and other pagan steppe riders from the east were only recently repelled before storming through France. From the Mideast and northern Africa, seemingly unstoppable, Islamic invaders were conquering in Spain, Sicily and southern Italy. Ireland, though small and relatively distant, shared in the dread of what may be coming.

The closest to contemporary sources used for this book were some Irish medieval annals and Scandinavian sagas. The annals, Irish and other, were yearly chronicles describing important events and people of the period. The sagas were often full of folklore, oral tradition and myth to accompany kernels of actual history. The Irish also had sagas of a type such as <u>Cogadh Gaedhehl re Gallaibh,</u> (War of the Irish with the Foreigners) which is excerpted above to illustrate its Irish and King Brian allegiance. <u>Njól's Saga</u> is a thirteenth century Icelandic work. Both cover the battle of Clontarf from different sides, though the latter contains many other stories as well. Interestingly, a Frankish monk, Ademar of Chabannes, who followed warfare of Christians with different pagan invaders around Europe including Vikings and Muslim Saracens, took great interest in the Battle of Clontarf in his 1014 Chronicon. This is another indication of its importance for Christiandom.

Wolf of Clontarf is a fictional account of several genuine historical persons and a culminating historical event. I have taken some liberties as a novelist by inserting fictional characters and using some taken from what may be embellished stories of legendary players. The same applies for the events in this book. The battles at Clontarf and Gleann Mamó however were real. In every case where I "made stuff up," I endeavored to nevertheless maintain historical plausibility. And I deliberately left out dragons, faeries and trolls – all of which I admire in other contexts. By 1014, a number of Vikings had become Christian, especially among the ruling classes. But most common Scandinavians held true to their old gods and there were examples of violent resistance to accepting the new faith on numerous occasions. There is, of course, no evidence the Irish adopted Spartan and Magyar tactics. But with a Greek Byzantine ambassador among them and the knowledge available from the continental network of learned Irish clergy, there is no reason that could not have occurred. (And it adds even more vim and vigor to an already rollicking tale.)

The Clontarf Battle has been something of a controversy for hundreds of years. Numbers of estimated combatants have varied from a few thousand to over forty thousand. Here, I selected roughly ten thousand on each side. Traditionally, a source of pride for the Irish nation and people, since the 1700s revisionist historians and elite members of the political, social and economic classes have tried to reframe Clontarf as just another minor internecine squabble among petty Irish kings with a few Vikings on both sides. This view seemed to prevail until relatively recently. In 2018, a British academic study employing quantitative network analysis methods revealed Clontarf was indeed primarily an Irish versus Viking affair. Still, there were some examples of each fighting on the opposite side (as in the American patriots versus British squabble in the 1770s.) By 1013, Danish King Sveyn Forkbeard, who already ruled much of Norway, had conquered all Anglo-Saxon England, much of Russia was ruled by Swedish Vikings and Islamic forces were on the offensive in southern Europe. Had the Norse prevailed at Clontarf, especially if Sigurd and Brodir held the reins, history may have been radically different.

CAST OF CHARACTERS
IN ORDER OF APPEARANCE

Likely Historical Persons *
From the Norse Sagas and/or Irish Annals **

Cael O'Cadhla - Irish Captain of Magyars

Teighe O'Kelly (Tadhg Ua Ceallaigh)*- Connaught Chieftain

Brian Mac Cennetigh (Brian Boru)*- High King of Ireland

Fergus O'Roghan - Irish Captain of Spartans

Malachi Mór (Mael Sechnaill)*- Irish King of Meath

Cormac Mac Mahon - Nephew of King Brian

Aoife - Irish orphan, Chief of Spies

Eoin - Aoife's brother Magyar rider

Pyrrhus Lakepeno - Byzantine Ambassador

Modolf Skalsun - Viking Ship Captain

Faolan an Trodach (Wolf)**- Irish War Chieftain

Thorbrand - Viking Warrior

Luta Einarsdottir - Viking Princess

Murcha Mac Brian*- Son of King Brian

Maelmora*- Renegade Irish King

"The Trainer"- King Brian's comrade

Cuarag MacMurchad - Grandson of King Brian

Sigurd the Stout*- Earl of Orkney

Thorwald Raven - Jarl of the Hebrides

Mornak Cennalath - Pictish Laochra warrior

Lywelyn ap Seisyll*- Welsh King

Basil II the Porphyrogenitus*- Byzantine Emperor

Bjorn - Beserker leader

Blamec Mac Goll - Irish Trainer of Hounds

Mael Coluim Mac Cineada (Malcom II)*- Scottish King

Domnal of Mar**- Scottish Warrior chief

Graeme - Scottish Cavalryman

Partha Brule - Pictish Boy

Palnatoki**- Jomsvikings Founder

Burislav**- King of the Wends

Thorkell the Tall*- Jomsvikings Leader

Ospak of Man*- Viking War Chieftain

Brodir of Man*- Viking War Chieftain

Helena Lakepeno- Byzantine diplomat

Donnchad*- Son of King Brian

Mothla O'Faelan*- Irish Munster Chieftain

Anrud**- Danish Prince

Griffen - Welsh Chief at Clontarf

Eorl - Renegade Saxon

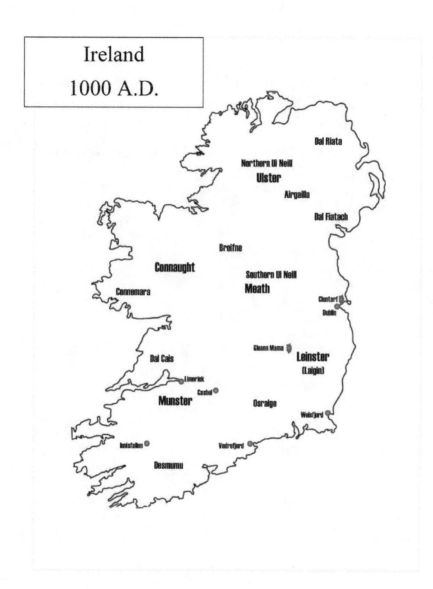

Ireland
1000 A.D.

Dal Riata

Northern Ui Neill
Ulster

Airgailla

Dal Fiatach

Breifne

Connaught

Southern Ui Neill
Meath

Connemara

Clontarf
Dublin

Gleann Mama

Dal Cais

Leinster
(Laigin)

Limerick

Cashel

Munster

Osraige

Weisfjord

Innisfallen

Vadrefjord

Desmumu

"Clontarf was too important to be left to the historians, so passed into the legend-maker's hand."

—Gwyn Jones, *A History of the Vikings.*

WOLF OF CLONTARF

Chapter 1
Dál Fiatach, East Coast, Ireland
1006 A.D.

A brisk wind blew across the craggy shoreline, thick with the briny scent of the gray Irish Sea. Cael and Fergus peered eastward, to where they knew the Isle of Man rose menacingly from the ocean, out there somewhere. They lay on their bellies amidst the long, branching fronds of bracken. They knew that old Celtic island was now a sordid den for pirates and murderers from the north. A bit inland, in a copse of trees, the older members of their small band sat and joked around a low fire. It was a splendidly bright day, the height of midsummer on Ireland's east coast. Yet, the seas were, as ever, an incessant slate gray broken only by frothy, sporadic whitecaps.

Fifteen years old, Cael O'Cadhla was of medium height with wiry, compact muscles on a lithe frame. He glanced north, toward the land of the Ulaid, and thought longingly of his own Connaught shores far to the west. His mother had taught him a bit of the geography of his home island. He knew of its five provinces: Ulster, land of the Ulaid people in the North; Leinster in the Southeast; Munster in the Southwest, birthplace of the High King and his fierce clansmen, the Dalcassians; Meath in the center, and Connaught in the West with its green peninsula of Connemara thrusting out into the great ocean. His home was there in the Connemara hills. He was here now with this fierce group of Munster Dalcassians at the behest of Teighe O'Kelly, one of Connaught's most powerful clan chiefs. The *Ard Rí,* Brian MacCennetigh, High King of Ireland was summoning young warriors from all over the island, and even Scotland, for some mysterious scheme designed by the king's almost mystical war captain.

As he scanned out to sea, Cael wondered how he found himself here. He had no idea what the purpose was, but he had grown up on stories of Brian Boru, crushing the Viking invaders again and again. The tales of the battles at Sulcoit and Gleann Mama, as told by Cael's clan bard, fired the Celtic blood of the men and boys who heard them. Even the young girls were stirred, and encouraged their brothers and cousins to train harder with sword, spear, axe and metal-bossed wooden shield.

Beside Cael, peering diligently eastward, Fergus O'Roghan, of Uisnech, was also fifteen. The redhead was taller and more massively built. Staring out to sea, he pondered why he was here. Fergus had responded to the call of the High King as a vassal of Mael Sechnaill Mac Domnaill, called Malachi Mór, King of Meath. Malachi himself had been *Ard Rí* but had recognized Brian's claim and given up the Irish crown four years ago. Fergus's father back in Meath had told him of all this, of how there were many "kings" among the many clans in Ireland. Yet each province had its own ruling king over the others, and over each of them reigned one, the *Ard Rí*, High King.

Cael and Fergus didn't yet know it but they were just two of hundreds, carefully selected to be part of new and innovative warrior groups. They would serve the cause of their God, their king and the Gaelic people. The unknown designer of this audacious scheme was even more outlandish than the plan itself, and he crafted its many parts with ferocious precision.

***

At first it seemed just a slightly larger whitecap on the otherwise unchanging gray seas. But the boys had the keen eyes of youth, and stared intently as the pale shape became a billowing rectangle, hovering above a sleek, dark form riding below. It cut swiftly through the waves. Almost abruptly, colors and shapes became distinct, most notably the long slim oars, mechanically sweeping along the sides of what was now clearly identifiable as a dragon ship. Round, burnished shields rested along the gunnels of the wooden hull. The fierce and despised dragon's head, eyes burning red and yellow, towering over the prow, told this wasn't simply a trading vessel.

"How did the Munstermen know the Vikings would show up here and now?" asked Fergus with a nervous whisper.

"We've been laying in this same spot for two days, so it's not as if we just showed up to greet them with perfect timing. I reckon Brian's men just guessed, and you know they're waiting for others to join them here. Anyway, we wanted red war and glory, didn't we now?" Cael replied, already rising to stand.

"I'm going to fetch the king's nephew."

With that, he bent low and ran back to inform the others of the approaching long ship.

***

Cormac Mac Mahon was the son of King Brian's long dead, older brother, Mahon. Forty-six years old, he was a hardened and battle-scarred war leader in his own right. He led this emissary of Dalcassian warriors which had been traveling and collecting groups of young recruits. There were many other such bands doing the same thing across Ireland and Scotland, searching for willing and selectively chosen volunteers, most from among the common people. Not counting the little brother and sister who had arrived yesterday, along with Cormac, Cael and Fergus, there were twelve Munster warriors, all of whom had seen years of bloody combat against the Norse and renegade Irish traitors.

Cormac, now crouching with the boys at their watch post, examined the ship with an experienced eye. "She's a *snekkja*. She'll have a crew of thirty-six, all of them fighting men. That's the Danish version, with a draft so low she can beach anywhere, and she doesn't need a port. They're making for Dublin no doubt, but will track along the coast looking for a bit of easy tribute for Sitric, the shifty Viking ruler of that accursed place. Sitric Silkbeard has been both enemy and ally to King Brian in the past but the rat-faced villain has never been one for any Irishman to trust."

He continued, "She's still a bit off but will surely come closer to us. Let's dangle some attractive 'tribute' where they can't miss it." Cormac smiled, told Fergus to follow him and dashed inland, instructing Cael to keep watch.

***

Aoife was thirteen years old with raven hair, the sparkling emerald eyes of an angel and milky white skin. Her brother Eoin was eleven. Four years earlier, they had lain in a hidden defile and watched as their little clutch of clan huts was set upon by armored, foreign-speaking demons. The marauders killed and burned everyone and everything, taking only a few sheep and some honey mead back to their three ships. A hard-riding force of Brian's allies from Connaught arrived too late. They mercifully took the two orphans along and later left them with a strong clan, bristling with fierce Northern Ui Neill warriors. Like wolf cubs, Aoife and her brother had grown tough and feral, yearning even then to join Brian's armies. Eventually, they ran away, only to be picked up by another traveling Dalcassian band. Riders from that group had brought them to Cormac yesterday with the intent to bring them back to safety in Munster. Now Cormac had plans that cheered the hearts of the little wolflings.

***

For the past two days the old shepherd had been happy to share his patch of land with this small band of warriors from Munster. He felt safer with them around. He didn't know why they were here, but he grew even more impressed when he learned one was the nephew of the High King. Sitting next to his little cart with his pony and small flock of sheep nearby, the shepherd stirred himself when he saw a grinning Cormac approaching with two waif-like children.

"Shepherd, I've come to ask a wee favor," Cormac said gently. "I want to borrow your flock, your cart and pony for a short while. Here's a bit of coinage to show my intentions are honest. When I return your property, you can keep some of this."

He passed the shepherd a jingling leather pouch. Opening it, the old man grew wide-eyed as he beheld more French silver coins than he thought might ever exist in Ireland.

"It's mid-morning now. I expect to have everything back to you well before dusk," Cormac said.

***

With the cart hitched, Aoife, sitting on its bench and controlling the pony, and Eoin driving the sheep behind them, the children followed Cormac toward a hill which overlooked the shoreline.

When he was satisfied the children and sheep would be easily observed as the long ship passed the gentle sloping hill, Cormac gazed down to the nearest part of the mud packed shoreline.

He turned to Fergus.

"The *snekkja* can easily beach there. It's a perfect spot just to the north of the hill. Our twelve warriors are back, not far behind, readying themselves. The other young lad, soon to be your weapon brother, is just above, looking down from that elevated promontory, tracking the ship's progress."

The grizzled warrior examined the surrounding terrain. The hill itself presented a meadow rising up its entire length from a small rocky cliff. The meadow was grassy and verdant, flanked by rows of low trees and shrubs.

"The Vikings will disembark and move down from the north along the beach. They will easily scale the little cliff and march up the slope, avoiding the clinging shrubs. But they won't be able to see this meadow from the ship's beached location."

Now Cormac took the time to mentally overlay his tactics on the terrain. With a predatory grin, he came to his decision and slapped Fergus on the youngster's broad back. Then the two ran to fetch Cael and bring him to where his warriors were assembled.

***

"They'll leave four on the boat and take the rest of the crew to seize some of the sheep and whatever else they think they might find beyond. Unless they're looking for slaves, they'll probably just ignore the children. We're not far from areas to the south they consider their own. They'll be fully armed and armored, and will move easily with deadly intent. We'll kill all of them in the meadow, then seize and burn their ship."

Cormac gazed at them, his steely eyes brimming with confidence and unfeigned enthusiasm. The twelve slammed swords and axes against their shields and growled ferociously.

"Holy Mother of God." said Fergus in a shocked whisper to Cael.

"There are fifteen of us, against thirty-two Viking monsters. How does this work?

"We two have not yet begun the training they promised, and our two hunting spears can't match swords and battle axes. What happened to the friends they were supposed to meet here today?"

Cormac glared at them sternly, reading from their faces the fear-tinged words Fergus had spoken. Then, abruptly, his visage and demeanor became softer.

"We shan't be just fifteen. While ye've been searching the seas to the east, I've been looking west. Our friends will be with us almost directly I'll wager. The "Magyars" move swiftly and stealthily." Cormac smiled at the twelve knowingly.

Cael brought his attention to the twelve Dalcassians for the first time since they assembled in this glen. All wore finely worked mail armor over their woolen tunics. Hanging from their wide leather belts were simple conical iron helmets with side plates to protect their cheeks, each helmet reinforced with crossed iron ridges to withstand axe and sword blows. Cael noted dents and scratches on all of the helmets. Most rested their large round shields against their knees while they stood listening to Cormac.

At that moment, four mounted apparitions burst from the tree line. The boys gaped in astonishment and clutched their hunting spears tightly. The riders wore headgear made of black otter fur over boiled and molded leather caps. Fitted leather jerkins draped over wheaten-hued, woolen tunics. To Cael's fascination, they had multi-colored leggings, much as the Gauls and Britons were said to favor in earlier times. They were armed with thin lances, each the length of a short man, which they carried on their backs.

Most amazing to the two recruits were the bizarre and weirdly bent bows which fitted snugly into wide leather pouches attached to their belts. Another leather pouch was secured to the mount's flank, stuffed with numerous feathered arrows.

Then Cael noted with pleasure the mounts themselves. He beamed and explained to Fergus.

"They're Connemara ponies, the tough, hardy little horses from my home. They're amazingly swift and agile, with tremendous endurance and surprising strength for their size. I've been riding them since before I could walk, with and without saddles and stirrups."

All four of the riders were of small to medium stature, lightly but solidly built, with simple rolled blankets to carry their scant belongings. Three had familiar Gaelic faces with round hazel or blue eyes, thin upcurved lips and rosy cheeks over light skin. The other was squat and much darker with a curly, blue-black beard, seemingly glistening in the sun. His eyes gleamed just as black and sparkling. And this one had the biggest grin.

"Ho, Pyrrhus." said Cormac with hearty vigor. "Ye've come just in time. I trust you and your horses have moved leisurely and you're well rested, as we've little time left. And where is himself?"

"He's just behind staying on established trails, following. That giant of a steed he favors can't move amongst the woodlands as readily as these dear little beasties."

The dark-skinned rider smiled and patted his mount affectionately. Then, with the same strangely exotic and sibilant accent, he asked, "Now then, Cormac, what is afoot?"

***

Modolf Skalsun guided his ship closer to land in the direction of the small flock on the hill his lookout had spotted earlier. He had led crews from Man to Dublin and back many times over the years, and knew the coastline and waters well. Now that they were closer to their goal, and the smell of livestock offal would linger for less time, he knew his sleek *snekkja* could take on a collection of fat Irish sheep for use as gifts and barter in Dublin. And if his passenger objected, that would be too bad, he mused gleefully. It was a welcome surprise to see the sheep so close to the sea and tended by what looked like two little wains. No matter, he thought, even if there were an entire clan of Irish shepherds, his crew of swaggering axe slashers would cut their way through them all to take what he wanted.

He knew Sitric's forces from Dublin would occasionally strike out north to this same region to collect tribute or pillage, whichever was easier. And that King Brian and the disturbingly uniting Irish were busily engaged in the west against other marauding Vikings and renegade Irish clans. So Modolf's chances of a short, rewarding raid were favorable.

"Hoi, you fat Walruses. Which of you wants fresh mutton tonight?" the Viking captain yelled. The crew laughed and pulled harder at their oars.

The dragon ship seemed to fly across the waters which became calmer as they approached the beach, north of the green meadow. For a time they couldn't see the meadow, the flock nor its small guardians.

"No worries you lazy bastards. We'll be upon them before they can scatter to the winds," the Captain hollered with a rapacious grin.

***

Modolf led his thirty-two eager Vikings across the narrow strip of beach to the rocky cliff below the meadow. Four had been left to guard the ship and its passenger, two of them ashore, keeping watch to the north and west. Despite thigh-length mail armor over padded leather and woolen tunics, the band moved quickly and silently. Most had burnished iron helmets, with visors and frightening eye slits covering the top half of their bearded faces — the unholy visage that terrorized all Europe and Russia. Extended in two columns as they climbed first the cliff then the slopes of the grassy hill, keeping watch to the treelines on either side, ready to deploy in a shield wall in the unlikely event of attack.

It was an easy gradient yet still a brisk march to the crest of the hill, from where Modolf could hear the occasional sheep bleating. A steady breeze blew in from the sea and the gulls screeched as they fought for prizes over the water's surface. Gradually the placid scene led some of the climbers to talk and joke among themselves in subdued voices.

"Nice to stretch cramped legs and breathe air that smells of good peat and green grass after nothing but biting salt air," said the youngest, a blonde haired, smiling teen on his first sea voyage.

His companions erupted into profane laughter and one teased the boy.

"Sit your soft arse on a rowing bench for weeks and weeks, from the northern snows of Norway to the parched hot beaches in the north of Africa before you complain about a short jaunt from Man to these Irish shores, you precious little princess."

The others laughed even harder as the now shamed youth blushed fiery red, plodded on and said nothing more.

Approaching the halfway point on the trek up the meadow, the band increased their pace, eager to get to the top and view the surrounding countryside.

One, then a second muffled and agonized groan erupted from the rearmost climbers. The lower half of the contingent heard the moans, and wheeled quickly to look behind. The two, in the rear, were down on their faces, long feathered shafts protruding from the mail on their backs.

"What in Loki's name?" yelled Modolf as his experienced veterans instinctively brought their shields up to just below their eyes.

Hoofbeats rumbled on the grass, and the Vikings saw two flying riders atop compact mounts ascending on their right flank, loosing arrow after arrow as their legs clutched their ponies' flanks, their arms working steadily drawing back taut bowstrings. Two more of the marauders went down, arrows in face and throat, too new and too slow to bring their shields up to cover against the aerial onslaught.

Amazingly, as the swift riders approached the crest of the hill, they twisted and continued to release volleys of arrows which had a reduced impact now that surprise had been lost. With a curse, Modolf called for his men to form a shield wedge and march quickly to the top.

Most of the Northmen were veterans of many a crimson battle on land and sea. All had seen death; grisly and brutal, and none feared losing their fellows to honest swords and axes. Yet not a one had ever seen arrows rain from behind before he knew the enemy was even about.

And no Vikings in Ireland, Modolf knew, had ever been harried by a duo of mounted ghosts twisting and turning on speeding ponies, wielding absurdly short and twisted bows; all the while dressed in otter skin caps and brightly colored Gaulish leggings.

Shields locked and raised, every one of the remaining twenty eight Vikings peered from behind slight gaps in the wooden wall, not knowing if the riders would come flying down to attack them again. Frustration and anger compelled them, involuntarily, to increase their pace until they were almost running, in heavy armor and tight interlocked formation, into a sun that was just starting to descend into the west.

Once again furious hoof beats. The Vikings leaned forward expecting the riders to come bounding down from above. Screams and groans erupted once more in their midst. Their helmets' mail skirts, which protected their ears and necks, made hearing difficult. It was difficult to accurately determine the direction of sounds. Only when one fell onto the man in front did they realize they were being attacked yet again from behind.

Slowing awkwardly, some turned and gazed upon two more of their members, staked into the ground by feathered shafts. Two mounted archers flew up from below releasing arrows furiously, one of which entered the mouth of a winded, gasping axeman.

"Are these the same two?" screamed one frustrated Northman.

"Who the hell knows? Just keep your shields up and let them come to us," shouted Modolf.

These two riders infuriated the Northmen by simply turning at the top of the hill and riding back down the same route. The dwindling formation turned to focus attention on the known threat. This time the arrows were stopped by thick oaken and metal shields. They were in easy range, almost point blank for archers, but the riders were seemingly too far away for the few Viking throwing spears the band carried. In a fit of rage, one Northman broke from cover. He threw down his shield, and with a burst of barbaric strength hurled a long-bladed spear at the nearest rider.

"I'll show them a blade doesn't need a bow to kill at a distance," he yelled in frustration and fury.

Incredibly, the spear flew true; range and deflection on target. Had the rider not dipped and bent under the pony's belly at just the right moment, he would have been struck and unhorsed. Even from this position, the archer brought his little bow in front of the straining pony's breast. He loosed an arrow which struck the spearmen in an unarmored leg. As he fell, the Viking bent to clutch at the arrow embedded in his calf. Seemingly out of nowhere, a shaft from the second rider whisped into his armpit, collapsing him immediately.

The two riders were to the left and behind the formation which had almost reached the hilltop. Modolf attempted to guide the Vikings' tight wedge formation into a true circle, but most remained focused on the arrows showering them from below. Before the circle could close, two more men on squat, muscular horses came thundering down along their right flank. One bearded axeman, who had been intent on the riders below, took an arrow in his left kidney before he could swing his shield to cover against this new threat. A big man, he knocked his shield mate to the ground as he fell with the mortal wound.

By now, all of the riders were below the circle of shields, with the wounded man having been pulled inside. The teams of riders formed a line of four, after reuniting and slapping each other on their backs amidst much jocularity. Now this line walked their horses slowly toward the enraged Vikings, stopping only when they were within easy spear casting distance of the bristling wall. For the first time, the Norse could see them, near and unmoving. None of the four could rise to the nose of the least of the Northmen. They carried lances strapped crosswise over their backs and shoulders, and their bows looked even more alien up close. Tellingly, only few, perhaps no more than twelve, arrows remained in the quivers of the four strange cavalrymen.

The four dismounted, and holding their ponies' reins, began laughing and taunting the armored giants so close to them. Modolf heard mocking curses in Gaelic, some of which he understood. A few of the Northmen snarled. Most couldn't follow.

"They're far easier to skewer from the saddle than scurrying squirrels," exclaimed a young rider to his companions.

"But they're fatter and slower than squealing pigs so it's no challenge a'tall, a'tall," replied another with a grin.

"But our darlin' pigs are not so ugly as these, Seamas."

"We're keeping the fields fresh and beautiful by scouring the land of these Godless, unclean vermin," retorted a third rider.

Now, one of the short, rosy cheeked men switched to Irish-accented Danish, repeating the same insults, and asked to see their vaunted female beauty; if only they would remove their helmets and armor. He grinned lewdly and winked flirtingly. All four horsemen laughed uproariously at that.

The Vikings immediately bellowed and stomped, tense and seemingly ready to explode.

"Hold." commanded Modolf loudly. Then, more quietly, he told them, "We'll rush them at my command."

One of the four removed his black furry cap and wiped his brow with it. The Vikings gaped then on no Irishman. No Celt at all.

He was short and darker than the duskiest of the Irish or Norse, with a curly dark beard and hooked nose. His ink black eyes seemed to incessantly sparkle as with some jest unknown to all but him. The dark man turned to his saddle and reached into a dirty woolen bag hanging across it. He rummaged through the satchel grasping for something, while keeping watch on the dangerously close circle of seething Vikings. Then, in perfectly articulated and almost melodious Danish he called out to them.

"Well now, you rank smelling sows must certainly be women, but these three may have been men."

His hand emerged clutching the long filthy hair of the severed heads of the three Vikings who had fallen at the bottom of the hill. He whirled and flung all three bloody trophies into the midst of the circle. They careened off raised shields and fell into the Viking cluster, rolling around tightly packed feet.

"My brother." screamed an infuriated axeman.

"My cousin Kari." bellowed another in rage.

No discipline could now hold fast the Viking circle, and two, then three, then more broke and ran out to slaughter the little men standing by their horses. Even as the first one sped downwards, the four horsemen grabbed their horses' reins, spun and began dashing down the hill.

As they ran and gained distance from their armored pursuers, they sprang onto their saddles. Remounted, the two teams of archers swung to either side and turned their horses once more. With blurring speed, the deadly little bows were drawn from leather cases. Almost immediately the ponies were above, behind and to either flank of the feverishly running group of blood-crazed Vikings.

The horsemen loosed eight of their remaining arrows. Seven found targets. Four of the fallen dropped without moving, feathered in backs and sides. Three others writhed and screamed in pain. Now maddeningly, the two groups turned downhill again, this time unslinging lances and leveling them at their sides. The ponies' hooves tore up the grass with bursting speed. Two of the errant Vikings were still running, seemingly out of control. Another stood unmoving, confused.

Modolf looked on in horror. "Get back to the circle. The rest of you hold."

Now, two spearmen were bearing down on the runners, their lances' pointed iron tips seeming just two more speeding arrows. The Vikings heard the hoofbeats behind, and tried to stop, turn and defend themselves. It was too much at this speed with both winded. One tripped to the ground. The other was barely able turn his head. Two lances wielded by riders on flashing, strong ponies crashed with incredible force through mail, wool, flesh and bone, immediately killing both Northmen.

The straggler flung down his shield and, despite his exhaustion, ran to regain the circle. To the rage and frustration of those remaining in formation, one of the riders leisurely trotted to each of the three wounded Vikings and efficiently used his lance to spike them through uncovered mouths and throats, dispatching them quickly. The two others slowly rode back to retrieve their bloody spears from the bodies of the gutted and obscenely splayed Viking runners. They slowly led their ponies uphill once again.

The last of the riders, the one with the shiny black beard, rode to the center of the meadow and dismounted. Dropping his lance to the grass, he uncased his bow and strung one of his two remaining arrows.

He looked uphill and calmly measured wind, range and distance. "A tailwind always helps," he whispered to himself in his own Mediterranean language, smiling. He drew back expertly on the recurved, bone-reinforced, little bow.

The terrified, running Viking, beardless and youngest of the entire crew, had thrown off his helmet and shield in his desperation to reach the safety of the circle. He was the youth who earlier had been so pleased to stretch his legs, tread upon the green, spongy grass and take in the scents of the Irish meadow. His long blonde hair was flowing in the wind and his blue eyes were open, bulging and filled with a fear he had never known. His comrades shifted to open a small gap for him.

As one Viking stretched out an arm to clasp the panting youth, an arrow abruptly emerged from the center of the runner's throat, dropping him, blood spurting onto the shield of another Northman. Such was the impact, this one fell with the grisly corpse over him. Before the arrow had even struck, the four riders had rejoined their line, lances leveled, and were slowly riding up the hill toward the wooden wall of Norse, who looked down in disbelief. Almost absurdly, one of the riders was making what were certainly insulting hand gestures in the direction of the gaping Vikings.

All eyes were on the deadly mounted line of small men and stunted horses when a deep, thunderously rumbling resonance rolled down from above.

"ABBBBOOOOOOO.."

The piercing cry was the ancient battle call of full-scale assault by attacking Gaels. Modolf looked up to the crest of the hill which his men had come so close to reaching.

He couldn't see it.

Instead he gaped at a V-shaped wedge of thirteen round shields crashing into his confused Vikings.

It was too late. The first Dalcassian axe flashed over a shield, insufficiently positioned to meet this new threat from an unexpected direction. The steel axe head crushed helmet and skull, splattering gore in all directions. Other attackers quickly slew five more Vikings, then the wedge of fiercely snarling Munstermen was in the midst of the circle, dealing arcing, well directed slashes and thrusts with axe and sword.

It was a slaughter. The Vikings' natural ferocity had been too battered by what four little men had done to them earlier, and now fierce, well-armed, infantry warriors were destroying them piecemeal. As they flayed in disarray, their circle dispersed by the wedge, they were horrified to suffer an additional insult.

Two of the horsemen were riding at a trot and jabbing at the backs of isolated Vikings, each of whom was fighting with two or more of the Dalcassians to their front. Three more Northmen went down.

There was only one arrow left. One of the small archers approached a Viking who was being harried by an Irish axeman.

"Hoi, Sven, do you still yearn to go a'viking?"

The last thing the wounded, but still fighting, Viking saw as he glanced toward the melodious Danish voice, was a dark, black-bearded little man loosing an iron tipped arrow into his open mouth.

All of the Northmen were dead but Modolf. He was covered with bloody gashes and his shield had been sawed to kindling by the repeated sword and axe blows of the Irish. He had managed to crush the shield of one of the Dalcassians with his heavy Viking axe and cause a deep but survivable blow to that one's shoulder. This was the only Irish loss.

Now he glared, staggered but defiant. His helmet slashed away, his face dark and bloodied. He looked grimly at the calm, circling group of Dalcassians, all with notched shields and bloody blades. To one side stood a burly red-haired boy, unarmored and carrying a simple hunting spear. The four horsemen sat astride their mounts, tantalizingly close.

"You'll not be having mutton tonight," said Cormac, approaching the last Viking with a measured step.

His broad shield on his left arm, Cormac passed his axe back and withdrew the long *scian* fighting knife from the scabbard on his belt. Then, with incredible agility, he dashed inside the arc of the Viking's rapidly descending blade and brought his shield up to deflect it. This same act broke Modolf's arm at the elbow. He never felt the pain in his arm since Cormac's *scian* thrust up and through the grizzled, blonde beard, into his upraised chin.

***

As the events on the meadow were drawing to a close, a small cart was ambling creakingly along the shoreline where the where the long ship was beached. It had come down from the north and the Viking guard posted there was the first to see it. He gazed at the approaching little wagon in amused surprise. A very young girl was driving it. She was accompanied by an even younger boy who was walking beside it. The guard could see the little pony pulling the cart was not used to walking along the beach. The poor beast was struggling with the effort of that and its apparently burdensome cargo.

The rear of the wagon was stuffed, full enough to allow a large woolen sack to be visible, rising above the wooden side slats. Like all the children here, this one was a pretty little thing, with the childishly upturned nose, ivory white skin, and large, green eyes of a young teen. Had the boy been older, he could have been her twin. The sentinel remembered seeing a little girl and boy tending the flock Modolf had coveted just before the ship beached. They looked just like these two, but he knew Ireland was bursting with dark haired, creamy skinned boys and girls.

He called to the two on the ship and the other guard who was watching the wooded scrubland to their west. "Let the others climb a hill and chase down a flock of bleating sheep. Our booty comes to us."

The guard seemed pleased at his joke. Unless the cart's goods were fish heads or cow manure, it was coming with them on their ship. He let the wagon advance, showing no signs of hostile intent. The other three Vikings looked on with interest and amusement.

As the cart continued, one of the guards on the boat said to his companion.

"That pony does not like walking on the shoreline. And why aren't those whelps frightened by our terrible dragon prow, nor by the giant troll who waits for them?"

The little party was now almost upon the big man just now described as a troll.

He moved slowly and casually to the side of the cart and the girl stopped it, looking up at him. The little boy stood and held onto the rear wheel.

"Now then my *cailín beag*, what is that fine cargo in the back of this little cart then?"

He had used the Irish words for "little girl" but was not surprised to realize she couldn't understand.

"*Tá….tá…mé….mé…,*"she stammered in a high, barely audible, trembling voice. Now finally, he could see she was clearly terrified.

He leaned forward, pointing to the back and asked in broken Irish, "*Cad seo?*"— "What's this?"- as she sat still, apparently shivering in fear.

At that moment, a startlingly large blackbird broke from the tree line and flew low overhead, cawing loudly just above them.

They all looked up.

'Ah then, Good Day to you Morrigan, and thank you for the visit.' said Aoife to herself, smiling mysteriously as the Viking cast his glance to her once more.

He looked down at her, perplexed. With lupine quickness, she reached into her sleeve drawing out a thin, glistening *scian.* In an instant, she thrust its length into the helmet's eye slit, and drew back again swiftly to slash viciously across his throat. He was dead before his armored body fell to the mud.

All three of the other Northmen had been watching the scene unfold. It seemed one minute their crew mate was bantering with the babyish girl, then there was a flash caught by the afternoon sun, and he was down without a sound. They wondered if he had broken into the mead barrel and poured some into his silver flask to enliven guard duty. But then, even from a distance they could see red geysers of dark blood gushing from his torn throat as he lay in the mud. All three screamed in fury as the guard ashore and the largest of the ship tenders rushed toward the strange scene, axes high and ready.

As they advanced, the young boy leapt back, while the girl sat, calmly watching their approach.

Aoife cast a glance at her little brother.

"Now then, Eoin, just smile at them. Remember Ma and Da and see what comes now."

The onrushing Vikings watched puzzeled as a gleaming iron blade sliced from inside the bag which filled the wagon's bed. The knife slashed quickly through the full length of the wool and disappeared again. Both stopped and stared curiously at the cart's now moving burden. Then a thundering crash assaulted the ears of the Vikings. They looked on in amazement as the wooden sides and back of the cart burst asunder, flying off in splinters.

An almost amorphous, dark and impossibly massive form seemed to slowly uncoil and rise from the shattered bed of the cart.

The torn woolen sack fell to the side. When the booted feet hit the ground behind the now half-ruined wagon, both Northmen could have sworn they felt the packed mud shudder beneath them.

The gargantuan figure stood erect to its full height and turned to face the two, its eyes burning, prognathous jaw grinning horribly.

Thorbrand counted himself the largest and strongest of the Vikings in the crew. He had been selected as guard because, Modolf thought confidently, Thorbrand could easily crush any five Irishmen who dared threaten their ship. He looked up at the approaching nightmare, which towered a head over him, and thought it could not be a man. It was clad in simple brown cowhide over a green woolen tunic which fell to the knees. Despite the lack of armor, Thorbrand saw that the black lacquered, and elegantly ornamented, iron helmet of a Beserker chieftain adorned the head of the giant. The thing must have ripped off the visor, because its terrible, scarred face was fully exposed.

No shield, nor axe nor sword served to arm the stygian vision. The Vikings could detect only a *scian,* appearing tiny at its waist, and a length of black chain dangling from a huge hand which clutched some implement. Almost immediately, the chain was released and the two could clearly see a lethally spiked, heavy iron ball, swaying loosely over the ground, as the thing toyed with its hide wrapped wooden handle. Both Norsemen backed away.

To their dread, they now saw both children were smiling, with horrible glee in their shining youthful eyes. Silently, the monstrous demon moved toward them.

"Ulf. …. Fenrir….. Brian's Wolf from Hel." called Thorbrand to his dispirited comrade.

"When we go now to Valhalla, our fathers' fathers will not disclaim us. Die now with pride and honor by my side."

Thorbrand roared an oath to Odin, and rushed the monster with shield thrust forward and flashing axe arcing above his head. In response, a huge muscular leg kicked forward, and almost casually forced the shield back and down, splattering Modolf's largest Viking unceremoniously onto the Irish mud. On his back, his shield arm broken in three places, Thorbrand looked up. He heard yet again the shrieking caw of the circling blackbird, and watched its swift dark passage. Then a whirring globe of studded iron crushed through the helmet and into his skull.

The man Thorbrand had called "Ulf" dropped the chain and spiked iron cylinder to the ground. He bent and retrieved the huge Viking battle axe from the dead hand of the mangled corpse. He wielded it with loose swings, and liked its heft. Then his green, golden-flecked, dagger eyes glared at the remaining shore bound Viking who had been moving furtively toward the girl on the cart.

With just one arm, "Ulf" brought the axe behind him and let it fly over his shoulder toward the Northman. Despite its immense weight and the distance between them, the spinning axe struck the upraised shield at its apex, and continued on to bury itself deep in the mailed chest.

Next, an arrow indignantly struck Thorbrand's already mutilated head. Another followed, and flew between "Ulf's" legs, embedding itself in one of the wooden wheels of the wagon. The pony brayed at the insult. The huge man quickly took the big Viking's shield and slid a thick arm into its sleeves. Holding it in front, he sprinted in impossibly swift and long strides. He reached the ship's side just as the next arrow impacted the shield.

He threw the shield aside, grasped along the hull, pulled, and with a leap, threw himself up and onto the deck. The last Viking guardian had thrown aside the bow, and was flying at him with an improbably huge broadsword. Too long and heavy for the Northman to employ with skill, he overshot his target and fell to the deck, where the absurdly hefty blade split a rowing bench.

As if dispatching a snared rat, the grim-visaged figure bent, took the helmet of the fallen guard in two hands, and twisted sharply, snapping the neck with a loud crack. He then stood erect, looked upward and roared out in a deep and booming voice.

"Now then Lord, there are four fewer of the bloody little heathens blackening Your and King Brian's holy Irish shores."

Chapter 2.
Beached Dragon Ship

After stripping the dead of all arms and armor, the Dalcassians piled
the bodies and burnt them. Cael and Fergus helped and noted with
interest the Munstermen were neither jubilant nor dejected. They
worked with quiet efficiency, only talking to assess the fineness of a
weapon or shield. In most cases, the quality of the enemy's kit was
vastly superior to that of the Irish. Both were aware though, Brian
had been importing, enlisting and outright stealing some of the best
craftsmen from all over Ireland and Europe to outfit his growing
Army.

Cael was still not sure it hadn't been just a violent dream, and
perhaps he was still sleeping at their high watch post of the last
several days. But the blood on his tunic and the smell of burning flesh
were real enough. He and Fergus had not been reunited until the
day's clash had come to its gory ending.

He reported excitedly to Fergus. "I was told by Cormac to follow
the orders of the swarthy leader of the little group of riders, and ran
behind them as they rode down to take positions waiting in the tree
line at the bottom of the meadow. I was then ordered to crawl to the
very edge, where the meadow met the trees, and signal when the
Northmen reached the center point of their march."

He was breathing hard, almost panting, as he told his story excited
and still afraid at the same time.

"It should have been wonderful and grand but Fergus...oh the
blood, the cries, the sounds of raw, red battle. I have to confess I
turned my eyes away a moment, not sure I could stand to watch. Fine
warrior I am."

He dropped his gaze to the ground, completely dejected.

Fergus replied, "I was assigned to Cormac himself. During the time when the Viking formation endured a shower of arrows on their happily difficult hill climb, all of the Munstermen were reclining comfortably on the grass, just over the crest of the hill. They were so relaxed and placid, the sheep came near enough to pet."

"My task was to take a concealed position where I could see the entire meadow and the Munstermen. When a certain signal was flashed by Pyrrhus' left hand, the Munstermen were to attack down the hill. I was to convey these signs to the waiting Dalcassians at the right time."

The big redhead put his hand on his friend's shoulder.

"Feel no special shame, Cael. When I saw what happened next, I wanted to run all the way back to my mother and father. The only thing that stopped me was that I was too frozen with fear to move."

So, when they rejoined after the battle, both recruits had observed the same series of events, each from his unique perspective. And both felt they had failed themselves and their friends by their fear. They hadn't had much time for discussion before they participated in the most unwelcome work of dragging and burning bodies.

Before long, two wagons, twice the size of the little shepherd cart, arrived at the top of the hill. Cormac had earlier sent word to the nearest allied clan chief to be prepared to take delivery of a gift from King Brian. The drivers of the wagons loaded the Viking arms and armor, gazing occasionally with disgust at the burning heap of Viking bodies. They also took on the wounded Dalcassian warrior to be attended by their clan's physician.

"Tell your chief, this boon comes with his king's compliments" said Cormac. "What he can't use, he can give to other good Irish Christians — just as long as you and they heed the summons when called by your king."

The recruits were surprised that this entire business of attacking and annihilating a full ship's contingent of Viking invaders, collecting their arms, and dragging and burning their bodies had taken remarkably little time.

Cormac did not give any specific orders, outline a plan of tactics, nor call for anyone to scout the way. With a knowing, feral smile he simply pronounced to his little army of infantry and cavalry, "Let us take a wee stroll down this hilly meadow and across the beach to pay a visit to the *snekkja*."

"But maybe it's already been burnt." he said.

As they marched in a surprisingly relaxed posture down the hill, Cael looked up and down the meadow — the scene of so much drama and death on this, the first real day of his new life. He shook his head and whispered to Fergus.

"Why are they simply walking, as if for some festive holy day procession, down toward that damned beached ship with its four remaining Vikings. Can those Norsemen not bring the ship to safety on the open water? I'm not sure what such a thing requires, but, still, approaching so blindly just seems dangerous."

The Irish band descended, negotiated the little rocky cliff, and then they were on the beach. None wore a helmet. Shields, axes and swords were all secured in slings and scabbards. Strangely, after collecting as many spent arrows as they could, the horsemen left their bows and quivers back with their ponies in the keeping of the shepherd, and not a man of them had more than a personal *scian* on his belt.

Cael pondered this apparent complacency on the part of grizzled and skilled warriors. *Either they know something I do not,* he thought, *or they trust Cormac with their lives completely.*

The stretch of beach between the meadow and the beached craft was minimal. A few steps more and they had a clear field of view to the north. The boat rested less than arrow range distant and appeared calm and undisturbed.

As they approached closer to the long ship, Cael confirmed his eyes hadn't lied. Nothing aboard stirred. One glance at the shallow-hull ship exposed its entirety to the viewer. No places to hide, and no "below deck." The recruits were instantly alarmed, yet their comrades were gazing around a bend to the north, toward a nearby stretch of the beach that jutted just a bit further inland. It hadn't been visible until now.

With a start, their hands tightening around their hunting spears, Cael and Fergus were shocked to see the two babyish siblings. Each was sitting in the packed mud, leaning against a wheel of the little cart. Both had their hands behind their backs, tied snugly to the wagon. Even more disturbing, each was also gagged with a swath of linen.

"At least the Viking beasts haven't yet butchered them." exclaimed Fergus. Both recruits braced and awaited Cormac's command to deploy for battle.

No such command was given. The entire band continued to walk at ease toward the bound children, The recruits' heads were swiveling fearfully in all directions. They bent low and followed the rest.

"*Fáilte.*"

The Gaelic cry of welcome rang out in an amazingly deep and resonant voice, shattering the relative quiet of the beach and its environs.

The entire band turned as one to the source of that greeting. Cael and Fergus stared in dazed wonderment as they discerned an enormous, dark figure, leaning casually against a rocky outcropping. He stood taller than any Viking or Irishman either had ever seen. He was holding an impossibly immense broadsword and twirling it in apparent curiosity. In the mud beside him, clad in the opulent and ornamented frock of a high-ranking Viking female, a young woman with shimmering blond hair knelt tied, her head bowed.

"She told me this amusingly large blade is of great ritual significance to the bloody little heathens, but the heft is all wrong."

The giant reported this to them as if in mere banter over weather or cattle. Then, he took the sword's hilt in both hands and whirled it in circles around the beach, finally loosing it. To the astonishment of them all, the broad sword flew high into the air, causing the gulls to screech and swerve. It splashed into the waves well out into the gray Irish Sea.

"Cael, Fergus. Come here" Cormac called grinning broadly, "I want you to meet my comrade, King Brian's war captain."

He put his big hands on their shoulders as they continued to stare at the fierce giant.

"Even King Brian calls him *Faolan an Trodach....* Wolf the Quarrelsome. And he is indeed our darlin' *Mac Tíre,* our own dear wolf. The bards and poets write of him, *'An Faolan a n-diaidh Danmare,* 'the Wolf who hunts the Danes.' He is the reason all of us are here. He is his royal foster father's planner, designer, and architect of the cursed Vikings' *Ragnarok.* That's the name they, themselves, call their coming destruction. He will serve Brian and create the means for the invaders' slaughter in blood, iron and fire."

Now the recruits were closer, and observed their newly introduced captain in detail. They were taken back to notice he appeared to have lived not many more years than themselves. Less than half the age of Cormac. His face was barbarically terrible, silver-scarred. Yet they knew Irish women and girls would consider it brutally handsome. Comrades would find that grim visage appealing and masculine, and take comfort calling him friend. And Vikings would recoil in fear.

"Now then, Wolf, what have you done to those sweet little children, and who is this fair haired, peacock hen kneeling in the mud? You never seem to do anything simply and directly. All you had to do was to slay four guards and take the ship."

With a mischievous smile, Wolf replied, "Sure'n you can see the ship is well taken. And as for the guards...Come here, you heathen wench."

This command was given in perfect Danish, and the blond girl immediately crawled toward him on her knees. Cormac could now see four round objects behind her. Adding to the day's horror, they were raggedly severed, bearded heads.

"She was a passenger on yonder vile scow. I found her cowering under a piece of torn sail cloth after I slaughtered the guards. Following a short and pleasant conversation, I learned she is the daughter of some damned Danish dignitary and was promised to some equally high-ranking heathen bastard who now sits in Sitric's court. Fine then, if we can't ransom her for half of Dublin, she'll make a proper, smoke-smudged, kitchen wench for some poor Munster family."

Cael gazed at the kneeling foreigner with curiosity. Curiosity soon turned to involuntary, compellingly magnetic, attraction. The young Connaughtman thought she was the most perfect and beautiful creature he had ever seen. Her abject posture only heightened her appeal for him. She was certainly his age, maybe a season greater.

This was too much, he thought. 'First I am present at as bloody and noble a battle as was ever sung by the bards of the ancient Milesians. Then I meet a terrifying giant who seems one of those ancient Formorian monsters of legend our mothers scared us about. And he to be our war chief. And now I see this angel who is, in truth, a pagan witch. God help us all.'

"And how, Wolf, does that explain what you've done to those innocent little cubs at the wagon?" Cormac asked with a wry smirk.

"If they're cubs, then 'tis wolf cubs they are. And you know that's a good thing coming from me."

The big young man flashed a mirthful grin.

"As I was conversing with this Godless foreigner, both of them swarmed aboard, rushing toward us, brandishing their slashing little *scians,* intent on butchery. They ignored my command to stop. It was only at the last moment I was able to catch them both up, and still they thrust themselves at her, cursing in a most un-Christian manner. All I could do was bind them, awaiting your arrival. Without a pause they screamed curses at her, until I gagged them to get some peace."

Wolf gazed over at the two tiny forms at the wagon's wheels, shook his head and laughed. "I like them immensely and want to bring them with me back to Cashel."

He cast his piercing green eyes back to the two recruits, visually measuring their worth in the late afternoon sun. He quickly discerned the reasons they had been chosen. The wiry, auburn-haired one was of medium height, and Wolf knew intuitively he would not grow taller. Still, the lad displayed an aura of endurance and agility, easily noted from the manner in which he carried himself.

In contrast his red-haired companion was already a head taller and would undoubtedly gain even more height and bulk. He walked like a proud young bull, straining to make its way through any obstacle. In very few years, he would be a bulwark of mass and muscle. Wolf could almost see the coming transformation through his own eyes even now.

"So then, I see a splendid swift "Magyar" and a sturdy stalwart "Spartan" before me. You've done well, Cormac. Now, let us burn that damned scow and hike to the top of that pretty little hill. After that, we head west once again."

Wolf had not claimed they were heading "home" since he considered the entire island of Ireland to be his home.

The Dalcassians cheered and rushed to throw newly lit torches on the beached *snekkja*. It was quickly enveloped in cheerfully cracking flames. They retraced their earlier route up the meadow, taking the still bound children and Danish captive in tow. Cormac moved off in a different direction, leading the shepherd's pony along another longer trail.

At the summit once again, they were met by another group of Dalcassians, who were traveling to the northeast to collect young recruits from among the ranks of the storied *Dál Riata*. This was the original Irish *Cenél*, the groupings of clans which had centuries ago crossed into Scotland and established kingdoms there.

These warriors cried out in cheerful greetings, happy to see their almost legendary war chief who had directed them to come to this place days ago. They were on horseback, and had brought with them a number of extra mounts, including two Connemara ponies.

Cormac led the draft pony to the shepherd, a mournful look on the Munster leader's face.

"I regret good shepherd your little cart has been damaged. But your sheep and pony are fine and fit."

The shepherd nodded and slowly retrieved the pouch of coins from a pocket. Surprisingly he seemed unconcerned.

"No matter, sir, 'tis a pleasure to do some small bit for me own king and country."

Cormac took the shepherd's hand and turned it palm up. He poured about half the contents of the pouch into the old man's hand.

"Here now, that should buy a cart and more for you," Cormac laughed and turned to rejoin his men.

The entire band now gathered around Wolf. He pointed to Cael.

"This one will go with Pyrrhus and his four riders to where the Magyars are training." Gesturing toward Fergus he added, "This red -maned bull will go with the Dalcassians back to Munster to become a "Spartan.""

"Yet again 'Magyar' and 'Spartan'," said Cael to Fergus in a low voice. "Does he not know we've not the slightest notion what he's on about?"

Pyrrhus now spoke up to the group's leader. "If you're indeed planning to take the wolf cubs with you, I've an idea to make everyone's life easier.

"Our Magyar training camp is in dire need of another kitchen woman. The captive will of course never be ransomed for what you demand Captain, so she should go with us. That way you can let the waifs accompany you without bindings, and there will be no Viking pagan for them to slaughter."

"That makes all the sense in the world," added Cormac. Wolf nodded in agreement.

To Cael's delight, the two Connemara ponies were brought for him and the Danish girl to accompany Pyrrhus' party. Then the seven riders set off west amidst a chorus of health and luck wishing *Sláns* from the others.

As they rode, Cael asked his first of what would be many questions to their swarthy leader. "And where will we find this training camp, sir?"

"Connemara, of course," Pyrrhus replied with a laugh, pleased that its location had been concealed from at least some of the local people.

Chapter 3.
Gleann Mama, Laigin, Ireland
30 December, Nollaig, Seven Years Earlier

Murcha Mac Brian, King Brian's oldest and strongest son, sat sweating in his saddle despite the frost of an Irish winter. It had been a brutal but glorious day. His father, for all his fifty-eight years, had fought like a lion amidst the ranks of the Dalcassian infantry. Brian was always most comfortable on his feet, surrounded by clansmen of the *Dál Cais*.

Murcha was equally at home standing stalwart in a shield wall or thundering through the glens on the back of a galloping warhorse. Cavalry was not common anywhere in Ireland though, and he'd never fought in a mounted column that exceeded twenty-five sword swingers. There were only twenty of his mounted clansmen with him when they first pursued the enormous wave of wildly fleeing Norsemen pouring out of the glen of the gap at Gleann Mama.

It was not long ago that the *Ard Rí*, Malachi Mór, from Ireland's central province of Meath, had come to an agreement with Murcha's father, Brian. The two of them would divide Ireland's rule between them. Malachi would remain High King and control the north and east. Brian would have the south and west. Though it was clear to all that Brian's ideas and the force of his personality were in ascendancy among the Gaels, this accommodation had worked well until recently.

Maelmora, king of the southeast province of Leinster, had chafed at the thought of taking a subordinate role to the Munster King Brian whose royal court was far to the west at Cashel. The men of Leinster, also called Laigin, had always been hostile to any perception of domination from kings to the north or west. Maelmora had decided to ally himself with the Norse in their long-established stronghold in

Dublin, and their ruler Sitric Silkbeard. For their part, the Dublin Vikings were eager to do anything to split the Irish, and impede what they could already sense was the increasing threat fueled by the fiery Dalcassian king. Malachi had sacked Dublin once before during a time of Norse weakness. That was in 980 when the Vikings caused some perceived offence to him. But even still, the Northmen had less concern for him than for Brian who, with his brother Mahon, had in 968 attacked, plundered and completely destroyed a strongly established Viking city at Limerick in the west. The Dublin Norse knew there had been no mercy shown at that time. Every Viking male had been put to the sword; all their women taken as booty. No Norse structure in Limerick had remained intact. Yet, over the years many more of their Viking kinsmen had nevertheless poured into Dublin.

So, in December of 999, the combined forces of Leinster and the Northmen in Dublin took to the field in rebellion, in defiance of both Brian and the *Ard Rí*. The Munster King had acted first, sending a rider to Malachi suggesting the Munster and Meath armies move immediately against the rebels and their foreign allies. Brian impatiently awaited the response from the High King. Finally, after what seemed like dithering on the part of Meath, the response arrived. Malachi would send his army south to meet Brian's.

Murcha had ridden ahead with his small band of riders to greet the Meathmen inside the borders of Leinster at the assigned place. His father followed, not far behind, with thousands of marching infantry from Munster and Connaught. The Munster riders were sitting on the top of a small hill, looking north, when they saw what they thought was the first contingent of the High King's forces coming toward them through the tree line. Murcha grinned and his men cheered, and rushed down enthusiastically to meet their allies.

There were two horsemen among the host from Meath, and they rode to greet Murcha's riders.

"*Dia daoibh.*" "God be with you all." cried Murcha, as the two formidably armed Gaels came closer. They slowed, then stopped, as one of the new arrivals introduced himself as war chief of the High King.

Murcha was pleased. It was always an honor to meet a fellow warrior and leader, especially if he was to be a weapon brother. He looked to the north again, expecting to see following contingents of warriors.

"My name is Murcha. I'm King Brian's son and one of his chiefs. I look forward to greeting the *Ard Rí* when he arrives with the rest of the army," Murcha said amiably.

The Meath chieftain couldn't hide his shame. He looked down for a moment, sighing. He tried to recover.

"King Malachi has sent his best warriors and trusts we, and King Brian's host, will crush the rebellion quickly. My men have been dispatching Vikings to Valhalla for years and with such allies as you Munstermen at our sides, we cannot fail to rid the land of them all.

"As for Maelmora and the Leinster traitors, they are simply sniveling vermin who once again will learn a lesson."

The Dalcassian was immediately furious and fought to control himself. His men, listening on, shared his anger, as they gazed at the still oncoming formation. Brian was marching fast to meet them, with multiple thousands of men. Malachi had sent only one thousand. The Leinster forces alone had close to three times that number. The Vikings could bring almost twice Leinster's three thousand. Murcha knew immediately the combined forces of Brian and Malachi would be outnumbered two to one, on hostile territory.

Turning his mount, Murcha told the captain to have the host follow his lead. The small force of Munster cavalry rode slowly to the southwest. Brian was always outnumbered, he thought, but this time could prove different. He cursed Maelmora's soul to hell for selling out his loyalty to his own people, and taking arms at the side of the damned Viking heathens.

***

The King of Munster, his son Murcha, Teighe O'Kelly of Connaught, and the captain of the Meath warriors, gathered about an oval, curiously symmetrical, rocky formation. Around them, was a series of large upright standing stones, each twice the size and twenty times the weight of a grown man. These encircled a large rectangular block of the same craggy rock, which almost seemed a feasting house's table. Aged stains and jagged cracks proved how long this place had existed. With a silent and reverential bow, King Brian of Munster gave hushed homage to those prehistoric Irish aboriginals who had come in the wake of the retreating glaciers. Those first Europeans, he knew with confidence, had built this stony altar, long before the arrival of the Celts and their Druids.

Earlier in the day, Murcha had pleaded with the king.

"Don't allow the Meath Captain to take part in our council. Malachi deliberately insults us with his paltry contribution against the combined forces we face. I believe it would have been better, Father, if you had assumed the High Kingship yourself and ordered Malachi as your vassal to deploy his entire army to our cause."

The Connaught chief, Teighe, laughed.

"Would you have preferred, Murcha, if no Meathman at all had come to fight and possibly die with us? Given our Irish temperament, it's a miracle we can ever have even two provinces at each other's sides. Here we have three."

O'Kelly continued with a smirk and pronounced, "I personally am not at all comfortable having to parley with two flea-infested, fat-bellied, flatulent Munstermen like yourselves."

At that, Brian broke into a fit of mirthful laughter until tears rolled from his eyes.

"Well, Teighe, please know we are humbled and blessed to be in the company of you and your pristine and immaculately groomed Connaught noblemen," which caused even Murcha to bellow along with the other two.

When the Meath war chief later joined them in the center of the stone circle, Brian welcomed him vigorously.

He outlined their plan in a concise and easily understood manner. The king explained that not far from them was Gleann Mama, considered an ancient stronghold of the Leinster kings.

At that moment, a robed clergyman joined them and draped a sheet of parched vellum, annotated with markings over the "table". This man was a tonsured monk, trained in map making, who had come from the monastery at Clonmacnoise. They all knew the good Christian clergy had little affinity for Irish kings who embraced heathen allies. Leinsterman or not, this one was Irish.

A quick glance showed their current location and Brian's entire plan in surprising simplicity. The Meath captain nodded in respect to the Munster king. Drawing his finger over the map, Brian outlined his sequence of events,

"The Leinster army has already assembled below Gleann Mama to await their Viking allies. The Norse are just to our east, still oblivious to the fact we've arrived. They will come down from Dublin as quickly as possible, passing between these little mountains and through this valley defile above which we now sit.

"Teighe will wait until the Vikings pass below, then take his five hundred Connaught madmen and move behind them behind to block any retreat. It will be late night or early morning when they appear. It's already our lovely Irish winter, cold and raining steadily, and the mist is hovering thick in the valley. Our three thousand Dalcassians will be just above them, but out of sight on the right slope as they pass. And King Malachi's one thousand best warriors will take positions to assure Maelmora doesn't spring on us from behind while we're engaging his Dublin allies."

Then, turning to the Meath captain, Brian added with genuine appreciation, "And it's glad I am to have your one thousand with us in this field. No matter what happens, please convey my gratitude to King Malachi when this is all behind us."

***

The Norse marched in multiple broken columns, with roughly a thousand sword and axe men in each. They were forced to break and loosen their formations by the narrowness of the defile. The driving rain, tenebrous darkness, and enveloping mist were of no great discomfort to these seafaring warriors. All had all been through much worse while pulling at oars during long ocean voyages with freezing rain, hail or snow assailing them as they strained.

At first it was just a murmur. Then, as they proceeded with heads bent, the sound of pipes became recognizable. Many stopped and gazed up at the black, steep hills to either side, just as the pipes broke into a loud crescendo and drums thundered.

From above, to their left they saw what seemed to be incandescently bright dragons tramping in the hills. These visions now appeared to by flying down upon them. With no time to react, the Vikings were stunned to watch flaming balls of fire crashing into their foremost thin marching columns. That was followed by the loud rumblings of large rocks and polished stones falling with force across the length of the dispersed groups. The fiery balls careened into men and set many ablaze.

Then, down from their left, and out of the darkness of the forested slopes, erupted an avalanche of screaming, cursing Irish warriors, falling on the scattered Viking marchers. Unable to maneuver or deploy in their accustomed shield-locked manner, the Norse were quickly falling in their hundreds to the flashing swords and axes of the wild waves from the hills.

The Irish commanders could see little from their vantage points on the hill. The night and the mist made for seeming chaos and confusion. They could only trust in the plan. But even in those times, at the turn of the millennium, there was a universal expression all real soldiers know well: *No plan survives first contact.*

The balls of flame had been simple round stones, wrapped with packed straw, bound with sinew, and doused with pine pitch. They had been intended to stop the forward movement of the Vikings, to encourage them to go back the way they came into the waiting shield wall formation of Connaughtmen in position in the defile behind them. Instead, the surviving Vikings ran to their front running wildly, around the still burning flames, escaping the Dalcassian onslaught. There were simply too many Norse to catch and kill. They poured out of the narrow glen, still in their thousands, spilling out in multiple streams rushing toward the east,

The force of Meath warriors was oriented facing east, assuring the Leinster army would not surprise them, when they heard cries to their rear. They had been deployed four deep and in two roughly equal sized formations. Almost as one, they turned about and were astonished to see in the now breaking dawn, multitudes of Vikings dashing in no particular order, being chased by the entire Munster army, who were running them down like vicious slashing hounds.

Shields locked, the Meath warriors moved vigorously to crush the disarrayed Dublin Norse between themselves and the Munster pursuers behind them. Even with Malachi's little army in the battle, there were still too many wildly scrambling Vikings to end it all right there. Hundreds of the Vikings were smashed under the blades of Meath and taken from behind by Munster sword thrusts.

Murcha's twenty horsemen, who had been commanded by Brian to deploy with Malachi's army, constituted the only real cavalry among the combined forces of the two Irish kings. Murcha knew his riders would not be effective on the slopes with the other Dalcassians. He also knew Brian wanted one of his own to monitor the Meathmen for any signs of treachery.

This general rout was where mounted cavalry was at its most effective. The fastest of the scrambling, winded Vikings was no match for the slowest of Murcha's horses. The score of riders were able to massacre the fleeing foe at will. When one of them might turn to make a fight of it, two or three of the Dalcassians would surround and quickly overwhelm the doomed enemy.

By now, most of the Dublin force had thrown away their shields and helmets and were running aimlessly eastward. Murcha, leisurely trotting behind, saw that the Norsemen were running in the direction of the main force of the waiting Leinster army. He watched a group of four Leinster horsemen break off from the formation and gallop furiously away to the east.

The stunned Leinster warriors could hardly believe their eyes. First they were amazed to see hundreds and hundreds of shieldless, fleeing Vikings pouring around them on all sides, bound for some imagined safety to the east. Could they really be trying to make for the walls of Dublin? Then they gazed with disgust and dismay at the sight of their king, Maelmora, and his mounted escort flying ahead of the Vikings in a dash to escape.

With that, Maelmora's dispirited army broke and ran to join the general retreat.

Eventually, even the Munster and Meath armies had to slow to catch their breath. Running and cutting down Vikings and Leinster traitors was exhilarating but exhausting. The combined rebel forces had gone off in three general directions. Throughout all of this, the five hundred strong blocking force of Connaughtmen back in the narrow valley had seen no combat. This group now marched up in smart formation to join their temporarily resting allies.

"Never did I suspect King Brian of Munster would be so dishonorable as to deliberately keep his Connaught friends from the glory of battle." said Teighe, only half in jest.

"They did the opposite of what I expected. Instead of withdrawing to apparent safety from whence they came, and into your waiting blades, they ran ahead through fire, rocks and the stones of the slingers to dash from the mouth of the defile," Brian said. "Presently, they and Leinster's army, and Maelmora himself, are all speeding toward the Liffey in wildly dispersed bands."

"And what now?" asked Teighe, grinning once again, his blood up for the pursuit.

"We've brought down fewer of the Leinster rebels than we have Vikings, they're fleeing in the center, the Norse are split in groups to their north and south. You take your men and hunt down the Laigin rebels. They are probably no more than three times your number by now; an easy morning's work."

Brian continued. "We and Malachi's men will go after the Vikings. I expect we'll find them trying to ford the Liffey at various places. We'll slaughter them all there."

***

Murcha had not been present during this discussion between Brian and Teighe. Earlier, on taking notice of the mounted escort flying out from the formation of stunned Leinster warriors, he had commanded his eager riders to follow at a gallop. He knew intuitively the fleeing detachment could be none other than King Maelmora and his guards. Murcha still burned with fury at the Irish traitor.

These Leinster riders had detected with alarm a force of twenty mounted Dalcassians, one of them holding aloft the banner of King Brian, coursing around the Leinster army and speeding directly toward them. Despite their lead, they inexplicably turned into a nearby wooded area.

Murcha knew his task would be easier now. The Dalcassians brought their mounts to the tree line and entered at the spot they had last seen the enemy. The woods were thick and the horses and men moved slow and gingerly, following a trail of broken branches. Before long, they were amused to see the unconscious form of a young Leinster rider.

"They were riding much too quickly and with too little control. This one must have knocked himself out on the stout branch of the tree above him," Murcha said to the others.

"I could tell they were panicked when they dashed into the woods instead of leading us on a merry long chase. Their horses are certainly fresher than ours. They should have had a good chance to escape."

Ignoring the boy, they moved on carefully.

With a cry of rage, two figures leapt from behind thorny black bushes to slash up at the riders. One of them succeeded in unhorsing a Dalcassian, before he was felled by another Munsterman's sword. The other was simply kicked in the chin by his tall intended victim before an upraised *scian* could thrust home.

"If the rest of the Leinster army fights as formidably as these, our infantry could be in trouble," the tall Dalcassian horseman laughed.

Soon, they came to a small clearing where four horses were contentedly feeding on the lush grass.

"Look at this tall Yew tree. It stands alone in this glade as if adorning the center of a small green garden," Murcha said as he examined the tree and its branches with interest.

Peering upward with concentration, his face changed to a countenance of surprise and amusement. "Can it be?" he said aloud, shaking his head.

The other riders watched as Murcha dismounted and leisurely bent to retrieve a stone the size of his fist. Without a word he strode casually to the tree's base and peered up as if measuring something. He then brought his arm back behind his shoulder, eyes glued to something above and near the trunk. He hurled the rock mightily with a muffled curse.

To the amazed disbelief of the Dalcassian riders watching, a body fell out of the tree, striking the ground unconscious at their chief's feet. He turned to his men.

"Bind the hands of the King of Leinster. When he awakens, tie a rope around his neck and secure it to my horse's saddle. We'll take him back to my father. Right now, I think some of us might have a bit of mead in our flasks, right? Well, break it out."

The youngest of them slid from his horse, grasping a twisted bit of hide. He securely bound the wrists of the prostrate turncoat. Rising, he stood and kicked the Laigin king hard in his well padded backside. The youth was pleased to receive a muffled groan of pain for his effort. Then he drank deeply from the jovially offered leather flask.

Chapter 4.
Ath-Cliath, Dublin, Ireland
1 January, 1000 A.D., Day One of the New Millennium

"They shall come to Gleann-Mama

It will not be water over hands. Persons shall drink a deadly draft around the stone at Claen-Conghair. From the victorious overthrow they shall retreat, till they reach past the wood northwards, And Ath-cliath the fair shall be burned after the ravaging the Leinster plain." *(Annals of the four Masters)*

The tiny settlement that the first invading Norse established in Ireland well over a century ago was expertly selected. The broad encircling bay on Ireland's central east coast protected the wide mouths of three rivers. They chose a spot on the south bank just beyond the opening of the middle river. They leapt out of their dragon ships, axes raised, almost as if they owned the earth upon which they tread. Neither men nor monsters rose to meet them. After sending swift, scouting runners into the surrounding countryside, they began to construct secure, earthen ramparts around this perfect little sanctuary which seemed to welcome them.

Over the years, more and more of their Norse brothers and cousins sailed down from the north to join them. Then, when all seemed secure, their blonde and red-haired women came to make their lives easier. For scores of years, they all thrived as long as they remained close to their sanctuary, only daring to conduct quick, flashing raids at soft targets around the island's coast.

They knew in the interior of this very moist, green and pleasant land, warriors, as fierce and wild as themselves, lived among ridiculously small and numerous patches of ground the Irish absurdly called "kingdoms."

The Vikings would never choose the stronghold of one of these kingdoms to pillage. Small, isolated clusters of waddled earth and thatched huts yielded much more easily acquired booty. The most attractive victims for the Odin-worshipping cutthroats were the abodes of the gentle Christian clergymen, who labored at well-tended monasteries and grounds, praying to their Jesus. They also sold perfectly cultured foodstuffs including mead, beer, honey and vegetables to their neighbors and parishioners.

Dublin grew prosperous, both from raw plunder and the lucrative appeal of commercial trade itself. Over the years, the Irish would occasionally retake the settlement from the invaders. But the Vikings would always return, either through force of arms or, more typically, because the Northmen were much more widely traveled and made the port settlement a center of Atlantic coastal trading that benefited both themselves and the Irish. Now, Sitric, the ruler of this bustling port center, had flown hastily to the north as the victorious armies of the two Irish kings descended on the city.

The walls of Dublin were constructed of raised and packed earth, topped with the spiked palisades of thousands of tree-trunk thick, wooden stakes. This barrier formed a semi-circle around the settlement's center with the walls running into the river Liffey. The invaders from Munster, Connaught and Meath now encountered hundreds of wattle and stone shacks and shops outside the walls, where peasants of no particular clan dwelt and made their livings providing services to the traders. They also functioned as middlemen in the commercial exchanges which occurred during times of relative peace among the Vikings and various Irish Kingdoms.

The three gates had been flung open by Irish servants within the city, who became wild and exultant as they looked upon the few small and ragged bands of Viking survivors slinking ignominiously back, trying to board any moored vessel within reach.

One ancient and wizened Irish servant cried out disdainfully at the fleeing survivors.

"Not long ago, you marched out from here. What happened to that fierce and indomitable band of northern supermen on your mission to crush your pathetic foemen? Have you met the *Nemain,* who brings fear and terror to all who threaten Ireland? Or did *Badb's* undead warriors spring up to meet you in the mountains?"

Inside the walls, the victorious Gaels found wooden longhouses with brightly painted doors. Some of these were immensely tall and wide and functioned as halls of commerce or barracks. Others were more finely made with opulently carved wooden doors and spacious courtyards.

These were the citadels of Dublin's elite. Into one, stormed Murcha with a few of his riders, all turned into infantry now that they were inside the city. With him, was his cousin Cormac, son of Murcha's dead uncle, Mahon.

The inside of the house was disrelished, as if some fierce wind had disrupted table, rugs, tapestries and chairs.

"I suspect this chaos is the vengeful work of Irish servants who no doubt hated the house's occupants. They took their fury out on the former masters' property before they too ran off to who knows where," said Murcha.

"Or perhaps the house's owners have simply knocked things asunder in a wild dash to get out. In any case we haven't yet seen a single Viking man or woman here," said Cormac in reply.

They expected this place to be as empty as the rest of the city. There were no Vikings, dead or alive, within the walls. They had all fled northward on horse or afoot, or in various boats and ships in hopes of finding refuge, anyplace but here.

While the homes of prosperous Irish clansmen were circular timber lodges, these Norse longhouses were of narrow width and impressive depth. This one was twice as wide as the breadth of one of their long ships and three times its length. It had been built around a wooden frame on a simple stone footing. Its walls were constructed of rough planks with wattle and daub.

"Do you think they've all gone off for good and we're well rid of them this time?" Cormac asked Murcha.

"I have prayed my father would do what he and your father did to the Vikings in Limerick those years ago. Kill them all, burn their dwellings and take their women."

Shaking his head sadly, he continued. "But he grows gentler of late, less filled with the rage of earlier years. I fear we'll indeed be forced to battle yet again with these accursed Northmen before our island is free."

As they entered, they noted the dwelling was divided into several rooms. Two rows of thick wooden posts ran down the length of the structure supporting the roof beams. These columns in turn divided the interior into three long aisles.

The long central corridor featured the packed dirt floor with which the Irish were familiar. Ashes from the fires of the house spread on the floor acted as absorbents. A long fire pit, now extinguished, extended for almost half the length of this central corridor which was clearly the main chamber. At its end was an imposing hearth with stones set upright from the ground. There were three smoke holes in the roof which provided ventilation and surprisingly bright illumination from the skies above. Three legged wooden stools, now tumbled onto their sides, were scattered haphazardly around the ashy floor.

On either side of this central cooking and gathering area, between the roof support columns and the longhouse's walls, were raised wooden benches covered by rough-cut planks. Some of these side corridors were further partitioned off to form several closed individual chambers. These rooms were for sitting, working and sleeping.

"Note the several small openings covered with animal membranes where the roof meets the wall," remarked Cormac. "This is the house of a high-ranking Norse family."

A number of stone-cut lamps were scattered about the side rooms, none of them lit. "They use fish liver or seal oil for fuel and cotton grass as a wick just as we do. Even without the illumination of the lamps, the light from the smoke holes and windows keeps the interior bright and almost airy. We could learn much from their builders," Cormac went on.

"My father has ordered all the homes of the Dublin ruling elite to be burnt but to leave the commercial buildings intact. He feels there might be value in allowing some Vikings to remain in Dublin and continue to bring the benefits of trade and commerce to the rest of the island. And that is why I know this fight is not to be our last." Murcha pronounced this with an air of resigned regret.

"Perhaps something or someone will arise to convince the king that the foreigners must be annihilated or absorbed. We cannot live alongside them as long as they call any part of Ireland their own," replied Cormac in agreement with his cousin's sentiment. "But at least we'll torch this vipers' nest of a house before we leave."

Some of the warriors began collecting Norse goods: stools, trestle tables, stone lamps, wooden chests, sheepskin bedcovers and woolen blankets; anything of use that the fleeing Vikings left behind. Brian had ordered these to be distributed to the poorest Irish families. Murcha's men discovered a vertical weaving loom, and that was brought outside to one of the waiting pony-drawn carts.

When these items were gathered, and the longhouse was emptied of anything of use or value, Cormac and Murcha kicked open a rear door and exited into the grounds behind, where they expected to find places of storage. There they discovered two additional structures of much more primitive construction than the elaborate longhouses or the commercial halls.

Cormac, who had spent some time visiting various Norse trading posts to barter Irish goods for Viking wares, explained to Murcha, "These are meant to store large items, or sometimes, as a means to house *praelars*. That's what they call their slaves and prisoners."

Each a third the size of the main house, these were sunken-floor huts, half buried in the ground. Made of stone and wattle with thatched roofs, one featured a central smoke hole, indicating a fireplace was within. Its door was torn off its leather hinges and, peering inside, Cormac could easily see the hut had been a lowly living and cooking place. Now it was obviously empty. Not far from the first, the other hut, its door still intact, had no smoke aperture. Incredibly, they heard soft murmurings coming from inside; a sad, yet soothing, voice. This was met by a rumbling low growl, which increased in pitch to a bellowing roar. Then silence again. The men looked to each other and drawing their swords from scabbards, they strode toward the last hut.

As they came closer, they observed this structure was more sturdily and securely constructed than the other. It was enveloped by two layers of heavy stones all around, extending to almost the pinnacle of its conical crown. From this central point projected a wooden beam which resembled the thick mast of a large dragon ship.

The door had been designed to be secured from the outside, and though it was still closed, they noticed a thick length of iron chain strewn on the ground. They slowly and cautiously pushed. It swung open with a high-pitched creak. The daylight illumined a small patch that barely penetrated the tenebrous darkness within. As their eyes became accustomed to the murk, they eventually were able to see a tiny stone lamp, with a paltry flame, casting an eerie phosphorescence. This allowed them to make out several ill-defined forms in the low-roofed interior.

"They came at him in a rage. He butchered them all."

The unexpected, subdued voice of an old woman with the lilting south Munster accent of Desmumu drifted from one corner just behind them. Both men stepped toward her. They could see she was sitting on a stool, staring into the dimness toward the center of the hut. Only then did they hear the deep, steady, and seemingly predacious, breathing of something hulking, just where her eyes were fixed.

Cormac gazed at a pale form, which appeared to faintly glow in the faint light the tiny lamp cast. It was either sitting or crouched there, leaning against the massive wooden mast which thrust up through the roof. Other indistinct forms were bunched around it. These were prostrate on the dirt floor.

Cormac called out to one of the men waiting outside.

"Fetch a lighted stone lamp from the longhouse."

A young warrior dashed back and returned clutching the requested item, curious and eager to join the two commanders inside. Now, to their fascination, the room revealed its grisly contents.

It was indeed an old Irish woman, dressed in a stained woolen garment, who had uttered those baleful first words. To their astonishment, the pale figure in the room's center was merely a young boy. He was improbably tall and rangy yet alarmingly thin. His wrists were encircled with metal cuffs, and these, in turn, were connected by short but thick links of chain. One ankle was cuffed and chained to the massive wooden post. He was naked but for a filthy leather loin cloth around his narrow hips. His hair was so deeply chestnut brown it was almost black, and fell in thick, long unruly coils to below his shoulders. From the top of that mane of wild hair to the swath of leather at his waist, he was covered in streaming rivulets of crimson blood.

What Cormac thought at first had been the sound of labored breathing, he now recognized as low, threatening growls, emanating from narrow lips which centered a powerful and thrusting jaw. Then, for the first time, the Irish warriors could recognize what was scattered on the floor around him. On either side, two corpses, adorned in the battle armor of Viking ravagers, lay outstretched, their viscous blood coating the packed earth of the floor.

Both were headless.

Between these, prone on the floor, directly before the cross-legged and growling apparition, an even more bizarre spectacle revealed itself. The body of an elegantly dressed, middle aged Viking woman lay face down, its head turned unnaturally to one side. Placed with precision in front of the women's unseeing eyes were the two severed heads of the slain Northmen.

"I'm a learned cook, an educated chef indeed. For fifty years I've been prized and treasured among powerful chieftains all over Ireland for my skills in a kitchen. Any maiden can prepare succulent beef, pork or mutton. I can turn badger, venison, squirrel, and even seal into elegant feasts beyond the imagination."

This sudden and incongruous exclamation from the old woman caused the three Irish warriors to gape at her with surprise. "Do not frighten or hurt him. God knows he's had enough pain in his young life."

She then began to tell the story in a soft but steady voice.

Chapter 5.
Viking Controlled-Dublin
Bondage and Fury

The woman began by reiterating she'd been an artisan among the class of roving artisans.

"I've never married, for scores of years I've traveled in the company of various bards and musicians. I've been employed by kings and chieftains who sought the best talent for their festivals, marriages and wakes. Two years ago, as I traveled with a handful of cheerful companions to the clan of an Osraige chieftain, our little group was set upon by a ranging pack of thirty pillaging Norse. They must have rowed their long boat inland as long as the river would allow."

Cormac and Murcha nodded as this was a familiar tale throughout their island.

"The Godless *Gaill*, foreigners, have no use for Irish poetry nor what they consider the droning of our majestic music. They promptly murdered the gentle and cheerful poets and musicians with slashes from sharpened, evil *seaxes*. They had no doubt pillaged the blades from some Saxon settlement across the sea in England."

Some of the young warriors, who had joined the cousins in the hut, winced at such an atrocity. The wandering artisans; poets, musicians and cooks, were highly valued and never molested by any of the various Irish clans and kingdoms.

"They found me hiding under my cooking tools and the others' musical instruments in the back of the little wagon our group had shared. They immediately surmised that I was a cook, and from the company I kept, most likely a skilled one."

"Even barbarians prize a talented cook" she said with a hint of pride, "especially when accustomed to their own food preparers, who have little notion to concoct anything beyond smoked fish. I was taken along with them and not long later sold to the master of this Dublin longhouse, a Viking of notoriety, and kinsman of the King of Norway, he boasted. I joined the small group of servants and worked under the direction of the master's hatchet-faced and barren blonde wife who treated us all with frustrated cruelty and disdain."

"I was kept with two others, a middle-aged man and woman from a clan of the Airgialla in the north. They had been captured as teens. While I cooked, these two fetched water and foodstuffs, and tended the sheep and pigs in the owner's nearby meadows. All three of us slept in that thatched hut yonder around a snug central fireplace on raised wooden cots which the servant man had constructed himself."

One of the warriors passed her a flask with cool water. She drank delicately, and continued.

"It was these two who told me the tale of the inhabitant of this always locked, darkened and unheated hut, which shared the grounds alongside our own. He had come when he was about five holding tightly onto the shoulder of his proud and beautiful young mother. They had been taken during a raid somewhere on the west coast of Ireland. That had been nine years ago, they told me. They related how the boy's father had been killed in the raid and then the two were whisked along with some other women and children onto a ship with a horrible dragon jutting high above its bow."

The old woman's eyes grew moist.

"For five years, the mother cooked for the master, his guests and frequent visitors, and she seemed to grow even more beautiful despite her captivity. She lived and laughed with her growing son and made cheerful company for her fellow captives. She assured them that they and the boy would someday be freed by the fierce Irish clans who lived in Munster and Connaught. She never acted the slave nor showed deference to any Viking, male or female. For some reason, she thought revealing their true names would dishonor both her and the boy, so she called herself simply 'mother' and he was her 'good boy.' "

"One evening, as the boy was approaching his tenth birthday, the master, his wife and the live-in warrior and liegeman of the Viking, were sitting around the trestle table in the longhouse being served by the boy and his mother. The two servants were preparing dishes of parsnips and turnips in one of the side alcoves. The wife noted the covetous glances the master cast upon the boy's mother. This seemed to be getting worse of late, especially when he returned from sea voyages."

"The wife had often boasted to the two servants that she was of high birth. She claimed she was a Viking princess and would not be dishonored by any Norseman's dalliances with an Irish wench under a roof in her own house."

The old woman went on as the warriors listened keenly to her words.

"Screaming, she accosted him, releasing her pent-up anger and demanding the cook and her whelp be sold before the master made a fool of himself. The master looked to his wife, surprised at this outburst, and for the first time, slapped her cheek sharply with a beefy calloused palm. The wife's shock was immediately replaced with an uncontrollable rage. She furiously grasped a knife meant to cut the meat. The boy's mother had been watching all this while standing at the wife's side in obvious discomfort, holding a plate of steaming mutton in both hands."

"In a flash, the enraged Viking matriarch plunged the knife deep into the breast of the servant woman. As the young mother fell, plate of mutton spattering the table and floor, the scornful wife rose and rushed to exit the front door in disgust. The two Viking men had watched all this in unexpected astonishment. It had happened too fast for them to react."

"The 'good boy' let loose an ear-splitting howl and exploded into motion. Leaping over a stool, he rushed with death in his eyes, intent on slaughtering the fiend who had thrust the long shearing knife into his mother's chest. He knew intuitively his mother was now as dead as his father. His fingers turned into claws as he closed on the wide-eyed wife."

"Just then, the enormous Viking liegeman put himself in the boy's path. Too fast for the eye to follow, the youth grasped another sharp knife from the table and reaching forward, slashed at the man's brawny face. This left a long bleeding gash from above the left eye, across the nose and down the right cheek. The blow would have been lethal had not the master taken the boy from behind, encircling his thick arms around the waist of the tall and supple young attacker. It had taken both men to bring down and bind this nine-year-old Irish child who never ceased snarling his fury at them. His eyes flamed murderously at the woman who stood inside the door watching. Then the two men took him to the dark storage hut and chained him to the post at its center, the liegeman constantly wiping at the blood which seeped down his face and blurred his vision."

***

Entranced by the story, the band of warriors was now sitting cross-legged in rapt attention.

"Well, there's no doubt she has spent much time amidst bards and poets. If she can cook as well as she weaves a tale, she's a treasure for sure," whispered Murcha to Cormac.

"He never again stepped foot into the longhouse, nor the little hut he and his mother had happily shared with the other Irish people. More ominously, neither the servants nor the Vikings ever heard another word of Irish or Danish out of his mouth. Before this, he had been a healthy and loquacious child quickly absorbing both tongues. For the five years which passed since that black and evil day, he was never unchained, spending every hour when not laboring locked in the squalid storage hut. Now, the only sounds which passed his lips were feral snarls and, more disturbingly for the Norse, deep, inhuman growls whenever any Viking approached."

"His tasks now became mean and strenuous. He cleaned the human and animal offal from the master's holdings. He pulled and hauled. As he grew bigger and stronger, he carried the heavy and fetid wooden waste barrels to pits, which he had dug with the flimsy planks he was given for that purpose. Even then, his wrists were cuffed with iron and the heavy lengths of chain constantly rattled as he worked. He could not be left alone outside. An armed Viking man or youth attended him at all times, until he was taken back to the unlit storage hut and bound with iron once again at the end of each day's tasks."

The woman held back a sob and continued.

"He was always accompanied by an armed guard, usually some Viking who was bondsman to the master. It may have been easier to simply kill him but the wife insisted he be kept alive, that she could revel in his torment."

"The servants explained to me that the master controlled three large Norse trading ships and they arrived frequently at the port of Dublin, brimming with goods from Scandinavia, the French coast and even from the sun-lit shores of the Mediterranean. As the years passed and the boy aged, he was used as a laborer, stowing and retrieving the huge chests and sacks of various goods the ships transported. By the time he turned twelve, he was able to easily lift as much as any grown man. The men on the wharves looked on in wonder. He was one day put to a test and managed to lift and carry a burden that would require two of them."

Cormac and the others Irish warriors looked at the tall but pitifully emaciated and blood covered youth in disbelief on hearing this.

Murcha bent to Cormac's ear, "If he were healed, tamed and trained, he'd no doubt rise to greatness as the hero warriors of the old tales. But alas, his mind seems sadly gone west."

Cormac was not sure he agreed with his cousin in that last part of his assessment.

The woman continued. "Because of his immense size and strength, and more menacingly because of his ferocious mannerisms and the snarling when he was among them, the Vikings on the docks gave him a name, *Ulf, Ulf Hreda*, "Wolf the Quarrelsome," he was called with a strange combination of disdain and a bit of reluctant respect from the heathens."

"Now, these developments began to disturb the master and his wife. The boy grew spectacularly large and showed no signs of physical damage despite the horrendous workload they forced on him. Though he appeared to have mentally deteriorated, losing any apparent will to speak, his body flourished beyond anything any of them had witnessed. As he entered his thirteenth year, he became as tall and brawny as the greatest of the Dublin Norse. When they saw the boy's massive sinews expand enormously, straining under the tremendous loads he carried, they grew even more concerned."

"So," the old woman continued, "for the last six months they had cruelly reduced what food he was given. At this point, I too was here with them. I would sneak to his hut at night and toss in bits of meat through small openings I could find in the rock and mud walls. During these times I attempted to soothe him, cooing softly with the old songs and stories from our ancestors."

Cormac wished his people had such a fine story teller as this woman when he was a young boy.

"Frequently of late, the master's wife herself came in the evenings with a stone lamp and evil-looking length of knotted blackthorn. I would hide in a bush nearby and could hear the whooshing cracks of the lash and his savage snarls of defiance as each blow struck home on the poor chain-bound boy's tall, thin body. Over the course of weeks, scars which I know will never completely fade, covered his shoulders, chest and face."

"Despite his lack of nourishment and frequent beatings, he was forced to work as always. Eventually, even his phenomenal physique began to dissipate as he grew gaunt and hollow-eyed. The guard who accompanied him on his labors told the master he stumbled often under the massive burdens he sadly continued to carry."

"I was sure his life would be numbered in weeks, when one recent morning I watched with some alarm as thousands of coarsely singing, Norse warriors left Dublin marching to the south. They bristled with axes, swords and spears, leaving only a few old men and boys behind. Among the armored columns were the master and all his liege and bondsmen. We were all frightened as there had been talk by both good Christians and the vile pagans about the coming dawn of a new millennium and the expected end of the world in flames and bloody death."

"Not two days later, on the first day of the new year and the new thousand-year, the Viking women who had stayed behind and we Irish servants gazed in wonderment from Dublin's earthen walls as some paltry few hundreds of scattered, fleeing Vikings rushed aimlessly into and around the city. We were all terrified and were sure the hounds and demons of hell were storming behind them in their hundreds of thousands."

Cormac could hear the cold fear in her voice as she relayed the superstitious dread they had all felt as the dawn of the millennium approached.

"All of the Irish went wild in their initial panic. Unmindful of the scrambling Norse survivors and the Viking women, the Gaels deserted their dwellings and, flinging open the city's gates, rushed out and away in any direction that might offer hope. Ships and boats were already manned by some of the exhausted Vikings. They pulled with a last effort on familiar oars which carried them to safety. That snake, Sitric Silkbeard himself, was among the first to flee and his ship led the mad cruise out into the bay."

"I watched as the two servants from Airgailla, who had by now spent most of their lives in Dublin, fled with the rest, leaving me behind and the boy locked and chained in his hut. Not long after, I spied from a hiding place the master and his scarred companion striding toward the locked little storeroom, axes clutched tightly, deadly intent in their cold blue eyes. They did not care about me, nor the two others, but like all Vikings they knew never to leave alive a hate-filled youth of the enemy, who would undoubtedly live and breathe for one purpose — to kill them both."

Cormac looked at the faces of the young warriors who had gathered around them in the small hut. Their transfixed eyes told him they were now listening to a far better saga than any yet recited by their own clans' bards.

"They quickly removed the chain and kicked open the door of this hovel, bending to enter. I no longer cared for my own safety and dashed in behind to run to a corner, peering into the gloom. The master's axe was already flashing down toward the pale, pathetic form crouching and chained in the center of the hut. Somehow, with just the bit of light from the open door and a tiny, flickering stone lamp, I could see as the boy leapt toward his attacker, brandishing the tightly extended length of chain between his two wrists to deflect the axe. At the same time, he kicked with his big unshod foot directly into the master's groin, toppling him hard to the packed dirt ground."

"His ankle chained to the center post, the boy could not move far, but he was able to snatch up the fallen axe in the blink of an eye. Ignoring the groaning Viking at his feet, he brought the axe handle up just in time to parry the second Norseman's descending blow. Then he simply held the axe before him and pushed forward with a terrifying snarl, the blade splitting the ugly face of his attacker, dropping him in a shower of blood."

Strangely, her voice seeming much younger now, the woman was caught up in the excitement of her own tale.

"Never stopping, with a fluid motion and savage roar, Wolf brought the red dripping axe over his shoulders and viciously down onto the exposed neck of the dazed master. The bearded head fell to the side and dark fluids gushed."

Cormac noted she had herself for the first time referred to the boy as "Wolf." He decided the Viking's name for him had proven apt.

"Panting, the boy dragged the other body closer to him and swung again, removing a second Viking head from its shoulders. He then leaned back against the wooden center beam with the master's bloody axe in his hands."

"It was this horrific scene of carnage that met the wife as she entered the hut, perversely desiring to gaze with satisfaction upon the results of her husband's intended actions. As her eyes recognized the reality of what had happened, she let out a shrill, mad scream. Her sanity apparently stolen by what she had seen over the last hour, she threw herself at the boy, arms outstretched, hands clawing."

The old woman caught her breath and continued.

"Strangely, almost calmly, Wolf dropped the axe and, to my astonishment, his lips curled into a feral grin as the Norse wife flew towards him. His long, thin arms extended, two calloused, cuffed hands closed around her throat before her nails could dig into his scarred face. He squeezed.... slowly, very slowly. With ferocious pleasure, he smiled as she, in horror, seemed to realize her fate for the first time. Her features bulged as his fingers crushed inward, preventing air from reaching her lungs. As the light began to dim in her cruel eyes, he clenched his fingers together and I heard a loud dry snap. She crumpled to the floor at his feet, and he fell to a sitting position against the post, her body directly in front of him."

The old woman had been witness to the whole violent drama which had taken only moments since the Vikings first kicked open the door.

"I watched as the boy reached out, collecting first one, and then the second Viking head. With a precise and almost tender intent, he positioned both of the grisly trophies directly before the dead staring eyes of the woman who had murdered his mother. Then he sat back with a sigh as I began speaking softly to him as gently and comfortingly as I could. Apparently, not having even noticed I was here, he growled fiercely, his body tensing, before he sat back again and closed his eyes."

"With all the horror I witnessed over the course of this, the first day of the millennium, I knew with certainty whatever monstrous horde of demons had slaughtered the Viking army would soon be pouring into Dublin itself. So, I continued to try to soothe the poor doomed boy. I wanted to make his remaining short time in our world as comfortable as possible. Despite my prayers, l couldn't eliminate the tinge of fear I heard in my own voice."

It was at this moment, she said, the two Dalcassian cousins had suddenly burst into the hut. She closed her eyes and made the sign of the cross as she had done so many times over her life. When she realized the two huge invaders had not decided to immediately slaughter them, she looked up.

Her nose alerted her before her eyes. There was a scent among different peoples. She had sensed this when she had first been captured by the Norse. They simply smelled bad. Even when they were fresh from bathing or swimming, there was an alien stench that assailed her nostrils when she was close to one of them. She was a cook. Creating and assessing aromas were part of her craft. Her own people smelled of Ireland's green hills, the sweet butter which came from its cattle, and the delicious honey produced by their much respected bee keepers. At least that is what she thought. Even unwashed and disheveled, her skilled nose found the poorest Irish preferable to the foreign heathens.

These were neither demons nor Vikings. They were her own people and they carried the mighty weapons of Ireland's most formidable warriors, Dalcassian axes. She took relief in the warmth and openness of their hard but handsome faces, so unlike the bestial features of the Norse men. She spoke something to them which she couldn't remember even uttering later.

At her words, they turned their attention to the "good boy" who sat breathing deeply, surrounded by the carnage he had wrought. They peered unsure of what was there and one called to someone outside. Another Irish warrior rushed in with a burning lamp. This one was younger, perhaps five seasons older than the chained boy. All of them now beheld in grisly detail the results of the events she had witnessed.

Amazingly given the surroundings, all of the Irishmen had been sitting comfortably against the stone walls of the hut. In the flickering yellow shadows from the two lamps, and the bit of now lessening daylight pushing through the open door, they listened with fascination as the woman related her story with as much skill and eloquence as any bard who had ever tread Ireland's verdant soil. Thus, they learned of the sufferings and hardships of the one who would eventually become their weapon brother, their friend and the war captain of all Ireland.

The beginning was told as something out of a myth from Celtic antiquity. Tragic, full of pain and misery, there had still been defiance and heroism as with all Irish tales. God had seemed to take them all this far including even the sad, pale youth who sat, eyes closed, among them. What was yet to come, they could never imagine.

Chapter 6
Innisfallen, Lough Leane, Ui Fidgente, Ireland
1000-1002 A.D.

The year one thousand was a time of unfathomable confusion, fear and superstitious dread for Christian Europe. The Pope in Rome was a Frenchman. He was also a scientist and mathematician. Many Christians considered him a heretic and warlock, while others considered him a living saint. Rome itself was ruled by a German Saxon emperor, who was an exceedingly devout young Christian and had been tutored by the French Pope himself. The Britons of past years, especially those in Wales and Cornwall, would have found it incomprehensible that the savage pagan Saxons who had pillaged Britannia after the Romans left, were now the stalwart defenders of Christendom against marauding enemies on all sides.

Indeed, the grandfather of the present Saxon Emperor, Otto the Great, had by force of arms and through many bloody battles hurled back Danish and Norwegian Vikings in the north, Slavic Wends to his northeast and, worst of all, the mounted hordes of Magyars to his southeast. These last were known as the "scourge and terror of all Christendom, enemies of God and humanity." Adding to this nightmare for the Christian west, the Mediterranean was controlled by invading Islamic Jihadists who occupied most of Spain, Sicily, Corsica and parts of southern Italy. The eastern Christian Byzantine empire was almost completely surrounded by Khanates, Emirates and Caliphates, all peopled by ferocious enemies seeking to conquer and kill or convert the Christian infidels.

It was precisely at the turn of the millennium, during this frenetic age, when King Brian's victory at Gleann Mama against the Dublin Vikings and Leinstermen took place. In a world torn by savagery, this was just another local eruption amidst the incessant turmoil of the period. And for the fourteen-year-old, now liberated, tall Irish boy, this was just the beginning of the epic events that were to come.

Incongruously, given what had already occurred and what lay in the future, it began quietly and studiously in the most bucolic of settings. After an Irish smith had been found to remove the chains from the wrists and ankles of the boy, the old woman cleaned him with a strip of clean linen and fresh warm water. She shuddered at the sight of the many scars on his face, shoulders and back, and the deep red striations where the iron manacles had cut into his limbs. She spoke softly and gently, telling him he was safe and in the company of strong men of his own people who would protect him. Wolf continued to breathe deeply, and then gradually seemed to almost imperceptibly relax.

Not much later, he and the woman were brought to King Brian. Cormac had found a woolen tunic amidst the booty from the longhouse and soon Wolf was adequately clothed, though his thin body swam in the garment of a huge Viking. Spurning any shelter within the walls of the now conquered city, the king was, with a few advisors including Teighe of Connaught, sitting and talking pleasurably in a simple leather tent in a field outside Dublin.

Though he spoke no words, even when directly questioned in both Irish and Danish by Cormac, the boy had accompanied them confidently and without any signs of anxiety or duress as they left the city's walls behind them. Brian graciously received the old woman and looked questionably at the startlingly tall, gaunt figure of the scarred, dark haired young boy. Murcha then asked the woman to please re-tell their story to the king, knowing his father would be moved by such an amazing tale.

The king and his advisors listened with keen interest to the descriptive and eloquent words the woman spoke. It was obvious she had spent much time in the company of bards, poets and musicians, and her tale rang almost musically with love, sorrow, and furious drama. When she finished, all of the battle-hardened listeners were visibly impressed, many with moist eyes. These were men who had spent the past hours taking reports of the day's atrocities from various sub-commanders among the allied Irish forces. Despite the courage and ferocity which characterized those glorious martial accounts, they had been even more mesmerized by the chronicle of these few lives of captives in Dublin.

Brian gazed at the woman now with respect and open admiration.

"Graceful lady, you have once again made me so proud of Ireland's women and our people. You are as much a hero to me as any of my warriors who have driven the Vikings and their traitorous Irish allies from the battlefields at Gleann Mama and beyond." He stepped close to her now, bending to tenderly kiss her forehead.

"Dear sweet chef, you are heartily welcome to stay with us at Cashel for as long as you would like. Though I'd miss your company, and no doubt your cooking," the King added with a genuine smile, "you are free to travel to honor with your presence any other Irish hearth and holding, and you will go with my blessing and recommendation."

At that, the woman bowed slightly and accepted the King's hospitality with gratitude.

Brian now looked to the pale youth who stood erect and steadfast. The King's hazel eyes shone with a combination of pity and amazement at what this boy had suffered over the years. And more poignantly, over what he had done in the last few hours in the hell of the Viking hut.

The two were of equal height, notwithstanding that Brian was considered an inordinately huge warrior among his people. Unexpectedly, the king placed his hands on the boy's shoulders and hugged him to his breast. To the surprise of both Cormac and Murcha, the "Wolf," who had this day savagely dispatched two armored Viking plunderers while bound at hands and feet, stood calmly, head bent, as the king whispered into his ear.

So it was that King Brian of Munster was able to declare to his assembled captains.

"You now stand in the presence of my foster son. He is to be taken to the isle of Innisfallen on Lough Leana, our 'Lake of Learning,' in the south of Munster. There, he will receive a classic Christian education, as have many of the sons of southern Ireland, including Cormac, Murcha and myself.

"The learned and traveled monks there will impart to him the knowledge of science, history, mathematics and religion, which we Irish took from the Romans and Greeks and preserved through the darkest ages as the rest of Europe descended into flames and ignorant barbarism. These same devout clergymen now also keep the scholarly lore of our people's Celtic druidic past; though the Pope in Rome would consider all of that just more pagan idolatry."

The assemblage laughed at the last part.

Cormac laughed loudest and addressed the group with unabashed joy.

"Sure then, Uncle Brian, we're all good Christians and we respect the mad Frenchman's papal authority, even if our happy and colorful Celtic rites aren't strictly in accordance with some of his sterner decrees. We'll sing, dance, fight, feast, frolic, hunt, make love and play as we always have since long before good Patrick arrived on our isle."

***

The "good boy" did not get to see the seat of the Dalcassian King at Cashel. He and Cormac rode together on sturdy and well-trained war horses across the interior of Ireland, which now made for a pleasant and safe journey under Brian's kingship. Cormac chuckled at first as the gangling youth sat awkwardly astride the saddle of his mount but over the few days of the trip, he noted approvingly how quickly the boy seemed to become one with the large horse. Wolf's long bony knees and strong pale hands mastered and calmed the animal.

The boy still had not spoken a word to Cormac, despite questions, stories and jokes from his older companion. For this reason, Cormac found it strange when the youth bent forward to scratch his mount's ears and utter fond words. Too soft to detect, the sounds were deep and low. The horse bizarrely seemed to nod its head in understanding.

"He's a good Irish horse. Don't insult him by spewing heathen Danish gibberish into his delicate ears," Cormac said with a grin, as he watched for the third time the conversation between the boy and his mount.

Slowly, the boy sat back in the saddle, back erect, and turned with a knowing wry and amused countenance to Cormac.

For the first time, his companion saw a hint of a sparkle in Wolf's bronze flecked, green eyes, as the thin lips curved slightly upwards. Now, Cormac knew, the boy's mind had not been hopelessly damaged by the horrors he had experienced in Dublin. There was an undeniable gleam of intense and innate intelligence along with youthful curiosity in those open and honest eyes. And, to Cormac's pleasure and relief, he also noted a mirthful humor responding to his words. This convinced him, despite all the torture, murder, and physical pain he endured, the youth had not descended into a simple, comfortable world of pure hate and vengeance. This "quarrelsome wolf" would recover and grow healthy again. Already, he was eating like his namesake and recovering the rosy glow in his ivory cheeks which characterized all the native people of this island.

***

The abbey was on an island in Lough Leane, one of three lakes in the area. Innisfallen was founded in 640 A.D. by Saint Finian the Leper. The king had sent word before Cormac and his charge arrived. Two monks were waiting as their little hide-covered curragh boat delivered them to a small wooden dock. Waiting with them was a grizzled but powerfully built older man who was clearly no monk. Cormac spoke just a few words to the company which had been assembled to greet them, and then turned to the boy.

"I'll be back to collect you in two years. Brian will expect you to know how to read and write in Irish and Latin by that time. The good monks will also teach you numbers and science, as well as the history of Ireland and beyond. The king also sent another to work with you here," Cormac gestured toward the older man.

"He has fought at Brian's side since the two of them slept in bogs as boys, hiding from the Vikings. He is as tough as leather and hard as steel and don't be fooled by his age."

That was all that was said. Cormac returned to the little craft and the oarsman set off toward the opposite shore.

Six months later the first report arrived at Cashel from Innisfallen. Cormac received it with interest. The writer, who was no doubt one of the boy's primary tutors, was able to effectively summarize the youth's progress. He later read aloud the author's words to the entire assembled court.

"As you expected, the boy began to speak words in the first few weeks. He eats with vigor and goes to classes with other students close to his age. He sleeps alone in a rocky hut he calls his 'beehive.' Though small, his stony abode has a central fire pit, a sturdy wooden chair and desk, a cot with a thin but comfortable mattress of straw and sheepskin, and two stone lamps. He tells us it is warm and surprisingly well-lit when both lamps are burning and a peat fire crackling."

A number of the men in the court nodded, remembering their own times, good and bad, at Innisfallen, but all recollected with comfortable nostalgia their spare but cozy quarters there.

"Despite his renewed conversational ability, he has still not seen fit to tell anyone, teacher or student, his true name. Everyone continues to call him *Faolan* — Wolf. He seems quite comfortable enough with that. He quickly mastered reading and writing, but I'm disappointed to tell you he is no better than middling at other subjects. He takes his spiritual guidance seriously, prays devoutly and attends Mass each morning."

"His keenest fascination is history, especially the military aspects of the past and present. He listens intently, and asks cutting questions of his teachers. Now, one friar, Brother Tómas, has become his personal tutor, and teaches the boy what has transpired in the world around him for the last hundreds of years. He is intensely interested in how the Vikings came to Ireland, how they are able to stay, and most importantly, how they might be defeated.

"We taught him the Vikings came as seafaring raiders in 795, initially content to pillage soft targets and leave quickly. The Gaelic chieftains were constantly fighting among themselves, as you know, and some of these foreign incursions have succeeded in developing into Viking strongholds, especially at Dublin, Vadrefjord, Weisfjord and Limerick.

"Based on what he saw after Gleann Mama when our allied forces of Munster and Meath defeated the Dublin Vikings, Wolf is especially attuned to King Brian's history in fighting the Norse. He learned in detail how the king had conducted a guerrilla war against the Limerick Vikings and their Irish allies as a prince of the Dalcassians. Later, with his brother Mahon, he fought a pitched battle at Sulcoit, which led to the storming and destruction of the Viking settlement at Limerick. With Mahon's death, we informed him, Brian has become King of Munster, and gradually, through force of arms and diplomacy, brought most of southern Ireland under his control.

"Wolf is also deeply concerned with what is happening outside of Ireland and what he might learn from that. He was especially fascinated when one day one of the monks who had recently returned from pilgrimage to Rome showed him a parchment map of Europe as it is known by the Pope's scholars. Ireland is a small, almost inconsequential spot in the northwest of this chart. Next to it is the island of Britannia, somewhat larger and broken into multiple kingdoms of Danes, Saxons, Hebrides and Orkney Vikings, and what Wolf is taught are his fellow Celts in Scotland and Wales. Further to the East is an enormous expanse of land with almost too many nations and people for the boy to comprehend. He casts dagger eyes on the homeland nations of the Vikings — Denmark, Norway and Sweden.

"We taught him that what the Danes and Norwegians had done to Britannia and Ireland, the Swedes had done to the lands to the east, establishing an enormous empire there called the land of the Rus. At one point the region's native Slavs had asked the Vikings to come rule them. Wolf was disgusted on hearing that, muttering about 'bloody little heathens.' Some of these Vikings have even gone further south to serve as mercenaries, known as Varangians, for the eastern Christian Byzantine Empire."

One of the king's old and now retired officers bent to Murcha's ear and said, "I do believe the writer of this missive knows exactly that it will be read aloud to all in the halls of the king. He no doubt wishes to impress and influence us with his wise counsel and advice as much as relay tidings of the boy."

Cormac continued, "He learned that fierce, mounted Magyar horsemen from the east had stormed into Europe and established the duchy of Hungary. Pillaging, bloodthirsty pagans, claiming they were a tribe of the ancient Huns, they threatened all of Europe and have only recently converted to Christianity, though their neighbors still view them skeptically. And he now knows to the south are various groupings of dusky Arabic and African peoples, all of whom share the same strange and violent faith which seems bent on destroying Christendom."

The old man tugged on Murcha's sleeve, "And now he is giving us warning."

Cormac stopped and looked at the old man and his cousin for a moment before going on. "Wolf has learned that Ireland is but a tiny speck in the cold northwest in a world that is immensely large, infinitely dangerous, and constantly threatening. He has vowed to himself and to us, he and his foster father will save and preserve Ireland and its peoples from the foreigners of the world."

The report included all that Wolf had learned in class, and went on to detail the rest of his training thus far. The old warrior had been specifically sent to Innisfallen by the king to prepare the boy physically, mentally and militarily to assume his place in the

Dalcassian army. So, along with academic and spiritual education, the youth went through intense martial drills to maximize his warfighting strength and prowess.

The writer humorously explained how, since the boy would not give his real name to the old warrior, neither would the man tell the boy his true name. So, they were both called simply "Wolf" and "Trainer."

"Trainer began by assuring that the boy eats correctly to include meat, grains and whatever vegetables we have seasonally available. First, he began running around the circumference of the island with the trainer exhorting him to move faster and, crossing inland, meeting the panting youth at various spots to rudely inform him of his unacceptably poor performance. Eventually, Wolf saw through this and was able to anticipate where the trainer would meet him. The boy would sprint there first and intercept the older man by dashing from the trees unexpectedly. The trainer smiles to himself, but doesn't allow his approval to be shown to his charge.

"When Wolf could fly around the island so quickly, he frightened both us and the other students, the trainer added another challenge. The boy continued to run as he had, but now he was forced to carry a robustly thick tree trunk across his shoulders while he exercised. At night the trainer placed obstacles — boulders, fallen tree branches, hastily dug trenches, sharp little stones and stinging nettles — across the running paths. Thus, Wolf has learned to examine the terrain, react with agility and resilience, and avoid painful falls as he flashes across our green little island."

Some of the younger warriors among the court members smiled knowingly in approval, remembering their own harsh but valued lessons under the tutelage of that same trainer.

"The next step was to learn to swim in the chilly, almost black, waters of our lake. He was taught swimming strokes that are intended for endurance not speed; just short distances on his side at first, enabling him to build up a tolerance to the frigid temperatures. Then longer stretches with the trainer beside him in a small boat.

Eventually he would swim to the opposite shore and climb up the bank to lie in the sun until the trainer came to collect him."

"Though this physical regimen, Wolf has grown rapidly in height and bulk. Once again, huge musculature appears on his shoulders, arms and legs. His skin exudes a healthy glow from the brisk Munster air, frequent cleansing rains, and the nightly steam baths he and the other students take while reciting the day's lessons."

The report concluded with one note of possible concern. Despite the fact he could not or would not reveal his true name, the boy was genuinely open and cheerful with his fellow students and his teachers. But when the conversation turned to foreigners in general and the Vikings in particular, a dark gleam became visible in his molten green eyes. His pupils narrowed and his thin lips curled back behind prominent jaws, revealing his predator-like teeth. He seemed to focus intently at those times, and whatever that intent might be, it did not bode well for any outlander *Gall.*

Cormac related the monk's report with enthusiasm in the great hall at Cashel so King Brian, his sons and captains could also take pleasure in the progress of the formerly pathetic figure they had all first met in the tent outside Dublin. The king, most of all, nodded with joy as his nephew regaled them with the tales of this wild Irish wolf.

***

Six months later, a second missive arrived at Cashel. The same learned scribe, who obviously knew Wolf very well by now, penned the report with identical eloquence and skill. It covered every aspect of what Wolf had experienced over the half-year.

Again, Cormac was pleased to read the chronicle aloud one evening after the members of King Brian's court had consumed a feast of venison and trout in the great hall.

"The boy has continued his studies at a measured pace, neither exceeding nor falling behind his fellow scholars in the required subjects. He has become attached to the sacred rites of the priests and the liturgy, though more as defender than active participant. He plays the role of stern taskmaster among other students who might not approach their spiritual obligations with sufficient vigor. Wolf is not demure about letting them know how fortunate they are to be raised in the true faith when heathenism and evil seem to reign in the world. He cuffs them sharply, with a blow from his thick palm, if they do not exhibit sufficient devotion. Yet his keenest interest remains as always, the history his well-traveled, clerical tutor relates to him on a daily basis.

"When the boy exhausted his questions about the world that surrounded him, he pushed his teacher assiduously to tell him how the present day had evolved from the previous ages. Why was Ireland such a distant outpost? What had happened in that distant continent that put them and the rest of the world in this precarious position where even their simple existence was threatened? And always most critical to him, he asked, what could the past tell us about how to crush our pagan enemies and preserve our people."

A murmur rose from the assembled audience and the old "war horses" among them smiled at the words.

"This monk shares the youth's love of history and rose to the challenge of the question. One recent morning as the two sat by the banks of the lake, its dark waters sparkling with dappled sunlight in the warm summer, our tonsured scholar told of what had passed ages ago.

"He began with the Greeks. Wolf was aware of them because the Latin tongue he now studies has been heavily influenced by those Hellenes. By now, the tutor knows, regretfully, he must pass over philosophy, arts and the foreign pagan mythology that the boy finds distasteful. The Greeks had a glorious past of epic warfare which entranced Wolf. He learned about the enemy Troy, and a Greek ruse which allowed them to annihilate their long-time foes. He was not the least impressed by the accompanying tales of individual Greek and Trojan warriors battling, but only how Troy was destroyed."

"His favorite lessons were those of the Spartans. He learned they were Dorians, and his tutor thinks these people must have been Celts since they originally came from the North. They were a nation of pure warriors who trained vigorously as does Wolf. They employed spears and huge bronze-faced shields and wore head-covering bronze helmets when they advanced to engage their enemies. The tutor told him that the Spartans did only two things: train to fight, and fight. Wolf finds that intensely admirable and never stops talking about it to motivate his classmates."

More smiles beamed on the faces of the assembled warriors, and now the hilts of *scians* and swords banged against wooden tables in enthusiastic applause. At the same time, some of the few educated men and women who specialized in conducting the king's diplomatic missions listened on with some concerned skepticism.

"Are the monks creating a learned Christian scholar or some monster who will destroy us all?" one gentle older woman asked her neighbor softly.

Cormac's voice drowned out any answer. "The boy's favorite story was of the Spartans at a narrow battlefield well to their north in a place called Thermopylae. Just a few hundred of them met an advancing monstrous alien army from the east and stopped the invaders for just enough time to allow the Spartans' countrymen to band together and throw the Persians out of Greece. This story resonates with Wolf, as he compares that to what Ireland now experiences at the hands of the Vikings."

"Our brother monk moved on to teach the attentive boy about the rise of Rome and how this small city had become a military behemoth. Wolf was delighted to learn that what the tutor described as his Celtic ancestors had desperately fought the Roman invader. The fact that they lost didn't dismay him. His mind is already churning with a future intent to learn from earlier failures."

"Hannibal of Carthage used Celtiberian infantry allies as simple chaff to draw the Roman legions into the Carthaginian trap at Cannae. These Celts had died in their hundreds to allow the Nubians and other North African warriors to envelop and annihilate the Roman legionnaires. Wolf was dismayed at the fate of those possible forefathers, but he has learned from the ultimate destruction of that Roman army."

"As he pressed his tutor for more specific details on the military aspects of the Romans, Wolf was gratified to see the gentle monk seemed to warm to the request. Despite his pious and learned demeanor, our tutor is an Irishman whose heart is roused by such stories."

"He learned that an ancient Celtic King, Brennus, had invaded and sacked Rome hundreds of years before the time of Our Lord. Instead of destroying every vestige of the growing threat, Brennus simply accepted a gold ransom price, and returned home, north of the Alps. This hideous mistake also made an impression on our oversized scholar.

"Wolf discovered the small stabbing *spathas*, the sword of the Roman legions was derived from his own people's craftwork. The Romans knew that thrusting into the entrails, throat or face of an enemy took less effort and was more deadly than simply hacking from above. He was told even the Spartans had short bronze thrusting swords to thrust into the foe when their spears were sundered."

"The tutor told him how Rome had been forced to endure the invasions of Huns from the east who had pillaged both the eastern and western empires. These were short, squat, scarred marauders, mounted bowmen from Asia's central plains driving all before them. At first, they simply dashed with their swift little ponies around the timbered outposts which served as Rome's outermost barriers. They plundered plush Roman villas and primitive German villages alike, dragging off prisoners and other booty before the defenders could react.

"I myself witnessed how my brother monk became animated as he continued his martial instruction. Even though these mounted archers seemed invincible, history made clear they could be defeated. Alexander the Macedonian had conquered the Persian horsemen by simply advancing and letting the archers run themselves out on the shields of his phalanx. The Macedonian King knew that the secret of cavalry was not in offense. Mounted warriors were better employed in distraction, deception, and most effectively in cutting into and dissecting a fleeing army."

At that one of the grizzled old warriors commented to his neighboring comrade," 'Tonsured monk,' my arse. Whoever this writer is he sounds like some maniacal cross between warrior chieftain and sagacious bard, with only a bit of the pious cleric in him." He and his friend both cackled in chuckles.

Cormac went on.

"What Wolf has learned from these stories is that cavalry should never become decisively engaged with a well-placed force of infantry. In a flanking attack, and especially an attack from the rear, mounted horsemen would kill five times their number. But the key point our future warrior realizes is that a fleeing enemy on foot can be destroyed in multitudes by just a few mounted warriors with bows and sharp iron tipped lances."

As Cormac completed reading aloud the section of the report, he called the "history lesson," he wondered, not for the first time, about the clerical author. Could the writer be the history tutor himself? Was there some lesson, some agenda, the author was trying to get across to King Brian's court? Could the boy's "keen interests" really be the result of some "gentle monk's" own heartfelt cause heavily influencing a young mind? Could this simply be a case of some frustrated clergyman in robes who deeply aspires to be a great warrior, another Saint Columba of Iona?

Cormac shook his head and smiled. It was no matter. Nothing he read disturbed him in the slightest and he felt the boy was getting an exceedingly exceptional education. He continued reading from the parchment.

"The boy's physical training has become even more arduous. And now he is drilling with real weapons. The trainer began with the heavy round wooden shield, making clear it was not simply an implement of defense, but a dangerously lethal weapon in itself. Wolf now has to carry his shield with him during runs around the island, slashing with it at tree branches and crashing into the thick tree trunks themselves. He leaves splintered brushwood all over the grounds of the abbey, which we and the students collect for our fires. He broke several shields until the trainer procured a massive new one for him, constructed of thick oak planks and plated with bronze on its front. None of the students and only few of the clergy can lift it.

"He was next trained in the use of the spear. Despite the presence of axes and swords on every battlefield, the trainer explained the spear was the most common weapon used in all wars. It required much less metal, and was cheaper and easier to produce than other weapons. The overwhelming majority of Irish warriors and many of the Vikings use the spear as their primary weapon. We Irish have two basic types: a heavy, thickly shafted one with a leaf-shaped tip that was a head taller than the man who carried it, and a shorter lighter one with a long narrow point, sometimes called a 'dart'. The latter is used for throwing and Wolf compares it to the javelins which he knew the Romans had employed to such great effect. The trainer told him the Vikings used their own heavy spear for both throwing and in infantry combat. One of their techniques is for a man to run forward at a sprint, and when sufficient momentum has been reached, he throws two heavy spears."

"The boy smiled at that, and commented that after flinging his weapons away in such a manner, the winded and unarmed Viking would be easy to kill. The trainer cautioned him yet again about never underestimating an enemy. Wolf learned to use both types of spears and grew capable of throwing even the heavy one to great range.

"He was then introduced to the Dalcassian axe. This was a modification to the feared two-handed Danish battle axe. King Brian himself has influenced its development, as you undoubtedly are aware. The Vikings primarily wield their axes in overhand swings from behind their shield walls. The large blades cause massive injuries, but their bulk makes them slower to employ in repetitive swinging strokes. Our Dalcassian version is essentially an upsized hand axe with a smaller but still lethal blade, which was designed to be used both in slashing and, with a deadly point at its crest, capable of thrusting directly forward, dagger-like. It can be held in one or two hands and is incredibly quick and agile. Such axes as these have shattered Viking hosts into broken remnants all across Ireland. This axe is also less costly to construct than a sword."

The same old warrior, who had been well into the mead for some time, now cried out in a loud and amused voice to the entire assembly.

"This writer monk seems not only a skilled and magnificent leader of warriors and learned scholar but a thrifty and cunning merchant to boot. I do believe good King Brian, you should immediately step down and we should summon him to lead us."

The entire court, including Brian and Cormac, erupted into bursts of laughter.

As the joviality subsided, Cormac continued.

"The trainer taught the boy to master the simple sling and stone weapon, which has existed since antiquity and was mentioned in the bible as a "giant killer." Against armored Norse behind their shield walls, such a weapon can only serve its purpose as a distraction. Nevertheless, Wolf has learned to become deadly accurate with the primitive sling and enjoys using it."

"Finally, he was given a sword, the weapon of nobility and honor and a gift from King Brian. These are dear and take time and skill to construct. Even among the Vikings, swords are handed down from father to son. Most have to settle for spears or axes. The Irish sword has a long pedigree evolving from the Gauls and Celtiberians. It is straight, and somewhat leaf-shaped with a hilt twice the width of its user's hand. Most have a simple, round pommel to achieve balance. Thus, unlike the Viking's own swords, which are considered the pinnacle of the craftsmanship in our world, ours can be wielded in one or two hands. In the grasp of a sword master, it is deadlier than spear or axe, and its thrust can penetrate the mail armor of the Norse.

"As he approaches his sixteenth year it seems no physical task is beyond him and whatever challenge the trainer throws at him, Wolf attacks with vigor. He swims the lake's waters in all but the most frigid weather, but now he swims with the heavy shield and sword strapped to his back. The weapons' great weight forces him to stroke mightily just to keep his head slightly out of the water and propel himself forward. When he reaches the opposite shore, the trainer is waiting with white linen swaths and grease to ensure the weapons do not rust. As soon as he and they are dry, both teacher and student are back in the little boat paddling to Innisfallen. In the middle of the lake, the youth will stand in the bow on the gunnels with shield and sword swinging, thrusting and parrying in feigned combat. The intent of this drill is to instill a sense of balance and awareness of his body, and to ensure he doesn't topple the little craft and send them both into the water. As he practices these natural and fluid motions, the trainer continues to stress the superiority of the thrust over the wild slash. Both have their place but a sword thrust requires less effort, can be rapidly repeated, exposes less vulnerabilities, and if directed well — face, throat, heart — will kill with even minimum penetration.

"Tenacious endurance has been instilled into Wolf's mighty frame through these icy, long distance swims. The trainer uses other methods to complement the speed, agility and balance the youth displays. He began by hitching the boy to a large wagon filled with ten or more students, and having him act as draft horse, pulling his fellows all over the island until he was a mass of sweat and rippling muscle. When that became too simple, the wheels were replaced with simple slats such as those used on sleds in winter's snow. The wagon was then filled with students and large rocks they'd been instructed to bring with them. To drag this requires herculean effort, but now tracks of this weird conveyance are found all over the island as the robust 'draft horse' has mastered the sled as he had earlier the cart."

Cormac had also wondered whether the trainer himself had written these letters given the detail of martial knowledge and physical training techniques described. But he knew the tough older man could neither read nor write. Could he have dictated to a scribe at the monastery? Would the monks take part in such a ruse? Again though, it meant nothing as there was nothing in either of the missives on the youth's progress that was cause for alarm or doubt.

Cormac completed reading the comprehensive second report from Innisfallen to the assembled Dalcassians and guests in the great hall of Cashel. All of the women and many of the men believed it resounded like the ancient legendary tales of Finn Mac Cool. But those stories originated from somewhere between superstitious fable and ancient history, while this was real and happening now. So, before he had even taken his place in the court of Cashel, among the elite of the Dalcassian warriors, the saga of Wolf the Quarrelsome was born.

***

When the next year had passed, Cormac rode out alone, taking with him another horse to collect the king's foster son and bring him back to Cashel. He left both horses with the ferryman's family, and the little boat took him on the short trip over the cold, black water to the verdant green island. Waiting for him there were several monks and the chancellor of the abbey, as well as the tough old trainer. Standing in the center and dwarfing them was an immense and, at first almost unrecognizable, gargantuan figure of a man. This one was armed and carrying a round, metal covered shield and heavy sword with snarling wolf's head pommel visibly extending from the scabbard which was strapped to his back.

The king's nephew could hardly believe this was the same thin, pale and mute youth he had delivered to this place two years earlier. In all of the Munsterman's travels, he had never seen such a massive and robustly built man.

"Dia dhuit agus fáilte romhat." "God be with you and welcome," exclaimed the young man in a deep bearish voice which belied his barely seventeen years. Wolf bound forward and bending down,

grasped Cormac's hand and shook it with an enveloping grip, as he flashed a broad toothy smile.

"So, you've learned not only to speak but to do so in proper Irish. "Cormac grinned back and shook the other's hand with vigor.

"*Ceart go leor.*" "Right enough," and I can do the same in proper holy Latin or the filthy Godless tongue of the bloody little heathens."

The young man's eyes sparkled with mirth and he was prodigiously happy to be with the man who had liberated him from the hell of Dublin in what now seemed an eternity ago in another world.

Listening to this exchange, two of the monks shook their heads, as they had already told Wolf more than once that many of the Norse proclaimed to be Christian in recent times. They also explained his fluent knowledge of Danish was a gift that would help the king and reflected well on him. Each time upon hearing these admonitions, Wolf merely spat on the ground and ended the conversation.

There would be no long departure ceremony. The young man turned and walked to the clergymen, clasping two of the monks in his huge arms and bringing them to his breast. They were of course his beloved history teachers, and Cormac was told by the abbot that one of them was the scribe who had written the long eloquent accounts of his time on the island. Wolf bent and murmured to them expressing his gratitude for the lessons he would never forget, and his thanks for mentally preparing him for what was to come. He then shook hands with the chancellor abbot and bowed his head slightly in respect.

Cormac stepped closer to the monk he had been told wrote the chronicles of Wolf's educational progress. He clasped the man's shoulder fraternally, gazed knowingly into the younger man's eyes and bent to whisper in his ear.

"Very well written, we may have need of your counsel in Cashel at some future time, dear Brother."

The robed clergyman blushed deep red but beamed a wide smile in acknowledgement.

Wolf then moved to his trainer and bowed once more. But he could not hold himself back, and clutched the older man in a bear hug which threatened to snap his spine.

"Before I came here, others tried to break me and see me withered and powerless. They almost succeeded. You, most of all, have healed me, have restored my strength and will. Your training is part of me now. You and those two scholars have taught me that my mind is my greatest weapon, and that keen intellect and deft skill will prevail over all the efforts of our bestial enemies. I hope to honor you in the years to come."

With that Cormac and his charge walked together to the landing place to meet the ferryman. Abruptly, the old trainer ran and clasped the young man's arm. He looked up and for the first time told his student his good, Christian, Irish name.

"Thank you for that master. And I am *Faolan an Trodach*, Wolf the Quarrelsome."

All three of the men laughed heartily as the ferryman looked on in confusion and some trepidation at the sight of the approaching scarred Goliath.

Chapter Seven
With the Dalcassians, Cashel and all Ireland
1002 A.D.

On the journey back to the seat of the Munster court, Cormac now took the time to explain the origin of the sword Wolf wore strapped to his back. Cormac reminded Wolf that Brian himself had selected this sword for him and, sitting relaxed in his saddle, told him the story.

"It was created by an Irish smith living alone in the wildest parts of Connaught. The man had once been a minor chieftain himself, it was said, but his little clan's settlement had years ago been attacked and horrifically destroyed in another of the long series of Viking raids. The chieftain had been away trading with another clan, noted for their ironwork, when his own people had borne the descent of the marauding pirates."

"Later, in agony, after surveying the ruins of his home, he returned to the neighboring clan's abode and humbly asked the other tribe's master iron worker to teach him how to create the finest edged weapons. After a few years, this former clan leader moved up into the Connemara hills with his iron-working implements. He called a cave home and began to craft only one type of ironwork — the most lethal blades, spears, swords and axes in Ireland."

Wolf's eyes seem to glow as he took in the words of this man he respected so much.

"It was during a trip into Connaught, meant for both diplomacy and show of force to impress the local kings there, that Brian first met the cave-dwelling smithy. The king sat at the older man's fire and listened to his story. He was delighted to examine some of the weapons the former chieftain had crafted. The sad old man combined superlative strength and stunning beauty in the creation of these implements of death or liberation, depending on their use. There were inscriptions in *Ogham* runes in old Gaelic on most. Instead of round iron pommels, the swords' hilts were adorned with artful bronze, end-pieces of nature — swans, wild boars, seals, eagles, badgers, dragons and horses. One of these, and certainly the largest, stood out to our Dalcassian king. This was because of its massive weight and heft, and the snarling, fang-bared, finely carved wolf's head which finished the hilt."

Cormac glanced to Wolf's shoulder where the same weapon's hilt was visible behind the boy's massive, long haired head. He continued.

"Brian deftly held and wielded the huge weapon, swinging in a few testing arcs. Then, with a smile said, well friend, I'm considered a very large Irishman, and I've fought and defeated more than a few of the Viking invaders in my time, but this beautiful sword must be intended as a work of art, no? Even the greatest Norse swords aren't so substantial."

"The older man looked back at his visitor and shrugged his shoulders."

"Munsterman. Note that the sword blade itself is shorter than both ours and theirs yet denser and, I believe, keener. It's heavier at the end but not enough to unbalance its heft, rather just enough to give it the crushing force of one of your Dalcassian axes. I had a dream not long ago. The dragons the Vikings display on the prows of their long ships are meant simply to terrify. At the beginning, as you can see, I shaped dragon hilts as well. But in our world, there are no dragons. We have something more fierce and noble on our island. We have fine, strong wolves which at times plunder our sheep and cattle but have never threatened our people. Our wolves are real. Their dragons are simple pagan idolatries to frighten good Christian folk."

"The old ironsmith, now animated, continued. 'In my dream I saw all of us...we Irish...as wolves. Like us, they care deeply for their pack members, tenderly care for their young, and fight viciously to defend their families. But as a Christian I know we're created in God's image and not really animals. Still, we can be like them and can be vicious enemies to the invaders. So, yes, the blade is beautiful and colossal, but it's made to crush and tear into the Vikings' armored bodies, even if it would take one of the old Celtic gods to wield it.'

"At that, he grinned up at the king with a uniquely Irish twinkle and winked. Brian ran his hands over the assorted weapons the man had placed before him. Despite a hard life, he has an eye for beauty, and when it was combined with what the king knew was prodigious militarily effective craftsmanship, it warmed his heart."

Wolf smiled at this as he shared the same ironic love as his king for both beauty and finely constructed implements of war.

"You, sir, make me staunch and proud yet again, as so often happens when meeting and spending time with new friends among our people. Alone, you seem to embody all we now need: Artist, Clan Chief, Craftsman, Warrior, Historian, Blacksmith, and, from your eloquence, Poet and Bard."

"The King put his hand on the old man's shoulder and bowed his head."

"If you would ever deem to join with us, we Irishmen, from all over our island, and with me in Cashel, I would be honored. I have spent my whole life to make us one and keep us safe. My people have been slaughtered, as have yours, by the invaders. I would have it otherwise."

Cormac had concluded his tale and continued riding in silence. There was now only the sounds of the songbirds and buzzing bees, along with the soft clops of their horses' hooves to serenade them.

The "good boy" had listened with keenly attentive eyes and almost spiritual interest in this newest tale Cormac so poignantly told him. Wolf guessed the old smith might have been of his own extended clan but had no way of ever really knowing. After having spent the last year learning the most efficient use of the spear, the axe, and the novelty of the sling, he was almost casually handed the sword which had been forged in that Connemara cave. This was the sword his foster father, the *Ard Rí* of Ireland, had deliberately selected for him.

Upon receiving it those months ago, Wolf had at first taken the huge weapon in one hand and was pleased to feel its dense heft. As the trainer had looked on with interest, the young, tall, and increasingly muscular youth moved gracefully forward, swinging the massive blade from side to side, up and down. This was the first time the trainer had ever seemed to hear the air itself audibly broken, with a noticeable *swish* caused by the violent descent of good Irish steel.

And so, the island had then experienced the outlandish phenomenon of a young giant dashing over its grounds with ponderous metal shield and massive broadsword, slashing and crushing trees, bushes, fallen logs and even the lake waters themselves.

Those were good memories for the young warrior. He yearned to use that same magnificent weapon to crush Ireland's enemies in the years ahead.

***

As the two riders passed through the gates of Cashel, Wolf immediately noted the differences between this much smaller seat of power and Dublin. Both were walled by palisaded, earthen mounds, wooden spikes thrusting up and out in defense. Just outside Cashel's gates, however, there were green meadows, some enclosed with small rocky walls, where sheep or cattle grazed contentedly on the rich tender grass. No peasant huts, commercial shops, nor merchants' tents surrounded Brian's ceremonial capital.

Inside everything was splendidly and sturdily built. Most were stone structures, braced with timber from the countryside. Unlike the gaudy, daubed multi-colored paint which decorated Viking dwellings, these were simply the staunch blue-gray of natural stones, set off with resin-oiled brown planks at their sides. Some were topped by thick golden thatch to fashion their roofs, while others had long, thick wooden planks connected by tongue and groove technology which had come from the continental Gauls.

There were verdant fields and corrals for grazing and a huge barn to shelter horses. Wolf gazed on a tall and narrow structure with a cross at its peak, and knew this was the chapel where solemn weddings and funerals occurred, along with daily Mass. Other structures resembled more the longhouse commercial and administrative halls of the Vikings, but without the ostentatious colors and wooden carvings.

They stopped and dismounted at the largest of these places. Cormac explained this was the great hall of Cashel and King Brian waited inside. Both had already detected the flurry of activity all around as they rode in. Cormac knew plans were already underway for the Munster King's tour of *his island.*

Young men rushed out to take control of the two sturdy horses which had effortlessly carried them from Innisfallen. Two fully armored Irish warriors opened the huge oaken doors for them, nodding with familiarity and respect at Cormac, and casting their eyes with wonderment at the enormous man with him. Both had heard the tales of Brian's foster son at the abbey, but this vision exceeded even those stories. Cormac greeted them with a few courteous words and Wolf followed inside, shield and sword strapped across his expansive back.

Upon entering, the two were immediately in the midst of animated and good-natured conversation among the fifty or so men, and about half that many women. The discourse immediately ceased. There was a hushed silence, and the two were taken aback as every eye looked upon first the familiar and beloved Cormac, and then with disbelief at his companion.

In 1002, King Brian was sixty-two years old. His deep red hair was streaked with wisps of silver as was his beard. But the king was still a stolid, powerful warrior who carried himself with dominating presence. Always among the tallest and strongest of his age, he now gazed at a vision that stood half a head above his own, and seemed to make even the mighty Cormac a dwarf beside him. He immediately recognized the hilt and wolfish pommel of the great sword he had received from the Connaught ironsmith years ago. This was the same deadly blade he had sent to his foster son, concluding he was the only one that could wield it in battle. And that smith still lived among his people here in Munster with honor and comfort.

"God be with all of us here. I hope I haven't discomforted you by beckoning your return to us, Wolf the Quarrelsome."

Brian had always maintained a sometimes sad but usually mirthful sense of humor. He appreciated the name the Vikings, who had been the boy's captors, gave to him. And he was delighted to see the fearsome young warrior break into a grin when he heard the king's words. Both of them knew the name might confuse and make fearful many of those here, but that was part of their shared joke.

"Buíochas le Dia." "Thanks be to God, my king. I am proud to be back with you and the warriors I see in this place. I thank you for seeing that I was educated and my liberator, Cormac, for tending to me on my return."

The assembled Irish in the hall who had heard the storied tales of the king's foster son at Innisfallen had not been told of his arrival. With great enthusiasm, they realized it all was true. Standing before them was a spectacle from the mythical Celtic stories. Neither Finn Mac Cool nor Cú Chulainn himself, this was a living, breathing, almost supernatural, Irish hero who stood in their midst. He had slain two armored Vikings while he was still a child, chained, starving and near death. Now he was back and as strong, massive and formidable as any could imagine.

The thin silver scars which crossed his face diagonally from forehead to chin both repelled and attracted the girls and women in the room. His immense height and physique impressed the men, who were even more pleased by the sly grin and mischievous gleam in his sparkling green eyes. Cormac tried to introduce him to them all but there were too many for Wolf to remember their names. He looked around himself and was suddenly awash in a first pleasure. These were not all students, scholars or monks. Scores of them were scarred and battle-hardened warriors, young and old. Even the women appeared to him haughty, healthy and proud, as he had been taught Celtic women had always been.

For a moment he thought of his mother. These women had the same fire in their eyes and natural pride as she did. After two years with only men as companions, he was both comforted and slightly excited having them around him.

The king arose from his seat and walked toward the new arrivals. He first took Cormac's arm and put his hand on his shoulder.

"Well done."

Cormac demurred that it was not he, but the monks and the king's trainer who had brought the sad Dublin captive back to vibrant life. Brian knew the trainer was on his way to another abbey which specialized in producing young warriors.

Then Brian turned to face his foster son. It was the first time in his adult life he had to look up at another man.

"You have turned out to be a man beyond the expectations I had when I sent you to the abbey. I merely wanted to see you come back to us healthy and cheerful. Your tall stature even then foretold great strength and power. So, I sent my friend and weapon brother to teach you the art of war, along with the monks' arts, science, history and of course our holy faith."

Wolf gazed solemnly into his benefactor's hazel eyes. "Sir, I have indeed taken to heart the lessons of my trainer, my history teachers and my priests but I confess science and arts were not my strength. I hope I haven't dishonored you."

With a widening grin, the king replied, "No, Wolf, no indeed, seeing you now, I have a purpose for you. You and I will together save our people, our island and even those beyond our shores; we will throw back the foreigners of the world."

***

Over the days and weeks, Wolf took his place in the company of what the Dalcassians called the *Laochra an Rí* — "Warriors of the King." All of the multiple tribes of Munster now rallied and considered themselves one with the Dál Cais. For the first time, Wolf was assigned to a barracks with the king's best and most trusted elite. Despite their fascination with their new weapon brother, they were intensely involved in preparing for some mission of great importance the king was mounting.

The "good boy" had been happily impressed by all of the Munster army. They had crushed Norse and traitorous Irish alike over the course of years and multiple battles. He was now immersed in the midst of this smaller and distinct band of the Munster forces. These were made up of King Brian's widely ranging extended clan, those relatives who were most dear and devoted to him. Fascinating to Wolf, these also included "hostages."

Taking hostages was an ancient practice, not confined to the Celts. These young men were here now, and freely delivered to Cashel by the most noble of the tribal and clan chiefs across Ireland, Scotland and even from Wales. No servants were they, and certainly not slaves, they flourished under the king's protection and training. "Hostage" was merely a term of mutual respect among kings and chiefs in Ireland. These young men assured there would be less animosity in an island whose clans and chiefs continued to assail each other.

Being a hostage assured the youth grew fully devoted to his host king and clan, while never relinquishing ties to his own people. It was a practical arrangement, considering those days of inter-tribal warfare. Brian asked for and received the best of Ireland's clans' sons to join him. Even the Ui Neill sent strong young tribesmen to be trained and educated by this Munster king, who had fought and crushed the Viking invaders again and again.

Wolf knew he was not truly a hostage, but he cherished the time with his high-borne companions and the blood relatives of his foster father. They, in turn, seemed to both enjoy and stand in awe of their new addition. As he lived, ate, drank and slept among them, the bit of fear turned to deep respect and later love for their strange, gigantic barracks mate. It didn't take long for them to look up to him as a leader they could follow.

Then, despite the king's preparations for a long march to the north, came a threat from the south. Limerick, to Wolf's disgust, had been reborn. After its destruction following the battle of Sulcoit in 968, Brian invited local Irish people to rebuild its walls, fields and buildings. Still later, some Viking merchants from the Orkneys petitioned to become trading partners with the Dalcassians. Brian saw fit to allow them to return and re-establish their lucrative trade. This time they would be under Irish masters. Since all of the fiercest Vikings had been slaughtered, their wildest and proudest women given to Irish warriors, a few Norse merchants could do no harm, and Brian welcomed them.

Now the numbers of Norse in Limerick had grown, and though the trade, as always, benefitted both sides, many of these Vikings looked to the other Norse settlements at Dublin and Vadrefjord, which still maintained a degree of independence and self-rule, and chafed at their forced subservience to the Irish in the midst.

While at Innisfallen, Wolf had learned, much to his distaste, that after the battle of Gleann Mama and the sacking of Dublin two years earlier, Brian had allowed the Leinster king, Maelmora, to not only keep his life but to retain his crown. Even worse, Sitric Silkbeard, Dublin's former Viking ruler, survived unscathed and was attempting to come to an agreement with the King of Munster himself.

At Cashel, Wolf discovered Cormac and even Brian's son, Murcha, shared his revulsion at treating traitors and foreign enemies with such undeserved grace. The young man was certain he would never be a politician or diplomat. He found the arranged marriages among Ireland's kings and chieftains repellant, especially when some of these involved unions with Vikings. He had no interest in political discussions and was most comfortable when conversing on military and historical subjects. One abiding ambition overrode all others for him — driving the Vikings and other foreign invaders out of Ireland.

The new threat arose once again from the Vikings. Not sharing his father's trust in Vikings or Irish who had proved disloyal in the past, Murcha had established a sophisticated intelligence apparatus, which extended across Ireland into Scotland, Wales and even the Saxon and Danish parts of Britain. He recruited human sources, most motivated by loyalty to a free Ireland or even a pan-Celtic fealty. Some of them were motivated only by wealth, and Murcha was not above paying for information. He knew never to trust the accuracy of just a single report from one of his sources, but to have information confirmed by at least two others before taking action.

Cormac complemented this human network with small contingents of swift, mounted scouts who were employed to conduct wide-ranging reconnaissance and serve as a messenger service for the small army of spies across both islands.

Separate informants had reported on newly arrived Viking long ships at a hidden cove on the Shannon river below Limerick. There were three of them, each brimming with armed Viking warriors with not a tradesman among them. Fast riding scouts confirmed the report, exclaiming the ships had not been there more than a day and a half, and they were being joined by some of the Limerick Norse.

It was not difficult to deduce they were planning on retaking Limerick for themselves, and evicting the Irish living and working there. Wolf's eyes glistened with deadly intent when he heard this news. Here was a chance for him to pay back some of his debt to his foster father.

The scouts and spies reported the ships' warriors were to march along the northern bank of the Shannon toward Limerick, where they would link up with hundreds of the port's "Norse traders." The cove where they hid was amazingly close to the home ground of the Dál Cais, another sign of their apparent lack of fear of King Brian. Apparently, they forgot he was a warrior before he became a diplomat.

In the great hall, the king and his advisors discussed their response to this affront. Murcha wanted to march south with the bulk of the

Dalcassian army, crush these new invaders at the cove and burn their ships. Cormac agreed, adding that they would move immediately thereafter to Limerick and round up the disloyal Norse assembled there.

The king's newly arrived foster son, without hesitation, asked to speak. Looking intently toward Brian, he made his case.

"King. I esteem the experience and knowledge of my kinsmen, but please grant me a boon. Allow me to march with the sixty young warriors who share my barracks to meet these ships. I have trained with them over the last months and we have become close. They are all your blood kinsmen, or your loyal, proud hostages. And, please allow me to take the ten or fifteen younger wains who watch us train when not at their studies. They already are little masters of the sling, and delight in providing us "weapons support" during our drills. Counted among them are your grandchildren and other future Irish heroes. I promise to return these little ones all safely to their families, and the tales told of them later will resound and cause dreadful fear among our enemies."

The other advisors immediately yelled protests, most adamantly over the scant sixty barracks mates intended to engage the Vikings. They also were alarmed about the mere mention of the nine to thirteen-year-old "slingers" being exposed to the rage of Viking plunderers. Murcha pointed out the numbers — the three ships would carry one hundred and eight battle-hardened marauders. Even if they intended to have the long ships sail to meet them in Limerick later, each of these required only a crew of six to navigate such a short distance on a river. That would leave ninety Vikings opposing Wolf's sixty young fighters. And the addition of the little ones made a bad situation yet worse.

The massive young man stood erect and unmoved as he listened to the elders' voices of opposition, his keen and confident eyes never leaving the king's. Brian seemed to gaze upon some enormous, steadfast figure from the pantheon of the old Celtic war gods. Wolf's ponderous shield and the splendid sword were strapped, as always, on his back, reinforcing the image of indomitable martial prowess.

"It shall be as Wolf the Quarrelsome has requested, including my grandchildren with him."

The king's words rang out clearly in the hall. Most of those present gasped, but Cormac caught Wolf's glance and nodded in pleased agreement.

Brian instructed Wolf to collect his mates and the wee ones and move out at once. He directed Cormac to take three hundred Dalcassian veterans to deal with the Limerick Norse. Murcha recovered from his opposition and a sly grin just faintly crossed his face. He was comforted to see his father resorting to his warrior instincts as opposed to the diplomacy which had seemed to rule of late.

***

Upon first learning the news of the three long ships, Wolf had summoned the scouts and a learned scribe from Cashel's little school who specialized in illustrating detailed schematics of the countryside. The stout clergyman listened to the scout's report, asked more than a few questions, and quickly produced a charcoal etched map on a thin piece of flat cowhide. Wolf had seen similar depictions in the library of his history teacher in Innisfallen with ancient battles and maneuvers prominently displayed over the various features. Now the ground around the Shannon, the cove and the route the Vikings must take became a clear and vivid image in his mind.

As the map made clear, the easiest, flattest and quickest way for ninety Vikings to get to Limerick was to simply walk along the river's shoreline. Not a long march, it was narrow but firm with a pebbled little strand and low rocky hills along the northern flank. This would conceal their approach from shepherds or farmers above, as they marched to meet their Limerick accomplices in a field, just east of the settlement. They could advance two or three abreast at an easy and rapid pace.

Wolf noted, with keen interest, there was one bend in the river, almost a ninety degree turn inward, where the shoreline opened. If the scout and the scribe recorded it all accurately, he knew he could place a solid shield wall of five wide and eight deep to meet the approaching enemy. He knew forty eager and hot-blooded Celts, all of them among the most formidably armed and armored of the Gaels, could halt and crumble even ninety of the bloody little heathens. To assure that, of course, he would be in the middle and foremost of their iron wedge.

He had detected a gap between the rocky hills, behind where the first of the oncoming Norse would meet his surprise as they rounded the bend. Another twenty of his warriors would position themselves in this defile.

Wolf and his bristling sword and Dalcassian axe wielding defenders would drive with ferocity into the marching Viking column, and advance unstopping and slaying. Their enemies would fight and push forward viciously for the first moments, then enraged, push harder still. But they would not succeed. Eventually, the rearmost would pull back, retreating along the way they had come. And his waiting twenty warriors would meet and destroy them from behind.

It was just like Thermopylae in Greece a millennium ago, but this time the smaller, defending force would attack and annihilate the invaders from their rear. Wolf then considered the tough little contingent of wee lads who had earlier begged him to come and watch, even as he first told them the news of the unwelcome Viking ships. They too would play a role.

***

The column of Vikings had set out leisurely in mid-morning exactly as planned earlier with their fellows in Limerick. It was an easy, though narrow beach walk and they formed into slim formations with three abreast, sometimes cursing in jest as one or more had to splash through the surf. Each of these columns represented separated contingents of about thirty shipmates who knew each other well. At their front were their battle captain and a huge Norseman from Limerick, who they knew was no mere trader.

For the last several days they had camped on the cove's little beach aside their three ships. The concealed location had not fooled the locals and, to their surprise, nearby farmers came by to try to sell them eggs, cheeses and bread, as well as fine fowl. The Vikings gladly paid the paltry price the countrymen had asked, and explained they were just waiting to take on cargo and passengers from Limerick. Brian's peace had prevailed in the West, and they suspected their Irish visitors would have no reason to fear or doubt them.

So, it was a determined, but less than furtive, march along the banks of the Shannon that morning. The rocky little hills and outcroppings to their side sheltered them from the wind above, and they could occasionally see sheep and cattle across the river though no people.

As the first contingent approached an inward turning bend, a youthful voice, brimming with glee, called down from above.

"And where are ye off to, my fine, fat, filthy, herd of heathen hogs?"

The two leaders looked up to their left to gaze into the eyes of a young Irish boy. A spritely, redhaired youth, no more than ten, with pale and coltish limbs protruding from a simple woolen tunic, grinned down at them. He was leaning against a large standing rock midway up the stony incline.

Laughing, the big Limerick Viking translated the boy's greeting for his fellows. These Vikings did not share his mirth and grumbled. In guttural, Danish-accented Irish, the local Norseman informed the boy they were going to Limerick.

"An' sure, ye must have my grandfather's permission to cross our pretty little riverbank, do ye not?"

The same gravelly voice laughed once more and bellowed out that no Irish grandfather, nor father, nor priest, nor mother could halt them, and that the boy should go home now, lest he disturb these fine Norse visitors.

The boy stood upright with shoulders back. "My name is Caurag Mac Murchad. I am the son of Murcha Mac Brian, who is the son of my grandfather the King of Munster, Brian the Conqueror. You have now displeased me, and should immediately go back to your foul, fishy-smelling scows and leave our island."

Even the Limerick Viking became angry at his. When he translated it for the others, they demanded the boy be beaten. The fleet's captain turned and ordered one of the younger warriors behind to climb up and bring the boy down. Amidst Danish cursing and pounding of shields, the Norse warrior, passed his shield and axe to mates, and scurried up the rocky slope like a squirrel. The boy continued to peer down at the grumbling warriors below him.

Three steps before the advancing Viking would snag his prey, five more wee Irish lads sprang up from the crest of the hill, twirling slings around their angelic little heads. When they released, four round stones impacted. Two bounced off a mailed chest and one struck the top of the visored helmet with stunning force. But that didn't matter, one stone, with tremendous velocity, entered the panting mouth of the climbing Viking, crushing the throat tissue then strangling him, resulting in quick death. He tumbled awkwardly downhill, and lay splayed amidst the startled invasion force.

Suddenly, stinging stones rained down even harder as the boy ran up to join his fellows. At this point, the stones were nothing more than a nuisance to the armored column and the Viking captain told them to move on. Death came easily, even if dishonorable from a simple slung stone. The objective was to take Limerick once again. Later they would return and kill these little annoyances, their parents and their clans. Shields upraised, the Norse moved forward more rapidly now.

As they rounded the bend of the riverbank, hoping to outdistance the distracting rain of stones, the skulls of the first three Vikings, including the Limerick Norseman, were crushed in a red shower of brain-smashing fury. Before the gore had even splattered the following three, they were down from sword thrusts or the crashing arcs of Dalcassian axes, with one severed head flying back to fall between the shields of two advancing followers. Their dead chieftain grimaced up horribly to their stunned horror. These two were dead before they could register the shock.

The forty elite of the *Laochra an Rí* had set up a shield wall in the form of a wedge, with their fearsome barracks mate, now leader, taking the spike position. These young warriors were the closest Ireland had to nobility. Unlike the mass of their fellow Irish warriors, they all had some type of armor — mail or boiled, fitted leather over thick wool and linen. They also wore thick iron, studded and slatted helmets, in the simple conical shape of their ancestors. Many of Brian's kin had received and been trained in the use of the Dalcassian axe, and they yearned to show they could kill Vikings as well as their elders. The hostages all owned their own wonderfully crafted Celtic swords.

This was not simple a unit of random peasant Irish tribesmen with spears and clubs. This was a force to meet the best of the Norse foe. They were young, hot-blooded and well-led and became a killing machine behind the slashing, thrusting, plowing whirlwind who mangled and turned to a grisly pulp all who stood before him.

The Vikings stormed forward to be massacred. They were unable to form their own wedge and their first ranks became a shamble of maimed bodies before they could be supported from the rear. The Irish formation never even moved forward beyond a few initial steps. Their intent was to draw the invaders in. As one member of the Gaelic wall was stunned or wounded, another came forward. But that happened only rarely. The enraged, ripping giant who led them slaughtered so many of the foe, his comrades simply moved on to the others to each side, flaying them with fury.

Making the Norse advance even worse than the nightmare it had now become, the furious flying projectiles from above were now joined by more stinging stones from their front. Wolf had placed the remaining little slingers to the rear of his wedge. They were able to whirl and fling the round stones directly into the faces of the second echelon Vikings. As the "good boy" had learned from his trainer, the slingers may not kill in their hundreds but distraction and deception help in battle.

By now, the original Viking ninety had become much fewer. Confused and pelted with stones, a bloodbath of their falling comrades to their front, the rearmost retreated back from whence they came toward the refuge of their long ships.

These rushed to the rear, happy to be free of the constant stones falling upon their helmets and shoulders. Then, in their haste to withdraw, they stumbled into another wall of thick Irish oaken shields. As the Dalcassian axes descended, the slaughter became horribly complete. The riverside was now a chaotic maelstrom of wounded and mauled bodies of Norsemen.

When the two contingents of buoyant Irish met at the banks, no Viking lived. Wolf inquired about his shield brothers and was informed one had lost an ear, and another had an axe blade cut off a big toe. Six others had simply passed out from exhaustion. The blocking force warriors were angry since so few of them had even become winded. This is what Wolf the Quarrelsome had dreamed, suffered and lived for during his hell in Dublin. This was just the beginning. The bloody little heathens and all the invaders of the world would be crushed under Irish steel. Wolf's mother would look down from heaven at Blessed Mary's side, and watch as he eradicated every vestige of the foreigners from their holy island.

***

Not much later, the remaining eighteen Vikings from the hidden cove took their three ships to the Limerick pier. Calling out with ribald curses, they greeted their shipmates awaiting them in their gleaming mail corselets and familiar fierce helmets. Springing up and onto the docks, a lanky Norseman ribaldly called out, "Are there wine, women and booty left for us?"

One of their awaiting brothers, even taller and more immense then they had remembered him, was the first to greet them. The captured Viking axes rose, wielded now by Viking-clad *laochra*, and fell with a steady precision. All eighteen would-be invaders were dead before the smiles had scarcely left their bearded faces.

***

With the problems in Limerick dealt with, the planned tour of the North could commence. The intent of the long march was both diplomatic and a show of force. The combined forces of Munster and its Connaught allies were to take part. The key objective of this display was to impress the powerful clans of the Northern and southern Ui Neill. Brian felt confident Malachi and his Meathmen were already sufficiently impressed by the military prowess of the forces at his command.

Despite the fact that most of Ireland was now nominally under the control of Irish chieftains, there were still small pockets of hostile Vikings at various places along the coast, and especially on some of the small islands offshore. During a late-night meeting with Cormac and Murcha, Wolf suggested a means of eliminating these pirate nests that would occur simultaneously with the march of the main forces.

"The three *snekkjas* have been docked in Limerick and I've made sure they are kept secure. It is my intent to use these long ships to sail north along the west coast, mirroring the king's land tour with a cruise of his Irish navy."

Wolf found Irishmen from Dublin who had sailed with the Vikings, some as servants, and others as willing freebooters, to raid the land of the Saxons. These men would teach some of the *laochra* how to sail and navigate, and these strong, virile young men would easily adapt to pulling the oars of the swift ships.

The naval training passed quickly, with several trial cruises on the Shannon, and the warriors came to embrace their dual role of sailors and naval infantry. The painted dragon heads on the bows of the ships were considered too blasphemous for the good Christian crews however. So, Wolf ordered them to be replaced with the likenesses of fauna native to Ireland. Skilled artisans and woodcutters combined to produce three new beautiful and naturalistic prows: a sleek swan, a regal stag, and, for the young leader's flagship, a ferocious wolf's head with fangs bared. The warriors found this last amusing and absolutely logical.

All of the veterans of the battle on the Shannon became crew members, and others among the various barracks competed to fill the remaining numbers needed to bring the maritime force to a total of one hundred and ten eager sea dogs. The Irish shields fit in place as well as any of those of the Vikings. Only Wolf's metallic plated huge shield was kept from the sea mists and waves, snug in a leather wrapping, when not on the massive broad back of its owner. From a distance the three ships looked exactly as before, and this was intended to be the case, since it was expected the sight of these ships would not automatically alarm any of the Norse scattered among the islands and coves of the coast. The warriors did take some shameful and mischievous pleasure however in knowing that their crafts' appearance along the coast would cause a degree of panic when observed by their own countrymen.

As they observed the boats getting underway out of Limerick in the early morning, Murcha remarked to his cousin.

"It may be hell itself we've unleashed here this day. I swear they look as terrifying as any fleet of Norse dragon ships afloat."

"No cousin," replied Cormac, "tis merely a band of merry monks off on a holy pilgrimage with a big, happy and saintly abbot at their lead."

Both laughed with gusto, breaking the calm stillness of the sun-lit morning. Then, they turned their mounts and galloped off to Cashel.

So it was that the huge land army marched north and the three *snekkjas* bristling with armed and enthusiastic crewmen sailed out of the Shannon and turned north, always keeping close to land.

***

Murcha's intelligence network had lately reported that two Viking ships and about ninety marauders used Achill Island, just off of Connaught's northwest, as a staging area for lightning raids on the least defended clan dwellings. These Northmen were supposedly not affiliated with any of the Vikings in Ireland, who were now nominally subject to various Irish kings and chieftains.

The three long ships timed their arrival at Achill to strike from the west at first light. They disembarked and marched hurriedly up the banks to the fields above. They had expected to meet their foes prepared for battle in the field, but amazingly, the Norse had posted no watch on the island's western side since there had never been a seaborne attack by the Irish on any Viking stronghold in Ireland. So, the band of *laochra*, ninety strong, moved swiftly in a column four abreast toward the eastern part of the island where they knew the two ships were docked.

They caught the Norse unaware as some of the Vikings were conducting maintenance on their ships and others were at repose, having eaten a breakfast of fish and porridge. Splitting into three columns, the young barracks mates let loose an ear-splitting war cry and fell to battle behind their colossal leader to wreak havoc on the foreign invaders. Wolf massacred the first four of the enemy before any other Irishman had a chance to thrust with sword or swing a Dalcassian axe. It was over quickly and none of the Vikings emerged alive.

Immediately afterwards, flushed with battle lust and adrenaline, one of the young Irish warriors jokingly complained.

"This day has been far too easy and not as honorable as red, bloody battle should be."

Wolf cast a harsh, disapproving gaze at him, immediately stilling the banter of the others.

"There is no honor in any Irishman dying in combat with these bloody little heathens. Our duty is to kill them all in any manner possible. Guile and deception are much preferable to bloody 'honorable' battle. And I've no use for single combat duels. We must always fight together as one unit with one purpose: completely and decisively crush any who stand before us."

The tall leader continued. "We drill in fives, tens, and thirties. Others may simply throw themselves in a disorganized mass at a formidable enemy. That has been the way of our people and we've lived to regret it. All of Europe and beyond was once, long ago, the land of our distant ancestors and now we are a simple little outcropping in the cold northwest reaches of the ocean."

Wolf the Quarrelsome became animated, warming to his subject while his weapon brothers looked on, trying to follow his passionately delivered history and tactics lesson. Because he was a gargantuan mass in their midst, splattered with the blood of ten or more dead Vikings, and oozing red from his own wounds, his words moved them deeply.

"Our Gaulish forebears conquered Rome long before the time of Our Lord. They stupidly allowed their blood enemies to simply pay tribute and live on unscathed. These same Romans later invaded north to annihilate and absorb all of their conquerors' descendants. The foreigners did this through superior equipment and tactics, though they were fewer in number. They fought as a well-ordered unit, and that is what I have tried to instill in training in the fields of Munster over these last months."

Now all eyes shone with unswerving attention toward their eighteen-year-old chief who seemed wiser, more experienced and more believable than any of their elders.

The deep, stentorian voice of their formidable young teacher enthralled them.

"My lieutenants have reported eight of our brothers have fallen, and three more received unnecessary injuries at the hands of these unprepared Norsemen. That is to our shame. Never leave the sides of your unit in battle. Even in broken terrain and confusion, always stay with your brothers, even if only five of you. All of the fallen were overcome with the battle fervor which has led to so many of our defeats over a millennium. They engaged singly or, worse yet, allowed themselves to be outnumbered by two or three of the heathens, as these fine Irish warriors sprinted ahead to gain "honor" and "glory"."

With that Wolf spat on the ground.

"Honor and glory are ours when we win and they lose. It is when they die and we live. It is when we return to relish the company of our weapon brothers and our families, and their corpses rot in red, dripping gore where we crushed them."

The "good boy" then turned and walked back to where his three ships waited. He had ordered that all the Viking bodies be left where they fell to serve as a deterrent lest any other band of northern pirates come to this island. All of their ships were put to the torch. As the *Laochra an Rí* marched off, some gazed back at the scene of carnage and destruction waiting to meet the eyes of the next marauding fleet of dragon ships that dared to come to Achill island.

***

The small fleet of Irish long ships — swan, stag, and wolf — sailed north along the coast of Connacht, and then east over the lands of the *Cenél Conaill,* the *Cenél nEóghain,* and in Ireland's northeast the *Dál Riata.* The main army of Munster had been met first with alarm, and then relief, as Brian's huge mass of warriors marched through their lands with smiles for their people, and small but significant gifts for their various chieftains. The Ui Neill, who had dominated Ireland for so long, seemed pleased by this "charm offensive" and all were impressed by the devout Munster king who greeted them with friendship and Celtic warmth.

In strong contrast to this display of his king's grace, Wolf was distressed to learn that Viking ships from Dublin, purportedly King Brian's allies, had landed and pillaged the various lands of the *Dál nAraide* and the *Dál Fiatach* clans. These small but important Irish chieftains, whose lands encompassed Ireland's northeast coast, had sworn allegiance to the *Ui Neill* and would submit to neither Viking nor southern Irish king. Wolf had assiduously avoided becoming entangled in the Dalcassian court's politics or his foster father's efforts at diplomacy.

He was repulsed to learn that not only had Brian allowed the Viking ruler, Sitric, to return to Dublin and administer the City under Munster control, but the king had allowed his beautiful Irish daughter to marry this pagan *Gall*. He had assumed the Dublin Viking, who had ruled during his agony in confinement, had either been dispatched by a good Irish warrior or fled to some cold, distant land in the north.

So, when the hospitable chiefs of the famed *Dál Riata*, the people who had made Scotland a proud Gaelic land, told him of the attacks on Irish people to their south, Wolf decided on his course of action.

As the Munster army marched south to the ancient seat of Irish kings at Tara, Wolf sailed east with his three *snekkjas*. The Viking presence in the Hebrides islands was an affront to the young man who had been taught by his monks that the foreigners had taken these islands from the gentle clergy and Celtic fishermen who had made their homes there. There was one island among many which might serve to repay two hundred years of attacks on the Irish.

This was the island that Sigurd the Stout, the corpulent, so-called "Earl of the Orkneys," had established as his trading post and staging area for raids into Saxon England, Scotland and Ireland. Sigurd held control over some of these western islands while others were claimed by Thorwald Raven, who styled himself "Jarl of the Hebrides." The monks had told Wolf that these islands were supposedly converted to the true faith by some Norwegian king in 995. When they told him this, Wolf retorted angrily.

"I've lived with the bloody little heathen savages. They embody evil and vile greed. Even if they are ever to turn to Christ, they will eventually adapt some heretical version of God's faith or revert to their true and natural Godlessness."

***

It was at still dark when the little fleet of long ships rowed leisurely into the well-situated port the Vikings had constructed on the island's west coast. As the morning light began to break, a few merchants walked out, rubbing their eyes, hoping to see a familiar ship or face, and especially cargo. The sun was behind them so they could observe the swan, stag and wolf prows — all had a bit of the Celtic on them — not the fierce northern dragon. *Strange.*

The ships avoided the docks and beached on the strand beside them. Then, without a sound, warriors leapt from the bow onto the beach and quickly moved up the banks.

"ABBOOOO."

In three formations, the invaders from the sea immediately rushed inland dividing the Viking settlement into thirds. The Viking merchants' skulls were split even before they could call out a cry of warning. The Irish, keeping to their tight knit groups after Wolf's warning, simply made a systematic cleansing of the port town.

All males over fourteen were slaughtered without compunction. The women and children were left for later retrieval. Pushing further in, the *Laochra* saw a Viking longhouse, many of them noting it was not much different from their barracks back in in Munster. This was where the fighting men would be just rousing from the night's revelries.

"Stad. Stop. A thunderous command from their leader rang out.

"Stop and let us wait for them to come to us. Going in would put some of us in positions we'd be hard pressed to defend. We'll move against them as they pour out."

Groups of enraged, murderous Vikings emerged wildly, spilling out of the longhouse like fat, white, somnambulant bears. The young *Laochra* in their tight knit groups, formed a semi-circle around the entrance. They thrust and cut their enemies down as if they were dried fronds of bracken.

Their chieftain watched, cautious for signs of either weakness or uncontrolled enthusiasm. They displayed none of that, seemingly now attuned to his commands. At last, one enormous *Danar* crashed out of the broken wooden doors, swinging two huge battle axes in sloping arcs over each shoulder.

The Celtic youth were taken aback at the sight of this solid monster of a Viking. His shoulders were twice theirs. The swinging axes occasionally smote the ground and shook the air. His nostrils flared like a cornered wild boar. Long blond hair hung to his shoulders and he was armored with shimmering mail. Burning eyes glared at them from the grim, visored helmet of their nightmares. His arms and legs were like mighty oaks, and they could hear and see the steaming exhalation of his monstrous breath as he stood before them posturing menacingly, both axes flailing.

With a predatory smile, Wolf stepped forward and bade two of his warriors to take positions, behind and to either side of him. Then, he ordered two more to take positions immediately to their rear.

"Now then, we are five. This bloody little heathen doesn't really need five Irish warriors to cleanse the world of him, but the lesson will be made."

Wolf turned to his mates and smiled yet again. He wore neither helmet nor armor, though he clutched his massive metallic shield and heavy sword, forged by the old Connaught chieftain.

"Hoi, *Gall Dubh* — black foreigner — how many of my people have you butchered?

"Now, you will die by the hand of one of the soft Irish sheep. Yes, I can see it in your eyes, you know me. Look closely and see your death."

To the complete surprise of the assembled Irish and the enormous Viking, Wolf threw shield and sword to the ground and leapt with exceeding speed onto his glaring enemy. Before either axe could descend, he was within their deadly arcs. They fell behind him. Two calloused hands closed around the thick, muscular Viking neck, squeezing firmly and slowly. Behind the helmet's visor, the blue eyes first expressed amazement, followed by unaccustomed and growing fear. The young leader's hands closed more forcefully, as he thrust one knee into the Viking's groin, crushing both bone and tissue. The strangling gurgle and the cry of anguish pleased Wolf.

As the monster's eyes dimmed, Wolf squeezed inexorably harder and he softly whispered, "Die in agony as I intend for all of you until you're gone from our lands."

The young warriors gathered around their captain and watched as the terrible creature slumped to the ground.

None would ever fear any Viking again, no matter how huge or menacing, nor would they view their leader in anything but awe from that time. The age of foreigners oppressing Irish was over. Their war chief displayed the freedom and unbridled physicality that every Celt yearned for from his or her core.

He was able to express it, more than any, through force of strength and valor. Such a thing had not happened in Ireland since the time of the ancients.

So, they left this one of Sigurd's islands. All of the Viking men had been slain but those who fled to the hills. Even Wolf would not allow the killing of the women or children. His intent was for the Norse women to be used as scullery servants or cooks for the Irish clans. The children would be given to those families who couldn't conceive on their own. These would grow up to be no different than any other Irish man or woman.

The three, now fully-laden, *snekkjas* were packed with the human booty Wolf had taken from the heart of the Orkney kingdom, and he knew this assault on their own would reverberate within the halls of the bloody little heathens. Unlike his foster father, Wolf had no desire for diplomacy or familial alliances with the Norse. His intent was steadfast since he'd seen his family's fate at the hands of the invaders. *Faolan an Trodach* meant to extinguish any vestige of Viking pestilence from not only Ireland but from all Celtic lands.

***

1002 was an eventful year in Ireland, marked most noticeably by the Munster king's long march across the island. Brian had succeeded in pleasing and impressing most of the northern Irish chieftains, especially the Ui Neill. His was no longer considered an upstart clan from a southern backwater. He now felt confident enough to send a message to Malachi of Meath that the High Kingship of Ireland was to change hands. King Malachi was a practical man, and knew without the Northern Ui Neill behind him, he had no chance against the huge force from Munster and Connaught which now marched comfortably in his direction.

The kings of Munster and Meath met in the ancient Irish capital of Tara in the east. Brian was diplomatic and gracious, neither haughty nor imperious. His vision was a united Ireland. Now at the age of sixty-two, he wanted all to live in peace together, even the still plentiful Vikings. He explained to his advisors they had been in Ireland for almost two centuries. They had come to marry into some of the best Irish families, as had some Irishmen taken Norse wives to themselves. He could prove how their skills at trade helped both peoples. Now, happily, some of them were becoming Christian as had the earlier Saxon pagans in England and on the continent.

Many of his most trusted chiefs quietly bristled at their king's soft words towards the Norse; principal among them were Murcha and Cormac.

The crowning of the new *Ard Rí* was accomplished with Christian ritual and Gaelic Brehon trappings. The ceremony captured the best of the learned culture which Irish missionaries had brought to Europe centuries before to impede that continent's descent into total chaos. Even Malachi seemed relieved to pass the reins to his ally and countryman.

Thousands had come to witness this passing of the kingship. Upon observing the regal bearing of the new ruler, and more poignantly, casting eyes on his enormous, well-armed, and battle tested army, they immediately understood this was not merely another ceremonial event. This was a genuinely epic juncture in the history of their people.

All had heard, since he never disguised it, King Brian intended to become the "Emperor of the Irish." There would be no more internecine slaughter among the Gaels. The Vikings would be equal partners and one folk with his own on the united island. And there would be natural allies overseas among the Celts in Wales and Scotland, and even among the Norse abroad, who would become Christian and peaceful.

Yet, during the ceremony, the king himself, reminded all of his unrelenting victories over foes, both Irish and Viking, since the guerilla days of his youth — Sulcoit, Limerick, Gleann Mama, and Dublin. All of this was meant to quell any notion of him as weak and appeasing. And, it did indeed convey a strong veiled threat to any who might oppose his design.

And thus, began a new era in Ireland, which gave impetus to a revived focus on art, literature and culture. Roads and bridges would be built, monasteries and churches repaired and expanded, and the way was shown by the High King to restore the scholarly preeminence of the country, which it had known centuries before. For twelve years the *Ard Rí* ruled wisely during one of the high points of Irish history.

Chapter 8
Fingwalle, Afon Dyfrdwy, Danish-occupied England, near the Welsh border
Late 1004 A.D.

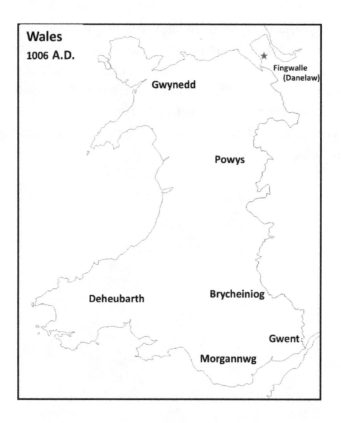

Wolf continued to train among the others of the *Laochra an Rí*. After the Munster king's assumption of control over the whole island, the ranks of these picked warriors had swollen with high-born volunteers, now including many from Scotland and Wales. It was among the new arrivals that their natural leader, the former Dublin captive, met his first Pict.

The Picts were an ancient people who had inhabited Northeast Scotland from before the time of the Roman invasions. They had established their own powerful kingdoms but had gradually merged, at first painfully and later almost peacefully, with the Scots of the Dál Riata who had come over from Ireland. Wolf found the dark-skinned young Pict, with long black wavy hair and sky-blue eyes, to be a short, yet formidable natural warrior. His name was Mornak Cennelath. He was delightfully full of cheer and jokes, which helped make the arduous training rituals pass with a bit less misery and pain for the striving recruits.

The warriors had learned much over the years from continuously struggling against the Vikings. Some of them, like their leader, had lived among the enemy and knew his strengths and weaknesses. King Brian had earlier developed some tactical and technical adaptations to meet the advanced threat presented by the Northmen. Now Wolf carried these further.

Unlike the vast majority of fighting men in Ireland who eschewed armor, these high-born youngsters arrived with their own mail or boiled leather jerkins and well-crafted swords. Some also had finely made spears, leaf-shaped steel tips glittering at the ends of shafts of white hazel. Elegant new Dalcassian axes were now being produced in Munster by skilled craftsmen under the tutelage of the very same old Connaught chieftain and blacksmith who had constructed Wolf's own immense and imposing broadsword. These axes were offered to warriors who wished to be trained in their deadly use. The axes were one of the king's own innovations. Now Wolf added more.

The Norse used spears and occasionally employed bows as well. But they used these weapons by necessity and not with any massed intent. The Vikings most feared and lethal tactic was to form shield walls or wedges, and advance with awesomely powerful downward blows of axe and heavy iron sword. The most lethal damage crashed upon the Irish from above. Savage head and upper body injuries accounted for the majority of Irish losses in battles.

Norse and Irish shield construction was similar - "two knuckles"-thick, circular wooden body with bronze bosses and leather arm straps. But even these sturdy defensive weapons could not always withstand the powerful crushing force of a violently descending axe blade. Wolf's own immense shield, armored entirely with metal, was too heavy for all but the strongest men to carry and wield in battle.

After consultation with the iron smiths and wood craftsmen, he devised a compromise for the elite warriors. Instead of having just a bit of bronze or other metal on the rims, they developed a means by which the top half of the shields would be plated with protective metal similar to Wolf's fully covered shield. Another variation, which offered even more protection, was to swag the top half with strong but elegant-appearing steel chain. They were much heavier and the odd balance took time to wield without awkwardness, yet eventually all of the *Laochra* were laboring under their weight. They prided themselves on their ability to master the new, more powerful, weapon they'd been provided through the wealth of the *Ard Ri.* Now, though the axe blow may still flash down with devastating force, the shield would almost always stay intact, allowing its owner, if he could withstand the impact, to thrust or slash into his extended enemy's flank, face or legs.

Local smiths also altered the construction of helmets which would be offered to the elite warriors and Dalcassians. Simple conical iron helms were modified to shield the back of the neck, and with a short extension on the front which covered just the bridge of the nose. The most important innovations were the thick half loops of steel which formed a cross, overlaid and melded onto the helmet's surface. These were intended as additional protection against axe and sword blows from above. Combined with thickened linen padding inside, this made the helmet heavier but much more effective in surviving the type of combat that was most common.

With the addition of the new shields and Dalcassian axes to his comrades' order of battle, Wolf took the time to be everywhere on the training fields instructing the young fighters in the efficacy of the simple thrust with sword point, or the specially designed crest of their new axes. About half of trainees chose to adopt the Dalcassian weapon, but even they retained their long fighting *scians* to be used in backup. The leader also impressed upon them that their new heavy shields were now even more lethal when used in offense. He demonstrated how they could be used to push up into an enemy's helmet, crushing nose and cheek bones and severely disabling if not outright killing the opponent.

As always, the combative Wolf stressed to them to keep tight in their formation of fives, tens, twenties or larger, depending on tactics adopted. In strong contrast to the tales of their youth, the stories of historical Gaelic champions, and the expectations of many of these high-born, proud young men, he spoke adamantly against engaging in single, ritual combat. Repeating they were too few, he related the lessons of how madly rushing Celtic warriors, flooding without organization as individual fighters, had been annihilated by disciplined Roman legionnaires, even when the Celts had advantage in numbers.

"That must never be repeated when we meet the Vikings."

The main armies of Munster and Connaught warriors, now increased by volunteers from Meath and the north, were formidable enough. The multiple hundreds of these young, exceedingly hard drilled, elite fighters would prove a devastating force multiplier in times to come. Through it all, the young leader imagined even more....

***

Building roads, bridges, and churches and maintaining standing military forces required great wealth. The king was reluctant to take more in tribute from his vassal clans and tribes. For hundreds of years Ireland's resources had been pillaged and looted by succeeding bands of Danish and Norwegian Vikings. Wolf decided the time had come for the nascent Irish empire to gain recompense from their erstwhile marauders.

The Vikings had long been active in Britain with even more success against the Saxons than they ever achieved against the Gaels. Enormous swaths of England had been consolidated under their control in what was called the Danelaw. The Saxons now only held the southeast of their country, while the Welsh continued to maintain the independence of their small western holdings. Now Murcha's intelligence apparatus reported a lucrative opportunity.

Welsh allies of King Brian had informed the Irish of a small but bustling trading center on the west coast of England, just to the northeast of Wales. This was in an area controlled by the Danes and they called it *Fingwalle*. It was on a little peninsula along a river the Welsh referred to as *Afon Dyfrdwy*. Murcha's network of scouts and informants was able to determine the Danes established this settlement as a storage and transshipment point for the booty they took in raids against the Irish, Welsh, Scots and Saxons.

One morning breakfasting with the High King, the "good boy" informed his foster father of his bold plan.

"I intend, with your permission, to take the three *snekkjas*, with handpicked volunteer crews from among my weapon brothers and visit this foreign trading center. I will return with whatever tribute we can fit into the long ships, and we will leave the Danish settlement in flames."

Wolf looked to the older man, expecting to find resistance or at least deep concern. He could only detect a sparkle of admiration and pride in those piercing hazel eyes.

"There are several young Welshmen training with us now who are familiar with the area, the terrain and the desires of the local people. They tell us our Welsh cousins would be pleased to have this nest of pirates destroyed entirely."

Later, when the chiefs and advisors at the court in Cashel heard of this plan they were first taken back, and then pleased by its simple audacity. There were no moral considerations since it was a foreign

Viking-controlled town. By now, they had become familiar with the young Wolf's cunning and martial prowess. But just before permission was granted, newer, more detailed reports arrived which called the operation into question.

There were one thousand Vikings in the settlement since it had assumed new importance as a western outpost of the Danelaw. Seven hundred of these were considered to be fit enough to fight on sea or land. The rest were women or old men. The marauders had taken to raiding small Welsh coastal settlements and seizing entire populations of these little enclaves to be used as chattel slaves for the Danes. Even more disgusting, many were sold to Islamic traders during Mediterranean voyages. The hundred or so Irish warriors Wolf could disembark from his three long ships would never be able to storm ashore and prevail against such odds.

King Brian's diplomacy must come into play to give any chance of success. Celtic Wales was composed of small provinces and kingdoms similar to Ireland. The Welsh also shared the Irish curse of not just armed incursions by foreigners — Danes and Saxons — but they too fought among themselves in pitched costly campaigns. The most recent ruler of the two westernmost Welsh kingdoms of Gwynedd and Deheubarth was a wise chieftain named Llywelyn ap Seisyll. He and Brian had exchanged ambassadors as well as hostages.

Through a series of dispatches Brian and Llywelyn came to an agreement in which the Welsh would send a force of five hundred of their veteran warriors to march on *Fingwalle* over land. This was unusual for the Welsh who preferred to keep their armies within their own borders to repel attacks and exploit their own familiar internal lines of communication.

Synchronized timing on the part of the seaborne Irish and their Welsh allies was essential. Otherwise both forces could be destroyed piecemeal. The cunning Wolf developed the details of the combined plan of attack.

There was great disappointment among the young Irish warriors who were not selected to take part, but their leader comforted them, explaining there were only the three ships and they would have ample opportunity to join him in the battles that were yet to come. Wolf chose some veterans of his previous expeditions against the Vikings, but he also took along untried young men as well. All of them had excelled in training. Getting blooded for the first time in a foreign adventure would accrue to their later benefit.

**

The three long ships disembarked several of their members in a secluded cove, away from any local settlement, along Gwynedd's northern shore. This small party of young Irish and Welsh warriors immediately set off at a trot toward the wooded area by the border with the Danelaw, where they knew five hundred eager and armed Welshmen awaited them.

The small Irish fleet stayed in the cove to give the Welsh forces time to make the half day march to approach *Fingwalle* from its east. During this time several of the men on the ships fashioned crude woolen sacks and bits of wood and paint into the form of dragonheads to slide over the stag, swan and wolf prows adorning the swift craft.

"Well they won't fool any of the bloody little heathens from up close, but they'll get us into the dock before there's any alarm. And they are gloriously ugly." Wolf grinned up at the menacing visages and slapped their artistic creators on their broad backs.

Five hours later the *snekkjas* got underway. They traveled east until they reached the mouth of the *Afon Dyfrdwy*. As they cut through the waters with furled sails, rowers straining over their oars in a measured pace, Wales was off to their starboard and the Danelaw shore to their port. It was mid-day when they first sighted the little harbor which sheltered eight ships. Each of these was much larger than the *snekkjas*. Two were alongside one of the several docks, and the rest had been brought up onto the sandy beach. The fortified town of *Fingwalle* was a short march from the dock, and they could see the tracks of the carts and wagons, which brought goods from the ships to the settlement.

***

Following Wolf's plan, by now the Welsh force was marching along a path which led directly to the Danish town. They had deliberately marched in the open, even singing old war songs in their lilting Celtic language. There was no doubt any Dane who saw these columns would speed to *Fingwalle* to alert the Vikings to the strange band of advancing Welsh. The Northmen knew the terrain around them well by now, and knew exactly where to bring their warriors into wooded ambush positions along either side of the path. They had the advantage in numbers, and had no doubts of their ability to annihilate the brazen invading Welsh columns, to swarm over them in deadly surprise. *Fingwalle's* palisaded berms had been left with a token force since no threat from the sea could even be contemplated by the arrogant Vikings.

The Welsh too knew this terrain since it had been stolen from them first by the Saxons and later by the Danes, who expelled those earlier English invaders. Most importantly, the Welsh knew enough to halt before they marched into a wooded killing zone. And now they stopped, formed four-deep lines on either side of the road, and simply reclined in the meadow, eyes peeled to the wood line before them, where they knew hundreds of cruel, axe wielding Vikings waited, yearning to slaughter every one of them.

The Vikings peered from the trees, confused at this turn of events. Then, after a few minutes rest, the entire Welsh force arose, turned about and marched back the way they had come, parallel to the road. The Danes were strung out in pockets extending along both sides of the road deep to the rear in ambush formation, and could not quickly form into columns to pursue the apparently retreating Welsh. Adding to the confusion, a cry arose from the rearmost of the Danish lines...smoke was seen billowing from the direction of *Fingwalle.*

***

As the score or so of Danes working in the little harbor looked on, the three *snekkjas* deftly slid alongside the waiting docks. Two of the men on the docks exchanged glances as they focused on the almost childishly crude dragonheads on the ships' prows. Their amusement quickly dissipated as the crews of all three ships leapt over the sides and swarmed over the harbor and its beaches. One hundred fierce warriors, many carrying strangely formed axes, began to cut down the unprepared Danes, who only now understood what was happening. It didn't last long, and before the last one groaned and bled out, the Danish ships were in flames and the Irish formed a column with their huge leader at point. They trotted up the road into the trees and toward *Fingwalle*.

Wolf expected only a small group of Vikings would be remaining inside the earthen mounded compound. He had no intention of taking time for an elaborate ruse. Now in a wedge formation, shields up, the Irish simply slammed into the main wooden gate with a tree trunk ram they had brought from their ship. The few Danish guards rained arrows and spears on them from above but none found an opening.

In no time, the main Irish force was within the walls. They split into three groups with the general intent of killing any who stood before them. Wolf took a group of ten and moved rapidly to the compound's center. The other groups systematically deployed to sweep through every quarter of the small town. Groups of two or three Danes hurled themselves on these formations of tens and fives and were surrounded and slaughtered like cattle by the quick flashing axes.

One group of the *laochra* burst into an exceedingly large longhouse, only to find more than one hundred bound and miserable Welsh men, women and children huddled together. These screamed at the sight of the fully armored Irish warriors who had erupted into their midst. From among these fierce intruders one clear Welsh voice rang out.

"Freedom. We're friends and your countrymen are on their way now to us."

The young Welsh hostage took off his helmet, shook his long chestnut hair and grinned broadly at his still confused kinsmen.

"Let's get these bindings off you."

The former prisoners were taken out and given food and drink, looted from the houses of the Vikings, as all armed resistance had quickly been overcome. Wolf had ordered all adult Danish males of fighting age to be killed on sight, and the women and children bound. Except for a few ancient wizened men, all that remained of Danes in the open were hundreds of mostly blonde and red-haired women and their tow-headed little children. These were herded into the longhouse that had held the Welsh, and its door was then chained shut. Only two structures remained to be taken, and Wolf's ten moved toward them.

One was a stout, well-built and colorfully adorned oaken longhouse — thick log walls with mud daub mortar under a huge arched roof. Its front door seemed more secure and robust than the gate to the town had been. The other was poignantly familiar to the massive leader of the assembled Gaels. It was a smaller and more primitively constructed version of the elaborate one. It had no adornments and no color, but was simply a wooden hut, partially overgrown with moss and other vegetation. Wolf approached it without hesitation and slashed his enormous shield in a crushing blow onto lock and door, sundering both.

A soft glow emanated from the hut's center. There was a small table with a hunched figure sitting on a stool, bent over a parchment, stylus in hand. He was not chained, but clearly a prisoner of the Vikings. With five young warriors assuming a semi-circle at the walls behind him, the "good boy" moved slowly forward.

The dim light revealed a linen-robed, middle-aged man, totally entranced in his studious endeavors. He was shorter than most Irish and Vikings but powerfully built. Curly rings of deep black crowned his head and his raven beard shone with the same tint and texture.

Seemingly unconcerned, the little man looked up into the scarred face of the huge apparition which peered down at him.

"Your northern stench is more tolerable than the Saxon English, and far less offensive than that which exudes from these verminous, foul Vikings. So, you great ugly ape, what new species of barbarian spawn oozing out of these cold, wet lands are you then?"

This seemingly insulting query was conveyed in faultless Danish, while peering unblinkingly into the hard and piercing green eyes of the armed giant with the massive shield and impossibly huge broadsword. There was not the slightest hint of fear in the speaker's dark, sparkling eyes and Wolf was happily surprised to see those same eyes twinkled with genuine good humor as a mischievous smile lit up the beaming, bearded face. Though the big Irishman had not the slightest idea what an "ape" could be.

He bowed slightly and replied with equally unaccented Danish, "My apologies, Your Majesty, I am so gratified my malodorous essence has only slightly assailed your delicate senses."

With that, both men laughed explosively while the five warriors, understanding not a word, looked on perplexed.

"Well, you speak quite elegantly in that pig-grunting Danish tongue, but you are most certainly not one of them. I suspect either Scot or Irish as I've yet to meet any of them. And I know you're not a turbaned Islamite heathen, I can smell them at great distance."

Wolf turned and addressed the Pictish warrior who was part of his band of five. "Mornak, is this regal person one of your people? I've not seen his like."

The good-natured Pict removed his helmet and looked closely at the grinning, sitting man with the thick curly black beard.

"Captain. *Faolan.* I am offended. Can you not see how much more beautiful I am than this wooly haired troll?"

He shook his own long mane of dark hair and ran his hand through the curly locks.

"Take notice. How smoothly my hand runs through these soft tresses, not like the oily black barbs on that one."

All three were now grinning and the older man, hearing the words, acknowledged, "Ah, yes, I've never met a native speaker but I've heard the Danes try to speak your language. You are Gaels, and that means Christians. Welcome."

Mornak spoke no Danish but would not have taken umbrage at being called a Gael. He and the others could only listen without comprehension as the short-bearded man addressed their leader.

"I speak seven languages fluently, including Arabic and this barbarous Danish, as well as the civilized and cultured tongues of Greek and Latin, but yours is not one I am familiar with. My name is Pyrrhus Lakepeno, born in the Peloponnesian region of Laconia in Greece. I am a trusted ambassador of my emperor, Basil the Porphyrogenitus, slayer of Fatimids and Bulgars, who rules from central Italy to the Caucasus and from the Danube to the borders of Palestine. I have served as emissary for three years with the formerly savage pagans and recently good Christian Magyars in the Duchy of Hungary. Two years I spent at the court of the continental Saxon King Otto, and for the last miserable year, I've been among these foul Danes. As you can see, they have neither the culture nor the intelligence to appropriately host a royal ambassador."

He laughed and stood gesturing around the tiny disrelished and locked hovel that had been his prison quarters.

"But I must admit, after a number of months I could not disguise my disdain and disgust for these vile pagans. Our relation-ship...shall we say, has soured."

His smile was so prodigious that the glow from the little stone lamp made his big teeth seem to shine with their own gleaming luminescence.

Wolf looked down at him and laughed.

"Well Sir, I too have spent time in just such an abode as this, surrounded by the same foul Viking wardens, but yours is a palace compared to the one in which I was chained as a boy."

Pyrrhus looked into the eyes of the young giant and, becoming serious for a moment, nodded in understanding and empathy.

Wolf smiled again and concluded, "We will have time to talk and drink together later if you would like, but now we have more Vikings to kill."

The huge young man and his five companions left the little hut and strode toward the larger structure. This had no windows just thick walls of timber and earth. The lone door appeared formidable. Wolf sent one of the *Laochra* to fetch the largest axe he could find.

The Greek had joined them, and had even been provided a sword which Mornak had retrieved from one of the slain Norse. The Pict handed it to him with a grin.

"They smell like rotten fish, grunt like pigs when they speak and are strangers to soap and water, but they do construct brilliantly fine blades," Mornak told the dark-haired man.

The ambassador made a few thrusts and slashes in the air to test the heft of the sword. The Gaels could immediately discern that he had a keen familiarity with the use of such a tool.

Pyrrhus now addressed Wolf. "Do you know what waits behind that door?"

"Either Vikings to slay or booty to gather, or if we're lucky we'll find both."

"Before you batter down that door, let me tell you a bit about the *bare-sark*, the ones without armor."

The learned Greek related what he knew of the beserkers, the fiercest and most savage of the Vikings. Fanatical members of the pagan cult of Odin, they were employed in various capacities as shock troops and as the guards of Norse chiefs and rulers. They believed they had the souls of animals, especially bears. Even when wounded, they continued the battle in a bizarre frenzy, their only purpose to kill. They painted their faces and wore animal skins instead of armor. Only their leader wore an iron helmet, painted black and fashioned after the head of a badger, wolf or bear, with frilled pointed ears and a swivel-down, metal visor which extended in the form of a fanged muzzle.

Fingwalle had a contingent of twelve of these savages attached to the Danish leader's guard force, and under direct command of an older beserker called simply Bjorn. As the Danish warriors were marching out to meet the advancing Welsh, and Pyrrhus was being led to his locked quarters, he had noticed all twelve of them had filed into the longhouse which was the abode of the chieftain, and where the most precious of stolen coins, jewels and clerical artifacts were kept. The Danish leader had less fear of the oncoming Welsh warriors than he did of one of his own kind stealing these riches during his absence at battle. The beserkers were fanatically loyal and would slaughter anyone who tried to enter but their chief.

To Pyrrhus' astonishment, the scarred and fearful countenance of the giant young Gael beamed lustily when he heard what was inside. He translated the Greek's story for the ten warriors with him and they too cheered and clashed their swords and axes against their iron-reinforced shields. Pyrrhus was certain the Irish would bring their full force against the long house, but, to his surprise, two-thirds of them were already outside the walls awaiting the arrival of the main army of Danes, who by now must have seen the smoke from the multiple dwellings the Gaels had torched.

Wolf instructed his small band to assemble in a wedge of ten. When he had cut through the door, they would form behind him and drive into the building. Knowing their blood was blazing with Celtic fire, he ordered, yet again, that they maintain a compact wall of shields and not break to engage on their own. Mornak was to be at his side.

It would have taken two normal men with axes a good deal of time to hack through the sturdy oaken door but the giant hewed with four mighty crushing blows and the wood was in splinters. He was able to kick through the beam which latched it shut from within and he led the first line of five into the longhouse's entrance.

The building was long and relatively narrow; stygian dark, with the expected small alcoves to either side of the extended central fire pit. When all eleven were assembled inside in a tight wedge formation, they peered down the length of the long hall. Near the end a small stone lamp was lit. It allowed them to see the forms of amorphous shadows rustling there. They heard at a distance deep rumbles and a guttural snorting which sounded a cross between bear and boar. Sunlight shining in from the smashed door barely illuminated two-man lengths into the structure. They moved forward as a group, eyes and ears fixed on the vague movements and sounds ahead of them.

From above came a deafening thunder of piercing snarls and two of the warriors in the rear rank were down. Black forms were on top of each as snarls and screams intermingled. In a flash, Mornak's Dalcassian axe caught a bit of sunlight in its downward arc. A grisly, soot covered head with filthy long hair flew backward, and the axe blade crushed through and into the packed soil of the floor. Two warriors were thrusting with their swords down into the back of another sooty and demonic form, causing more blood to splash over them all. But it was too late for the fallen Irish youths; one had a broken neck from the impact of the huge beserker, and the other had been pierced multiple times with a stabbing *seaxe*, undoubtedly taken as booty from the bloody hand of its former Saxon owner.

Wolf had only briefly looked back, and then returned his eyes forward to the threat ahead. The three survivors in the rear rank kicked the bodies of the dead Vikings into the light nearer the door and gazed down at the sprawled beserkers. Both were naked, covered from head to toe in blackened moist charcoal from the fire pits. Mornak spat in disgust.

Wolf knew they had sprung down from the overhead beams, which had been turned the same dark color from the constant smoke of the cooking and warming fires. These savages had presented a virtually invisible and deadly threat from above.

With a curse the huge leader whispered a new order.

"Two lines. First of five and second of three of the tallest of you, all behind me. First rank look to front and sides, second rank keep watch above us. There will be at least two more of them in the rafters and you'll only see the whites of their eyes before they spring, and that only if we're lucky. Second rank, drop shields now and be prepared to thrust up as high as you can when the beasts fall on us."

The *laochra* listened to their commander intently, trusting without reservation that following his orders would save their lives. Wolf continued.

"First rank, there will be several of them springing out of the side alcoves toward the end of the hall. When they do, form a circle and let them impale themselves in their rage on your blades, crush them with your shields and kill them quickly. Second rank will support you if needed. I count three hulking forms, seemingly tethered, at the back of the hall, and a larger one, lurking silently behind them. They are mine."

It happened almost exactly as Wolf predicted. It was if the Gael had choreographed the movements ahead of events. As they approached the center of the room, two more giant specters fell on them, growling like beasts from above. This time the lanky youths in the second rank were waiting and as the first rank raised shields over heads, the second reached up and thrust the pointed ends of their swords into the descending bodies, ripping soot-covered torsos and spilling greasy entrails. Both naked beserkers were dead when their bodies struck and rolled off the raised shields.

The lines moved forward with the second rank a bit further behind, and still oriented to what might come from above. As they approached the rear of the longhouse, curses and growls erupted from both sides and four huge bearskin clad monsters, with enormous battle axes sprang upon the young warriors. These formed a shield circle as commanded and braced for impact, their swords and axes ready to thrust.

Even in this horrific moment, Mornak's wildly exuberant humor could not be repressed, as he called out to his weapon brothers.

"At least these ones aren't naked."

The huge axes crashed down on the upraised shields. Though these held intact, the enormous force drove two of the *laochra* to the ground. One lost grasp of his shield and was crushed by the next axe blow which easily penetrated his boiled leather tunic. Mornak thrust the tip of his own Dalcassian axe into the armpit of the insanely grinning beserker and the demon crumpled as the tip pierced his heart. The others were now pushing back with their reinforced shields into the three remaining berserkers, deadly sword blades pistoning in stabbing thrusts.

While this mayhem was savagely playing out, Wolf dashed forward with unbridled fury toward the back wall, toward the snarling dark forms. In the dim light, he could see the flash of a blade severing lengths of rope which had bound the waiting beserkers to overhead beams. Even as he leapt to meet the first one, he knew this had been done to assure they were even more enraged. But he was on them too rapidly, before they could fully adjust to their newfound freedom, and his massive broadsword's blade slashed through two screaming throats, spurting showers of blood in the dim light of what was now a slaughter house. He turned just in time for his shield to strain under the blow of another axe. Wolf braced his heels then thrust his shield forward into the blue painted face of this attacker. Nose and cheekbone crushed, the wild man fell back and Wolf pushed his blade point deftly into the thick chest as he descended.

Before he could turn about to face the last spectral form, the one who had freed the others, both his ankles were encircled roughly by a length of chain. He felt his feet pulled out from under him and he crashed to the floor on his face. Knowing he was an instant from death, he rolled in a flash onto his back and brought his mighty shield up into a protective position.

Just in time. The first crash of the battle axe was so forceful it pushed the shield against his face, splitting the bridge of his nose. Recovering, Wolf braced both huge, muscular arms as blow after blow rained onto his metal covered shield, denting it amidst the cacophonous howls of the monstrous demon who was bent on his destruction.

Wolf inched both hands up toward the top of the shield, removing one arm from its straps. Just as another blow impacted onto the shield, he clasped it from the top, lifted and with enormous strength flung it downward from his body toward the legs of his assailant. The metal rimmed shield struck the beserker chief in both shins, breaking them with an audible cracking sound. Axe upraised, he fell onto the prostrate giant lying below him who, almost calmly and smoothly, brought up one massive arm which was clutching a long black blade, Wolf's own *scian dubh*.

The keen blade pierced through the bear skin and deep into the falling Viking just below his navel. Wolf jerked up tearing until he reached the breastbone, and tossed the body off of him before he was covered with spilling intestines.

Sitting up, the young leader examined, for the first time what had snared and brought him down. It was a simple length of iron chain, wood and leather handle at one end, and a viciously spiked metal ball at the other. He had never seen such a weapon and knew he was lucky that while the chain had caught him, the spiked end had simply ended in the air; otherwise he was sure his own shin would have been broken. He also took notice that this Viking must have been Bjorn, the leader. He removed the dead man's black enameled iron helmet with its pointed iron wolf's ears and fanged muzzle visor, and looked at the savage face which was almost totally covered by thick black whiskers, even the eyebrows grew together in one hairy arch.

With no time for further rumination, Wolf unwound the chain from his ankles, clasped the ball and chain in his hand, lashed the helmet to his belt and moved to his comrades. The red wave of combat which had swept the longhouse had left shattered tables and smashed benches. The packed earth floor was now drenched in pools of crimson blood, pouring from the bodies of mangled beserkers. The leader counted seven of his original ten standing amidst the dim gore. All twelve of the beserkers were slain.

"You've a nasty, bleeding gash on your beautiful nose, *Faolan*. That might leave a scar," Mornak exclaimed with a grin.

Wolf wanted to be angry since they had lost three of their brothers, but the Pict's humor was contagious. He would counsel Mornak later, but for now he grinned back.

"There are still about seven hundred unblooded Danes, no doubt rushing toward us as we speak. Gather our fallen and let us get out of this heathen pig sty."

***

They emerged from the long house and into the light to a clamorous commotion. The leader of the band of thirty that had taken the town was the grandson of a Connaught king. With the grounds within the walled enclosure secure, he had positioned his men along the palisade facing toward the east, from the direction they knew the furious Danes would be rushing when they saw their settlement in flames. They could hear much shouting, and see some of the men dashing to open the east gate, into which poured the other two groups of the *laochra* who had been sent to detect the returning Danes. All about them individual dwellings were on fire, and most of the outer buildings were burning as well. The smoke could be seen all the way to Wales.

"They're not far behind us, and they don't appear happy," shouted one of the Celtic warriors, as he sped through the gate.

Immediately, Wolf began posting the men at various positions along the palisaded earthen wall, where he assumed the Vikings would strike hardest. He ordered some to collect wagons and any other debris to shore up the two gates into the town. He was pleased to see there was no pandemonium, as each of the young men sprung to his task with brisk alacrity. Now he began to hear the furious war cries of the onrushing Danes.

Just then, off toward the base of the eastern wall, he noticed the Greek shouting furiously at the royal grandsire from Connaught. The Irishman looked down at the dark man perplexed, his red-blonde head tilted at an angle like a yearling hound.

"I've no idea what he's saying. I think he's on his fourth language now, and this one I recognize as Latin but I only know my prayers. *Pater Noster* didn't help," he explained to the war chief.

"I've been telling him to take down from the walls the Viking captives he's placed there. These damned heathens don't care whether they kill their own. Maybe a son, brother or husband might spare one, but the typical scurvy sea cur, who spends his life pulling an oar, will obliterate anything which stands before him and his enemy," Pyrrhus said to Wolf in Danish.

The huge captain looked up to the ramparts. Three bound Danish women and two old men were standing facing east, surrounded by armored *laochra* with shields deployed. Immediately assessing the situation, Wolf knew the grandson had concluded with gentle Christian logic that the Danes would back off when they saw that their kinsmen and women were being held behind the walls.

The former captive knew that logic was wrong.

"Take the Danes down from there." Wolf said in a deep voice.

It was too late. An arrow, loosed from distance, struck the breast of one of the old men, and a young woman had her torso impaled by one of a shower of spears hurled by the charging Danish horde. These two fell in a crumpled heap, and the Irish quickly cut the bindings and sped the other captives down to safety.

The Connaught leader looked on in disgust, and quickly rushed up to join his men on the ramparts. Wolf and the Greek were at his side. Before taking position with the others though, the "good boy" removed the black beserker helmet that had been lashed to his belt, and placed it on his head.

Mornak, Pyrrhus, and the giant grisly figure of the Irish commander with the hideous and bizarre fanged helmet stood in the center of the Irish line on the walls. Wolf kept his sword strapped to his back, and carried his now severely battered but still intact shield at the ready. In one hand he held the leather handle of the spiked ball and chain.

The Danes were pouring from the wood line and running in an amorphous mass across the field toward the walls of the town. Quickly responding to the spectacle of the burning dwellings, and the fact that they had been strung out in ambush positions awaiting the Welsh, they did not have an opportunity to adopt an orderly formation and measured plan of attack. Wolf knew that would work to the great advantage of the Irish and their allies in the coming battle.

There was a scattering of Viking bodies, those who had arrived first and tried to storm the walls on their own. About a score were splayed below, some of them draped over the sharpened wooden spikes which extended out from the walls. These had been felled by Irish spears, or in hurling themselves against the shield wall at the top.

Like a raging flood, without clear lines or formation, the Danes threw themselves up the steep earthen incline and onto the swords and spears of the waiting Gaels. They outnumbered the defenders nearly seven to one but had the disadvantage of unfavorable terrain and angle. Adding to their travails, the sun was beginning to set in the west and their eyes were straining to see the enemy through the glare as they looked upwards.

The Irish quickly expended all their light throwing spears. Some of these had found targets, to lethal effect. Now, the young elite were shoulder to shoulder and shield to shield, thrusting and slashing down into the wave of heathen Danes trying to displace them.

From behind, a rain of stones, pots, pieces of metal and branches were flying over the heads of the Irish shield wall and into the faces of the massed Vikings as they struggled up the inclined walls. Fifty or more Welsh women, no longer captives, were flinging everything they could find at the hated Danes from directly behind their Gaelic protectors. Further behind them, a score of Welsh children, both boys and girls, were whirling slings the Irish warriors had given them, all with stinging stones gathered earlier. The Irish were pleased to see the little Welsh wains could use a sling as well as any of them. A few of the Welsh hostages among them, had recruited about twenty of

144

the adult Welsh men and equipped them with arms and armor taken from the slain Vikings who had remained in the settlement. This score of very motivated, Norse-garbed, Welshmen took their place on the walls alongside the Irish, and called curses down on their hated enemies.

All of this wreaked psychological havoc on the morale of the attacking Danes. They had started their day with the iron confidence of their people. Trusted scouts had given them advance notice of a motley group of Welshmen marching from the east, but now their stronghold was in flames.

The main body of Danes stormed in waves against this bizarre group of Gaels, which for some insane reason included the giant beserker, Bjorn, fighting in their midst, slaughtering their comrades horribly with his whirling studded iron ball just as they reached the top of the wall. As Viking bodies piled up in heaps before the ranks of the enemy, the Danes were even more confused and horrified to see that a contingent of twenty of their countrymen, part of those who had been assigned to safeguard Fingwalle, had joined the ranks of the foe. They could recognize the markings on the Viking shields, and the even some of the individual weapons of their comrades. Through all of this, they were getting pummeled from above with stones, wood and metal debris, which, while not lethal, distracted them, and made them more vulnerable to the slashing and thrusting blades of the savage Irishmen.

By now, two hundred Danish bodies littered the walls from base to the summit. The remaining Viking leaders called back their warriors to restore order. Thus far it had been a disorganized melee, which the Gaels had taken advantage of. Now, they formed into a massed wedge of hundreds which would concentrate on one point on the walled defense and press inexorably up and over the ramparts. Even from outside the walls, the Danish leaders knew they still had vastly superior numbers and the Irish could not stop what was to come.

It was at this point that Wolf removed his helmet and pried off the fanged visor with his *scian*. He placed the helmet on his head once more and cried out in Danish with a deep and rumbling roar.

"Now. You bloody little heathens can gaze with awe, and without obstruction on my beautiful Irish face.

"Your people named me *Ulf*. My wolves and I have just now slaughtered your beserkers, and I took this helmet from their leader after I gutted him like the pig he was. Two hundred of you lie now dead and rotting in front of us since this day began. Come and join them."

With that, more than one hundred Celtic warriors on the wall slammed swords and axes against shield, again and again, crying **ABOOO. ABOOO.** — a thundering and piercing clamor which sounded across the fields.

A few of the Vikings murmured among themselves.

"Fenrir" and "Ulf." were repeated in superstitious fashion…as was *Ragnarok*. The Danish leaders called out hoarsely, trying to restore order, and it was at that moment that a boisterous and jubilant cheer went up from those on the ramparts who looked to the east.

The Welsh had returned.

They had formed into two separate formations of four deep and fifty wide. Their dragon pennants flying overhead, some of them were blowing on horned instruments which sounded liltingly like the pipes of the Irish. They marched in perfect order, shields locked, toward the oppositely-deployed Viking wedge.

Unlike the Irish or the Norse, the Welsh were skilled archers and knew the value of massed arrows. Their marching formations were followed by half a hundred bowmen, moving shoulder to shoulder.

Wolf knew these young Welshmen had learned from their elders who had been fighting Saxons and Danes for centuries, and Roman legions before that. Five hundred of them covered the length of the field impossibly fast, before the Vikings could reform. With a thunderous clash of steel on steel, they were on them from behind. The storm of battle swept over the field. And arrows, more lethal and accurate than the stones and debris, rained down on the wheeling Danes.

From the ramparts, Wolf called for the western gate to be made clear. He ordered two groups of thirty to form wedges, and placed the Norse-clad Welshmen in their midst. The other group of thirty under the command of the royal Connaught grandson would continue to defend the walls. The Gaels had lost surprisingly few of their number to the chaotic and disorganized assault of the Danes on the wall. Even those few were wounds from which the injured could recover. Now, two reinforced armored wedges of *laochra* struck out with heated intent in a semi-circular arc around the length of the walled town, and positioned themselves to strike the Danes from the north against their exposed flank.

With yet another impassioned war cry, the Irish wedges struck in surprise against the Danes who were occupied with the Welsh attack from the east. From his position behind, the commander of the Welsh archers had observed the Gaels moving from the north and ordered his archers to shift their points of aim to avoid harming their allies.

The Danish Viking warriors who had proudly manned Danelaw's western stronghold at Fingwalle now bore the brunt of red rage of Celtic fury. Welsh and Gaels thrust, slashed and tore into them. The slaughter was horrific. Bloody vengeance was savagely taken for centuries of grievances and atrocities. No quarter was given or expected. Wolf was leading one of the wedges with Mornak at his side, and both were surprised to find the stocky, powerful Greek had somehow found a shield and was directly behind them, lending his strength to the onward crush of Irish steel.

It was soon over and except for a few who may have reached the safety of the forests, no Dane walked the field. Less than fifty of the Welsh lay dead on the field and fewer than ten of the Gaels had been slain. In glaring contrast, the Vikings had been annihilated. Wolf looked to his comrades and then over to the leaders of the Welsh. He raised his sword in salute to them and his men cheered lustily. The exuberant young Welshmen returned the cheer and their horns sounded in unbridled celebration.

Not much later, they split what booty they could recover between the two allied forces. More than any treasure, the Welsh were happiest to recover their countrymen and women, but Wolf assured them they could take anything that had been stolen during raids except for what was in the home of the Danish chief. Wolf and some of his men returned to the bloody longhouse and retrieved multiple chests of jewels, coins and stolen clerical chalices, enough to fund more of what King Brian needed to restore Ireland to its splendid past.

They burnt every vestige of Fingwalle before they left. The Irish marched to their ships carrying their treasure and the bodies of their fallen. The Welsh marched east and then south to their homeland, carrying with them whatever possessions they had retrieved, their liberated kin, and the captive Viking women and children. These would be held for ransom, or else put into servitude in the Welsh villages.

As they were sailing across the Irish sea, Wolf the Quarrelsome enjoyed long, exhilarating discussions with his new Greek friend; each educating the other about the ways of their known worlds.

Chapter 9
Munster, Ireland
1008 A.D.

The conversations between Wolf and Pyrrhus that took place on that sleek long ship were just the beginning of protracted and fruitful exchange of ideas which continued without end. When they arrived at Cashel, Wolf introduced the Byzantine ambassador. King Brian received him with hospitality and honor, and intellectual fascination. The King spent as many long hours with the Greek as Wolf did.

Brian was interested in politics, religion and the various alliances which existed throughout the Europe of the millennium. The Irish king learned much from these lengthy and illuminating conversations with the learned and amiable emissary. They both spoke in Latin but the polyglot Greek was learning Irish rapidly with the same incredible skill he had already mastered all of the other tongues he commanded.

The young man, who was rapidly becoming war chieftain of the entire Irish people, was only marginally concerned with the strategic and political knowledge imparted by Pyrrhus. They were important to him only as they gave insight into a military design of technical and tactical advantage.

Wolf was impressed to learn their guest was not only Greek but from the same region where the vaunted Spartans of antiquity had dwelled. The "good boy" had loved those classical stories of Spartans and Persians learned in Innisfallen. Now he was delighted to have one of those Dorian warriors right here in Ireland at his side. When he confessed this joyful revelation to his Greek friend, Pyrrhus replied in answer.

"Not for the first time, I have observed what a wondrous thing is the Irish imagination. You fight reasonably well but you are all hopeless romantics. I am as far removed from a Spartan as you from one of the ancient Gauls. Nevertheless, I thank you for the compliment, you crafty wolf."

The Greek explained the training of Spartan warriors was inordinately brutal and began at seven when the boys were removed from their families and put into training camps. Beatings and insults were administered by their elders to remove any degree of individualism and make the aspiring *hoplites* totally dedicated to the Spartan nation.

Wolf, listening with great interest, said, "Well based on my own experience, I find beatings and insults repugnant. No Irish youth will ever be subjected to such trauma while I command. But I am sure it was the physical trials and mental stress the Spartan trainees endured that made them so formidable. That we can and must incorporate into our own training."

He learned about the Spartan spear which was two heads taller than a man and was fitted with a butt spike on the opposite end. He was fascinated to learn that the spike was for use if the blade was sundered, and more often to push down to dispatch wounded enemies as the Spartans advanced across the field. Unlike the broad, almost sword-like, leaf-shaped Irish spear points, these where long, triangular and sharply pointed to thrust through openings in shields and armor. The Spartans attacked the enemy with spears over their shoulders thrusting forward, though sometimes they deployed a first rank to thrust up from below.

The Spartans had only one other edged weapon besides their deadly spear, the *xiphos*. Pyrrhus described this to his big friend with some degree of boasting.

"Their swords were almost ridiculously short and wide. They were less than the length of one of your Irish fighting *scians*. These nasty little blades were meant to encourage the Spartan warrior to close with and eviscerate his enemy while their eyes were locked."

Wolf's own green shining eyes lit brightly at that description.

The two decided this means of Spartan combat might work to effectively take away the Vikings' advantage in technology and tactics. The young *laochra* were already well advanced in their own infantry training which took into account the best of the Irish and Viking fighting methods. There was a need to create a new corps, and new group of colossal young Irish Spartans who could meet and defeat any Norse shield wall or wedge. These must come, Wolf knew, from the common young Irishmen who had no chance of ever otherwise gaining elaborate armament and tailored training. Wolf enthusiastically decided to send emissaries to recruit these burly young men. Later, he and Pyrrhus would train the trainers.

***

After his march from the site of the battle of the meadow, Fergus arrived at the Spartan training camp, situated on a hilltop between Cashel and Thomond. His new friend, Cael, had ridden off on a splendid swift pony with the band of Magyars and the captive Viking woman. Fergus had walked on foot, as he had his whole life, with a band of Munster warriors. They were all led by the enormous scar-faced giant and Cormac, who had led the attack, which had unbelievably resulted in the annihilation of an entire crew of Viking pagans.

Along the way they picked up more burly young clansmen who joined their party, and these quickly also became Fergus' friends. The red-haired youngster from the midlands was among the first fifty Spartans who occupied the wooden barracks at the hilltop Spartan encampment. Over the next two years, they would grow to two hundred. With most from Munster and Connaught, Fergus was one of the few Irishmen from the Ui Neill. But they were all robust and sturdy when they arrived and they became enormous, almost frightening, heavy infantry warriors with training and diet.

They were provided the same heavy shields and reinforced helmets as the *laochra* elite. King Brian's many ironsmiths, under the tutelage of the old clan chief, who all had come to cherish, produced finely wrought Spartan spears, their construction directed by Pyrrhus, and robust new fighting *scians.*

These humble lads had never envisioned even holding such weapons. More and more Spartans reported as training grew. Wolf would often ask older members of the Munster army and some of the elite *laochra* to form up in six deep lines with their own shields on the Spartan training field to help his experiment. The Spartans would assume line of battle without spears or any other bladed weapon. They would move across, four-deep, at a walk, then a measured lope, and finally at a furious sprint. For the first few months they would crash against their countrymen's formed ranks and smash themselves into the ground, occasionally breaking bones and gasping from suddenly emptied lungs. Wolf would always encourage them, shouting how well they did, and ordering them to move back and form again for the next charge. With such a massive, and to most of Ireland, still legendary leader exhorting them on, the Spartans would ignore the blood and do it all again, bellowing even louder.

After a year of this, none of the regular Munster army, nor the *laochra* wanted to stand before the Spartans. So long rows of plank-connected wagons were placed before them and weighted with heavy stones, a reminder of Wolf's own training. Now they had their spears, and the first rank thrust up and into the groins of the painted strawmen attached to the wagons' sides, the others pushing above into the eye slits of the illustrated Norse scarecrows.

These young men had been well selected. They would have grown on their own into widely recognized strong and formidable men. Wolf took the advice of Druidic physicians and the learned Christian priests and monks to turn them into hulking pillars of muscle and speed. They were provided with beef and cow's milk four times a day, as much as they could eat. The constant activity insured they didn't grow fat, and berries, parsnips and turnips promoted their overall health and growth.

By 1008, Fergus had grown to a magnificent and intimidating Celtic warrior. His biceps were as thick as his thighs, and those were like stone pillars. He now had a full and thick red beard to go with his long, curly crimson locks. With natural leadership abilities, constantly manifested during intensive training, he had become the commander of the two hundred Spartans. Pyrrhus was even trying to teach him Greek. Wolf measured his weight at not much less than his own. The Spartans, every one of them a common Irish farm boy on arrival, were now pleading to take the field against Ireland's enemies.

***

Aoife and her brother Eoin had been treated almost like prisoners for the first bit of the trip following the meadow battle. As the other party trotted off on their handsome little ponies, the huge giant who had first clutched, then bound, then gagged them, released both with a huge smile. Aoife looked penetratingly into that towering scarred face, with its two deep green eyes which beamed down at her. He had not even thought to take her own little *scian*, but she had no mind of that now. With the same sweep of the two massive arms that had torn them from ripping the throat of the Norse woman, he gently picked both of them up and sat them on his enormous chestnut horse.

For the first time since their parents had been slain by the monsters, the little orphans felt safe and secure in the company of these wild Irishmen from the west. Even the northern Irish clans had sometimes had business with the Vikings. After what the two youngsters had seen that day, these big, bruising men hated the Norse as much as they did.

"Don't worry Eoin. We can trust this Fomorian giant. Don't you remember Ma and Da used to tease us about being Fomorian foundlings, discovered wailing in a dried well when we were babies? Well then, maybe he's our long, lost older brother."

Eoin grinned back at her, pleased at imagining he was one of that legendary race of strange giant warriors from Ireland's antiquity.

Both children were put into the hands of the teaching clergy at Cashel. Over the years, with impressive innate intelligence, both siblings thrived and became intellectual leaders among their classmates. Aoife, however, remained untamable. Eoin was expected to be a warrior, but she knew she would be an even better one. The emerald eyed, raven haired, wild girl stole out at every opportunity to watch, and then try to join the elite hostages in their training. The officers quickly sent her back with a gentle scolding.

Eventually she learned to combine her wholesome, magnetically attractive Celtic beauty with her feminine wiles. She somehow managed to cajole smiths and warriors to "lend" her a shield and the reinforced helmet of the elite. She had traded her little *scian*, with its elaborately carved hilt for a simple large wooden-hilted fighting knife. She learned to move furtively into the training ranks of the elite and take her place in line. Through the worst of the grueling drills, she kept up on her own, exhibiting no revealing weaknesses. When breaks occurred, she moved off to the side, uttering in a comically deep voice, that she had to pee. Each evening, she'd break off, hide her equipment, wrapped in linen, in a thatch of fronds, and return to the snug cottage she shared with Eoin and the old couple who cared for them both.

Even though this subterfuge was primitively unsophisticated, the Irish warriors felt secure in their surroundings and had no suspicions about this strange hostage in their midst. And Aoife was mostly silent and ferociously agile and aggressive in training. She was able to maintain this charade for almost a fortnight.

One day, Wolf was not just observing, but standing in the middle of their training wedge as they exercised in mock battles against their comrades. He noticed one of his weapon brothers directly before him had neither axe nor sword, but just a long *scian*. As he observed more closely, he noted legs more rounded than those of the surrounding companions. More disturbingly, even under the thick woolen tunic, this one's bottom appeared recognizably heart shaped and curved. Then, he noticed long dark curls spilling out from behind the sturdy iron helmet.

Jutting two heads above his brothers in the training formation, Wolf bent forward and gently, but deftly, removed the helmet from the warrior before him.

With a tremendous resonating shout, he commanded "Halt training."

Aoife had quickly brought the shield up to cover her face but it was too late. Wolf brushed the shield aside and gaped in amazement at the small figure standing before him.

Over the years, the young leader had visited the school classes of the two orphans on occasion and been pleased to see them progressing so well in classical and religious studies. But at the moment he was in the immediate presence of a strong and beautiful young woman he could barely recognize as the wailing little wolf cub he had tied and bound along with her sibling two short years before. She was now fifteen, nine years younger than him, and she was a well formed and robust vision of Celtic pulchritude with raven tresses, creamy white skin and luminous and vibrant eyes. Despite his astonishment and resentment at this disruption in training, he could not prevent himself from grinning down at her.

"Must I now tie and gag you once again, little cub?"

Aoife glared back at him defiantly, eyes shining with intensity and resolve.

"For two weeks, I've trained as hard as any of these mewling whelps. I'm at least their equal and probably a better warrior than most."

As those around her began to laugh, she thrust her shield to one side and pushed her arm forcefully out to the other, spilling the two warriors standing next to her unceremoniously on to the spongy, grass-covered training ground.

The entire formation burst into riotous cheering at that, and Wolf was laughing now more than any of them. Aoife stood unmoving and boldly in the center of the formation, her eyes glancing around challenging anyone to confront her.

"Well, Aoife, you are not meant to be one of this crew of young hounds, but I've received reports of your superior mental and scholarly accomplishments. And for two weeks you've apparently trained and exercised with these fighters without a one finding you wanting. If you'd accept, I think we can find a position of some use with Pyrrhus, myself, and a few others which will exploit your skills and enthusiasm. But that's only if you really want to help me drive the bloody little heathens out of Ireland."

Aoife gazed earnestly into the face of the enormous Irish leader, a face that had been etched into her heart since the incident on the beach two years before. The defiance and resentment that had kindled in her eyes were now replaced by something deeper and warmer as she replied in a clear and steady voice.

"Yes, Captain. I accept your offer, *Faolan an Trodach.*"

Chapter 10
Cúnna an Cogaidh — The Hounds of War
Spartan Training Camp, outside Cashel, Munster Ireland
1009 A.D.

Wolf never regretted his decision to bring the orphan girl into the fold of his small circle of friends and advisors. Her energetic vitality, formidable intellect and driving sense of purpose inspired and motivated those who came to know her. Aoife despised the invaders as much as the chief himself but never displayed bitterness or morbidity. She was creatively persuasive when convincing others to follow her lead. She would convey her intent with logical reasoning. Sometimes with men that didn't work. She would then resort to using her femininity and beauty to entice and prevail. When even that failed, she would call into question the manhood of her opponent. As she became more widely known as one of Wolf's trusted companions, she seldom had to cajole those around her. Her magnetic personality and honest enthusiasm worked wonders among the diverse and naturally unruly and resistant clans of Irish across the island.

As the months passed, Wolf's confidence in her grew, and she sometimes accompanied the wandering groups of Dalcassians who were recruiting the various specialized contingents of King Brian's growing Irish army. While the men talked with the chieftains and priests and assessed the qualities of the potential young warriors, Aoife would spend her time conversing with the women and girls of the small camps and settlements they visited. She was also recruiting but to a different purpose.

After six of these recruiting missions, which had spanned the length and width of Ireland, she sat one evening with Wolf, Cormac, and Murcha around a cheerfully blazing fire pit inside a large tent constructed of brown leather, draped over supple oaken rods. Smoke rose from an opening in the center of the tent, and stone lamps provided additional light. They had convened at the Spartan training camp. Murcha was passing on updated reports from the spies and scouts of his extensive intelligence network. Aoife had heard such informational briefings before from the king's son and they left a strong impression on her. When Murcha was finished updating the disposition and composition of the Viking forces in Ireland and across the waters, and the situation among the remaining defiant groups of Irish who had not fully accepted Brian's vision of a united land, he drank deeply from the tankard of honey mead he'd been nursing.

It was at this moment that Aoife withdrew a parchment from a pocket in her linen tunic and placed it across her knees. At sixteen, she was now literate and educated thanks to the monks and nuns of Cashel, and the three men noted the parchment had been written in her own hand.

"This is a list of names of three score good and dedicated Irish women and girls who have sworn to me their intent to do everything possible to secure the king's vision of our various people and clans as one mighty nation. I think we could certainly add these motivated Irish to the ranks of the all-male spies and scouts." Aoife looked at the others with earnest intent, clearly prepared to defy any protest.

"Women are able to go places and do things without attracting undue notice where a strange man would immediately be cause for close scrutiny. They can pass, almost unseen, as cooks, cleaners and field workers because, in many cases, that's exactly what they are. I watched some of them ride like the wind on their own ponies, and it is these I have instructed once every three months to bring me tidings of the events in their provinces, especially as concerns the Vikings or any other enemy of Ireland. In my absence, they will report to the captain." She nodded toward Wolf.

The three hardened Celtic warriors gazed on the animated girl with respect and admiration as she passed the single page of manuscript to Murcha. He examined the neatly scribed document, noting with pleasure how the names were associated with far flung districts across the entire island. Several were in and around Dublin and other Viking settled areas in the Southeast of the country.

Murcha handed the document to Wolf, and turned to Aoife.

"These brave women and girls will be a welcome addition to our corps of scouts and spies. They will significantly increase our ability to have our eyes and ears constantly focused on our enemy's actions and intent.

Looking at the others in the group, Murcha continued, "I now will rely on Aoife to assume direction of all of our intelligence efforts, of spies and scouts, and detailed knowledge of our enemies. I thank you Aoife and will tell my father of your initiative and dedication to our cause."

The girl cast her eyes to the huge young captain who was grinning warmly and with obvious pride. She lowered her head and tried to conceal her own contented smile.

***

A few months later, Aoife approached Wolf late one Morning as he had been observing the Spartans undergoing shield drills. The girl told the leader there was someone she wanted him to meet, and the two of them walked outside the walls of the encampment, where a little old man was waiting in a green and pleasant field. The man was dressed in the rough dun-colored woolen trousers and shirt of a simple country farmer. Sprawled lazily on the grass around him were three enormous Irish hounds; two red brindles and a wheaten. Both man and dogs gazed up at the huge warrior with his big, well-worn metal shield and broadsword strapped across his back.

"God be with you," the old man said in a cheery voice as the dogs came to their feet, their tails wagging in long, swishing arcs.

"My name is Blamec Mac Goll, and this is Brendan, Cuilinn and Ronan."

He patted the great heads of the hounds as he mentioned their names. He whispered some quiet word and all three approached Wolf and nuzzled against his flanks, their tails' movement displaying their obvious joy, as the tall warrior patted each and scratched behind their ears.

"I'm afraid you've a bit too many years to be recruited into the ranks of these young Spartan Irish, friend Blamec, or did you come to have these three fine Irish fighters put into the ranks?" Wolf said this with pleasant humor as he continued to stroke the big, wiry haired beasts.

"That's exactly why he came," Aoife replied with no hint of a jest.

The girl then described how she had met Blamec on a recruiting trip not far away on the border with Connaught. He lived with his son on a small farm where he tended a few cattle and sheep. He was known for his way with dogs and helped train the various Irish breeds as shepherds, guards and hunting dogs for his neighbors, which earned him a bit of additional wealth. She had watched the old man training two huge mastiffs as guard dogs for a local chieftain when an idea came to her.

She observed how fierce and powerful these mastiffs were and how they could be trained to either incapacitate or kill any potential thief. The Irish hounds, which had been bred to protect Ireland's flocks and herds from wild wolves, were as large and ferocious as the mastiffs. But unlike the bulky guard dogs, the hounds were incredibly swift runners, combining graceful agility with ferocious strength. Blamec had a small pack of seven such hounds on his little farm. She was serious about enlisting these and many more of the noble and formidable hounds into the king's military service and told the leader exactly that.

Wolf was a keen student of martial history and he knew the Romans, the Gauls and the Germans had all used war dogs for various purposes. But they had seldom been employed in a pitched battle between two forces with slashing weapons and thick armor. He appreciated the novelty of the idea but told the girl and old man he could not bear to watch such beautiful and splendid creatures as these be slaughtered by well-armored Vikings, who wore linked mail down to their thighs, and carried heavy shields and flashing axes.

The two conspirators exchanged sly grins and asked the tall young warrior to witness a small demonstration. Then Aoife whistled in a loud and most unfeminine way and two fully armored Vikings came out of the camp's gate walking toward the assembled group of Irish people and dogs. Instinctively, Wolf's big calloused hand flew to grasp the hilt of the sword at his back, and he had already started to assume a combat stance when the old man and girl began to laugh uproariously.

The two Norse ambled awkwardly toward them as Wolf looked closer. They both wore the elegant armor of a well-off Viking plunderer with sturdy shields and classic Danish battle axes. Their helmets were expertly made; fierce looking with visors and mail curtains down the sides and back. From head to mid-thigh, they were as armored as land crabs and would strike fear into any who laid eyes on them.

Aoife assured him they weren't really Vikings. The arms and armament had come from booty taken over the years from Viking dead, and delivered to be stored at the Spartan camp to be issued to scouts and spies as needed. They had simply borrowed some of that for this event.

When the two savage forms approached to a certain distance, the hounds' demeanor immediately changed. They bellowed and growled, deep and rumbling, and sped toward the oncoming Vikings with an apparent uncontrolled rage. As the "Norse" deployed their shields and raised their axes to defend themselves, the three beasts stopped and continued to growl fiercely.

Then the men advanced toward them at a run and the dogs bounded away, easily staying out of range of the lethal axes and charging Vikings. The two hulking forms turned and began to run back to the camp and all three hounds sprung after them with bursting speed, almost upon them and within striking distance in moments. Suddenly, the men stopped and turned to face the snarling dogs. In mid leap, all three of the hounds swerved aside and immediately ran back, stopping out of reach, growling and howling even louder.

The two Vikings now made a wild dash toward the camp's gate, as fast as they could given their armor and weapons. Once again, the pack of three huge, fierce hounds rushed after them. This time there was no turning around, and the dogs, each weighing as much as a large man, sprang onto the backs of the fleeing Vikings, crashing them forcefully to the ground. Blamec, Aoife and Wolf ran to the scene as the huge jaws of the hounds were working to crush flesh and bone. The hounds had been trained to attack only two points on the body: the throat exposed under the helmet, and alternatively, to close their jaws around the thigh, underneath the mail skirting. Blamec later explained that was intended to sever the large blood-carrying artery, causing instant incapacitation and ensuing death in very short order.

"Stad."

The hounds immediately recognized the tone of Blamec's voice, and obeyed as he attached leashes to each of their collars and led them away. Wolf was concerned for the health of the poor lads who had played the role of Vikings and bent to help them. Both cursed and struggled to their feet, throwing off helmets. Each wore a thick layer of leather around his neck, and these leather collars had been filled with lengths of chain mail for even more protection. The two peeled these improvised collars from their throats and threw them to the ground. Finally, each bent and unwrapped similar bindings of leather and mail which had been wrapped around their thighs — the reason they had walked and run so awkwardly. Aoife grinned mischievously at the two angry and frustrated young Spartans.

Wolf quickly detected two things. One of the Spartans was the big redhaired leader, Fergus, and both of them reeked with a foul fishy odor. Wolf could not conceal his own grin at the youths' obvious discomfiture.

"She talked us into carrying out this ridiculous stunt." Fergus said.

Aoife went on to explain how the hounds had needed little training to consider the Vikings hated threats. They sensed the Norse difference from the Irish by sight and scent. The Viking armor and helmets provided the visual display and, as added indignity, the two Spartans had been forced to smear fish parts over their faces and hands. They also had to drink a cup of fish oil. All was meant to approximate the foul natural scent of the Norse.

"We refused to do the fish smearing until she would do it herself." Fergus's companion told Wolf with the same resentment that his friend expressed.

"And did you really cover yourself with fish offal, Aoife?" Wolf asked.

"It was the only way to convince these two bawling, great cherubs to play the part Blamec and I planned. And it wasn't that bad at all, certainly nothing to whine about."

Glaring at Aoife, Fergus clasped his friend on the shoulder and both dashed to the camp to douse themselves with water and then take a long steam bath in the structure dedicated to that purpose.

Blamec, who had now returned to the group, laughed with the others as the two huge young Spartans ran through the camp's gate.

And so it was decided. Blamec would accompany some of the recruiting tours to enlist hounds from all over Ireland. In this, he would be aided by Aoife who would also be collecting young healthy puppies and yearlings. The Connaught chieftain Teighe O'Kelly, who kept his own pack of well-bred Irish hounds for hunting and companionship, had promised to donate ten of them to the cause. When they had recruited enough canine warriors, Blamec would establish a formal camp close by the Spartans to formally train both this army of dogs and a squadron of Irish handlers, who would assume the role of pack leaders.

Now, Wolf's only task was to convince Cormac, Murcha, and the King, that he had not finally succumbed to the mental derangement they had feared years ago. Then again, the giant warrior thought, it might work to his advantage if all thought he was just a wee bit mad.

Chapter 10
Magyar Training Camp, Hills of Connemara
1009 A.D.

Pyrrhus had recounted to Wolf not just tales of woe and disgust about his time with the Vikings, but also some of the pleasant experiences he had as Byzantine ambassador among other peoples. He had grown especially fond of the Magyars while at the court of the Duke of Hungary. The Greek related how these savage riders, storming in a red rush out of the east, had been the scourge of Europe, raiding as far west as the French coast and driving deep down into southern Italy. They had even threatened the Byzantine empire itself. It was only relatively recently, in 955, that they had finally been stopped by the Saxon King Otto at Lechfeld.

Almost en masse, the pagan Magyars had converted to Christianity, and ironically became allies of the Emperor Basil. Pyrrhus explained further.

"This was a masterful diplomatic move for the emperor, as the Magyars on the Hungarian plain can keep a check on the unruly Bulgars. I spent three years living with these newly minted Christians, and was accepted as brother by them.

"I thought I was a skilled horseman until I rode with an army of their bow-wielding warriors. To the Byzantines, heavy cavalry is a critical component of our military forces. The horse is seen as an implement, no different than helmet or shield. Byzantine horses are intended merely to carry lance and sword wielding riders into the battle, with the expectation the rider will fight with skill, astride his mount.

"The Magyar and his horse move and fight as one. Their warriors live in the saddle. They eat, sleep, fight and defecate while mounted." Pyrrhus said this last bit with a grin.

"Their horses are smaller than those of the Byzantines and Saxons, but swift, strong and imbued with tremendous endurance and tenacity. They carry thin lances and short stabbing swords but their primary weapon is the bow — what we call the Asian reflex bow."

The Greek's intellectual curiosity was never sated, and he spent fascinated hours watching and working with the Magyar craftsmen who constructed these powerful bows. They were built from maple saplings. They used deer sinews for the backing, horn of gray cattle for the belly, and deer antler for the bone plates. This construction was much more refined and complicated than what was needed to construct the simple wooden bows the Vikings and some of the Irish used. The results were worth the effort as the Magyar bows were shorter and lighter, with equal or greater range and accuracy, than those of their enemies. Most importantly, they could be easily employed while riding, and used in massed cavalry formations they could let loose a massive aerial shower of death against opposing infantry or cavalry.

The primary Magyar tactic was to bypass heavily armored formations and attack their logistical sources and lighter forces in an attempt to isolate the main force. The horsemen harass and try to draw the enemy out of formation and envelop them from all sides. Because of their speed, mobility and shock, this technique almost always prevailed.

Just as he had fought with the Irish against the Danes, Pyrrhus earlier went into combat with his Magyar hosts against various contingents of Bulgarians, and even against some of the Kievan Russ Vikings. He proudly carried a Magyar bow he had crafted himself, and learned to shoot and ride as well as his Hungarian comrades. Those were glorious and memorable days for the amiable and spirited Greek.

They had developed the idea of a corps of Spartan Irish heavy infantry only a few months earlier and already had close to two hundred recruits. The Irish leader had split his time between training with Pyrrhus and the Spartans, convening with the King's council of advisors, and visiting his comrades among the *Laochra an Rí.* He was confident he and a few of the most tactically and physically advanced young leaders among the Spartans could continue growing and developing the heavy infantry force. Pyrrhus' accounts of the Magyar army and their battles had given Wolf another idea, and he thought he might have another use for his trusted Greek friend.

Pyrrhus tried but couldn't hide his smile when the huge Irish youth told him he had plans for a new type of Irish warrior. If there could be Irish Spartans, then surely there could also be Irish Magyars. And no one would be better than Pyrrhus to train them.

"Well, Faolan, what a wondrous idea. You're a wellspring of innovation and vision. I'm honored."

Wolf immediately detected a hint of obvious sarcasm in the Greek's words.

"I see you've taken advantage of my formidable Irish creativity and imagination to plant seeds to further your own ideas. Well, in this case, I will not beware of Greeks bearing gifts but rather happily accept yours." Wolf laughed.

"And it's a good thing you have, since I've already found the perfect mounts, your own Connemara ponies, and the perfect place to train, Connemara itself. Your allies in Connaught are already at work constructing stables and barracks and they've given us the first squad of recruits, along with their mounts," Pyrrhus replied with the customary twinkle in his eyes.

***

It was a warm, shining day, mid-summer in the year of Our Lord 1009, in the green and tan hills of Connemara. A gentle breeze carried the briny scent of the ocean, which meshed pleasantly with the earthy musk of the dark brown turf in the fields and the blooming, fragrant grasses and wildflowers. Cael had called this place home for almost three years, and in his case, Connemara really was home. He was nineteen-years-old. Pyrrhus had promoted him to a position of leadership within the contingent of Magyar cavalry, now grown to almost two hundred swift and agile riders on their perfectly matched mounts. He loved the land, his friends and weapon brothers, the deadly little bow he had come to master, and especially the horses.

Strong and sturdy, thickly muscled, and with incredible endurance, they were large for ponies and small for horses. Perfectly adapted to the harsh landscape, they were resilient and sure-footed, able to dart among rocky outcroppings and uneven, hilly terrain. There were still wild herds of them in Ireland's west, and Pyrrhus could not stop remarking about how lucky they were to be among these intelligent and loyal creatures.

The Magyar bow also fascinated Cael. Pyrrhus had arranged to have four hundred maple staves delivered from Wales. He taught two of the recruits how to create the artistic and formidable little bows by combining the maple with local sinew, cattle horns and antlers from red deer. The arrows were constructed from white hazel and other local varieties of wood. Most of these were fitted with iron bodkin tips, designed specifically to be effective in piercing mail armor. The young Magyar Irish recruits learned to live and fight in the saddle, their ponies an extension of their legs, their bows and arrows an extension of their arms.

Along with the accoutrements of battle, there was another special source of wonderment and captivation for Cael here in his Connemara hills. Since he had first laid eyes on her at the beach three years ago, the Viking girl had become an alluring fixation for him. He had tried to speak gently to her on their original shared journey to this place. But, while she wasn't hostile nor apparently even frightened, she had seemed distant and resigned to submissive silence. As the months passed and Pyrrhus did indeed employ her along with a few of the local women and children in the kitchens of the camp, Cael had found every excuse to somehow be around her.

Her name was Luta Einarsdottir, and Wolf's decree assured she was never accosted by anyone. As she became accustomed to the rhythm and regularity of life among the hard-riding youths and the company of the simple country people around her, she gradually found her place. Her gentleness and kindness to all caused some degree of consternation among the red-blooded young recruits, who were being trained to slaughter the despised Norse invaders with the utmost force and violence. How could this one seem so pleasant?

Even more astonishing to Cael was Luta's presence at Holy Mass every Sunday and her obvious knowledge and devotion to the liturgy. Though the Celtic rites varied somewhat from continental Christianity, she was comfortable and easy with the familiar rituals.

Cael had once asked Pyrrhus about this apparent aberration. The well-traveled Greek explained. "Many of the princes and nobility among the Danes and Norwegians profess to have converted to the true faith. But the vast majority of their common people reject, sometimes violently, any deviation from worship of Odin and the Nordic pantheon of their lesser gods."

"Some of the Viking women can be good Christians, but their men can only thrive within the heathen superstition of dark barbarism. The Magyars, in contrast, have become devout followers of the faith. I'm convinced most of the Vikings will eventually become Godless apostates and heretics, soulless and emasculated without the fiery forge of Odin to give spark to their otherwise savage natures."

Watching Luta interact with the priest and two nuns who visited the camp, Cael had doubts about the Greek's opinion on that subject, at least in her case.

He had also posed a question that had been nagging him since he'd first seen the giant Irish champion, and later learned more about him during the leader's occasional visits to observe the Magyars training.

"Why does Wolf constantly refer to the Vikings as 'bloody little heathens'? They are not all heathens as you told me, and they certainly are not little," asked Cael with genuine confusion.

Pyrrhus laughed and informed Cael that he'd been asked that question before.

"I've thought about it and developed a few theories. Compared to the giant Wolf himself, the Norse are indeed small. He grew up under horrific conditions amidst a family of pagan Dublin Vikings and considers them all the same. He uses this derisive term specifically to inspire and drive out any terror from his fellow Irish warriors, who've been taught since youth to fear the great pillaging monsters from out of the north." The bearded Greek laughed.

"Or more likely, he just loves to insult the Vikings in their own tongue. 'Bloody little heathens' serves many purposes for Wolf the Quarrelsome."

Cael was relentless, and over the months Luta slowly grew accustomed to his youthful attempts to compliment and comfort her. She eventually accepted his invitation to teach her to ride the beautiful ponies which were always around them. The two took long ambling excursions over the hills, where Luta advanced her knowledge of the Irish language. Cael taught her how to be one with her mount and move effortlessly along with the gentle and obedient mare.

These delightful interludes occurred far too seldom for the newly minted cavalryman, who now carried the added burden of leading a squadron of Magyar Irishmen. The training was rigorous, and Pyrrhus constantly compared them to "real" Magyars, admonishing the recruits that they couldn't last a day with the riders from Hungary. Their Irish pride challenged, the youthful Gaels, all from common peasant families, pushed each other harder and harder to show the damned Greek what they were made of.

They could now all hit a target the size of a man's heart at a distance of one hundred twenty-five paces while at full gallop. Pyrrhus would never admit it to them, but they were now indeed as skilled, hardened, and swift as his former Magyar comrades, and their ponies were even better than those back in Hungary.

***

Pyrrhus had been away for a full week. He returned on a splendid summer day with a companion riding beside him. Cael watched the two as they rode up and into the walled encampment. When they neared, Cael was sure he had seen the other somewhere before but couldn't place him. He was a short yet athletically built youth of about fourteen, perfect for apprentice duties. The youngest among them did the least appealing work, which of course included cleaning out the stables. Cael had done it himself for months when he first arrived.

"Cael, do you recognize this fine little Magyar?" called the Greek as he trotted closer. The Irishman cast his gaze again to the face of Pyrrhus' companion. Could it be the wild, wolf cub he had first seen those years ago at the beach? At fourteen, lean and lithe, he was no longer the babyish wain.

"Bid greetings to Eoin, sister of Aoife, she who is now trusted advisor to the captain, and leader of a corps of spies and scouts. I believe he should tour the horse stable first, don't you?"

Cael nodded his head jovially, as Pyrrhus walked toward the small stone house to take a steam bath and wash off the dust of the journey.

"And I think Eoin should work until the stables are sparkling clean before he gets to wash and eat. It builds character, doesn't it, Cael?" the Greek said, pleased as always with his own wit.

Chapter 11
Emperatus Scottorum
Scotland 1010 A.D.

"Saint Patrick, going up to heaven, commanded that all the fruit of his labor, as well as baptisms as of causes and of alms, should be carried to the apostolic city which is called in Irish Armagh. Thus, I have found it in the books of the Irish. I, Máel Suthain, have written this in the sight of Brian, Emperor of the Irish; and what I have, he has determined for all the kings of Maceria."

Máel Suthain (The Book of Armagh)

In mid-summer, Wolf was summoned to Cashel by the king to attend a unique council of Brian's most senior and trusted diplomatic and intelligence advisors. By now, Aoife was considered a member of this small circle, which was critical to implementing the aging monarch's plans for the Irish people.

Within the confines of a well upholstered leather tent, gathered around a snug fire on sturdy wooden stools sat the king; his ambassadors to Wales, Scotland and Brittany; Aoife Captain of scouts and spies; along with Murcha and Wolf. Excluding the huge scarred battle captain, there were no purely military leaders, present at the meeting. Cormac was overseas, traveling with Irish clergy to make a pilgrimage to Rome.

Wolf had been told he was there to represent the *Laochra an Ri*, the Spartans and the Magyars. Most reassuring to Wolf, except for Murcha, there were no members of the king's family in attendance. Brian's other sons and daughters, and especially his wife, Gormla, were viewed as distractions by Murcha and Wolf, as these kin too often tried to influence the king to gain this or that personal benefit. Gormla, the half Viking sister of King Maelmora of Leinster, former wife of a former Viking king of Dublin, Olaf, with whom she bore

Sitric, the current Viking king of Dublin, was also married to King Malachi of Meath, before divorcing him to marry Brian. This convoluted drama of interbreeding and diplomacy through targeted marriage was repugnant to both Murcha and Wolf.

Aoife simply found it amusing and had once given her opinion to the quarrelsome giant. "I think it's just stupid. I wouldn't marry any man I didn't love and I'd kill myself before I'd let any foreign devil touch me, or more likely, I'd kill him first."

Despite his poor choice in wives, King Brian had been an otherwise clever master of diplomatic strategy. Unlike everywhere else in Christendom, the Irish church was not dominated by bishops or cardinals, but rather around monasteries headed by powerful abbots, who were usually members of the royal dynasties of the provinces in which their monasteries were located. Among the most important abbeys was Armagh, closely associated with the powerful Ui Neill clans, who had traditionally held power in Ireland in the past.

Five years earlier, after having been established as High King, Brian had donated twenty-two ounces of gold to the Armagh monastery, and announced that Armagh was the religious seat of all Ireland. He further decreed that all other monasteries should send a portion of funds they collected to the abbot there. This move cemented the relationship between the Munster king and the Irish clergy in the North. The Armagh clerics knew they would only hold the title of religious capital and maintain their wealth and influence as long as Brian remained High King.

In the passage inscribed into the "Book of Armagh" at the time, King Brian was not referred to as *Ard Rí* but as the Latin designate *Emperatus Scottorum* — "Emperor of the Irish." Wolf was intelligent and trained in Latin. He knew that the clergy and Brian assumed the title meant that he was to be the one king of all Ireland with no subordinate kings. But the word *Scotti* was used in Latin to describe both the Irish and the Gaelic speaking Scots in Britannia's north. Whatever dream Brian had of a united Ireland, Wolf imagined even more. The empire he envisioned was not just of the Irish but of all the Celtic people — Scots, Welsh, Cornish, Bretons and Irish.

Along with their manifestly superlative fighting skills, one of the traits of the ancient Spartans which had most impressed the "good boy" during his studies at Innisfallen was their stoicism. They were taught to speak little and listen much; to only interject when they had something of critical relevance to say. Now this may have seemed improbable for the hot-blooded disposition of the Irish, but Wolf nevertheless endeavored to master it. So now he listened.

The king had determined the moment was rapidly approaching when the red storm of full-scale war would erupt decisively on Ireland's shores.

"Despite our victories over all our enemies and our construction of a formidable and deadly Gaelic fighting force, I am painfully aware the odds are enormously against Ireland surviving as a sovereign Celtic and Christian nation." The king told them this with sorrow and anxious concern.

"I am aging. Many of the subordinate regional rulers among the Vikings and even some of the more restive Irish clans have only grudgingly submitted to our authority. I had hoped to convince them all to join with us as countrymen and become one people, but I am running out of time."

Upon hearing these words, Wolf grimaced. He had always been convinced this sentiment was drastically wrong and terribly dangerous. Any foreign incursion into the small island, if allowed to remain with its own alien customs, language and culture intact, was like a disease which festers in a human body, causing first discomfort, then heated fever and finally agony and ultimate death.

Wolf knew there could be no co-existence with pestilent foreign invaders. The Vikings had to be demonstrably crushed and forced into total submission. The survivors would be offered a choice of death or absorption into the Gaelic fabric. Wolf had read of the fate of the Celts in Britain and Gaul. They had joined voluntarily, been annihilated, or simply melted into the Roman or Germanic populations. In none of those cases had they emerged as a free and independent people.

King Brian continued. "The purpose of this limited council meeting is to make an assessment of which among the various peoples of Ireland and Britain will be on the side of the Gael, which will join in battle against us, and which will remain neutral. There is no intent at this moment to develop a military strategy. That will come later. This council is intended as a means for us to understand the correlation of forces for the coming conflict."

After all present, but Wolf and Aoife, had given their reports based on their individual experiences and expertise, Brian had a better understanding of how dire the situation was.

In Ireland itself, Brian could count fully on only the clans of his own provinces in the Munster homeland and those of southern Connaught. Northern Connaught held more affinity with the northern Ui Neill than with their provincial kin to the south. King Malachi and Meath would be allied but only so far as it was in their own interest. They had shown limited support at Gleann Mama ten years ago and that would likely be their model for any future battles. The various northern clans including the Ui Neill had always resented both Meath's and Munster's ascendancy to dominance. They would not actively engage against Brian, unless they scented weakness. It was assessed though that none of the northern clans would actively take the side with the foreigners and take up arms against the High King.

Leinster remained the least loyal, and Maelmora burned with indignation at how he had failed in the past. To make matters worse, he himself was half Viking and despite the impression he conveyed that the Dublin Vikings under his nephew King Sitric were his trusted vassals, the opposite was true. Maelmora was merely a pawn of Sitric who pulled the strings in the east and who maintained deep and abiding kinship and contact with the Norse chieftains in Manx, the Hebrides and Orkneys kingdoms, and even Denmark and

Norway itself. That meant Dublin and Leinster could bring armies dwarfing Brian's to the field.

As far as the ambassadors were concerned, no Norse, not even those who were ostensibly Christian, could be counted on to support the king. The Christian Saxons were fighting for their lives against the Danes in their homeland. And all knew, in their hearts, no Saxon could ever be counted on to aid or even abide any Celt anyway.

The good Welsh would support the king, but they were unlikely to send any but token forces to his aid, as they were reluctant to leave their little kingdoms unguarded. Several hundred volunteers, veterans of the Fingwalle campaign, could perhaps be dispatched.

Scotland was another case altogether explained the ambassador to Alba. Since the Scottish Gaels had joined with most of the various former Pictish kingdoms over many years, they had grown stronger together. Despite being harried by island-based Vikings to their north and west, sea-going Norse raids from Scandinavia along their east coast, and Danish and Saxon threats from the south, the Scots had expanded their holdings, kept their Christian faith and Gaelic language and become a proud people who, the ambassador said, admired what King Brian had accomplished in Ireland, their ancestral homeland. He felt they could be convinced to join the king with significant forces if treated properly by the Irish.

Even with possible Scottish assistance Brian knew, the combination of multiple branches of Vikings allied with the treacherous Maelmora, leading Leinster, would overwhelm the armies of Munster and Connaught, given the lack of complete loyalty by Meath and the Irish north.

It was at this point when Aoife asked to speak.

"My loyal network of women and girls has been reporting to me for years in confidence. The women in the south of Leinster claim their men folk feel betrayed and alienated by Maelmora who spends much time in Dublin and only comes to the south to visit the Viking coastal enclaves at Vadrefjord and Weisfjord. The men of Laigin will be less than responsive in the event of call-up, especially if we are prepared to support them."

Aoife continued with calm certitude. "Many of the women of the northern and southern Ui Neill have told me their young sons and brothers have run off to join with the king's loyal allies in southern Connaught, and have been eagerly welcomed by many of the small clans there.

"The young warriors of clans from all over Ireland, those who train with our *Laochra an Rí*, our Spartans and Magyars, have been sending letters home to their families, flushed with pride in Ireland and the king. While the Spartans and Magyars are for the most part common folk with no knowledge of writing, they have easy access to monks, who put their words to paper and carry the messages to their homes. These constant reports from their sons, cousins and brothers generate fiery spirit and longing among the lads and lassies. Our women are confident ever moreyoung and highly motivated men from all over the island will come to us to expand the ranks of our forces in Munster and Connaught."

Her summation gave room for hope. The enthusiasm and optimism of the seventeen-year-old girl brought smiles to the faces of all the men assembled there. They made plans to send a large and generous delegation to Scotland.

***

A sleek *snekkja* and a heavier transport ship conveyed a rather sizeable Irish diplomatic mission to a narrow strip on Britain's west coast. This small bit of coastline lay above Danelaw territory, and below that controlled by the Hebrides and Orkney Norse kingdoms. It was a thin slice of land controlled by the Scots. Though it would have been vulnerable to attack by either Danes or island-based Norse, both left it free, as both also had advantages in trading with the Scots and a corridor to the sea worked to the commercial advantage of all.

Mael Coluim Mac Cineada, or Malcolm II, was the King of Scotland. Like Brian, he was referred to as *Ard Rí* of the Scots and was, like Brian, surrounded by nominally subordinate sub-kingdoms. He had defeated a huge Norse army within days of his coronation in 1005. Given the similarity in the threats facing them, and their shared Gaelic pedigree, it was only natural the two great kings should be allies.

The unusually large size of the delegation showed the importance the Irish held in securing a military alliance with the Scots. With Cormac in the diplomatic lead, the party included Wolf, Aoife, Cael of the Magyars, Fergus of the Spartans, and the amiable Pict, Mornak, of the *Laochra an Rí*. Mornak's parents were expected to be at the Scottish court to greet their son.

Along with the principals, there was an assortment of warriors from each of the Irish fighting classes. To impress the Scots, Brian had decided to also send Pyrrhus, who would be announced as the Byzantine ambassador to the Irish court. And Luta, who had by now become a beloved sister figure to the entire Magyar camp, had accompanied them. This last was only after Cael's shameless pleading to Pyrrhus.

The reason the bulky transport ship made the journey was to carry the gift of the Irish High King to his Scottish counterpart. Pyrrhus had selected twelve of the best Connemara ponies from the Magyar stable to present to Malcolm in Brian's name. Of course, the Scots had their own horses and ponies but the sturdy steeds from Connaught seemed almost designed to be ridden into battle. They would master the Scottish Highlands as well as they did the rocky Irish hills.

The Scottish court had prepared a feast to meet the occasion. As the leaders of the Irish delegation marched into the king's hall, drums and pipes called the court to attention. All Scottish eyes however were fixed on the giant and foreboding figure of the immense armored colossus, whose beardless and scarred visage peered out from a black enameled helmet with the pointed ears of a wolf.

Some of the experienced Scots warriors recognized it as the helm of a beserker chief, its visor torn off. The huge man had to bend as he passed under the wooden support beams. A massive metal shield was strapped to his wide back, with the sheathed leather blade of a Dalcassian axe over one shoulder, and the wolf-headed pommel of an impossibly huge sword over the other. Wrapped around a wide leather belt at his midsection was a length of chain and a strange studded black ball of iron. In a scabbard at his waist was the same fighting *scian* Scots and Irish warriors kept close at all times.

Until now, Wolf the Quarrelsome had been considered just another myth, another tall tale from the storied imaginations of the many warriors who told of him. But at that moment the Scots gazed with their own amazed eyes on the nightmare of the Norse, the raging Celtic beast of the west.

"It's not just a tale. That's himself, the 'Wolf who hunts the Danes.' The fat Saxon merchant who sells us wine didn't lie," whispered a Scottish chief to his wife.

As Cormac and Malcolm went through the almost ritualistic words of greeting, Aoife was delighted to see several hounds, similarly formed but sleeker than the huge hounds which graced most royal Irish hearths. Fergus and Cael wore the distinctive garb of their units, both of which appeared strange to the Scots. With the courtesies completed, Malcom introduced Cormac to Domnall of Mar. Domnall was very close to Cormac's counterpart, the nephew of the king, and a storied, grizzled warrior in his own right. He was the regent of a province in the north where he was trusted to act as a bulwark against frequent raids from Norway and Denmark.

With tankards of good Danish ale and juicy slabs of venison piled upon wooden plates, Cormac, Wolf and Domnall sat together around a smaller table to discuss the hard realities of the Irish visit. Off to the side, Pyrrhus was regaling King Malcolm with his experiences across the known civilizations of the time. The Scottish king listened enthralled, trying to learn of things and events outside his world.

While the king and Pyrrhus discussed philosophy and history, the warriors at the smaller table set about the serious business of assessing what the state of the world meant for Scotland and Ireland.

"We all agree our survival is at stake. The situation remains precarious and there are multitudes of dark forces poised and yearning for our destruction."

Domnall despised the Norse as much as his two Irish guests and continued.

"No matter how forcefully we repel their incursions, they come again and again. The Vikings from the islands to our west and north are not to be trusted in the long term. The trade they now conduct with us will turn to rapacious invasion at the slightest scent of weakness or disunity on our part.

"I swear to you now. No matter what good King Malcolm might say, I stand ready to come to Ireland when King Brian has need against our common foe. Even if only my own little army of two thousand ferocious highlanders, my veteran brothers over long years, are all to go with me."

King Brian's nephew then made his own vow in turn.

"We will never allow Scotland to go down under pagan Norse axes. Call and we will come when the need is most dire."

Cormac rose and clasped hands with the Scotsman, and Wolf stood above both, grasping the shoulder of each.

While this war council was ongoing, the music in the hall was delightfully festive. The stringed instruments, flutes, and various drums, including the Irish-type *bodhrán*, were familiar to the visitors. The Scots pipes were different from those in Ireland, louder and more piercing. The music was fast and frenetic, and warriors, sitting to their tankards, pounded their *scians* on the oaken tables to the driving beat.

Already, the young men and women were dancing like the wild elvish folk of the old days. The *Tuatha Dé Danaan*, in their glittering halls under their fairy mounds, could not hope to equal the revelry of the Scots and Irish cousins feverishly spinning to the uniquely Celtic music.

Cael wasted no time and took Luta in his arms. Both laughed with glee, their eyes sparkling as they lost themselves in each other.

Fergus awkwardly approached a buxom Scots girl with hair as fiery crimson as his own, and she caught him and dashed to the center of the hall. The two joined the fevered prancers there, as the warriors threatened to crush the tables with the pounding of *scians*. Even Mornak's stately parents were dancing, and the young Pict found a pretty second cousin to escort to the floor. Undeterred, King Malcolm and Pyrrhus continued in conversational bliss as they sat alone and entertained each other with great sagas.

A small but vivacious figure appeared at the table where the three great captains of Gaeldom sat and planned their futures. Aoife, reached down and firmly clasped both of Wolf's thick wrists with her small ivory hands and pulled up with all the vigor she could muster.

He didn't move.

"Now then, you great ape, you'll arise and dance with me this moment."

Pyrrhus had told her what an ape was but he had not yet shared that description with Wolf. Aoife had laughingly thought the description of a giant, powerful, and hairy man-monster described the "good boy" very well.

For a moment, Wolf glared at the brazen girl who had disturbed them. Then, filled with joy at the arrangement that had been made with Domnall, and noting the poignant emotion in the eyes of the teenage girl, he picked her up in a massive embrace as if she were a kitten. Never letting her down, he joined the others on the floor, dancing wildly, lifting his great knees and flying around the room with unabashed pride as if she were a shimmering goddess, encircled protectively in his arms.

Aoife's eyes never left his, and the two of them seemed to blend into the pure and atavistic Celtic ecstasy of the music, the wild dance, and the eternal communion of the Gael.

***

There were a lot of old stories shared and news exchanged between the Scots and their visitors during the course of the night's revelry.

One tale was on the lips of all the Scots. It had started just months ago and become stranger over time. Cael and Luta sat by the central fire with several Scots couples and listened with unbridled interest.

A burly, auburn haired Scottish warrior told the tale.

"In the Viking-held lands to our west, traders have relayed tidings of demonic attacks on isolated Norse dwellings. The pattern is always the same. In the early hours before dawn some 'thing' steals a single head of cattle or a sheep from whatever enclosure shelters the livestock. Worse, if there are adult men at the location, they are sought out and murdered in their sleep. Their heads are crushed by some heavy blunt force. There is never any mutilation or wanton destruction, nor are women or children harmed. The marauding creature is only seen as a shadow. The terrified women and children who catch fleeting sight of it as all describe the phantom as dark, silent and incredibly fast."

Knowing he had the rapt attention of the young Irishman and his pretty Danish companion, the warrior continued.

"In reaction, the Norse mustered large groups of mounted riders to comb the hills looking for the creature in caves and woodlands and valleys. Now we know the Vikings are more at home at sea than on horseback in the uneven terrain of our heather. They move slowly and clumsily, and are no doubt loud enough to scare off any quarry well in advance of ever seeing it. Nevertheless, the search parties seem to have been successful as the attacks there stopped, and no further reports of sightings have come from the Norse."

The Scot's tall, handsome wife, whose hair was as golden as Luta's, picked up the story.

"Now some of our own cattle and sheep have gone missing. For weeks, Scottish farmsteads have become the larder for whatever this creature is. Only now, no man is ever attacked, and strangely, small trinkets of various types are left at the scene of the theft."

This last addition to the story caused both Cael and Luta to think they were being made gullible victims of their hosts' tall tales, yet all of the Scots swore it was true. The next morning Cael discovered most of the other Irish had heard similar stories from other Scots and the details were exactly the same. An idea formed in Cael's head, which might further cement good relations between the two groups of Gaels. He rushed to see Cormac.

"I want to borrow back seven of our ponies for a few days. And I want to take two of my Magyars, and Mornak the Pict with me, along with Luta, who leads the support element at my training camp."

The young cavalryman went on to detail his plan to seek out and kill or capture this "demon" that was terrorizing the hills.

"With a small force of picked riders on mounts which we know are perfectly designed for this rocky, hilly terrain, we will be faster and more silent than any horde of blustering and raucous Vikings. I'll take two of the best Scottish horsemen to display the unique traits of the Connemara ponies our king has gifted to them.

"I sat with these two last night," he added.

Cael noted Cormac's apparent puzzlement on aspects of his search plan. The older man's eyes narrowed quizzically at mention of Mornak, and especially of Luta, the erstwhile captive.

Trying to appear as earnest as possible, Cael explained his reasons.

"Mornak has spent time visiting the Magyar camp in the company of Wolf and has become a proficient rider, even if he never learned to use the Magyar bow."

"And," the youthful Connaughtman noted, "Mornak will prove useful if we are to run into a band of uncivilized Picts which are still rumored to exist. As for Luta, she will be helpful in assuring the families at these isolated homesteads will not be panicked at the approach of a group of riders which includes a gentle blonde woman among us."

Hiding his smile, Cormac only nodded in feigned assent. He believed none of this — "leader of the support element at the training camp," indeed.

This whole "plan" was simply an opportunity for the young Magyar to embark on a small, exciting foreign adventure, surrounded by close friends and a beautiful woman. Cormac knew Mornak, the Pict, had a rare gift. His natural ebullience, sparkling humor, and eternal optimism made him a sought-after companion by all the men and women who met him. And, Cormac thought, the lad must consider him a benighted imbecile if he believed Luta was only along to calm frightened children. After watching them last night, Cormac knew Cael was trying to make the most of this time with the young woman to whom he was obviously already deeply attached.

In any case, it would do no harm, the older man decided, and he could use the time to continue to talk and make plans with the impressive Scottish chieftain, Domnall. He told the eager Magyar, whose eyes pleaded like a puppy's, that if the Scots agreed, they could leave at mid-morning.

**

They had ridden for hours and were now well into the remote hills where the thefts had taken place. Graeme, one of the young Scottish warriors, led them to the farm that was first targeted by the phantom thief. An old man invited them in and shared some locally produced mead with the party.

"The one taken was an older sheep. The rest of the flock was undisturbed. The poor old thing was on its last legs, and due for just one more shearing," the farmer said. "There were no signs of bloody attack. The sheep was simply gone."

"In the center of my pen, with a fence of small boulders I collected myself, I found two little treasures which had been placed on a flat rock on the ground. One is a delicately carved, beautiful white seal. I recognize the local hornbeam hardwood from which it was crafted. It shines brightly like ivory in the light from the stone lamp. The other is a primitive looking necklace with bits of colored rock, polished bone and crystal arrayed along a strip of sinew."

The old farmer who normally had no use for trinkets was especially proud of these two. He rushed to fetch them and held them up to his guests for their inspection.

"That seal looks like a toy I played with as a child. May I see it?"

The farmer handed it to the Pict, who now spoke with an Irish Gaelic accent. Mornak broke into a big smile, and the others knew the sculpture had no doubt awakened pleasant childhood memories in the now fully grown and fierce warrior.

"My mother told me the only way she could get me into water in a wooden tub or a river was to let me take my seal in with me."

Everyone laughed at that, including the old farmer. Cael had also played with carved animal toys, mostly in the shapes of the hounds and ponies of his Connemara homeland.

The farmer went on to explain there were a series of farmsteads spread in a circle around the small mountain which dominated the landscape. About once every fortnight for the last two months thefts had occurred, and now four separate farms had been visited. All had suffered the loss of one of their stock, and been left with similar trinkets. It had been half a month since the last, and there were two other homesteads yet unmolested. The farmer gave them directions to the nearest. They thanked him and rode off swiftly.

It was just before dusk. Before they got in sight of the next farm, Cael halted the group.

"Graeme and Luta will ride to the homestead, explain the purpose of our visit, and ask to be granted shelter for the night. I'm sure that if they are observed they will appear to be visiting relatives in the eyes of any furtive onlooker who may be watching from the slopes."

"Meanwhile, the rest of us will diverge, and move up the slopes of the mountain then across to look down from above on the farm and grounds. We'll move silently and take positions where we will keep vigil for any activity down by the livestock. A full moon in a clear sky will hopefully be our ally in this nightwatch."

***

Seven hours later, a few hours before dawn, a dark figure emerged from a pit that had been dug into the field the previous night. It was covered with a roof of thatched branches and heather to match the surroundings. With no sound, but with amazing celerity, it was quickly in the midst of the sheep. A blow from a heavy cudgel dispatched the intended target, and with little effort, the carcass was hefted onto the thief's shoulders.

As the marauder ran, almost as swiftly as before, toward the slopes of the mountainside, five horsemen burst from hidden locations above, converging on it with wild cries. They had already decided they were not going to kill the "demon," but take it alive back to Malcolm's court to display their prize. Their bellows had awakened the family inside and they burst out from the house along with Luta and Graeme. The men of the family carried torches.

The thief had dropped the booty and tried desperately to find a way out, but even its speed could not match that of the galloping ponies, and two of the Magyars came alongside and roughly picked it off the ground to fly between them as they rode like the wind. Eventually they circled to where Cael, Mornak and the other Scot warrior stood and waited. They flung the thief into their midst and the three pounced on the struggling figure and secured it with coils of rope. It took all of them to subdue it.

Graeme held his torch close. Now all could see the monster in detail. It was draped in a roughly sewn tunic of thick black wolf hide. Both feet were covered with squirrel hide. Its hair was black, long and bristling and its face was pasted with dark charcoal soot. Hair, skin, and furred raiment alike were liberally smeared with some rank, gelatinous grease. The creature smelled like a particularly foul sheep.

With more torches now illuminating, Luta bent to examine more closely its face. Two clear blue eyes peered fearfully up at her.

"*Tá sé ach buachaill beag é.* ""He's just a little boy." she cried to the astonishment of all.

***

It was mid-afternoon when the seven ponies returned to the stronghold of King Malcolm. Days before, the arrival of the Irish delegation had caused a stir among the king's extended family, and now there was another rare spectacle. One of the ponies bore two riders. Mornak rode double with a black, hairy figure.

At first, Pyrrhus thought the party had indeed captured some form of Scottish ape. As they dismounted, it became clear the figure was no ape but a short man. The Pict kept one arm protectively around the figure, and led him into the round main hall of the king where the senior Irish and Scottish dignitaries had been made aware of their arrival. The rest of the party followed.

The court and the visitors were seated at a U-shaped wooden table into which Mornak strode with "prize" in tow. He bowed his head slightly to King Malcolm and nodded to Cormac and Wolf. He was also pleased to see his parents sitting with the other high ranking persons around the table. When he had the attention of all, he began the tale.

It was another all too familiar story of heartbreak, death and misery that was the lot of many of the common people at the time of the millennium. The boy was a member of one of the few still existing, only semi-civilized, small isolated Pictish tribes. His family had hailed from a remote peninsula in the extreme north of Scotland. Three years ago, a pillaging band of Vikings had come, not from the sea, for which his tribe had prepared routes and means of flight, but from the land corridor to their rear. This was a group of Norse marauders from the Hebrides kingdoms, and they could easily approach by land march up the coast from the west.

As had transpired all over Europe for hundreds of years, the merciless Vikings, slaughtered and looted rapaciously, killing all the men, the old people and babies, and taking the women and young children who could walk. The boy had been ten years old, and watched from a refuge cave his father had prepared amidst a pile of large boulders in case of such an attack. He had been trained by his father, and was digging for mussels when he heard the first screams. He ran instinctively to the hiding place hoping to find his mother waiting for him. It was too late.

Cael looked to Aoife and Wolf, knowing both would be deeply moved by Mornak's report of the boy's vile experience at the hands of the *Gall*, given their tragically similar backgrounds to this boy's.

Aoife's eyes were filled with tears, and even the fierce and indomitable Irish giant gazed at the boy with empathy and pity.

"His name is Partha Brule. He speaks no Gaelic, just an old Pictish dialect which I can only understand with some effort. Partha's father was taken down by three axe wielding Vikings, after he slew the first two attackers with a stone-tipped Pictish hand axe. His mother was taken in chains along with other women and children. The Vikings marched west and Partha followed behind secretively, hoping to somehow find a way to help his mother escape."

Mornak went on with the tragic story.

"For days they marched and he followed, eating mussels or bits of edible seaweed when he could find them. They turned south and, after one day, were met by a larger group of Norse with horses and wagons. On foot now, he had no chance and was soon too far behind to ever catch a glimpse of his mother or know her fate."

"Over the weeks and months, he had to spend more time foraging just to eat, drink and survive in the harsh climate. His father had taught him to hunt with snares, and fish with bits of sinew and bone. He was not above scavenging the hide of a recently dead wolf to replace his frayed woolen tunic, and he used the skins of the squirrels he snared to make rough shoes. He told me he had no idea the world he lived in was so large, having never been more than an afternoon's walk from his home. Partha searched for his mother looking down on some of the coastal Viking settlements, but never catching a glimpse of her or any other of his people."

"His father had taught him to hate the Vikings even though he had never seen one until they came to his settlement. But his father had also told him that his people were allied with another group of foreigners. These were called Scots."

There were murmurs among the audience and all heads nodded knowingly in approval.

"The months turned to years and Partha realized eventually he would never find his mother, so he decided to not only survive, but take revenge on the people who had destroyed his clan and family.

Along with edible plants, snared squirrels and birds, he learned to supplement his diet with livestock from Norse farmsteads on the coast. He could fly over the rocks and hills at tremendous speed, and he said his muscles became taut and wiry. He moved from place to place, finding crevasses in the rocks or deep copses of trees in which to shelter."

"He spent days scouting some targeted farmhouse to determine who lived there, where the livestock was, the schedules of the people, and, most importantly, whether he would have a chance to get revenge on some Viking man. He had already decided not to harm any woman or child. On the night of the attack, he would cover his face with soot, then smear his body and hide coverings with grease and droppings from the sheep he stole. This was intended to mask his scent from dogs, and allow him to sneak up on the sheep without them bleating."

One grizzled old Scottish chief cried out, "Smart lad you are."

"He crafted a stout wooden cudgel which he carried in a sinew binding around his waist. He would slip into a window or gouge a hole through a thatched roof. Then he would descend silently into the interior and bludgeon the man or men with mighty blows to the head. He would dash out silently and swiftly to retrieve the carcass of the sheep he had already killed. Most times, he claims, he was so phantom-like he could crush the man's skull without waking the wife sleeping next to him. But sometimes, they awoke screaming to see a black and vile figure speeding off into the night as the man lay with blood trickling from ears, mouth and eyes."

Some of the ladies present gasped at the graphic description.

"Several months ago, the Vikings sent large groups of warriors on horses and these surged all over the countryside looking for him. They were loud and slow, and he could always elude them before capture, but still they came on. His only recourse had been to flee to the east to still new territory. At some point he noticed there were no more riders around him."

By then, Mornak made clear, Partha was in Scottish lands.

"He had come to our country and discovered farms and flocks once more, but the people he observed were different from the Norse. He said they were gentler in demeanor, more pleasant to gaze upon, and their language was different and softer. They could be the mythical Scottish friends his father had told him about, he thought."

"He had to survive so he would take their weakest livestock, but as his customs from childhood had taught him, he must always leave some form of payment in return. He found he loved to carve and craft little wooden figurines with a small knife he had stolen from one of his Viking victims. He had seen his mother make necklaces with stones, bones and seashells and tried to emulate that as well. When he now slipped into a farmstead, covered in soot and grease, he would take only a sheep, harm no one, and leave a gift as hopeful recompense."

All of the women in attendance as Mornak spoke were weeping openly now. Even some of the men were trying to hide moist eyes. The Pictish warrior had to stop for a moment to let them gather themselves. The story of Partha's capture by the Gaelic hunting party was almost anti-climactic, as Mornak concluded his oration.

A Scottish woman of royal blood rushed out with a plate of cheeses and bread and enticed the boy to sit by her at the table, where he was given a large cup of buttermilk to drink. She hugged him to her breast, smearing her elegant white silken tunic with grease and soot, to which she cared not one wit. The boy ate ravenously, not having understood one word of Gaelic Mornak had spoken, but intuitively able to feel he was now among friends.

The discussion on the boy's fate was animated, since he seemed to be considered a treasured guest by all. It was decided that he would be raised by Mornak's parents, which pleased the *Laochra an Rí* hostage, since it meant he had a new brother, and, no doubt, fellow warrior in the not too distant future.

Wolf, noting his deeply similar origin to this boy, insisted he would send funding to help ensure the boy was given a full and classical education by whatever clergy the Scots and Picts might have. They assured him they had highly cultured monks and nuns who had been taught by both Celtic and Roman church masters, and that Partha would speak flawless Gaelic and Latin when the Irish returned on a future visit.

***

As the Irish delegation, now without the twelve ponies, marched west to return to their beached long ships, Cormac and Wolf were satisfied with the diplomatic and military relationships they had established with the fiery chieftain Domnall above all.

They turned to wave *slán agaibh*, and were delighted to witness a smiling young boy in an ivory woolen tunic. He wore a golden torc around his neck, and had long, curly black locks falling around a rosy cheeked, blued-eyed, happy face. Partha Brule stood proudly erect, with promise of glory to come, and Mornak's parents stood equally proud on either side of him.

Aoife had quietly been extending her network of female spies, women who shared her vision of sovereign Celtic lands, free of Viking, Saxon or any other foreign incursion. She had sought her connections among the common women, the cooks and cleaners, and the wives of farmers and merchants. She'd learned at King Brian's court that royalty meant intrigue. The families of the higher born were more interested in position and status than patriotism. Her Scottish network would be an advanced means of gaining early warning of troubles abroad.

Cael couldn't help just a wee bit of gloating. With Luta at his side, he moved up to walk next to Cormac for a bit.

"So now, dear master Cormac, do you still think my wild escapade simply mischief and adventure, or did we indeed assure a fortuitous ending and abiding alliance with the Scots and Picts?

"Was I off for a bit of *spraoi* or was I indeed furthering our king's and *Faolan's* plans?"

Cormac cuffed the Connemara youth good-naturedly on the side of his chestnut-hued head and laughed boisterously.

Chapter 12
"Jomsvikings."
Jomsborg, Southern Shore of the Baltic Sea
1011 A.D.

Sometime in the 970's, a series of events around the shores of the Baltic led to the establishment of one the most feared and powerful pagan mercenary orders the northern world had yet seen. The cast of characters swirled around myth, legend and recorded history.

Palnatoki was a fierce Danish leader and chieftain of the island of Fyn. He was an ardent supporter of the Norse religion to which the overwhelming majority of the Scandinavians held, despite the experiments with Christianity some of their royalty undertook. Palnatoki raised Sveyn Forkbeard, future conqueror of the Saxon English, who would become king of Denmark and England. Burislav was a king of the Wends, a savage Slavic people living in the lands east of the continental Christian Saxons. Burislav decided to provide an island off his northern shore to Palnatoki if the Dane could establish an armed presence there to serve as a buffer against raids by Norwegians and Swedes.

Palnatoki seized on this chance to establish a pristine warrior cult populated by fanatical and devoted servants of Odin. He had no preferences regarding his warriors' ethnicity, and ruled only that they follow the fundamentals of the traditional Norse beliefs. Scandinavians of all stripes joined, along with "men from the east," including Slavs and Turkic tribesmen. The island's central fortress became known as Jomsborg, and the warrior cult was known as Jomsvikings.

Not long after Jomsborg was established, a young and motivated Swedish Viking named Stybjorn took over command of the

Jomvikings. Palnatoki had envisioned a stern code for the cult members to live by, and Stybjorn enforced it sternly.

Recruitment was selective. Jomsvikings were between the ages of eighteen and fifty. In order to be admitted, volunteers had to engage in ritual combat with cult members. This was called the *holmgang.* If they exhibited weakness or lack of skill, the Jomsviking opponent would kill them with no remorse. If they fought valiantly, they were spared death and admitted. If they prevailed and showed superior fighting skills, the combat was stopped before further bloodshed occurred, and they were welcomed with cheers.

All had to swear dedication to Odin and the order itself. They were to defend their brothers to the death, and avenge any grievance against the order or the Norse gods. They were not to show fear or retreat before an enemy, unless the foe was larger in numbers. All booty was equally distributed among the brothers.

Upon pain of death, no women were to be allowed within the walls of Jomsborg where the warriors must always stay when not on campaign. If any individual warrior was outside the walls alone for more than three days, he was subjected to severe punishment. However, on campaign, treatment of women encountered was horrific. Rape and murder were the rule to assure there was no distraction from the objective of the raid — destruction and pillage to gain spoils and wealth for the order.

The Jomsvikings had suffered some losses in major battles throughout Scandinavia, but in 1009 they began to raid England and Scotland, where they gained both riches and notoriety. Thorkell the Tall was the leader of the Joms in these attacks against the Saxons and the Scots. Early in 1011, he landed with a large fleet of warships near Ipswich in the Saxon held lands, on the shores of a river near Nacton. His forces annihilated a huge Saxon force which had been sent from Ipswich. To dissuade further raids, the Saxon English were forced to pay an enormous sum of tribute on a regular basis, the *Danegeld,* so despised by the many the of victims of Viking atrocities in southern Britain.

It was Thorkell who sat in the leader's throne in the hall of the Jomsvikings on the shores of the Baltic when the delegation from Ireland arrived. They came in three ships bearing gifts, including wool, horses, mead, silver and gold. They assured no women were in their party.

Their leader walked confidently through the center aisle of the hall and bent his head toward Thorkell in greeting. The pagan chieftain looked down at the visitor, his fellows and the gifts strewn before him. On all sides, fiercely bearded members of the order glared at those from Ireland, who had come into their midst.

Sitric Silkbeard, King of Dublin, daughter of Gormla and son of King Olaf, stood proudly before the Jomsviking leader.

"Hail, cousin. You've brought us honor in the east and the glory of Odin has prevailed. Yet, further west in Ireland, the Christians grow stronger under a powerful king. He dares advance in battle against not just our strongholds in Ireland, but against Sveyn in England, and he probes into the Hebrides seeking weakness. I swear Ireland has more riches than England and France. If we control it all, there is no hope for our enemies here or on the continent."

Thorkell smiled at this Viking king from the west who had honored him by this visit. "Please sit by me, cousin, and let us discuss this," he replied with genuine interest.

The two laid plans as Sitric explained the situation existing in the western abode.

"King Brian's nominal rule over the island is nothing but a myth. The Irish can never unite. The strongest of the chieftains are in the north, the Ui Neill, and their thousands of warriors will never join in battle on the side of Munster and Connaught. King Malachi's warriors in the Meath midlands will only be reluctant allies to the king

"The Leinster king, Maelmora, who happens to be my uncle," Sitric said with a wink, "is weak and will obey whatever order I give him. Our now subdued but restive Viking towns in Ireland –

Vadrefjord, Limerick, and Weisfjord burn with righteous Norse indignation at being held to Brian's leash."

Thorkell grunted at that and smashed a big fist into his open palm.

"I have summoned other Viking allies. I've also recruited a force of five hundred rogue English Saxons who have foresworn Christianity to return to the worship of their old faith and Woden, who is, of course, none other than our own Lord Odin. The Saxons have sworn not to take the field against their own people but yearn to kill the Christian Celts, as their ancestors did not long ago."

The Dublin king told Thorkell all would be ready within three years. Then a scarlet, foaming torrent of furious Viking fire would mass on the western island and extinguish all Celtic resistance. The servants of Odin would control the North, the West and the East in Rus. They would crush the Christian Saxons, Greeks and Latins they encircled, and then move south and east. Nothing would stand against them.

Thorkell replied, "My brothers of the order are already raiding throughout England and Scotland. We could quickly turn our attention to Ireland if the price was right."

The order was dedicated to extending the realm of the Norse gods, to gaining riches for the brothers, and to the joy of battle. Sitric's plans offered them all of this beyond their most fervent dreams.

Chapter 13
Ospak and Brodir
Isle of Man
1012 A.D.

Almost midpoint between Ireland and Britannia, the strategically located Manx island was controlled by two strong Viking brothers, both of whom lived on the isle's western coast, Ospak and Brodir.

Ospak was a follower of the Norse gods and considered by all who knew him to be the "wisest of men." He was not only intelligent, but insatiably curious. He would have been considered a scientist in later centuries. He was also an anomaly among the Vikings; open minded and compassionate. Though he was approaching middle age, he was youthful in his deep interest in all that went on around him. He took time to closely examine what he saw, and make assessments about what it all meant to him and his world. His greatest joy was to ride around the expanses of the island with his family, friends and loyal elkhounds racing alongside. He led about six hundred warriors and their families, and was so close and generous to them, they came to share and unconsciously emulate his good nature over time. The Greeks would have called him a "benign" ruler.

His brother, Brodir, in contrast had converted to Christianity in his youth. He went even further and became a deacon of the Mass, a layman honored to serve in the Consecration of the Sacrament. Yet later, as he aged and became exposed to the most attractive sins of his time, he apostatized, and reverted to the worst of paganism.

Ospak was a tall, robust and healthy man, typical of his Viking brothers, with long blond hair, bristling moustaches and beard, and strong limbs. Brodir was bizarrely grotesque. Half a head shorter than Ospak, he was twice as wide and ponderously heavy. All of this bulk was chiseled muscle. His arms and legs were like the immense beams which supported the largest *skalli* long houses. His hair was unnaturally long, black as coal and covered him like a bear skin. Brodir's feats of strength resounded throughout Scandinavia, until no man, not even a beserker, would stand before him in ritual or actual battle.

Brodir called himself Odin's son and "Christ's dastard." He worshipped all the Norse gods, even the ones his people considered malign. By doing this, he was said to have become skilled in sorcery. One day, he appeared in a coat of blood-red mail and told all that no steel would bite him. His life's purpose, he now said, was to eradicate the white Christ in the world, and establish Odin and Loki as masters of men.

After a particularly savage raid on the Welsh coast, Brodir arrived home on Manx to find he had a single visitor. Sitting by his hearth was a familiar figure. Brodir and King Sitric of Dublin had engaged in trade in slaves, iron and foodstuffs over the years. Now, his commercial partner was asking for more from him than simple commerce.

In his calm and measured way, the Dublin king regaled Brodir with plans of future riches and glory to Odin which lay across the waves in Ireland. The Irish High King was weak and surrounded by enemies. Dublin was the launching point for an easy conquest of the entire island.

And, both to entice and further enrage Brodir, Sitric went on.

"This aged and worn out Irish king has commanded his people to destroy any vestige of Odin and the Norse gods in Ireland and Britain. He then plans to sail with his new navy against the Danes in England. This Celtic king intends nothing less than the annihilation of the Nordic world. His words are fantasy but still an affront to us."

Sitric requested that Brodir join him and the other Norse who would come to Ireland when the time was deemed right. Almost everything Sitric said was a lie, but the Manx Viking needed no more prompting. Still though, he had to ask about rumors he had heard.

"And what does your mother, King Brian's erstwhile wife, think about this plan?"

"My mother, who is half-Norse herself, most eagerly awaits the destruction of Brian, the Irish, and the Christians, and loves any good Viking chieftain who lends cause."

Brodir smiled slyly, having heard many stories of Gormla, the wife of Kings Olaf, Malachi and Brian. He asked then about another tale, oft recounted by his wild followers.

"What of this 'Wolf' the phantom, quarrelsome Irish giant, who supposedly exists only to populate our wives' nightmares, to scare our children, to rend us apart? Will he stop us from achieving complete conquest on his island?"

Brodir asked this in jest. He had heard the stories and knew his warriors loved sagas of monsters and beasts. He half wished it was true. Nothing would please Odin more than if Brodir, the fierce, were to slaughter a foreign, Christian champion in single combat. He had slain Welsh, Saxon and challenging Norse over the years, a legendary Irish nemesis would just add to his laurels.

Sitric became serious for a moment. He had also heard the tales. But he had not wanted to share them with his allies. His own Dublin Vikings remembered an almost supernaturally strong, boyish Irish slave who had apparently escaped after the disaster of Gleann Mama. Then there were tales of disasters in Limerick, and some of the little islands the Vikings had formerly held around Ireland. The most ominous was the story of the Danish annihilation at their stronghold in *Fingwalle*. The Norse survivors had told of Irish among the Welsh attackers.

One of these Irish warriors was said to be a beast from Nordic mythology. He had butchered a dozen beserkers, something unheard of. The ones who escaped murmured about *Ulf* and *Ragnarok*, and their stories were not to be believed. This creature was larger than any man any Viking had seen, and spoke Danish as well as themselves. He had been adorned with the helmet of a beserker chief, and his scarred face was displayed before them all to their horror.

The Danes who later returned to Fingwalle found only mangled Norse bodies and burnt dwellings.

The King of Dublin laughingly told Brodir that those stories were just more Irish blather. They would rule Ireland together when the time came. With a rapacious gleam in his eye, the Viking juggernaut from Man nodded in eager agreement and reveled in visions of his coming glories.

Chapter 14
Darkening Skies
Southern Ireland
1013 A.D.

Sitric Silkbeard became more confident as the results of his diplomacy progressed smoothly and advantageously. Danes, Norwegians, Jomsvikings, and the Norse of the isles were rallying to his cause. His recruited force of five hundred apostate Saxons operated from one of the Hebrides islands under the protection of Thorwald Raven. These pillaged the coasts of Scotland and Wales; and Sitric and Thorwald both profited from their raids, while denying any knowledge of them.

Yet the Dublin king knew that he had to have allies among the Irish themselves to distract and harry the *Ard Rí*, to force him to disperse and diffuse his armies. As always, his uncle, King Maelmora of Leinster, was the most malleable. Sitric and his mother, Gormla, now divorced from King Brian and living in Dublin, pressed the uncle and brother to throw off the yoke of Munster. Both were relentless, but Gormla was spurred even more by spite and bitterness as Brian had since taken a younger wife.

Maelmora sent messengers to the northern Ui Neills, to O'Ruarc, Prince of Breifne and to the Chief of the Carbury in Kildare, asking their support in ridding Ireland of the tyrant in Munster. These, in turn, returned word of their own resentment under Brian's rule, but stopped short of promising warriors to move against him.

Maelmora had even dispatched entreaties to Malachi of Meath, reminding him his title of High King had been usurped by Munster, that he was of the proud southern Ui Neill, traditional rulers of Ireland, and that the Norse had feared and respected King Malachi much more than they ever would this Dalcassian from the backwaters of the southwest.

Malachi defiantly rejected these fawning blandishments, replying that Brian had shown that the Irish prospered when they were together and united. He further admonished Maelmora, reminding him that Meath and Munster had crushed Leinster and its Norse allies before and could do so again if the Laigin king betrayed his oath of allegiance to the *Ard Rí*.

***

Shortly afterwards, sporadic probing attacks began issuing from the south, across the border into Meath. They were at first nothing beyond the traditional cattle raids that small clans of Irish had waged against each other for a millennium. Malachi, however, suspected something more pernicious than family squabbles was at play. He responded by sending forces to the southern border to confront the raiders. As his warriors were thus deployed, without warning, ranging groups of Dublin Norse exploded from the east, pillaging inland as far as Tara. These incursions were more serious and violent, with settlements and clan holdings put to the torch and captives dragged off.

King Malachi resisted as best he could but was eventually forced to go on to the offense. The Meath army was deceptively drawn into a pitched battle against both Leinster and the Dublin Norse at Drinan near Swords in an area long held by Sitric's Vikings. The combined forces defeated the host from Meath, leaving two hundred of them dead on the field, including Flann, Malachi's son.

The Vikings and rebel Irish followed up on this victory by marching into the heart of Meath, where they plundered the countryside. The Norse looted the monastery of Saint Feohin at Fore, where they violated the laws of sanctuary by seizing and carrying off woman and children from the very walls of the shrine.

Malachi found that he could not defend against so many enemies, especially with his northern Ui Neill kin unwilling to join in his defense. The Meath king was now forced to send emissaries to Brian, demanding the protection to which, as a subordinate king, he was due. His pleas were doleful. He explained to the *Ard Rí* that Meath was plundered, his sons killed, and Christian monasteries were debauched by the *Gall* and the treacherous Leinstermen. He beseeched Brian not to permit Maelmora, the Danes, and the men of Breifne and Carbury to come all together against him.

The High King knew that he was not yet ready for the ultimate clash. He had hoped Malachi could either defeat or come to an agreement with the Maelmora and Sitric. But upon hearing the alarming reports from the Meath king, and disgusted by the atrocities of the Norse, he came to his decision.

Murcha would drive south with the entire troop of Dalcassian clansmen and the general Munster army to take the Leinstermen from behind, as their deployed warriors were operating against the beleaguered Meathmen in the north. These home-based forces would total over three thousand men, mostly infantry, with an accompanying cohort of one hundred cavalry and scouts.

Brian ordered Wolf to move against Osraige. This was a small satellite kingdom to the immediate west of Leinster, nominally subordinate to Maelmora. For the first time, the entire force of five hundred *Laochra an Rí*, three hundred Spartans, and two hundred Magyar cavalry would campaign together in the field, under the overall command of the giant young warrior, now held in respect by them all.

The High King trusted his Connaught allies to protect his northern flanks against any threat from that direction and hoped Malachi could hold on to delay any incursion into Munster from the east. He immediately sent word to Malachi that help was coming, and urged him to fight as valiantly as ever for just a bit longer.

***

Osraige was just across the border of Munster. Wolf led his army of one thousand formidably trained and visually intimidating special warriors on a march from the north to the south of that small kingdom. His intent was to destroy any and all resistance against him.

There was none.

The first the local people learned of the invasion was when hundreds of fantastic, strangely-garbed, mounted specters stormed into and around their settlements, challenging any to defy them. The people were yet more confused to hear these strange men with otter skin caps and multi-colored breeches, carrying long thin lances and sheathed little bows, speak in multiple dialects — all of them familiar Gaelic lilts from across the island. When no resistance emerged, the riders sped south as fast as they appeared. One or two rode back the way they had come.

Not long later, tramped three marching columns of hundreds of heavily armored giants with solidly constructed iron helmets masking much of their faces, and wielding long, terrifying killing spears. Each carried an impossibly thick, metal covered, shield. They were led by an even larger and more robustly formed colossus, whose locks of red hair and thick beard spilled from his helmet. It was as if they knew none would stand against them. They moved with precision rapidly through the towns and settlements, looking neither right nor left. It was as though they were ghosts or visions, but for the earth-shaking rumble of their boots on the ground.

Incredibly, behind these marched a larger force of heavily armed warriors. They were not formed in compact columns but in a line of hundreds and hundreds, which spread like a wave over large swaths of the countryside. Unlike the others, these engaged in conversation with the people and searched through their homes and halls. They explained they were the *Ard Rí's* sworn legion, that the High King was not happy with the people of Osraige for siding with the heathen against their own people. Some asked the locals why these rebels should not all be put to the sword at once.

The same story emerged from the mouths of the terrified commoners. Maelmora had sworn to unleash the Dublin Norse on their homes and families unless they provided him men for his army.

They had sent some of their warriors but most remained home and hidden. The *laochra* came to believe this was indeed true, as they watched young men rush in from the countryside to protect their families. They were all left untouched. Yet the homes of the absent clan chiefs were torched, their possessions taken and put into carts, and their families, if any, delivered into the shelter of some other local homestead. The king was merciful and kind but some example had to be shown.

The same pattern continued from the north to the south of the narrow little province of Osraige. Through all of this march, Wolf the Quarrelsome, had been riding on his huge steed around the flanks of his army, giving orders and assessing the situation on the ground. With him, rode Aoife and a small group of five of the *laochra*, led by Mornak the Pict. As always, Aoife spoke with local women and girls while the men remained concealed. She was able to confirm everything that the frightened commoners had told Wolf's warriors.

Just to the immediate south of Osraige, the Viking port city of Vadrefjord, nominally subordinate to King Brian, lay astride the coast. Wolf quickly developed a plan to assure its continued submission. He knew he could not allow himself to enter the Norse settlement for two reasons.

First, he considered it wise to let the Vikings question whether he truly existed; to remain an amorphous, spectral threat to them. Secondly, he knew that his self-discipline had not progressed to the point where he could leave an armed Norsemen alive in his presence. He could not stop himself from slaying any Viking who came within sight. He was learned and logical enough to know this was a fault but honest enough to recognize its reality.

***

Five hundred strong, the force of *Laochra an Rí* marched deliberately up to the gates of Vadrefjord, King Brian's lion pendants flying above them. They were under the direct command of Caurag Mac Murchad, son of Murcha and grandson of Brian, the same little wain who had years ago taunted the Viking marauders on the banks of the

Shannon. He was now a powerfully developed warrior of twenty-one years

As Wolf expected, the gates opened almost reluctantly, and the resplendently armed unit moved inside, bristling with readiness for any sign of threat and displaying an aura of absolute control over everything. Inside, awaiting them, was the local Norse chieftain, surrounded by a number of his party.

"Your High King has invaded the lands of the Osraige and Leinster traitors and they are now being punished. He intends to move on Dublin when those lands have been subdued. He has requested that you provide us with food and drink, and whatever other sustenance we need before we move on," Caurag said in a ringing voice all could hear.

The Vadrefjord chieftain, no real friend of the Irish or their king, congratulated himself on having stayed out of any mischief in the north. His port city enjoyed a lucrative trade in maritime commerce, and Brian left them relatively free to administer that business. He bowed low and ordered his people to bring the Irish whatever they wanted.

Convinced now, there would be no treachery, the Irish warriors relaxed and made camp in the narrow streets and open spaces of the little port. Viking women and children brought fish, mussels and mutton as well as delicious barrels of Danish ale. Caurag conversed at some length and in close quarters with their chief, and counted himself fortunate that his quarrelsome leader had chosen to remain absent. He also counseled his warriors to drink sparingly of the ale upon pain of Wolf's wrath.

Outside the walls, this leader sat around a fire in a woodside clearing, among the Magyars, with Aoife, Pyrrhus, and Cael beside him. Mornak had accompanied his weapon brothers into Vadrefjord. Wolf had chosen to conceal the presence of the special warrior bands from the eyes of the Norse, until they could eventually be thrown against them as shock troops. Fergus and the Spartans had marched home when it became clear there would be no resistance. This and the general lack of any real combat in their "invasion" of Osraige had frustrated Cael and Fergus immensely.

Wolf counseled them.

"Pillaging defenseless Irish settlements would not be Christian. As much as I might want to sack and burn the heathen port city, I have sworn to abide by the king's arrangement with the bloody little heathens."

Pyrrhus, Aoife, and Cael, had to hide grins when Wolf used that now familiar phrase.

On a positive note, he assured them there would be clashing of spears and showers of arrows to come against the *Gall* in the near future. While Aoife and Pyrrhus seemed resigned to that, Cael's eyes lit with eager anticipation.

***

As Wolf's men were maneuvering in a show of force across Osraige, Murcha's larger army was ranging deep across Leinster. The king's son noted that Aoife's reports had been accurate. In the south, the Munstermen were received warmly by the people, and there were many men of fighting age working in the fields, indicating they had not joined the main body of Leinster forces pillaging Meath.

As he moved northwards, he found empty settlements. In each of these his warriors were ordered to seize whatever spoils were present from the properties of the local chieftains. On the grounds of one, they discovered an old man, hiding in a stack of hay. He told them the people had fled to the woodlands or to Dublin itself in terror of the oncoming hordes of the *Ard Rí*. They laughed and told him that the true king was far gentler in Leinster than Maelmora and the Vikings had been in Meath.

Ranging wider, they came across royal holdings of the Leinster King. These, they looted completely and left in ashes. Not desiring to be burdened with baggage, Murcha sent whatever was of value back to Munster where it would add to the king's treasury. Ironically, he knew some of the funds generated by those spoils would be spent to build roads, bridges and churches right here in Leinster. Brian was the King of all Ireland and he chose to bring prosperity to the entire country, not just his own Munster.

Like Vadrefjord, the Viking trading port of Weisfjord on Leinster's southeast coast had taken no part in the aggression against Meath. The Viking leader there sent out a delegation to meet Murcha's army as it was marching through the countryside. They brought gifts of silver coins and jewelry for the High King in acknowledgement of his authority.

Murcha accepted the coins but refused the jewelry or any other item that could possibly have been stolen from a Christian land. Since the emissaries could not exclude that possibility, they told the Irish commander they would return two days hence with proper tribute.

Just as promised, they arrived at Murcha's camp on the morning of the third day with a cart filled with exotic treasures. These included curious and sweet-smelling spices and oils, bolts of the smoothest silk, marvelously crafted carpets with intricate and beautiful designs, and bizarre curved swords of extraordinary workmanship with jewel encrusted hilts. These, the Norse call "scimitars." They declared these gifts met the Irish prince's demand in that all were stolen during Viking raids on Islamic lands in the distant south.

Murcha accepted these with good graces, but he later said to his lieutenants. "If God's holy angels dwelt on an island somewhere out in the great sea, the damned heathen Northmen would attempt to invade and plunder them as well."

***

The armed resistance shown by Malachi and his struggling Meath army stiffened when they were informed Brian had sent two separate armies into Osraige and Leinster. They counter-attacked with skill, exploiting their intricate knowledge of the terrain in their homeland. Small groups of clansmen whose settlements had been pillaged struck back from their forest refuges in deadly guerrilla raids.

When the warriors of Leinster learned of the two armies plundering their towns and settlements, morale evaporated, and they clamored to return home. Their king would not accept such a withdrawal as he knew they would be destroyed piecemeal if they returned in individual bands while Brian's forces were rampaging in strength. Maelmora begged his nephew, Sitric, to allow his army to withdraw to safety behind Dublin's formidable ramparts.

Sitric, though he would not admit it, was also worried about being away from his city with the High King's forces in the south. He was especially angry and disappointed that none of the other Irish chieftains had joined in the rebels' combined assault on Meath. He was coming to the conclusion that the Irish could not be trusted as reliable allies, and he must depend on his own kind even more than he had anticipated.

Without ceremony, the Leinster Irish and Dublin Vikings hastily departed from Meath, and rushed south to Dublin to put thick earthen walls and spiked palisades between them and the wrath of the *Ard Rí.*

***

In September, Wolf and Murcha's two unbloodied and intact armies met outside the walls of Dublin. They had been too late to intercept and destroy the rebel forces before they reached safety inside the city. The combined Munster forces assumed a blockade around the semi-circular walls, permitting no one and nothing to enter or leave by land. Wolf, however, was careful to keep the Magyars, and himself out of view of the Vikings manning the walls.

There was no siege equipment anywhere in Ireland, and strong walls and a prepared, defending force made taking any fortress extremely difficult. In Dublin's case the advantage was even greater for the defenders, since they could be resupplied by long ships plying the Liffey.

Murcha tried vigorously to lure the defenders into the open. His men challenged the sentinels on the walls, insulting their manhood and cursing them for cowards. The days turned to weeks, and Wolf decided to send the Magyars home. By now, even these hot-blooded specialists knew their foe was not coming out, and they rode west without complaint. The Irish then tried to deceive the men behind the walls by ordering the entire force of *Laochra an Rí* to march ostentatiously westward, in full view of the watching eyes of the Vikings and their Irish rebel allies. This too failed to lure the defenders out of their sanctuary.

In December, King Brian, arrived at the Munster camp to assess the situation. The weather was especially harsh and cold, and provisions were becoming difficult to acquire for the encamped Munster army. The garrison inside was warm and well fed, while his own men shivered. On Christmas day, Brian, Murcha and Wolf led their forces back to Munster. All knew that events were far from resolved. There was an almost palpable sense that a furious maelstrom was building to a coming crescendo.

Chapter 15
The Gathering
Northwest Europe
Early 1014 A.D.

Even before he had visited Brodir, the legendary and powerful Manx chieftain, Sitric had made a journey to the kingdom of the Orkneys, where Sigurd Hlodvisson, called "Sigurd the Stout," ruled an island empire that extended to mingle with Thorwald Raven's holding of islands in the Hebrides. Thorwald, also called Gilli, was a brother in law of the Danish king Sveyn, who was on the verge of crushing all Saxon resistance in the English kingdoms when he died in December of 1013. It would be left to Sveyn's son, Canute, to vanquish any remaining Saxon resistance in England and become its ruler. In strong contrast to others of their kind, the two Vikings of the isles, Sigurd the Stout and Thorwald Raven, cooperated. Their violent aggression manifested itself in plundering and pillage against Celts and Saxons, not against each other.

Of the two, Sigurd was by far the stronger. The Shetlands and Orkneys were his and the entire north of the Hebrides island chain was peopled with his followers. Sigurd yet sat uneasy. Not long ago, one of the newest of the Norwegian kings had ordered him and his entire people to immediately embrace the White Christ on pain of death and immediate invasion.

The Orkney ruler bowed and scraped and appeared devout at his baptism. When this newest upstart and royal pretender sailed off from his islands, he and his people immediately burnt the crosses and beads they'd been given. They retrieved the totems and carvings of Odin and Thor, and erected them tall and challenging on the coasts of their many islands.

So it was that when the Nordic king of Dublin's three sleek long ships docked at his port, he was in a foul mood. His temper was soon alleviated when he heard the bodings of the Irish-Viking ruler. He was thrilled to learn of the weaknesses among the competing Irish kingdoms, and of the yet to be harvested riches there. Ireland was full of untapped iron, silver, gold, and well-fed fat cattle — superior to any in Europe or elsewhere.

The reigning Irish king was resented by the multiple small rulers, and the land needed the stern rule of a proven Viking overlord. Sitric went on.

"I, myself, prefer to conduct our mutually profitable maritime trade out of my own stronghold in Dublin. This is the reason I ask you to come when the time is right, join with other Vikings, crush the Irish usurper and seize the crown of Ireland for yourself just as Danish warriors are doing in England."

The corpulent Viking had heard such stories before. He was not so naïve as to think the Irish were weak and submissive. He knew what King Brian had done in Limerick, at Gleann Mama, and in Dublin in years past. Yet he still smarted at the destruction of his trading port in the Hebrides those years ago, having been told that some wild wolfish chieftain of King Brian led that raid.

Sitric continued his narration.

"Their old king is fanatical in his hatred of everything do with the Norse gods. His only goal is to eradicate Odin and Thor and any other vestige of what he calls 'heathenism' from Ireland, Britannia and the isles."

At that, seething with rage just as had Brodir, Sigurd yelled, "First some effete, effeminate and newly appointed 'king' of our own people threatens us and tries to force me to abandon our gods. And now an Irish 'king' deems to destroy us from the west. Yes, Sitric, call and I will come with my thousands. We will crush the Christian Gaels, take their island, and defy any to oppose us, including whatever girlish man might sit on a throne in Norway."

Sitric thanked and praised the lord of the isles, and assured him of victory and glory.

***

In early March, Mornak and two of the young Scottish-born warriors of the *Laochra an Rí* crossed the sea in a small but sturdy boat to visit the stronghold of Domnall of Mar. They were enthusiastically received in the rustic yet formidably constructed seat of the Scottish Gaelic Viking slayer. The warriors there were amused to hear their fellow Scots of the *laochra* speak with the distinctive soft rolling trill of the western Irish, and jokingly urged them to remain in Mar until they could regain their proper Scottish tongue. The three received these good-natured taunts with light heartedness, but it soon became clear the purpose of their unannounced visit was far more serious than simple diplomacy.

First, they related accounts of recent events in Ireland, how Leinster rebels and Sitric's Vikings had invaded Meath and pillaged the countryside. They explained that King Brian's armies had driven the Norse and rebel Irish back inside the stout walls of Viking Dublin, after neutralizing Osraige and the south of Leinster. They continued by reporting to Domnall the latest intelligence assessment provided by the far-reaching corps of spies and scouts.

Mornak said, "By early spring, just weeks from now, massive forces of Vikings from across northwestern Europe will be on the move.

"Sitric Silkbeard, Viking ruler of Dublin, has secretively journeyed abroad and solicited the support of Ospak of Man, Thorwald Raven, 'Jarl of the Hebrides,' and Sigurd the Stout of the Orkneys. He even traveled to the Danelaw to meet Sveyn Forkbeard, as that one was wresting control from the English Saxons and extending his victories."

More ominously, they reported, "Sitric has journeyed to the Baltic itself where he met with mysterious groups of eastern Viking cutthroats. He showered them with promises of booty to be plundered from the Gaels."

Domnall trusted his allies. Their words echoed reports he had received from of his own spies. He immediately perceived the foreboding potential of catastrophic disaster, not just for Ireland, but for Scotland as well. If this massed horde of combined Northmen could eliminate the strongest vestige of Celtic resistance in Ireland in the west, the fate of Scotland and Wales would be sealed. All of northwestern Europe would be controlled by the heathen *Gall*.

The emissaries bade Domnall be prepared to come and aid King Brian, Murcha and Wolf on shortest notice from an Irish messenger. Domnall knew, if such a request arrived, it would mean the Norse to his north and east would be preparing for engagement against the Irish and their attention would be focused there. He could leave his lands under the protection of King Malcolm and join in the great struggle for survival against the merciless enemies of his people.

"Tell your king and my weapon brothers, Prince Murcha and Wolf the Quarrelsome, when word arrives, I will be at their sides, not later than five days hence, with two thousand battle-hardened, fire-breathing Gaelic Highlanders. Together we will drive the pagan foreigners into the sea and save our people."

***

In the first week in March, Llywelyn ap Aeisyll, Welsh king of Gwynedd and Deheubarth, looked upon the largest and most formidable warrior he had ever seen in his long years of hard living and harder fighting. He stood impossibly tall and massively built, with a Dalcassian axe and the wolf-headed pommel of an immense broadsword crossed behind his back. Beside him, stood one of Llywelyn's own grandsons adorned in the garb and weaponry of the *Laochra an Rí*. He was a hostage who had been exchanged with the Irish king years before. One of Brian's grandsons was likewise a member of Llywelyn's royal guard, and a charming and pleasant young fellow who everyone counted as friend.

The giant and the king conversed in Latin which both spoke well, having learned the same liturgical dialect of the romance language. Wolf reminded the king of the good relationship between the Welsh and the Irish, and that they both shared common enemies. He had traveled to Wales to give tidings of a gathering threat, which endangered the continued existence of both peoples. Vikings from all over the world were massing against the free Irish. Among them would be a huge force of Danish warriors to be sent by the Danish court in revenge for *Fingwalle.* Alongside would be hundreds of pagan Saxons, who had left the true faith to take arms against Christianity as they had in their not too distant past.

At that point, the Welsh-born *laoch* interjected in the dulcet, melodious language of Wales.

"Sire, this Irish officer is too modest to tell you. He was the leader of the Gaels during the battle of *Fingwalle* ten years ago. And it was his plan that liberated our captive people and eliminated that slaver's den on our border. I fought at his side that day as did five hundred young Welsh heroes who volunteered to cross our borders to join him. He has been my war chieftain, captain and trainer in arms, and his word is to be trusted without reservation."

There was a murmuring in the king's court among the onlookers at mention of *Fingwalle.* Some had fought there and one cried out that, as a boy, he was among the captives rescued that day. This one dashed to Wolf, reached up and clasped him on the shoulders and took his hand firmly in his own, his eyes fighting back tears. Wolf could not understand the words but recognized the conviction of heartfelt appreciation. He in turn rested his huge hand on the other's shoulder, smiled down at him and nodded.

The king knew he had been put in an awkward position. He could read the passionate sentiment that was building in the hall. The Welsh had traditionally not deployed warriors across the seas as a matter of defensive survival, preferring to protect their borders and fight on their own ground. But he had to do something. He stood and looking across the hall announced his decision with a strong and stirring voice.

"We are too few to dispatch our entire army to aid our allies and still be able to repel our many enemies. It pains me to admit that. But we sent volunteers to aid this giant warrior in years past, and that we will do again. I know thousands will rally to the call but, as King, I can only allow five hundred of our young men to sail to Ireland. This number proved victorious before and I trust we will prevail again."

A thunderous cheer erupted, nearly every man clamoring to be among the volunteers to aid the Irish. Wolf looked around at the blazing martial spirit he had ignited among the otherwise regal and serious members of the court. He bowed slightly to Llywelyn, and asked him to be prepared to rapidly dispatch the promised band of Celtic warriors upon word from the *Ard Rí*. As he and his companions left the hall, they were surrounded by exuberant Welshmen slapping their backs and arms in affection and comradeship.

***

One morning in the middle of March, a strangely constructed small ship made its way majestically along the River Shannon, underway to Limerick. Above the mast, flew a blue pendant with a thick white cross, intersected by diagonal white bars. Above the cross was the letter **P** in white. From a small staff rippling from the stern, another pendant, with a double headed eagle on a yellow background, waved in the gentle breezes which heralded the coming spring.

The arrival of this ship was no surprise. Plans had been made to greet its crew upon docking in Limerick. The best source of information for news from the continent was the network of Christian clergy which plied its spiritual endeavors far and wide. Irish monks, recently returned from Rome, had been asked to deliver word to King Brian of a visiting delegation from the Byzantine emperor. They had been precise as to the day and hour of its arrival but could provide no more details.

The Irish were pleased to hear tidings of these new guests, but Pyrrhus was strangely uneasy. Fifty of the *laochra* and fifty more Dalcassian veterans stood as honor guard at the head of the gangway as the foreign ship was secured to the dock. The greeting party consisted of Prince Murcha, Cormac MacMahon, and Pyrrhus.

Two bizarrely dressed, medium-sized men sprang onto the gangway, and made their way with broad smiles up to the waiting Irish. They were both garbed in brightly colored tunics of different hues falling to mid-thigh. Instead of trousers, they wore long satin skirts that fell to their sandal-clad feet. Unlike the kilts of the Scots, these were akin to the long dresses of Viking and Irish women, or the clerical garb of the priests and monks. They also displayed some familiar features. They wore otter skin caps and carried recurved bows in leather pouches, and quivers brimming with brightly feathered arrows.

Now Pyrrhus broke into a wide grin and began calling in an alien language which eluded them all. With long strides, he bound down to meet them and hugged each, kissing them on both cheeks. The Irish had never seen such a display.

The three arrived now at the landing and Pyrrhus animatedly introduced these visitors as his dearest friends from earlier days. They were, of course, Magyars, and he spoke their names which none of the Irish could ever possibly pronounce. They continued to converse in this exotic language, when Pyrrhus' smile froze, as he looked downward with some trepidation at the deck of the little ship.

A stately figure emerged from a cabin built into the stern. Elegantly dressed in a purple and gold, flowing dress, she was a tall, athletically-built, raven haired woman of unsurpassed beauty. Two more Magyars followed behind, each carrying a small wooden chest.

"Now comes the reckoning," whispered Pyrrhus in Irish to his friends.

Together they asked him who this radiant vision was, and why he seemed displeased.

"Her name is Helena Lakepeno and she is my superior officer in the diplomatic corps of our emperor."

"That name sounds familiar to me somehow but I don't know why?" Cormac announced perplexed.

"That's because it's my family name, you lumbering Irish dolt. She is my elder cousin as well as my ambassadorial chief."

When this second contingent of the delegation arrived at the landing, the tall woman, who had ascended the gangway in commanding strides, smiled with genuine pleasure at the two tall Irishmen. Then she looked to the black-bearded Greek, her eyes narrowed a bit, and she became serious. She nodded to him with a hint of some sterner discourse to come.

"My name is Helena and I am the senior ambassador of Basil the Porphyrogenitus, Emperor of the Byzantines. I come to convey to you the compliments of the emperor and deliver a small gift which may assist you in your coming trial against the pagans."

She spoke in mellifluous Latin which she knew educated Irish would understand. The two behind her, also Magyars, opened the chests, and the Irish cousins beheld an immense fortune in gold and silver coins.

"I am Murcha, the son of King Brian, and was sent to extend *Cead Míle Fáilte* — 'One Hundred Thousand Welcomes' — and escort you to Cashel."

Cormac's wife had died in childbirth years before. Too busy with fighting, training and recruiting to find another, he had been immediately mesmerized by this dark Venus who stood before him. He offered her a choice of riding in a specially prepared coach or on her own mount. She chose to take the horse provided if she could ride at his side, she told him, her brown eyes shining. Then she took his arm and he led her between the formed ranks of the armed escort and watched enraptured as she sprung expertly into the saddle.

The Magyars and the clergy that had accompanied the delegation followed behind and were also provided mounts. For the first time in weeks, the visitors from the Duchy of Hungary felt at home as they once again guided strong horses between their muscular calves.

***

During one of his voyages from Man to the Danelaw, Ospak had found a Saxon serving girl to help his wife maintain their estate. She was an exceedingly intelligent and hard-working little creature, and in a surprisingly short period of time she became a daughter figure to his wife and himself, and a sister to their two sons. Theirs was a happy and cheerful home to begin with. With the addition of this new arrival, it became even an even merrier abode. Her name was Cearo, and she was a devout Christian. She prayed each evening and morning in the little room which had been prepared for her, and carried a curious arrangement of wooden beads and a small crucifix with her at all times.

Cearo's presence among them made its strongest impression on his wife, who one day announced to her husband that she too had become a Christian. Unlike other Viking husbands who would have beaten her or worse, Ospak simply joked.

"I don't want any foul-smelling incense to be burnt in this house." Then he patted her round bottom and grinned.

The joy Ospak shared with his immediate family was not mirrored in his relationship with his brother, Brodir. The two Northmen were of opposite mind and disposition on almost every subject. When Brodir told of his meeting with Sitric of Dublin, the planned invasion of Ireland and how Brodir would take the crown, Ospak was not impressed.

"Sitric has always been a fool and Brian should have slain him seven times by now. The Munster king has maintained profitable relationships with the Vikings in Vadrefjord, Weisfjord and Limerick. Why would you want to fight against so good a king?"

Brodir responded to this protest with unveiled disgust and the two parted in anger. During the final weeks of February and early in March, the suspicious Brodir observed what he thought were signs portending some great coming calamity. One night a thunderous storm cast down sheets of rain, deep red in color; not the normal clear, cold sea rain. It was warm, driving and crimson. Another night brought a windstorm which wreaked havoc in the small ports splintering those boats and ships, which had not been adequately sheltered. Most ominously, the next night saw people and animals attacked by huge flocks of ravenous ravens. Such events had never occurred in anyone's memory.

When next the two brothers met, Brodir sought Ospak's counsel on what these strange events might portend. Ospak related that during prayers together, his wife and Cearo experienced visions of a mighty meeting of huge armies on green fields by a seacoast. Much blood would be shed on both sides. But the Vikings would die in droves and be dragged down into hell. His brother's words and these visions infuriated Brodir, who ordered Ospak to leave his home, return to his clutch of Christian women, and never return upon pain of death.

Now Brodir turned to his own sorcery, summoning acolytes and conjurers of Odin and Loki. One old mage augured, "If the battle will be on Good Friday, King Brian will fall but the Irish will win the battle. But if we fight on any other day all who oppose Brian will be slain."

Brodir now determined he must force the battle to take place on Good Friday. He believed the prophecy that Brian would fall, but would personally assure he and the Vikings would rule the battlefield at day's end. No man had ever prevailed against Brodir in open combat; not Saxon, Celt nor any other Northman. He would not have his destiny denied him by an ancient, doddering king of the Irish.

***

Knowing the breach between them would never allow Ospak and his family to remain safely in Man with the looming battle to come, Ospak dispatched a messenger in a swift craft to Limerick with a message for King Brian. Then, after a family counsel, he gathered his five hundred closest followers and gave them a choice.

"Brothers, join me in alliance with the good king of Ireland against the Danes, Leinster rebels and mercenaries from the east, or sail with my brother, Brodir, to certain death."

Such was the charisma, leadership and moral appeal of this greatest Viking of his time — all eagerly voted to follow Ospak even to the pits of hell.

***

Early one foggy morning in the second week of March 1014, fourteen long ships, with dragon prows and arching shield rails, sailed out of two ports from the Isle of Man with fierce Viking warriors. Unlike multiple scores of similar ships, with thousands of similar warriors, now crossing toward the port of Dublin from Sweden, the Baltic, Norway, Normandy, Denmark, the Danelaw, the Orkneys and Hebrides, and every other northern settlement, this fleet of fourteen was sailing to Limerick to take their place at the side of the High King of Ireland.

None of these five hundred Norsemen had any way of knowing that other ships with other types of warriors were also sailing to the aid of the Irish. North of them, ships transported two thousand ferocious Scottish Gaelic highlanders on the short trip across the northern Irish sea where they would make landing in the province of their forebears, the Dál Riata, and march south to join the forces of Munster and Connaught.

Not far behind them sailed yet another contingent of Celts. Exactly the same number as Ospak's Vikings, they were five hundred, seasoned Welsh warriors on an uncharacteristic voyage beyond their own borders to cast their lot with their Celtic cousins. Many of these were veterans of a place called *Fingwalle*, and all were eager to display their gratitude in raging battle against the invaders of the isles.

Chapter 16
Order of Battle
Dublin Environs
March and April 1014 A.D.

After Holy Mass, on the first Sunday of March, a small band of Irish leaders set out on a "Commanders' Ride." This was a proven military technique which allowed battle captains to conduct detailed and leisurely evaluations of their expected areas of operation prior to major hostilities. The intent was to conduct this reconnaissance and preparation of the battlefield in a permissive environment. That meant they did not expect to find enemy forces gathered in the areas they would cover.

This advanced detail consisted of Cormac, representing the *Ard Rí,* Wolf standing for the *Laochra an Rí,* Cael and Fergus who were the respective commanders of the Magyars and Spartans, and Aoife, who was now Prince Murcha's captain for all matters of intelligence. Murcha himself had stayed behind to attend to matters of diplomacy with the Byzantines and to meet another arriving band rumored to be sailing from the east.

No one would tell Wolf anything about these other visitors, not even Aoife, who seemed to be intimately familiar with all matters of importance. The giant warrior was perplexed at this, as he had been trusted with every other bit of intelligence reporting. He had been selected as an ambassador to the Welsh king, even though all knew diplomacy was not one of the fiery warrior's strengths. Wolf had succeeded at that mission, receiving a promise of a Welsh army disembarking from its own shores to come to aid of the Irish. He was well aware of the massive hosts marshalling to drive against his foster father and his people, and that was where his attention was now focused. He put any indignation out of his head, and concentrated on their preparations for the decisive battle to come.

**

When all the leaders of Munster and Connaught initially came together at Cashel in that first week, Cael and Fergus met each other again for the first time since the battle of the meadow eight long years before. They had been mere frightened striplings back then, laying side by side in the bracken, shivering in dread at the sight of an oncoming dragon ship.

When Cormac reintroduced them, each gazed on the other in amused disbelief as the older warrior looked on entertained. After much arm clasping and shoulder slapping, the jests began.

"I'd no idea back then you'd grow into a great plodding, red furry, mongrelized spawn of some bear and ox, or that you'd be wearing a round metal barrel around your ample girth when next I laid eyes on you, Fergus."

"Nor did I think I'd see you again sporting a court jester's piebald trousers and the little cap of an itinerant traveler. And you've not grown a hair since last we met. Are you indeed a dwarf then, Cael? And have you not heard of the Spartans?"

The commander of the Magyars looked up to the left and scratched his head with the dramatic flair of an actor in some Gaelic saga.

"Ah yes, were they not the squat, swarthy southern tribe of fig-eating, wee men whose sheep were always nervous? Right, the good monks told us about them. And has yourself not heard of the Magyars?"

The big Spartan looked at his erstwhile companion trying to control his own laughter.

"Indeed, Pyrrhus has told many tales of them. But what do yellow-skinned, slant-eyed, savage Pagans, who love their horses more than their wives, have to do with you then Cael?"

Laughing, Cormac said. "I'll leave you two outlanders to catch up. All this heathen talk of Spartans and Magyars leaves a simple

Christian yearning to confess to a good priest. Now then, there is recently plundered Danish ale in sturdy wooden kegs in the tent there beyond."

He pointed to the top of a nearby little hillock where scores of warriors were gathered with foam-topped, brimming tankards amidst singing and laughing.

***

That had been days ago and, of course, both knew the reality of what the other had been accomplished. Though together in Osraige, Wolf kept the Spartans and Magyars separated. The two leaders, despite their requests, hadn't met each other on that campaign. He wanted them to appear as separate and alien, perhaps not Irish. He knew tales of weird warriors from another time and place would appeal to the Irish and play to the superstitions of the Vikings, as long as he could maintain the deception.

Now they all rode together. Though the Spartans were the epitome of heavy infantry, Pyrrhus had insisted their officers were taught to become masterful riders. Fergus sat upon one of those same massive steeds, with enormous chest and flanks that Wolf rode. In fact, Cael secretly thought, excepting *Faolan an Trodach*, Fergus was the biggest man he'd ever seen. He was glad the Spartan from the center of Ireland was on their side. Then he chuckled to himself as he remembered that terrified redhaired boy. He had paled at the thought of the upcoming confrontation with Modolf and the raiders on that small hill on the Dál Fiatach coast.

They rode through the south of Meath, which had borne the brunt of the raids from Leinster and the Dublin Norse months ago. Recognizing the standard of the *Ard Rí,* Cormac insisted on carrying, the local people shouted friendly greetings, and cursed the rebels and the *Gall.*

***

They turned their horses' heads eastward at Tara and then down into the lands that had been so securely held by Sitric's Vikings until they had been thrown back by the king's forces. Now as they moved toward the coast north of Dublin, all was desolate. No Irish people had moved in to recover these good, green lands, and the small homesteads of the previous Norse owners still remained empty. Murcha had not elected to devastate them. They stood perfectly formed, as if the former occupants had simply disappeared.

With no one to oppose them, the small band of the High King's senior officers, now transformed to scouts, came to a grand forest along the coast. This was called Tomar's Wood and it extended below the high ground to its north, and west almost to the rocky coast where it met the long, tear-shaped peninsula of Howth.

Leisurely riding along the shore, they noted a narrow gap which allowed carts and people access through the neck of the peninsula to the widening lands beyond. The forest was thick and tall on the other side. They took the path and gazed south toward Dublin along the coastline. The path opened there into a wide expanse of beach which gradually turned to meadow. All of these leaders on the "Commanders' Ride" studied the terrain and nodded knowingly to each other.

They rode beyond to the few families that lived on the outer end of the narrow neck of land. These constituted their own clan. Six enormous families and one little church, they seemed to consist solely of scores of strapping young boys and numerous pretty girls. The entire clan was thrilled to see the riders from their king enter their small maritime province.

Murcha and Wolf had earlier spoken and were ready for the preparation of their expected battlefield. Cormac called out to a few of the smiling lads.

"Must the clan be connected to the mainland at all times? Would it cause much harm if ye' were to be cut off from the mainland for a bit?"

The answer came with shrieks of hilarity as one of the boys replied, "We have the purest, cleanest water in our sacred wells. Our crops thrive, and much of what we eat comes from the sea. The only reason we ever venture inland is to trade with the neighbors, good Christian and vile heathen alike."

But since the Norse were masters in Dublin, it was sometimes dangerous to visit their relations. Even when the Vikings paid for their wares, the foul-smelling *Gall* seemed an offense to Christiandom.

The western Gaels laughed with appreciation and Cormac announced their request.

"In less than one month's time, the High King will come with thousands of Irish and their good Christian allies. We will throw the *Danar* forever into the sea. Can we now count on ye' to provide a few strong and eager young men to help?"

***

With cheers from the entire clan, it took no time until forty young and enthusiastic men were at the narrow neck with the Irish scouts. Wolf explained they needed to close this small gap. They must gather rocks, logs, branches, bits of straw and bracken. Put driftwood and debris from the sea atop that. The key was to make it look natural. The heavier layers of stone and timber underneath should have coiled lengths of rope attached to allow them to be removed at the exactly right time. The fervent boyos leapt to the task. Cael and the others determined this corridor would allow four horsemen abreast to pour through.

After this pleasant interlude with their countrymen, the party was in high spirits trotting back to the Wood of Tomar. They rode south and crossed the insubstantial Tolka River, noting this was in reality but a trickling stream, easily forded by infantry and cavalry. They were forced to skirt west, as the Dublin Norse had recently started to reoccupy some of their homesteads closer to their stronghold. They observed bands of Vikings north of the Liffey River and kept to the woods and out of sight.

Eventually, they arrived at the Liffey, which was wider and more formidable than the Tolka. They wouldn't cross the one principal choke point immediately across from the walled city. This was called the *Droichead Gall Dubh* — black foreigner bridge. It was wide and sturdy, and they all saw the utility of denying it to the enemy.

Wolf became even more spirited and pleasantly impressed when he observed the skilled and determined intellect of his companions. He loved all of them, but had never been sure any had fully shared his vision. His entire life had been pain, suffering, slaughter and killing. Now he was in his right place among the closest thing to angels God had created — his fellow Gaelic men and women, along with the other Celts he had met in his travels. Abruptly and ironically, his thoughts returned to planning the formidable task of annihilating thousands of the bloody little heathens.

They rode to find a ford across the Liffey where their horses could swim. Once on the other side, they galloped back toward Dublin. The ground became higher. They crested a hill and peered below.

This was a good assembly area for an army to dominate the Viking city. There was water, cover and concealment, and lines of communication from the west. They could see that the Vikings below had also returned to their homes in the adjacent suburbs of the fortress. From this position, the Irish could slice down to strike the Leinster traitors moving up to support their Norse allies.

They all sat comfortably around a little campfire to discuss what their reconnaissance had revealed. To Wolf's pleasure, they came to the same conclusion.

Before setting out, Murcha and Wolf had convinced the king not to join the battle until its eve. Brian had protested, but all his closest family insisted. He was the heart and soul of Ireland. He had always prevailed. He had always been just. Now, his task was to watch his sons, grandsons and extended family drive the foreigners forever from Ireland. He should receive whatever allies came to Munster to assure their welcome. His captains would set the plans to repel the horrendous onslaught all knew was coming.

Aside from Cormac, the members of this small assembly of leaders were all in their twenties. The fact that their aged and beloved king trusted them to plan and prepare the coming battle for the fate of Ireland against hordes of savage Vikings weighed heavily on all of them.

All but Wolf.

He was filled with unbridled joy and confidence. He had no doubt of the final result no matter what the little heathens could throw against them. Enormous shoulders and biceps seemed to swell and shudder with his exuberance, now that some certain harbinger of victory seemed to, once again, envelop him.

"We'll burn everything south and west of Dublin. All those areas Brian told us to leave untouched months ago will now be set in flames all around the walled city. The Leinster traitors will have no way of joining their foreign allies. As the king has already told us, he intends to have his son Donnchad raid there once more with his thousand Munstermen, a third of them cavalry."

Wolf was warming to his battle plan.

"We can clearly see how difficult it is to cross the Liffey. So, after assembling here, the bulk of our armies will cross and take positions in an extended formation just over the little Tolka stream. We can cross that easily and still stay dry above the knees."

The giant war chief now was fully imbued in his martial subject. He went on.

"The masses of Viking hordes will flood the bay of Dublin and the Liffey with more long ships than ever before seen in Ireland. Neither we nor our allies can expect to impede them at sea or by surrounding Dublin. They will supply the city indefinitely from the mouth of the bay. The northern bridge will allow them to come out, but we will contain them there with a well-organized mixture of our own forces."

He nodded to Fergus, who reveled in the anticipation of coming combat.

"No worries, Spartan. After your behemoths slaughter a few hundred of them, even the Vikings will not be so stupid as to not find another way to come at us. You'll then be redeployed to find yourselves where the battle rages fiercest." Wolf smiled in a savage feral manner.

Aoife now took her turn.

"The Norse will do everything to deceive, confuse and outright lie to our forces opposing them. It is my assessment, based on our intelligence reports, and my own experience as 'Viking-slayer' and scholar, they will attempt to come at us from the sea."

She added the last part without boastful pride. Aoife's words were meant to remind her comrades that she too had taken down one of their foes in days past.

Wolf nodded to his "little wolf cub" with admiration and affection. He had already determined in concert with Cormac the beaches along the "Meadow of Bulls," north of Dublin, at a place once called Moynealta, would be exactly where the Vikings tactics demanded they must land.

Aoife unfolded a sheet of vellum and spread it on the grass, taking stylus in hand. She drew in graphic detail a layout of the terrain to the north of Dublin to include its rivers, streams, woodlands and beaches. Later they would use this map to brief the king and the other commanders on how best to deploy the armies of the Celts to meet the invaders.

***

A message had arrived at the High King's court days ago, requesting that Brian provide refuge for a large group of Vikings from the isle of Man. Even in times of shifting alliances, such a petition was unusual. Aoife's intelligence network, however, had already reported on the bitter fallout between the two leading brothers on that island.

They learned from clerical sources that Ospak's wife had converted to Christianity some time back with her husband's blessing. In return for sanctuary, Ospak would bring five hundred well-armed Norse to fight alongside the defenders. In contrast to his royal father, Murcha's natural instinct was to distrust overtures from any of the Vikings, but, in this case, he decided to rely on the assessments of the spies who told him Ospak was an honorable and plain-speaking man, even if he was a leader of the hated Norse.

So now, on a sparkling March morning, Prince Murcha waited with all five hundred of the *laochra* and another half thousand Dalcassian veterans poised along the docks of Limerick. Fourteen dragon-prowed long ships glided in to be met by experienced men of the harbor who secured each of the craft in its own mooring.

The first to ascend the gangplank was a tall blond Viking with an open, honest face, now lit in a broad smile. Murcha was pleased to see he was accompanied not by a bristling guard of warriors, but by a handsome regal woman and a younger girl who might have been their daughter. Behind them came two tall young men who were undoubtedly Ospak's sons.

"God be with you Prince Murcha. I am Ospak of Man and this is my wife, Dagny, and our foster daughter, Cearo. My two sons follow us. Thank you for your hospitality and most courteous greeting upon our arrival."

This was spoken in the Manx Gaelic dialect, which many Vikings living there understood. Some were beginning to adopt it as their primary language. Murcha noted curiously the Saxon origin of the name of the younger woman. He was relieved to see that there were a goodly number of women and children among the Norse, now coming up from their ships. It was unlikely the Vikings would suddenly erupt into raging battle while their wives were at their side with babes on their hips.

"Your presence and your service are most welcome, Ospak of Man. My father, the king, waits with pleasure to receive you at Cashel. It's an easy march from here but we've brought some mounts and carts for you and your family. Will you ride with me?"

The two warriors clasped hands and the unlikely band of Gaels and Norse made their way out of Limerick toward the seat of the Dalcassian king's court.

***

Near the end of March, the entire host of the allied Irish army swept in long columns out of Munster eastward. Leading them were three hundred heavily armored infantry with metallic shields and long deadly thrusting spears. First among these was an enormous red-haired officer with flowing beard. Following directly behind, marched one thousand of the older Dalcassian veterans, most of them had served with Brian since the guerrilla days. A third of these were mounted, with the king's son Donnchad among them. The Dalcassians were followed by five hundred superbly armed Manx Vikings. Ospak had explained that many of these were originally from Iceland, and had already adopted Christianity. The conventional Munster army under a captain named, Mothla O'Faelan, numbered twenty-five hundred common farmers, craftsmen and merchants, now once again become warriors. These marched behind the others at a leisurely pace.

To the north of these columns, moving on parallel course, were two thousand more warriors from Connaught under the chieftain, and long-time ally of King Brian, Teighe O'Kelly. Except for their clan leaders who were experienced and well armored fighters, most of these were similar to the conventional Munster forces — common folk with a simple desire to rid Ireland of the invader and fight alongside their king. Most carried simple hunting spears, with axes and swords wielded by a lucky few. Their only protective armor were their well-woven, woolen tunics, soaked in vinegar to toughen them against sword and arrow.

Marching with this northern contingent was the entire band of five hundred *Laochra an Rí*, Prince Murcha at their lead.

Screening to the front of the two huge columns galloped all two hundred Magyar light cavalry. Almost incredibly, there were four genuine Hungarian Magyars among the eager Irish imposters. These were impressed and delighted to be both mascots and weapon brothers to the wild Gaels who had assumed their tribal name. One hundred of the cavalry was to ride north to meet, and become escort for the two thousand Scots highlanders marching down now from the lands of the Dál Riata. Another hundred were to skirt south to a little bay in friendly southern Leinster, just above Weisfjord, where they would greet a small fleet, transporting five hundred experienced Welsh fighters, many of whom were veterans of *Fingwalle*.

When this entire host finally came together, they would number approximately ten thousand; ninety-five percent of them Celtic. They would be the largest assembled fighting force of Celts in Europe since the ancient days of the continental Gauls.

Chpater Seventeen
Prelude to Battle
April 1014 A.D.

Some of Sitric's people had returned to their homesteads around fortified Dublin, but the main body of warriors and others remained secure behind sturdy walls. Since the Irish armies had lifted their siege last December, Sitric had become more confident. Yet he was still too experienced and wise to push out again. Now that he had summoned them, he knew he could expect thousands of overseas allies, bristling with arms and armor, and thirsting for plunder and blood in just a few short days or weeks.

Early each morning, just as dawn broke and the sun came up gloriously behind him, the Viking king of Dublin would pace the ramparts of the city's packed earthen walls, and gaze to the west, wondering if the *Ard Rí's* forces would return before the fleet of dragon ships sailed into the bay. By early April, the verdant green had returned and the meadows and homes of the surrounding farmers, along with the few small wooden commercial establishments around Dublin, seemed once again peaceful and bucolic. After Gleann Mama and the sacking of Dublin fourteen years before, few native Irish had returned to their former small huts and trading sites around the city. So as more Norse came to Dublin, they simply took over those areas and it was these people, working at early morning tasks, Sitric now looked upon with a rare sense of peace in his heart.

One early morning, just before the sun rose, Sitric was again standing on his pleasant vantage point gazing westward. Curiously, he noticed sparks, then small sprinklings of flashing light among the houses and buildings. A Viking, posted as southern watch, bellowed a piercing call.

"Fires to the south. Much movement."

Sitric heard, and watched in growing horror as the small sparks and lights exploded in size. Every one of the dwellings became quickly engulfed in raging flames, and the hideous screams of their inhabitants were shrill. Silkbeard could now discern dark multitudes of men swarming like a surging tide around and through the suburbs, moving closer to the city walls.

A scream burst from his right. He gaped in shock as his long-time bodyguard, a fierce and powerful warrior from Norway, plucked in vain at an arrow which had come from below to pierce his chin and into his skull. He was limp and dead as he dropped over the walls. More screams along the ramparts.

Sitric then heard thundering hoof beats directly below him. They drowned out the groans of the dying Vikings beyond the gates, and the battle cries of the Gaels who were slaughtering them. Incredibly, hundreds of speeding cavalry were galloping along the walls, loosing scores of arrows at the guards above, who bent and looked down in the morning light at this alien and unexpected sight. The guards were perfectly silhouetted from below by the dawning sun and were easy targets.

Irish riders are few and they definitely don't use bows while in the saddle, thought Sitric. Just then an arrow narrowly passed over his shoulder. He drew back and looked behind him and below. By now the alarm had been sounded. Thousands of his own warriors were rushing to take positions of defense with which they were well familiar. Some were inside the walls and others reinforced the ramparts.

The flying column of riders completed their swift circuit at the base of the enclosed city then swept south, around and behind the burning suburbs below the city. The sun was fully up now, and they would not ride around again with their eyes into the glare. Sitric watched in anguish in the morning's light as these strange warriors rode over and lanced multitudes of fleeing Viking men who were vainly trying to escape to the woodlands. They left behind them scores more of dead and wounded guards on the ramparts, some of whom had been pierced with three or more arrows.

The brilliant sun now shone on many thousands of Irish warriors. They surrounded the entire city south of the Liffey. Sitric had never seen so many Irishmen arrayed as a single force in his life of arduous battle. They had destroyed everything outside the walls. No Viking man remained alive, and he could see streams of wailing Norse women and children being led toward the dark green forests to the west.

He had expected the return of the king. But he had not anticipated so great a force nor such a shock of sudden, swift violence. He cursed now that he had not deployed more outlying watch posts, and that he had seemed so comfortable behind his walls.

Some of the familiar banners of the Dalcassian High King flew over the invading army — the three lions on a field of crimson. They were directly in the center of the Irish host. But the Gaels, just as the Norse, also carried standards. There were artfully crafted, carved figures of boars, stags, blackbirds and hounds mounted on wooden poles. Above all, were crosses and crucifixes, raised high, accompanying each of the three divisions of forces which threatened Dublin. This combination of pagan idolatry and devout Christianity did not seem strange to either Viking or Irishman. The Pope in Rome would have another view entirely.

Now from due west, as the Irish host took defiant positions just out of his archers' range, a small mounted party rode before them. There were five riders. One carried Brian's pennant, and Sitric immediately recognized him as Prince Murcha, the king's son. He had no shield but two swords secured to the wide leather belt at both hips. Directly behind him, on a huge black stallion, trotted an impossibly large warrior with broadsword, Dalcassian axe and metal shield strapped to his back. Incredibly, he wore no armor, but bore upon his head the black lacquered helmet with the pointed wolf's ears of a Viking beserker chief. At his side rode a slight companion who carried yet another standard. This was a spectacularly carved and realistically painted, wooden wolf's head with bright golden eyes.

At first, its bearer appeared to be a young boy, but on closer inspection, Sitric and the onlookers on the ramparts were taken back to see a beautiful raven-haired woman at the behemoth's side. She was mounted on a strong sleek pony of the Connemara breed. Even with the long pole to raise the standard, it still only barely rose to the head of the huge rider. From a distance it appeared two wolves were ranging alongside each other.

Following this unlikely pair came two more riders. One sat astride the same proud type of tough, little mount as the woman. He was short and robustly built with dark skin and deep black rings of curls on his head and ample beard. Like his companion beside him, he was smiling broadly. He carried a strange triangular pennant with double-headed black eagle on a yellow background. A few cries erupted from some of the well-traveled Norsemen who stood on the earthen walls.

"The sign of the Emperor of the Byzantines. Are the Greeks now marching with the Irish?"

Beside the Greek, rode an armored warrior, helmet doffed, and attired in the familiar panoply of the *Laochra an Rí,* which the Vikings recognized as the High King's elite guard. He also carried a standard on a wooden staff. It was the carved head of a white seal of the sea. Several small pennants adorned the pole beneath the seal. Each bore runes and symbols not found among the Irish. More cries came now from Vikings who had come from the Hebrides.

"Those are old Pictish words, and seals are sacred to the Picts. That one has the face and form of a Pict as well.

"I thought we killed all the Picts?" yelled another Norseman.

The detachment of five riders now came to the center of the Irish formation and turned from the Norse to face their own army. None on the walls could make out their words but all could first see, then hear, then feel the thunderous response.

Thousands upon thousands of deep voices resonated in the ancient Gaelic battle cry. It almost seemed to shake the earthen walls and timber logs of the city.

"ABOO. ABOO. ABOOOOOO."

***

The Irish forces took up static positions surrounding the city, south of the Liffey. They deployed a small force of cavalry, carrying the purple and white colors of Connaught, and a larger force of infantry from the same province, to cross the river to the north and torch any dwellings there. The local inhabitants, having seen what transpired among their neighbors to the south, fled across the *Droichead Dubh Gall* into the city days ago. Surprisingly, the Connaughtmen left some of the larger storage buildings intact while other Norse structures were burnt to the ground.

At this point, the city was isolated but for its corridor to the sea. This secure approach to Dublin was expected by all within to be its salvation.

As each day brought more and more of the fierce dragon-prowed long ships of various types into the docks of the small city, morale rose, and the Norse warriors grew confident once more. Along with the familiar sleek *snekkjas*, there were larger and more powerful *busse* and *skeide* warships, and a number of huge lumbering, cargo-bearing *knarrs*. Men on the docks unloaded armor, weapons, horses and foodstuffs along with barrels of mead, ale and wine.

By now there were several hundred ships of various types in the harbor and the bay. One morning, forty long ships departed the city and sailed southward. Sitric had communicated with his uncle, the King Maelmora. They had decided to bring the Leinster forces in by sea to avoid forcing them to clash with the Irish around the city. The Dublin leader was disgusted that Maelmora was only able to persuade about one thousand Leinstermen to join in battle against Brian. He knew now for sure he could only really trust his fellow Vikings. The king of Leinster had failed to enlist any of the Irish leaders in the north to rally to his cause.

As the long ships sailed south with their skeleton crews to meet their waiting passengers down the coast, a separate formation of Irish warriors moved in disciplined ranks from the Irish encampment to the south. They could be clearly observed by the Vikings on the walls and Sitric had no doubt that was exactly what was intended.

They were led by Donnchad, another son of King Brian, at the head of almost three hundred mixed cavalry with seven hundred common infantry warriors marching behind. Above them flew the Dalcassian pendant along with banners representing various Munster and Connaught family clans. Pipes, flutes and drums accompanied them and added a stirring percussion to the martial tramp of hooves and boots, and the clinking of armor, leather and weaponry on the move.

Sitric knew they were striking south to once again plunder Leinster, but he had outsmarted them. Maelmora's army would be aboard ships and coming up to Dublin before Donnchad could close with them. He smiled and made his way down to the docks. Lookouts had spotted an enormous fleet of ships on the horizon approaching Dublin bay. He was sure it would be Thorkell the Tall leading thousands of fervently devout, Odin-worshipping Jomsvikings. He wanted to be the first to greet them.

***

The first day of the second full week of April 1014 saw even more Viking ships arriving to join their allies at Dublin. By now the docks were filled, and the ships had to anchor in the harbor. Smaller boats were used to transport men and arms into the city. Those in the Danelaw had never forgotten their losses to the Irish at *Fingwalle*. Now, Anrud, Danish Prince and nephew of Sveyn Forkbeard, the recently deceased Danish king, arrived with one thousand Danish Vikings from England. All were battle-proven veterans of successful campaigns against Saxons and Welsh. Every one of them burned for revenge against the upstart Irish.

Maelmora's Leinster army had already disembarked from the ships Sitric sent. The Dublin king noted most of these were stern-faced. They were primarily rebel leaders and their liegemen, whose homes and property had been looted and destroyed during Murcha's raid through the province the previous autumn. They had nothing more to lose, and as local chieftains and professional warriors, most were well armed and armored, unlike the common Irish soldiers they would face in combat.

Near the end of that week, the five-hundred Saxon pagans, who had been enlisted and supported by Sitric much earlier, arrived along with two thousand of their Hebrides allies under Thorwald Raven. Thorwald was pleased to find Anrud, the nephew of his brother in law, and both toasted King Sveyn, who was surely now battling with pleasure in Valhalla.

The total number of warriors in the city, including Sitric's Dublin Norse, was just under ten thousand men. They didn't yet know it, but they already outnumbered the Irish surrounding them. And the Dublin king knew that Sigurd the Stout and Brodir of Man had yet to arrive. They would bring with them close to four thousand axe-wielding, chain-mailed fighters from all over northern Europe. Silkbeard also remembered with glee, both Sigurd and Brodir relied on a few hundred savage beserkers to even further motivate their warriors.

***

During that second week in April, Murcha was pleased to welcome the Scots highlanders and the Welsh warriors to the Irish encampment. There was much joviality when Domnall, Murcha, and Wolf met again. And Wolf was highly gratified to see the Welsh were led by a strong young warrior named Griffen. This was the same man who grasped his shoulder at the Welsh king's court, and had given thanks for his liberation from the Danes at *Fingwalle*. Now the hard-muscled fighter from Wales was eagerly prepared to prove his appreciation, and take blood revenge on the pagan Norse as well.

The arrival of the Scots and Welsh took place out of sight of the Viking watchers on the ramparts. Sitric now knew he could not long hold back the bristling array of seething Danes, Saxons, Jomvikings and plunderers from the Hebrides. They would insist on bursting out of the city gates and plunging in to clash with the surrounding Irish forces.

The Dublin king called for a war council one night near the end of that second April week. Around his feasting table sat Thorkell the Tall, King Maelmora, Eorl, leader of the Saxons, Prince Anrud of the Danes, and Thorwald Raven. Sitric looked each in the eye and said, "I remind my cousins and brothers even more reinforcements are on the way. We will soon have irresistible strength, the likes of which have never been seen in Ireland."

The leaders understood this, but they chafed at the fact they were sitting like women behind sturdy walls, while the Irish taunted them from outside. They discussed various options for breaking out and striking the enemy. The three gates south of the city would allow them to pour out from multiple points, but each of these was narrow and angled, allowing only three men abreast. The largest gate opened onto the bridge over the Liffey. This would enable men to form lines of eight across. And it would allow a wedge of mailed warriors to storm across in numbers with sufficient width and depth. They would also initially be secure at their flanks if they struck from there.

"The enemy appears to be sparsest to the north just across that bridge, with only a few score cavalry and several hundred common warriors," said Thorkell, disdain in his voice. "My Joms could deploy in good numbers across that broad and sturdy bridge and annihilate them with little effort before they could be supported by the others."

For days, they all observed the Irish there, lounging amidst the smoldering ruins of the dwellings. Some had the audacity to set fishing lines along the river and lay with their feet up, basking in the sun. The Viking leaders reasoned the several large commercial storage buildings had been spared to provide the Irish shelter at night from the cool spring rains.

"Tomorrow, with Odin's blessing, I intend to cross that bridge and destroy the revelry of those bead-praying Gaels. Then we will march in strength along the beaches to the north and establish a beachhead to welcome Sigurd and Brodir."

The Jomviking leader's passion and confidence were catching. All around the table, they howled in boisterous support and drank deeply of the sweet honey mead.

***

At dusk the next morning, Dublin's river gate creaked almost eerily for the first time in weeks. The Gaels from Connaught, posted across the river, heard the tramp of armed men before the wood and iron portal was fully opened. The dawning sun glistened off the polished mail of the massed formation of axe-wielding Jomsvikings. They strode in precision movement, seven across, in an impressively stolid and intimidating phalanx.

As they approached the south side of the bridge, the Connaughtmen, their Chieftain Teighe O'Kelly at their lead, formed into their own wall of shields in the middle of the bridge. There were about two hundred of them clasping wooden shields with metal bosses. Some had swords and axes, but most carried simple hunting spears. Their small escort of mounted companions formed up on both flanks on the northern sides of the bridge. Few had anything for armor except their vinegar soaked woolen tunics. They braced themselves to meet the onslaught of the Baltic monsters. Teighe stood before them and made the sign of the cross. They all repeated the same familiar small ritual. Then he turned to the enemy once again and took his place in line.

As the Norse cultists stepped onto the bridge, the Irish could barely believe they were witnessing a human foe. All were armored from head to mid-thigh with sturdily built, interlocked shields and enormous axes. They came on in silence, the only sound the heavy tramp of their booted feet on the wide, thick planks of the bridge. Just as the onslaught came to spear length distance from the Irish, there erupted a thunderous growl, and the Jomvikings threw themselves against the shields of the Gaels.

The massive axes arced down in deadly blows which sundered the wooden shields of their foes. They moved relentlessly forward. Scores of the Connaughtmen fell, splattering froths of crimson showering their comrades. There occurred the occasional lucky thrust which found an opening beneath a Viking helmet or in thigh or calf, but there seemed no stopping the onrush of iron and muscle from the southern shore of the Baltic Sea. Teighe, had been the focus of the Joms' ferocious assault. He had been rendered unconscious by the simultaneous blows of two Viking axes striking against his shield and helmet. His countrymen quickly retrieved him and passed him through the lines to the safety of the rear, where he was taken up by attendants, and surrounded by his loyal Irish hounds.

Abruptly, a Celtic flute twilled with a shrieking, piercing note.

With a quarter of their fellows down, the remaining Connaughtmen, turned and fled back across the bridge, passing around to both sides. The Jomsvikings paused and tightened their own formation, preparing to surge forward again.

In an instant, still on their own side of the bridge, the Joms suddenly gazed awestruck upon a vision none had ever imagined. Such a thing had not been witnessed anywhere in Europe from the earliest Roman times. Instead of the woolen tunics, wooden shields and uncovered heads of the majority of the Irish warriors they had just forced back, they now gaped, through their helmet's visors, at a steel juggernaut which rivaled or exceeded their own formation in ferocious appearance.

Iron-strapped helmets with nose guards and skirts covered the new enemy's heads. They wore mailed armor falling to their knees. Their shields were swagged across the top with metal and chain. None wielded sword or axe. All clutched robustly built stabbing spears, with long, triangular steel blades. Over their armor, they wore flowing scarlet cloaks, which covered their shoulders and backs. All of these spearmen were huge. Their bulk seemed even more pronounced by the armor and red robes. At their center, in the lead, was the most enormous of all. Long red hair spilled below his helmet.

His thick beard fell to the top of his massive chest. None of the Jomsvikings had ever witnessed such a formidable and impressive enemy formation.

But the Joms were zealots to their gods and battle-hardened veterans. Once again, they moved forward silently until the inevitable roar and lunge at the new foe.

Fergus and his Spartans had trained for years exactly for this. To this challenge, their young lives had been dedicated. There was no need to give conscious thought on how to react. They braced and dug in their heels, each rank wedged so close against the one before it, the entire formation seemed one immovable bulwark, not three hundred individual warriors. The first line carried their spears underhand to thrust upward at unprotected thigh or calf. Their massive shields were held directly in front to bear the brunt of encroaching muscle and steel. The second rank raised their shields to protect the heads of those before them and their own. These wielded their spears over their shoulders as did those behind them, to thrust and advance, thrust and advance.

The Spartans met the Jomsviking assault like a stone-solid, unyielding wall, powered by arduously trained, muscular thighs and shoulders, behind impenetrable steel. As expected, the huge axe heads crashed down onto the iron defense. To the astonishment of the Norse, none penetrated. Instead, spear thrusts flashed up to stab into throat, chin, thigh, and under the armored skirts, driving into groin and gut. The first line of Vikings went down in bloody confusion. As the second reacted to the spears thrusting up by trying to lower their shields and swing the unwieldy axes in awkward underhand strokes, their faces, necks and eyes became vulnerable. The Spartans in the second and third ranks had spent months practicing to precisely stab their killing spears into small openings around helmet and mail. These ranks now slaughtered scores of onrushing Vikings who could not see what was happening at their front as their comrades fell to the ground or were pushed off the bridge by the melee.

After what seemed like hours but had only been minutes, the Jomsvikings pulled back toward the gate. Behind them they left almost two hundred dead. To their disgust, they watched as the red-robed demons lifted and threw the mangled bodies of their comrades into the river to clear the battlespace on the bridge.

Fergus was splattered with blood. The drenching fluid seemed not so prominent given the red cloaks they decided to adopt after Pyrrhus told them the Spartans of old adorned themselves in crimson. He was pleased to see there were fewer than ten casualties among his warriors, and most of these had been knocked cold from the impact of axe blows on shield or helmet.

For days, the Spartans had concealed themselves in the large warehouses in readiness for such a sally across the Liffey Bridge. Fergus most highly respected the small band of Connaught warriors who had volunteered to lure out the Vikings and take the first blows. Many of the now martyred men from the west had become his friends. He now readjusted the ranks and brought the freshest Spartans from the rear to the front. He took his place at their lead and in the center, awaiting the next advance of the enemy.

The Viking leaders observed all of this from the high walls along the river with disbelief. Thorkell had been the first to be slain by the giant with the red hair. The Jomsviking leader's body was now settling into the mud at the bottom of the Liffey, along with hundreds of his men.

The Joms came again three times over the day — hour after hour of butchery. By now the Connaughtmen were adding to the confusion by slinging stones from both flanks as the Spartans slaughtered the armored ranks from the eastern seas. Only as evening approached did the attacks cease. The survivors withdrew into the gate which was again closed. They had left behind almost seven hundred of their members, all of whom were now in watery graves. Those who remained alive cursed that they had not been able to maneuver on the confines of the bridge, not comprehending the irony that the historic strength of the Norse was that that their quickly moving shield walls did not let their enemies maneuver against them.

The Spartans had a score killed, all sorely grieved over. Another score were sent back to be treated for wounds. But they still numbered over two hundred and fifty confident warriors. Fergus did not expect the enemy to come again, and on this side of the bridge they were well out of the range of missiles from the city.

He had counted the enemy dead…seven hundred against twenty. The young Spartan captain from the center of Ireland was eager now to lay eyes once more on Wolf and, especially, Pyrrhus.

Thermopylae had been truly resurrected on Irish soil.

***

On the brilliantly warm, glistening and pleasant afternoon of Palm Sunday, 1014, another small group of Celtic riders rode north across the Liffey, along the high ground until they reached the edge of the Tomar Wood. Since the day of the battle at the *Dubh Gall* Bridge, Dublin's river gate had not opened. Murcha had ordered the Spartans and Connaught warriors to join the main army, leaving the lands north of Dublin empty, enticingly attractive for the Vikings to strike out across the bridge yet again.

They refused to take the bait. The Liffey's waters had run red for two days with the blood of hundreds of spear-sundered Jomsvikings. Now it ran clear again. No doubt, the heavy, perfectly formed chain mail of the Norse settled deeply into the mud, burying the wearers in fine Irish mire.

***

Murcha, Cormac, Ospak of Man, Domnall, Griffen, Mothla, and a bruised but still formidable, Teighe O'Kelly sat around a senior leaders' council fire back at the main encampment, trying to decide the next step and when they should summon the king.

It was a much more youthful and vivaciously exuberant band of equally important leaders who conducted a joy-filled ride on that glorious day. Faolan an Trodach, War Chief of all Ireland; Aoife, holder of best intelligence on the pagan enemy; Fergus of the

Spartans; Cael of the Magyars, and Mornak, the Pict, officer of King Brian's royal guard, the *Laochra an Rí*, sped across the green turf, riding toward the tallest copse of trees on the highest hill. At twenty-eight years, Wolf was their elder. His companions were in their early twenties. To these, the High King had entrusted much. The fate of Ireland and Christiandom was in their hands, as their comrades now gathered around fires in the rear.

The hard-riding band finally reached a singularly tall coniferous tree, towering over its neighbors. Standing at its base was a raven-haired young man, dressed in the unique garb of the Irish Magyars. Two muscular Connemara ponies munched contentedly on the grass a short distance from the big pine.

A round stone suddenly fell from the tree, only inches from the Magyar. It was covered with a piece of vellum parchment.

"He's now almost brained me three times with these damned rocks."

Eoin, Aoife's younger brother, peered up at the visitors with a mischievous smile and bent to pick up the message laden rock.

Reading the words impressed on the parchment, he looked up again, his face no longer so jovial.

"Sails. A hundred or more. He says they cover the sea. All of them *Gall*."

The riders nodded. They all knew this was to be anticipated. Young Eoin had not been fully informed of what they knew would come.

The riders gazed upwards at the tree as they detected a swift, scurrying movement in the branches. There were no red squirrels in Ireland so large to make such a commotion.

From somewhere above, a dark, powerful figure dropped unceremoniously to the ground.

"Well, it's a good *Peine Albanach* — Scottish Pine — so I felt quite at home up there," said the young man. He rose gracefully and grinned at the newcomers.

All but Aoife and Cael were astounded to look down upon the now legendary dark demon of Scottish and Norse nightmares.

Partha Brule, the former scourge of all Britannia, was now a healthy and robust warrior, seventeen years old, and dressed as a proper Scots highlander.

Mornak leapt from his warhorse and wrapped his new brother in his arms. Wolf beamed with approval and admiration at this addition to their host of warriors.

The huge red-haired Spartan now called down, "Mornak, is that yet another barbarous Pict who joins our ranks?"

"He's slain bigger men than you, you greasy Greek." Mornak retorted with gleeful certainty, fully aware Fergus was a Celt from the isles, as were they all.

The Spartan retorted, "Well, at least this one is not as bloody ugly as you."

For a moment, Mornak the beautiful, was dismayed, then he remembered who spewed that vile insult.

"The bottom of Wolf's boot is more handsome than you are, you great florid ape."

Pyrrhus had explained to all of the leaders except Wolf what an ape was, so the Irish giant could only shake his head, perplexed yet again. Aoife and the others burst into laughter.

Now serious once more, Wolf, green eyes flashing grimly, called the revelry to a halt.

"The ships are those of Sigurd the Stout and Brodir of Man. They'll be arriving in Dublin tonight with almost four thousand blood lusting little heathens who want to murder us all. We must ride back and prepare a fine Gaelic *Cead Mile Fáilte* for them."

Filled with the ebullience of youth and joy at being among their own blood, imbued with the passion of an avenging mission, and blessed by the good white Christ, the young riders all bellowed a fierce cry and galloped across the turf to the cadence of thunderous hoof beats toward the encampment of their main army.

***

There now seemed so many ships in Dublin bay, one could walk across the entire harbor without wetting a foot. Smaller boats ferried the Vikings of the isles to the docks of the city. Despite the fact that the fortress town was now packed with almost thirteen thousand warriors, along with women and children, there was no lack of provisions. Vast quantities of ale, mead, dried and salted fish and meats, and bushels of wheat and spring vegetables had been delivered over the weeks. Those fighters, who could not find a roof to sleep under, had no problem camping in the open courtyards and training fields in the pleasant mid-April weather.

Sigurd and Brodir met with the leaders of the pan-Viking alliance and were provided a detailed situation report of the events of the last several weeks. Brodir was incensed to hear of the debacle on the bridge, the death of Thorkell the Tall, and the routing of the Baltic Odinists. He refused to believe the description of huge, heavily armored, spear wielding infantrymen in scarlet cloaks.

"I never had any confidence in the mongrelized Jomsvikings anyway. Too many damned Wends, Slavs and Turks pretending to be good Northmen."

Brodir spat this last with palpable venom in his growling voice.

The native Dane, who had taken over command of the remaining Joms, thought briefly of unsheathing his sword and launching himself at the Manxman. But he mentally measured the monstrous figure before him, and, having heard the stories of his invincibility, simply replied, "You'll see before the week is out how Jomsvikings slay like no others, and you will rue your insulting words of this day."

Brodir merely grunted and the conversation turned again to the upcoming plans.

***

In the Irish camp, which was due west and out of sight of the walls of Dublin, Wolf had finally been informed of the arrival and alliance of Opsak and the five hundred Vikings from Man and Iceland. Murcha and Cormac sat alone with him in a small leather tent, expecting an explosive eruption of protest from the Norse-hating giant. They told him all of these newly arrived allies were either born into Christianity or had taken baptism since coming to Limerick, and that their leader was an honest man who was kind to all who knew him. Many had come with their wives and children, and all had severed any connections with other heathen Vikings.

The Prince and his cousin held their breath, anticipating a raging firestorm.

"Well, let's make sure we keep them away from Blamec Mac Goll's slashing hounds. Those great and beautiful Irish beasts very much despise the bloody little heathens."

With that, Wolf bowed slightly and took leave of his friends and comrades. Murcha and Cormac watched as he had to stoop to exit the tent, and looked to each other in relief and bewilderment. The "good boy" never failed to amaze either of them.

***

After making his way out of the tent and ruminating on news of Vikings in their midst, Wolf had to clear his mind of distractions and stay focused on the days ahead. He would simply not think of Ospak and his men. He would avoid them if possible. His intent was to close with and crush as many of the Norse as his sword, axe, shield and flashing studded ball of iron could smite. Hate and vengeance would abide no accommodation, no nuance. He had tolerated King Brian's arrangements with the various Viking vassal towns, but had never taken part in any dealings with them. A clear vision of raging combat sweeping over the battlefield; ripping, stabbing, thrusting and slashing; drenching the lush Irish soil with the gushing red blood of the invading *Gall*. Just visualizing this image filled the massive Irishman with a savage satisfaction.

Looking up, he noticed Aoife smiling and walking purposefully toward him. She was now twenty-one, confident and beautiful, with the same ivory skin, raven hair and wee button of a nose. When she grinned at him, as she did now, he could still see the little girl he tied to a cart years ago. His pleasant brutish fantasies of slaying

Northmen dissipated for the moment, and he could not help smiling back at her.

She took his huge hand in her small one and urged him to follow. He had already been told Mac Goll had arrived with ten companies of well-trained, fierce Irish hounds. Each unit of ten, was led by a mounted Irish officer who had been schooled by Blamec himself.

They walked a good distance into the wood, until they arrived at a pleasant green clearing which was bisected by a small, fast-flowing, bubbling stream. Wolf was beguiled to see one hundred of the powerful, sleek war hounds, lounging in little circles around a human leader, who sat in their midst. It was almost as if there were ten little independent clans, come together for a happy reunion in the field. Some were lapping from the rivulet's clear pools and a few were chasing each other in play. Most were simply splayed on the grass and sleeping contentedly, which Wolf was told was the normal state of nature for these beautiful, loyal creatures.

As they approached, several of the large, sleek hounds stood up and walked toward the couple, shaking their long, swishing tails in sweeping arcs.

"They certainly don't look like savage killers, do they now?" Wolf said as he bent to stroke the flanks of the two around him.

"You'll see just how sweet they are when we get orders to set them on the *Gall*, Captain," said a leader of this particular clan of hounds. The young man's Connemara accent could not be missed as he gave the couple a beaming grin.

Wolf immediately liked this pack leader. He had to admire his audacity and confidence in himself and his canine charges. And then, all ten of the men, eager to lay eyes on and meet in person their still mysterious chieftain, made their way toward Wolf and Aoife. Many of the hounds loped alongside them.

The couple was amused to note the incongruity of the experience. It was as if they were surrounded by a hundred fierce approaching beasts with slashing teeth and powerful muscles. Yet the reality was a grand show of genuine affection. The hounds came in all wiry-haired hues — red and gray brindle, blond wheaten, deep red, and some with coats as black as Aoife's dark mane. Two dogs were pure white. Blamec never took to the superstition about albino animals or men. All of them were God's creatures and he had personally trained these two.

In the splendid company of these eager young warriors, Aoife and the hundred spectacular hounds with their expression-filled eyes, Wolf completely forgot Ospak's Norse foreigners assembled elsewhere in his camp.

***

Back near the large command tent where Murcha, Cormac, Teighe, Pyrrhus and the other senior leaders were making the final decision to send for King Brian and receive King Malachi and his army, Cael took the opportunity to re-introduce Fergus to Luta. He described her as the "Chief of Logistics" for the Magyars.

Fergus held back his grin, seeing clearly through the ruse. The Danish girl may help with provisions and cooking, but the redhead knew Cael had been smitten with her since that first day on the beach years ago. He was a bit jealous to see the genuine, shimmering affection the two held for each other. Luta had bright golden hair and was nearly as tall as her Irish lover. She spoke perfect Gaelic now, and wore a Celtic cross upon a delicate silver chain around her ivory, swan-like throat.

She exuded a magnetic personality and it was impossible not to like her. Fergus wished they had captured two Viking wenches that day long ago. The conversation turned to the battle at the Liffey Bridge. No longer merely a secretive rumor, Fergus and his Spartans were now renowned heroes, held in esteem by the entire Irish army. Even the common warriors, essentially farmers with hunting spears, felt a new confidence in themselves and their simple wood-shafted thrusting weapons.

Luta had heard of the Jomsvikings and had no sympathy for them. She knew they despised and sought to slaughter those of the Norse, who, like herself, had converted to become Christians.

249

Cael remonstrated that his Magyars had feathered scores of Norse watchmen with their deadly arrows on the Dublin walls during that first surprise attack.

"But it was not seven hundred." replied Fergus, with the brimming pride of a newly-blooded young leader. Then he slapped his friend on the back and winked at Luta.

"No worries, Cael, I'm sure you'll have a chance to catch up in the days to come."

Luta made the sign of the cross and looked disapprovingly at the two as they seemed to joke about killing and death. But she was also dreadfully concerned about the fate of all of those she had now come to love.

Chapter Eighteen
Cath Chluain Tarbh
Battle of Clontarf
Easter Week 1014 A.D.

By the early morning of Easter Thursday, most of the allied Celtic armies had made their way out of their encampment west of the city. They crossed the Liffey and the Tolka to move into assembly areas in the high ground and Tomar woodlands which looked down on the beaches of Dublin bay. They had marched well out of sight of the lookouts on the Dublin walls, and had left behind a token force to keep the campfires lit and conduct the occasional display for the city's guards. The Vikings posted there could only look out upon the ruins of homes, buildings and fields surrounding Dublin on all sides. Some still smoked, and, to their disgust, they could see the bodies of Vikings caught outside the gate putrefying in the sun. Since these were assumed to be pagans, the Irish had not seen fit to give them a Christian burial.

At mid-afternoon, Irish watchmen arrayed along high, concealed vantage points noted scores of small boats ferrying men out to the hundreds of ships in the bay. Larger long ships were also departing from the Dublin docks close to the city. Mounted scouts sped back to report these events to the leaders, who were in the rear with the main armies. By the time the senior officers arrived to gaze out into the bay, many of the dragon ships were well underway, sailing westward.

Wolf, Cormac and Murcha watched as almost the entire fleet set sail. The Norse demons manned the rowing benches in an apparent mass withdrawal from Irish waters to return to whatever hell holes they had come from. Aoife gave some final orders to the officer in charge of the scouts and lookouts, and the entire band of Celtic leaders, with the Viking Ospak among them, turned back to greet King Brian and Malachi Mór, who were expected to arrive in the early evening.

**

Sitric, Brodir, Sigurd, Thorwald and the others had decided on their plan of action just one day earlier. Their advantage lay in their ability to form their huge army in massed lines along a wide front, not in sallying out piecemeal from apertures in the city walls. Brodir was obnoxious, complaining to Sitric that the perimeter outside the city should have been secured before the arrival of the Norse allies. The Dublin king merely nodded in agreement, content for now to let the Manx leader howl and bellow, as long as he and his killers would later play their parts against the Irish.

They would attempt to deceive the Irish into thinking the overseas Vikings were returning to their Isles. Or maybe the Celts would believe the Norse were simply setting off to find a softer target elsewhere. They would sail out in the afternoon. During the night they would come about to storm ashore along the beaches north of the city in early morning. Even if the Celts detected them returning, they would have to leave their encampment and attempt to deploy their forces over the two rivers to meet the landing. By then, the Vikings would have been ashore, securely deployed in battle formation, and on the move to crush any resistance.

Sitric would keep one thousand warriors in the city to support when needed, but two thousand more Dublin Norsemen, and Maelmora's army of one thousand from Leinster would also be aboard those ships.

**

This time Murcha did not curse when King Malachi came with a force of only one thousand men. Meath had still not recovered from the depredations of Sitric's and Maelmora's invasion the previous autumn. King Brian, now seventy four years old, had arrived with but a few retainers. He greeted Malachi warmly in the large leather tent, which had been set up for the leaders to conduct their council.

There was no feigned emotion between the two old Irish kings. They had come to know and respect each other over the years, and those feelings had blossomed into true affection and friendship.

King Brian was also delighted to meet in person Prince Domnall the Highlander, and Griffen, the leader of the Welsh allies. These two gazed upon the aging, but still tall and nobly erect, King of Ireland with awe and admiration. No single Celtic leader had ever defeated the Norsemen so often and so decisively as the Dalcassian lord. His long hair and beard were silver yet still flecked with crimson streaks, and he carried a huge broadsword on his belted hip with authority. His eyes sparkled with youthful mirth, and his wide smile made the Scot and Welshman feel as though they were his kin.

The council gathered around a large map stretched out on a great wooden table. The map had been drawn by Irish monks who specialized in terrain manuscripts. It featured Dublin and all the adjacent lands to the north and to the sea. The fields and beaches of Clontarf were at its center. Aoife's spies had confirmed what military logic had already dictated. The Vikings were not leaving. They would be back at dawn and bring their ships to the beaches where thousands could come ashore, hoping to surprise and flank the Celtic armies.

Most at the table argued they should be engaged at their weakest point, as they struggled from the surf onto the sand. The massed Celts could then slaughter them more easily there.

"If we did that, they would certainly just turn their ships to the sea once again, and we would have to go through this all over again. This issue must be drawn to its final conclusion now. This is the time for us to annihilate them all, to purge Christiandom of this vile heathen scourge forever."

All eyes turned to the speaker of these words. Wolf looked to Brian and Murcha with an expression that signaled "with your permission?" Both nodded for him to continue.

"We will emerge in formation from the high ground and forest, moving down through the fields and beaches. There will be three divisions and a reserve. On our left flank, Domnall and Griffen will position their much appreciated and welcomed warriors. Behind them, in a position to maneuver at my command, will be the Spartans and Magyars, with Blamec's war hounds behind them."

All except Ospak smiled at that. The hounds had thankfully appeared to hold the Scots and Welsh in as much affection as they did the Irish. Only Ospak's Norsemen had not yet laid eyes on the *Cúnna an Cogaidh*, and that was by design.

"Mothla and the main body of Munster will be deployed in the center, with the Dalcassian veterans at their front. Behind them will be the *laochra*, prepared to move out at my command. On our right flank Teighe and our trusted weapon brothers from Connaught will take the field. At their front, due to their superb fighting abilities and excellent armor and arms, will be Ospak's men."

Cormac gave a cautious but not unkind look to Ospak. He and Wolf had already spoken to Teighe O'Kelly. The Connaught chieftain had been ordered to be prepared to butcher the Manxmen and Icelanders from behind at the slightest hint of treachery.

"King Malachi and his Meath warriors will take the high ground behind our right flank as the army's reserve, to cover the bridge and river crossings and be prepared to assist if required. We will allow the enemy to land unmolested and form ranks. Before they have completely finished, we will emerge from the hills and woods, and take positions across from them. Then we will close and cut them down like fields of ripe wheat. We will drive them into the sea, and they will sink into the blood drenched waves. They have never given us quarter, and they know that at this point our only goal is to kill them all. Those, my friends and brothers, are the field orders for this holy day, Good Friday. Please let us know now if there are better ways."

The giant leader looked each earnestly in the eye, encouraging any honest alternatives or ideas. None came. Instead, these seasoned warrior leaders pounded the table with the pommels of their *scians* in hearty approval. Aoife, the only woman around that table, gazed at her heart's love with moist eyes full of pride and emotion. Then, she too loudly banged her deadly *scian* on the wooden surface. Murcha and King Brian looked to each other, and nodded in satisfaction.

***

Even before the first hint of sunrise, lookouts posted in the tall trees, Partha Brule among them, observed the return of the Viking fleet. The Norse had attempted to maintain strict light discipline and for the most part succeeded. But here and there, wisps of flickering flame from small stone lamps on the decks of the long ships, provided a barely visible contrast to the darkness of sea and sky. The eagle-eyed young watchers, from their perches high in the pine branches, dropped signal wrapped stones to the ground. All contained the same message. The Vikings were returning.

Dawn's light was just rising as the ships hit the beaches, and the fierce occupants leapt out amidst raucous commands from their leaders to form ranks. They drew the ships up onto the sand and then rushed to join the massed formations. As the last of the fleet's ships came ashore, their leaders were pleased. It seemed their ruse had worked. They were able to form into three cohesive divisions unmolested by defenders.

On their right, Brodir, his bodyguard of beserkers, and his veteran Manx pillagers took positions, Anrud's Danes and the five hundred Wotan-worshipping Saxons directly behind them. At the beach's center King Maelmora and his Leinster traitors were arrayed alongside his nephew's two thousand Dublin Vikings. Silkbeard, himself, had decided to stay inside the walls of Dublin. Behind these were the survivors of the Jomsvikings, still a large and formidable band. On their left, the two armies of the Vikings of the isles, under Thorwald and Sigurd the Stout, joined to form the numerically largest of the three Norse divisions — five thousand well armored killing machines.

Just as the ranks were closing, and before the marching orders could be called, the piercing wail of hundreds of Celtic pipes, accompanied by the percussion of deep-timbered oversized *bodhrán* drums, crashed down from the higher ground inland, assailing the ears of the Vikings. From the forests' edges and behind the hills to the south, thousands of enemy warriors marched down toward them in well-formed ranks. There were three divisions roughly confronting the Vikings' own formations.

The sun was fully up now, high over the sea behind the Norse, beaming down on King Brian's army which appeared to shimmer in the golden morning light. When they were just beyond archers' range, all three of the oncoming formations halted. The braying of the pipes and clash of drums ceased. The two opposing armies glared at each other. The abrupt silence was now broken only by the familiar cries of sea birds and gentle rise and fall of small waves lapping upon the beaches. The host of eleven thousand Norse fighters and their thousand Leinster allies stood opposite nine thousand warriors who had aligned themselves with the High King of Ireland. Among them, and further back, covering approaches to both rivers and bridges, was the army of Meath. The Viking leaders knew a force of yet another thousand Irish cavalry and infantry was somewhere to the south, led by the king's son, Donnchad. Still another thousand of the Dublin Norse remained with the city's walls.

On the Norse right, Brodir and Anrud, and those around them were astonished to gaze up at the scores of pennants rising above the formation facing down at them. There fluttered the blue and white crosses of the Scots in Alba and the *Y Ddraig Goch* — the crimson dragon symbol of Wales. Beautifully carved seals and badgers, prized as spiritual protectors of Picts since antiquity, were also born aloft on long shafts. Along with these standards were the ubiquitous crosses and crucifixes of Christiandom. The Danes and Saxons could not detect a single Irishman among the twenty-five hundred foes facing them. They looked upon Scots highlanders, standing alongside sturdy Welsh infantry. There was no mistaking the different garb worn by the Celts of Britannia.

In the center Maelmora noted the familiar banners of Munster and the Dalcassians. The renegade Leinster king took the time to point out Prince Murcha, and others of the Dalcassian leadership to the officers of the Dublin Norse and Jomsvikings.

On the Viking left, the greatest surprise and consternation met the stunned gaze of the Vikings of the isles. Thorwald and Sigurd looked up to see Ospak of Man, standing next to a tall Gael who carried the maroon and white banner of Ireland's west, Connaught. Behind these two were massed five hundred superbly armored Norse Manxmen in perfectly disciplined tight ranks. To their rear thousands more wild Gaelic warriors from the far west stood defiantly.

For some reason, there now occurred an unexpected and almost involuntary delay in hostilities, as both sides took time to reflect and prepare for what was to come. Christian clerics with acolytes took positions at intervals in front of the three divisions. They began to celebrate the sacrifice of Holy Mass in the field, and the Vikings looked on as the fierce warriors opposite them, knelt, stood and made signs of the cross at the appropriate times. To the horror and disgust of the Vikings from the Hebrides and Orkneys, Ospak and the Manxmen joined all the others in venerating the Sacrament. A gentle breeze blew from the west and the scent of ritual incense, drifting down to the sea, assailed the nostrils of the Norse.

The hasty Masses were completed, and the clergymen rushed back to the rear of the lines. A hushed silence came over the allied Irish ranks, as a single rider, astride an enormous stallion emerged from the center formation. The steed moved at a stately, almost regal, pace. Its rider was a tall, noble figure with intricate chain mail armor, worn over a pleated linen shirt.

On his head was an ornate, yet robustly functional, gleaming crested helmet. Long silver hair and beard could be seen at a distance. He held a large golden crucifix, affixed to a long wooden shaft in one hand, and a huge shining broadsword, reflecting brilliant rays of sunlight, in the other. The horse responded to the familiar nudges of his knees and muscular calves, with no need for reins. An impressively deep voice called out to them all across the fields.

"My brothers, my sons, my beloved family in mind and heart, as are all of you now. Gaels, Celts and dear Christian allies from Man and Iceland. On this day, our Lord and Savior, suffered and died on a cross for us. His sacrifice was ordained so that we might live in freedom in the light of Christ, with the hope of joy and salvation for all eternity. His bloody execution was ordered by warriors of an invading army, according to their pagan rituals and traditions."

The huge and erect figure thrust his sword backward to point down to the sea, to the beaches and fields there, and to the massed ranks of ferocious armed foemen.

"There stands another invading army. There are pagan hordes who strive to bring darkness and destruction to you and your lands. But you now fight for your God, your families and your people. On this holy day of veneration, I promise you now, whether you perish in the crush of battle or live to see our final victory. All of us Christian warriors and brothers on this field this day, will share eternity with me in God's heaven."

A roaring cheer erupted from thousands of Christian throats, as Brian Mac Cennetigh, High King of Ireland, rode slowly back to disappear into the ranks of Munster once more.

At the rear of the formation, the king met his foster son.

"I have calmed and assured their souls. Now you go out and fire their blood. *Nár lagaí Dia do lámh.* — May God not weaken your hand."

Nár lagaí Dia do lámh.

Now another rider, even taller and more robustly built than the first, burst from the ranks of Munster to take a position in front of the assembled divisions. His was not a slow, regal pace, but a swift, deliberate and controlled canter. Mounted atop an immense chestnut horse, he appeared some dark, avenging giant of the ancients. He wore no armor but a simple green woolen tunic. On his head was a black, lacquered, iron helmet, with the crafted ears of a fierce wolf.

A massive iron shield on his back partially obscured a Dalcassian axe and impossibly large broadsword, strapped and crossed over his huge shoulders.

He trotted his horse in circles to allow as many as possible to see and hear him.

"Weapon brothers. Our king rightly cares for our souls. I appeal now to our fires of righteous rage and revenge, which burn like molten steel in all of you. I don't want you to go into battle with prayers and peace alone in your hearts, but also with the fury of vengeance."

He turned his horse about and gestured toward the Norse lines, his deep voice booming in loud furious curses.

"There are the hosts of the bloody little heathens and their sniveling traitors to the Gael. On this day, we will smash and crush their skulls. Their brains will coat and clog our axes and swords. Our blades will tear their still-beating hearts from their armored breasts. Our flashing spears will rip their bellies and spill their putrid entrails onto the rich Irish turf. They will suffer their own agonies now as just repayment for hundreds of years of pillage and slaughter of Christians."

"My promise to you, my brothers, is this. By day's end, we will crush every one of the foul invading vermin now standing so fiercely before us. Their bodies will litter the fields and beaches. Thousands of them will fall under the arcing blows of our steel. Even the sea will run red with their blood. Their cursed dragon ships will go up in flames."

He violently pulled the reins of his steed and rode much closer to the Viking lines. To the amazement of both sides, he now repeated the exact same fury and doom-filled words of bloody annihilation of the Viking foe. This time in perfect Danish, ferociously directed at the wide-eyed, gaping Norse below.

Galloping back to the Munster lines, Faolan an Trodach, the colossal War Chieftain of the assembled Christian forces, bellowed once more in clear Irish Gaelic.

"It is for us. Here now. We on this field of bulls will win the power and the glory. Not just for us, but for our nations' people. And for the people of our blood in Scotland, Britannia and France. No damned foreign heathen will ever master any Celt anywhere after this day."

***

Amazingly, after this display of threat and defiance, the Norse lines still didn't move to battle. Instead, insults and taunts arose from individuals on both sides. Many recognized hated enemies on the other side. Others just called challenges to individual combat. One chief among Anrud's Danes announced he had lost a father and brother years before at Fingwalle. He sought any of the Welshmen who had been there that day.

Griffen, hearing the challenge, burst from the Welsh ranks and stormed out to meet the Dane. The two came together just in front of the Viking lines, but it ended almost immediately as the Welsh leader deftly stepped under the furiously descending swing of the axe and thrust his sword point in a sideways lunge into and through the Dane's neck, splattering the first blood of the morning on the mixed field of sand and grasses. As Griffen turned and walked back to his lines with a broad smile, a huge blonde giant burst from the ranks with two throwing spears and hurled them toward the Welsh leader's broad back.

Griffen went down without a chance to even face his enemy amidst the outraged curses of the Scots and Welsh. Now the leader of the rogue Saxons ran out to stand beside the body of Griffen and called out.

"Where is Domnall? Is he a coward like all the Scots of the highlands? His people were the enemies of my blood of old, and always shall be forevermore. Come out, you lice-ridden cur. Face me now."

Domnall could not hold himself back and rushed down to meet the challenger. He retained enough wit to stay beyond spear throwing range. He let the Saxon move up to him to a spot equidistant between both armies. This was now sword and shield against sword and shield, almost as if they were two gladiators of ancient Rome. The Saxon was broader and stronger, yet shorter and slower than the tall, rangy Scot. When a feint to the head caused the Saxon to raise his shield too high, Domnall lopped off his leg below the knee. As his opponent fell screaming to the ground, the Scot moved to stand safely above him, and deftly found an opening to thrust his bloody sword point into the Saxon's jaw, stilling his screams forever.

***

Wolf, unaware of any of these events, was in position in the immediate rear with Aoife and four mounted and trusted warriors of the *laochra*, one of whom was Mornak the Pict. His command post was between the main body of the *laochra* and the Spartans and Magyars who had been posted behind the Scottish allies on the extreme Irish flank. From that direction now marched four of the warrior hostages, who had been among a group of fifty in the woods to cover against any attempt at surreptitious assault from that quarter. These four were escorting about twenty weaponless warriors, clad in the Saxon manner.

A young Irishman with an accent of the northern clans, spoke.

"Captain, these are deserters from the Saxons. When they saw the priests holding Mass before the Scots and Welsh, they realized the utter evil of their apostasy. They moved off in groups of two and three to their right, and dashed into the wood. We found them as they fled toward us. None were armed. They ask only for a priest to confess, and to die in righteous combat against the heathen foe."

"Find a priest for them, and deliver them to Prince Murcha and the Dalcassians with my compliments," replied the giant with amusement. The Saxons looked up at him in fear and awe.

King Brian had been persuaded to return to a leather tent in the rear to the north. This came only after his kin assured him his well-chosen leaders would carry the day for Christ and King. At seventy-four, the Dalcassian leader had already fought and won enough

261

battles. Now it was the turn of the younger leaders. Wolf was relieved their beloved king would be out of harm's path as battle grew closer.

New riders galloped in, flying toward the command party. They cried loudly.

"Individual combats are breaking out all over the lines. Champions on both sides are fighting and dying."

Wolf was incensed. He learned that Griffen was dead after slaying a Danish chief. Domnall had killed the leader of the Saxons, and was now engaged in single combat with the monstrous Brodir of Man.

By the time Wolf arrived to the front of the Scots/Welsh line, Domnall was dead at the feet of Brodir. The Scots were screaming that the Manxman had attacked him before he could recover from the fight with the Saxon. Now Wolf could hear Brodir yelling for Murcha the Gael to meet him in combat. Wolf could not allow that.

The command group dismounted. Wolf told Mornak and another to follow as he moved down to the Viking behemoth, who positioned a muddy booted foot on the dead body of the noble Scot. At spear throw distance, Wolf ordered his two companions to hold their ground.

"Take note of this, Mornak. This is not individual combat which I have ordered forbidden. You two are part of my formation, covering my flanks and rear, and we now fight as a unit against the bloody little heathen. Now, do not move forward, whatever takes place."

Filled with cold rage, Wolf wanted no part of taunting this broad bear of a Viking, he meant to slay the heathen quickly and order the main battle to commence. With a roar, he exploded in a sprint to clash like a juggernaut, shield to shield, into the evilly grinning Northman. For the first time in his life, Brodir was not simply put to the ground, but struck so violently, he rolled, head over arse, several times down the slope.

Standing groggily to his feet, he knew he had only been saved by the plush padding of layered linen and thick blubber under his red-tinged mail armor. He had not believed any human could muster such strength as this Irish giant, who wore the mangled helmet of a beserker chief. He dropped his axe and withdrew a short stabbing sword from its scabbard, intending to withstand the next blow and thrust into the unarmored Irishman's exposed side.

The next clash of shields was even more violent, and though prepared and expecting it, Brodir rolled down the hill yet again, trying to shake the shock and remain conscious. This time, when he rose, he ran as fast as his shaky legs could carry him back to the safety of the Norse lines.

Wolf watched, and felt a warrior's shame to witness the pathetic retreat of the cowardly heathen. He had no time for rumination and dashed back to join his small unit. Mounted once more, he galloped to the rear and retrieved a bright scarlet cloth from his tunic, waving it high over his head. A piercing shrill burst from scores of Irish pipers at that moment. At this signal, for the first time in Ireland's history, almost nine thousand aroused voices burst out all with the same cry — **ABOO. ABOO. ABOOO.**

On a wide front, extending from across the Tolka to the Tomar woods, thousands of furious, vengeance-filled Celtic warriors, five hundred Christian Northmen at their sides, stormed down the slopes to thunder into the massed ranks of the Viking invaders.

***

The initial collision of arms and warriors impacted as an explosion of iron and muscle, accompanied by the ringing of steel and guttural grunts of ferocious men. On both sides, five hundred men went down in a shower of blood in that first clash, and then the battle developed its own rhythm, as all battles do. The long day progressed over blood-filled hours until mid-afternoon. The Irish center and right divisions, outnumbered more than two to one by their foes, fell back grudgingly. On the Irish left, the Scots and Welsh had the same strength as the Danes, Saxons and Pagan Manxmen opposing them. The highlanders and Welsh pushed slowly forward, filled, as much as the Irish, with vengeful fury toward the hated foe. It was at this moment that groups of young men from the Howth peninsula, who had sneaked behind the Norse, tugged on the ropes which had been concealed beneath the debris placed there weeks ago. They broke open the corridor. This allowed the Magyars to storm through on their ponies and turn to come around the Norse ranks.

As the last of the riders passed, the remaining Irish were stunned to be set upon by scores of howling savages wielding axes maniacally. Early on, Sigurd had decided to order all of the beserkers among the various Viking contingents to join together and sweep around the right flank to set on the foe from the rear. Now the Irish had conveniently opened a corridor for them. There were one hundred raging wild men altogether. The youngsters from Howth fled back up the neck toward their homes, and the few *laochra,* who had helped to open the gap, withdrew back to their lines.

The maddened beserkers, now exultant, poured into the opening after them, only to be unexpectedly confronted by a solid wall of scarlet-robed, heavily armed behemoths with long, stabbing spears thrusting out from an iron wall of shields. What happened next was simply a red slaughter. More than two hundred Spartans advanced into the undisciplined mob of wild men who mindlessly threw themselves in vain against the unstoppable juggernaut. The beserker flank attack evaporated in minutes in a rolling sea of crimson, which splashed unnoticed onto the scarlet cloaks of the Spartans.

The Spartans now turned to support the advancing Scots and Welsh by assaulting the flank of the Viking right. The Norse right division began to crumble rapidly, and the remaining Danes shifted left to join the Dublin Norse and Leinstermen as they advanced.

Now a new threat to the Norse swept swiftly into the corridor, around and behind the long, massed divisions. Two hundred galloping Magyars flew along the beaches and fields, loosing volleys of arrows. Hundreds of Vikings and Leinstermen fell, completely oblivious to the Irish cavalry in their rear, deadly shafts protruding from their backs.

Wolf was everywhere on the battlefield. At the head of nearly five hundred *laochra,* he swept into the flank of the center Norse division which had been pushing back the Munstermen and Dalcassians. Murcha, battling furiously with broadswords in each hand, personally watched as *Faolan* sought out and slew King Maelmora, as the renegade leader struggled among the few remaining Leinster traitors. The tide turned and the Dalcassian elite began to butcher the disorganized Dublin Norse and Jomsvikings from one side, as Wolf and his *laochra* pushed in from the other. It was too much, and the Norse survivors now turned to flee to the safety of their long ships on the beach.

This was what the Magyars had awaited as their arrows were now mostly spent. The entire rightmost division of Danes, Saxons and Brodir's men had been destroyed piecemeal by Scots, Welsh and Spartans. The few survivors now moved to join the other divisions still battling. The Magyar force of two hundred began to ride down the fleeing foe, thrusting with their lances. There were only two hundred riders, and still thousands of fleeing Norse when a new horror flew down the beach, baying with fierce howls. One hundred enormous beasts, all with slavering fangs, sprang onto the exposed backs of the fleeing enemy. Snarling, well trained jaws closed on blood-gushing throats and beneath the armor to crush hard pumping veins and arteries in muscular thighs.

Somewhere in this melee, Prince Anrud, nephew of the Danish king, found Prince Murcha, who was surrounded by heaped piles of Viking corpses. This new personal battle was slower and more awkward as both were now nearly exhausted from the day's trials. Finally, Murcha pulled the splendid mail jerkin of the Dane over his head, and thrust down with a killing stroke. Before he crumbled, Anrud was somehow able to thrust his dagger in a final burst of energy into the Irish prince's side. Murcha fell dead on top of the Dane.

By now, on the Irish right, which was most heavily outnumbered, Ospak, his two sons, and Teighe O'Kelly had all been slain along with many hundreds of Connaughtmen and Christian Norse.

Teighe's body was still precariously floating in the shallows but slowly descending into the water from the weight of its armor. A squad of four leering Vikings, seeing a chance for mindless revenge by mutilating the corpse of the valiant Connaught chieftain, rushed to pluck Teighe from the waves. As the first of the Norse reached down to grasp the flowing dark hair of the fallen chief, a ferocious apparition burst from beneath the water's surface.

An enormous Irish hound, its muscular body covered with strands of wet seaweed, given it a weird green shimmering appearance, sprang on the bending Northmen, closing powerful jaws around the warrior's neck. Blood gushed and the Viking crumpled as the hound gently took Teighe's woolen tunic collar in its mouth and dragged him onshore. The huge beast, still covered in fronds of seaweed, stood guard over the body of the slain hero, snarling defiance at any Northman who dared approach.

The three Vikings wisely decided to join their comrades, leaving the loyal creature to stand guard over his master.

Elsewhere, Sigurd and Thorwald's forces had advanced the deepest into the Irish ranks, yet now their only thought was to flee south over the rivers to the safety of Dublin.

Just then King Malachi and the Meath army finally joined the battle against the desperate Vikings. This final assault by fresh warriors effectively ended the battle, as Sigurd and Thorwald were cut down with the remaining few thousand of their Norse plunderers by the rejuvenated Irish and Manxmen. Just over one thousand Norse were able to somehow cross to Dublin. As Wolf had promised, the fields, beaches and waves were strewn with mutilated Norse bodies.

***

King Brian had released all but one of his guards to take part in the final route of the invaders. He knelt, heartbroken in prayer, having been informed of the death of Murcha and thousands of other Irish, including many from his clan. A moan, from outside his small tent interrupted the stillness of the quiet woods. Unheard by the king, his one remaining protector fell with two arrows in his breast.

Kneeling in prayer, Ireland's most magnificent king had just given himself over to his God once more when a dark, furtive figure silently entered the tent. The king felt no pain, and at the last sensed his father Cennetigh, his brother Mahon, and son Murcha approaching to greet him along with a familiar and peace-filled presence of incredible light.

***

After getting pummeled by the Irish giant, Brodir had slunk off furtively into the woods while his army was dying behind him. He had four savage beserkers alongside and hoped to move unseen through the fields and forests, to somehow reach Dublin. He could not believe his luck, and praised Odin when he stumbled on to a small tent, with only a single guard and the *Ard Rí's* banner flying over it.

His sword blade was already descending and clashing onto the silver head of the praying king before the tent flap had closed. He burst from the tent, and in a maddened, exultant voice cried out.

"Now let it be said to the Irish and all the Foreigners of the World, that Brodir of Man has slain Brian Boru, King of Ireland."

The four beast men around him, two of them naked, covered only with grime and muck, howled insanely. Then the small party moved once more toward the hoped-for refuge of Dublin. They didn't get far.

***

When he learned that Murcha had been slain along with so many others of the Irish leaders, Wolf sped on horseback to the king's tent to protect and console him. On the way, a young boy appeared from the woods, eyes filled with tears and calling out. He was the son of a local shepherd, and had hid himself in the trees to watch the battle when he noted the king's retinue setting up a tent near his concealed vantage point.

Sobbing, he now gave Wolf and his four mounted companions his awful report. "Five savage Vikings crept from the woods and murdered King Brian and his lone guard. The murderers are even now moving south on foot through the forest."

Gentle of heart and emotional, Mornak burst into tears at hearing this news. Wolf's face became a mask of concentrated fury. With a muttered oath, He led the mounted party of four *laochra* on a wild gallop into the forest sweeping southwards. It didn't take long.

They moved in a line toward the tiring Vikings, approaching them through gaps in the trees. Wolf sprang from his saddle, as the others aggressively trotted forward and rode down the four filth-covered beserkers, crushing them under their mounts crashing hooves.

Wolf towered over the gasping Brodir and swiftly slashed his broadsword down in a sweeping strike that severed the thick wrist clasping the Viking's axe. Then the Gael struck the shocked heathen in the jaw with an open palm, dropping him to the ground, stunned. With the four beserkers now mangled and splayed dead on the forest floor, Mornak joined his chief and passed him a rope. The Viking leader felt his mantle of red-mailed armor pulled unceremoniously over his head by the Pict, who spat in disgust and threw it to the ground. Wolf dragged the dazed master of Man to a tree, and tied him by neck and waist as he slumped there.

He sliced deftly with his *scian* to carve a long slice in the Viking chief's stomach from crotch to breastbone. With a snarl, he clawed his hand inside and slowly pulled out the steaming, foul coils of intestines. Wolf wrapped them in loops around the huge midsection of the agonized murderer. The final gory coil was secured around the dying man's throat. Mornak returned to his horse and joined his companions who were looking on from a short distance.

Brodir's eyes began to lose focus and his agonizingly pained breathing began to slow. Wolf bent to whisper in his ear.

"Know you now what no living man knows. My given name is Caoimhin Conaire. My clan is from the far west of our island. A small, simple and noble clan we were. You will shortly be in the worst of hells. You will have to ask the nine bloody heathens my father slew, before he was taken down by a score of your pigs, to tell you our family name."

Wolf stood, and his sword flashed down again, severing Brodir's other hand to assure he would never again carry a sword, even in hell. The young Irish giant looked down in grim satisfaction, as a final shower of blood erupted from the monster's mouth and its eyes clouded and dimmed, forever empty.

EPILOG

The battle of Clontarf virtually annihilated the allied forces of the invading Norse. Perhaps eight thousand lay on the meadows and beaches. All of the Viking leaders were slain except for the architect of the invasion, Sitric Silkbeard, who stayed in his fortress city during the battle. Maelmora of Leinster was slain by *Faolan* and his army was destroyed.

On the Celtic allied side the losses numbered several thousand but the High King's extended family suffered terribly. Brian, his strongest son Murcha and many others of the clan never left the battlefield. Ospak and his sons, Teighe O'Kelly, and most of the Scots and Welsh leaders likewise perished. A united Ireland under the rule of the Munster dynasty was not to be. Malachi assumed the role of High King once more.

***

Seven days later, three *snekkjas* –stag, swan and wolf — were being made ready at the docks in Limerick. Despite the victory, Wolf the Quarrelsome was devasted over the loss of his royal foster father. He had conferred with his surviving friends and they had all come to a decision.

The Gaelic giant would lead a reconstituted band of warriors out into the wide world. They would be a diverse group of Irish, Scots, Welsh, Picts, Icelanders, and Greeks numbering less than one hundred. Aoife, Eoin, Pyrrhus and his cousin Helena, would accompany Cael, Fergus, Mornak and his brother Partha along with other survivors of the great battle.

As Wolf and Aoife and Cael and Luta stood on the foredeck of the wolf-prowed *snekkja*, Cormac, the oldest, joined them along with his Greek friend. All of the ships were in motion. Fergus was aboard one and Mornak another. They were underway in the late afternoon.

They sailed westward. Pyrrhus suggested turning south and raiding Muslim North Africa to arrive with riches and fame into fabled Constantinople. The Icelanders told enticing tales of a mysterious shimmering land far to the west where their kin told of riches to be taken. All of this appealed to the Gaelic giant as he faced the sea. Aoife looked into her man's eyes with the love of years and she was content to be at his side.

They were still discussing adventures to come as the three ships disappeared over the horizon into the descending sun.

THOMAS J. HOWLEY CONTINUES
THE SAGA IN BOOK TWO

WOLF THE
QUARELLSOME

COMING SOON FROM MOONSHINE
COVE PUBLISHING

A PREVIEW BEGINS ON THE NEXT
PAGE

Off the Coast of Gastonia, France
Late April 1014 A.D.

On a bright sunlit and nearly windless morning under a cerulean cloudless sky, a large hook-beaked cormorant glided effortlessly, eyes fixed on three sleek *snekkja* long ships skimming smoothly through the coastal waters below. One boat was slightly ahead, the other two abreast behind it. All three bore the unmistakable form of those feared dragon ships which had unleashed slaughter and terror all across the north and west of Europe.

Yet there was something different about this small squadron of swift wooden craft. Two were adorned with the gracefully carved heads of a sleek swan and a regal stag. These figures thrusting proudly up from the prows of the sturdily built *snekkjas* were crafted in the Celtic style harkening back to the time of the ancients. Their artists' work was meant to convey simple beauty, not to intimidate sea spirits nor frighten victims. If the elegant swan and stag seemed out of place upon these fierce Viking ships of war, none among their crews cared a rat's ass. Both of these boats were mainly crewed by Christian Celts who appreciated the beauty of God's natural creatures above heathen devilry.

The foremost of the three vessels however was bedecked with a snarling wolf's head thrusting high above it bow. Along with this ferocious figure, still more features seemed to indicate the Norse pedigree of the craft. Somewhat more blonde and red-haired oarsmen were sprinkled among the crew than on the other boats. Indeed, these were mainly Manx and Icelandic Northmen, good Christians who had allied with King Brian at Clontarf. They had fought against the Viking invaders who had swarmed from all across northern Europe to seize Ireland for themselves and their leaders. Now the bloodied survivors had thrown in their lot with the Celtic crews of the other two boats on a voyage to God only knew where.

Foremost among the rowers, taking his place among the oarsmen sat the formidable and inspiring leader of this seaborne enterprise. He had refused to take a single bench and rowed alongside the oldest of the warriors of this entire band of newly minted a. Still, most of the weapon brothers firmly believed Wolf could, alone at the oars, easily drive the entire ship through the strongest gale.

At 28 years, *Faolán an Trodach* – Wolf the Quarrelsome, once given the name *Ulf Hreda* by the Dublin Norse, sometimes seemed more a gargantuan and fantastic apparition of dreams or nightmares than a simple mortal man. He was a head taller than the tallest of any of them, as powerfully and heavily built as a raging bull but rangier. Supple and swift as his namesake, he'd pummeled enormous, bear-like, Norse *beserkers* to death with his bare hands over the last several years.

Long dark hair, so deeply chestnut hued it was almost black, hung unkempt to his shoulders. Green intelligent eyes which seemed to radiate spark-like golden flecks when he was in his battle fever, now shone with good humor and contentment. He eschewed the heavy beard favored by many of his crew, preferring, it was said, to have his scarred face displayed before his enemies for the same reason ancient Celts painted themselves with blue woad and worked lime into their spiked hair – to shock and imbue awe into the foe. Thin and faint silver scars diagonally crossed his broad face from hairline to chin; the result of beatings across head and shoulders with cutting blackthorn staves in his childhood. This, at the hands of his Viking captors after his mother had been murdered by a jealous and barren Danish matriarch. These would never completely disappear and were now joined by more recent battle scars, won at Clontarf and already healing. Ironically, the same scars which he unashamedly carried with martial pride also attracted women and girls and won him the admiration and respect of his own warriors.

He had deeply mourned King Brian, his foster father but only after savagely hunting down, smashing and legendarily executing the king's killer. Now Wolf resolved to carry Brian's example of freedom to other lands. The giant leader also knew his Gaelic blood and soul yearned for adventure and challenge. If he could help others, even strangers, win freedom from subjugation he trusted he would make both of his fathers and his mother, now watching him from God's heaven, well pleased.

After the death of King Brian at the moment of victory at Clontarf, the king's youngest son was now King of Munster. All of those who fought under Brian's banner felt the pride of victory and the heart-rending loss of a beloved father figure. A diverse band of hard-fighting and trusted veterans of the climactic battle – Irish, Scots, Picts, Welsh, Icelanders,

Manx and even a few exotics from the east of Europe – had pledged to follow the charismatic giant as he moved on. So, Wolf had called for a counsel of his most trusted friends and advisors and, with the blessings of the new king, they had sailed from Limerick into the expanse of the western sea. Once underway, they had discussed their path and destination in earnest while the three boats were lashed together during periods of calm waters. Many of the Icelanders urged they make for Iceland, provision at some good Christian port there and strike out west toward the unknown to gain riches and glory.

Wolf remembered talking early on to two of the Icelanders about these supposed riches in the far west while they all pulled together at their oars.

"Now then, tell me more about Iceland and what lies beyond. Our clan bards claim that there will be found *Tír na nÓg*, the island of eternal youth, a place with vast forests, flowery meadows, joy and abundance. Though they also say it can be dangerous for travelers who stumble upon its shores."

The two exchanged knowing glances, happy to be making conversation with this colossal natural warrior who spoke perfect Danish and was, by now, a mysterious legend both feared and loved across Europe.

"Well now," replied the youngest of the two, "Iceland is filled with volcanic rocks, geysers of steam, and just enough green to yield a paltry harvest, but then beyond to the west, hmmm." He stopped mid-sentence and looked up whimsically.

His mate picked up. "We've not been there ye' understand but we've swapped tales with some among our kinsmen who claim they made the voyage. The first Skraelings they found surely didn't match the tale of eternally young Celts."

The younger man laughed at that. "They were short yet sturdy and covered head to toe in some type of fur with only their little black eyes peeking out. At first it was thought they were sea creatures since they sat so low to the sea. They looked to be moving immersed in the waves though working their tiny paddles. Only later did our cousins learn they were piloting small, sleek hide-covered boats. They flew off when first they saw the dragon ships from afar. Once ashore on their islands, our brothers searched for them in vain."

His friend continued. "Finally, an old man came down from the hills to them, head uncovered. He reminded some of the *Sami* tribes who live in the far north of our people's old homeland, though much shorter and with black hair and strangely shaped eyes. Since the island looked so barren, and the old man not to be understood, they gave him some food and a small child's knife and departed to sail further west."

'I can tell their kinsmen must have been good Christian Northmen, otherwise they would surely have killed the old man and hunted down and slaughtered the rest out of long-time custom,' Wolf mused to himself.

"And later," chimed in the older one, "they came, or so they said, to a land so immense, any further sailing voyage west was impossible. And this land was as brilliantly green as Ireland and even more deeply forested than Norway or France. As they hugged the coast, large bands of tall and well-formed men, as fair as we and the Irish and clad in well-made skins adorned with colorful decoration shadowed them as they made their way south. These strangers brandished bows and spears and bellowed deep and ferociously, in apparent defiance. They almost seemed to welcome battle with our now depleted and famished kin."

"By this time," his mate continued, "they'd been underway far longer than any who came before them. Their diet of fish, the occasional careless seabird and water, and the salt sores which covered them, as well as the exhaustion and lack of free and robust movement away from the rowing benches, bade them return home before all perished. And so, alas, that's all we know about your *Tír na nÓg*. Mayhaps, had they made land and explored…well?"

This plan of journeying to strange and unknown lands held immense appeal for all the Celts who shared the Norse yearnings for exploration and discovery. Besides, the Irish lads announced to their Icelandic mates, good Saint Brendan had already traveled there, converted all the heathens to the true faith, and returned in time for Christmas dinner. The Northmen just shook their heads and laughed at that.

Wolf had been sorely tempted to follow that mysterious and entrancing path and voyage to some entirely new land, notwithstanding his long-held disdain for anything which even reeked of Vikings. However, the valiant and true Icelanders and Manx who fought the invaders at Clontarf by his side had severely challenged his beliefs on that subject. The young leader had come to reluctantly realize his hatred and distrust of all Norse had not always served him well. Such had the crew of stalwarts now straining at oars behind him certainly proven beyond doubt.

'But then,' he told himself, 'these true men and one dear woman, are good Christians and they've volunteered to follow me to hell if I but lead them. They are no longer, if ever they ever were, followers of pagan Odin.'

In accordance with the customs of Irish nobility, Brian had assured that Wolf, after liberation from bondage, had been classically well-educated by the good monks on the Isle of Inisfallen. Now he mastered the Gaelic, Danish and Latin tongues, was knowledgeable in the sciences, numbers, geography and engineering of the day, and held a deep love and interest for history and world events. He'd been taught there existed rampant evil and that good gentle Christians were everywhere under oppression across the known world.

So, he decided, they would raid and harry heathen lands along the route to the south and then east, and finally come to the majestic capital of Constantinople. There they would present themselves to Basil, Emperor of the Christian Greek Roman empire and offer their services in defense of Christiandom and free people everywhere.... or so Wolf believed, as did his enthusiastic band of battle-tested heroes.

***

"Well, my 'good boy,' d'ye reckon we'll ever round this thrusting French peninsula and make way our due south once more?' the grizzled older Gaelic warrior asked his oar mate. He used the term of endearment a noble old woman had told him Wolf's mother called him to conceal his true name from the Vikings during the time of their captivity.

Wolf laughed. "We hugged the coast of Ireland and Wales years back before striking that rat's lair of *Fingwalle* in the Danelaw on these same boats. And we were simple Celts with not a Viking among us. And that ended well for us now, didn't it?"

***

The wolf-prowed boat was first to make its way past the narrow tip of the promontory. As the lead pilot gestured with hand signals for the other pilots and helmsmen to turn once more, a keen-eyed, raven haired young Irishwoman standing up high at the bow was the first to see the unexpected. She peered intently assessing what lay before her eyes, before grasping the pilot's shoulder and directing his gaze to what moved on the waters not overly distant ahead of them.

There, on this almost completely windless day, sailing southbound with only the torpidly gentile currents to carry them, were three ships like

277

nothing she, nor any of the Celts had ever witnessed. Unlike the Norse craft, these were high, crescent shaped and wider with black triangular lateen sails, now drooping flaccidly in the absence of any breeze to fill them. No oars were apparent but the decks were manned by stygian-swathed figures who themselves appeared as alien as their strange craft.

The experienced Norse pilot turned to Wolf, his voice calm but filled with earnest and knowing intensity.

"Captain, we've come upon Moorish dhows. They'll soon spy us." With eager concern, he continued, "Those black sales give evidence they're slavers. Two of them will be teeming with fighting men, most likely Berbers, with Arabic officers. The dhow in the center will be carrying their cargo, no doubt Christian slaves. It will contain a few crewmen, guards, merchants and the miserable souls in their holds."

Even before Wolf could reply to that, the wise Icelander had already flashed urgent hand signals to double the speed of all three ships – the same deep slow and powerful strokes through the water but now wasting no time on the upstroke.

Soon, the Moors had detected their pursuers. A fair-haired young boy and limping woman were dragged onto the deck of the black-topped central ship. Wolf watched as two dark figures behind them raised enormous bulwars which caught the light of the full sun with an arcing flash. Two heads flew off the slight bodies and into the green-blue sea, a warning to the Norse ships to stay away.

Not just Wolf but all the allied veterans of Clontarf, men and women, were overcome with immediate and seething rage at the spectacle. All had the same vengeful and deadly urge as their captain raised his wolf-pummeled sword toward the monsters and shouted in a voice which thundered across the otherwise quiescent seascape.

"For God and King Brian. Crush these bloody little heathens."

Nearly a hundred voices rose in a resounding bellow which seemed to almost rip and tear the very ocean. **Abooo, Abooo, Abooo"**